PACK ICE
ERLINMEYER
ICEDANCE
SEA
PERMAFROST LINE
PIRATE
ISLE
SUNGSONG SEA
HAIN
KINGSKEEP
THE VICEROY'S CASTLE
TURNSHIRE
TURN HALL
SALT
CRYSTAL
CAVERNS
GWILFIFESHIRE
MOONCALL
SEA
LOST
LIBRARY
LONG
POND
VALLEY
OF
TOMBS
STOAT
HOUSE
URLAND
THE
EYERIE
CROW'S REST
GADOT
CINCH MOUNTAINS
SKIPPING LAKES
SWORDS
HEARTH
BRYSTOL
QUEEN'S
DREAM
RAINSLEEP
SEA

The Accidental Tales
Book Four of the Accidental Turn Series

Cover design by Ruthanne Reid and Rodney V. Smith
Edited by Kisa Whipkey (2018) and Donna Frey (2024)
Book design by Brienne Wright
Map by Christopher Winkelaar

Electronic ISBN: 978-1-7381485-3-0
Paperback ISBN: 978-1-7381485-4-7

PRAISE FOR THE SERIES

"Being a part of a family, however unconventional, is an integral theme of Frey's clever, adventurous, and endearing Turn novels. [...] The thought-provoking story discusses the stereotypical role of women in fantasy novels, but more focus is placed on the characters' struggles with their familial roles and relationships, creating depth and commonality."
—Publisher's Weekly

"I started reading and was captivated. This superb novel grabbed me from the opening sentence, and never let go. [...] The whole tale is several clever twists on the oh-so-familiar fantasies we've read before. I want more. *Books* more".
—Ed Greenwood, *Forgotten Realms*

"Let me start by saying [...] that I think that J.M. Frey's *The Untold Tale* is the most important work of fantasy written in 2015. It may be the most important work of fantasy written this decade, but I'll have to get back to you on that in 2020.
—Dr. Mike Perschon, *The Steampunk Scholar*

"INSANELYAMAZING! The Untold Tale tears apart the tropes of heroic fantasy and gives back what we need: true heroes, true love, and the astonishing realization that yes, real people are magical."
—Julie Czerneda, the *Night's Edge* and *Trade Pact* series

"This story is nothing short of fun, unexpected, and

a little bit queer. If you're interested in a Science Fiction/ Fantasy undertaking with all of the ingredients of a queer anthology, *The Untold Tale* is for you."
—Dallas Barnes, *Pink Play Mags*

"It's easily the strongest I've read in the last year. [...] The fictional world = real world trope isn't the only one Frey twists, however. She also plays with the ideas of the hero and heroic adventure, feminism, gender roles, and the role of the narrative itself, in innovative – and occasionally cheeky – ways. This novel has the potential to appeal to a great many readers, across genres.
—Violette Malan, PhD, *Dhulyn Parno* Series

"If I could mark this as 10/5 stars, I would, but that's impossible, so 5/5 it is, with much hearts and swoons. [...]*The Untold Tale* is delicious, each word meant to be savoured, breathed in, nibbled at, full of hidden delight and wonder. Frey has a beautiful writing style - all at once slightly old-fashioned and delectable, whilst also being modern and quick-paced. It's tongue-in-cheek and it's serious. It's like an epic fantasy and a modern YA all in one. It is a book for every bookworm or geek [...] But most of all, it is a book for writers - and Frey delivers."
—Ana Tan, *A Tsp Blog*

"John Scalzi did Redshirts. He poked fun at a beloved symbol of geekdom, and we loved it. Frey has done the same for the sacred fantasy tropes and it's fantastic. An empowered woman of color, thrown into the chauvinistic world of the epic fantasy today's geeks were weaned on, serves as the perfect narrator for a critical and wonderful look at fantasy in the modern world."
—Leah Petersen, *The Physics of Falling* series

THE
ACCIDENTAL
TALES
Short Story Collection
J. M. FREY

For all of you fellow Readers, fellow Dreamers, fellow
Fans, and fellow Creators—
What magic we can create together out of our love.

TABLE OF CONTENTS

Introduction

Part 1: Told

1 - The Tales of Kintyre Turn
2 - Ivy
3 - Ghosts
4 - Love Letter
5 - Home

Part 2: Remembered

6 - Arrivals
7 - Happiness
8 - Rhymes
9 - Lullaby

Part 3: Voiced

10 - Origins
11 - Deleted
12 - Health

Part 4: Authored

13 - Magic
14 - Pride

Acknowledgements

INTRODUCTION

So, here we are. At the end of a series, and the end of about five years of planning, plotting, scribbling, writing, editing, revising, rewriting, re-editing, re-revising, re-plotting, re-re-planning, and generally... just a *lot* of work.

What is it like to finish an epic fantasy series?

It's exhausting. Sure, thrilling, triumphant, terrifying, all of those things, but mostly exhausting. It takes a lot out of a gal to write a trilogy. What a lot of people don't realize is that writers are not only writing while they've got the pen in their hands, or their fingers on their keys.

Writers are thinking about their stories constantly, playing mental Jenga with scenes as they do the dishes, composing the perfect opening line in a boring office meeting, brainstorming how on earth they're going to get themselves out of that corner they wrote a character into while doing the bedtime routine with the kiddos. Writers are making notes everywhere—scrap paper, receipts, notebooks in purses, on whiteboards and chalk walls, on their hands while on the subway, and on sticky notes that bristle from the edge of their computer screens like a lion's mane. Writers are bouncing ideas off one another in chat groups, at pub night, on 3 a.m. phone calls, and around the next play on the hockey rink. In short, writers are *always* writing.

Until—suddenly—they're not.

That moment when you hand in that final manuscript, when you're not allowed to make any more changes, when all the notes in red pen have been addressed and all those plot holes sewn up, that moment when it stops being your burden is...

Wonderful. Freeing. Terrifying. Scary. Amazing. Tear-and-laughter-inducing.

Because you don't know if your editor, agent, publisher, secondary/beta reader, friends, mom, or local librarian will love it. That eats at you. But at the same time, it is such a relief.

You know you've done the best you can, and that you can stop carrying your little book baby all over the place. It has its own legs now; it can learn to walk. It'll be running soon enough, and then, if you're lucky, it'll be flying off the shelves.

Yeah, it's exhausting.

But it's also thrilling. It's wonderfully challenging. It's the culmination of years of hard work, and lost sleep, and having your creativity pushed in directions you never expected, bloomed in ways you never could have predicted, and bruised in ways you couldn't have mitigated (but that you would never wish to have unhappen because you learned from it). It's amazing. It's *magic*.

The thing is, though, I was never meant to know this feeling. True story. Like Deal-Maker Spirits, literary villains stepping off the pages into the real world, and magic leaking into the world through scars, *The Accidental Turn Series* wasn't supposed to exist.

With a working title of "Feminist Meta-Fantasy Thingy," (evocative, I know,) this series began as a rant I wrote in my personal journal about the intended audiences of classic Western fantasy, and those current writers who were inspired by it. It was framed as a woman, standing on a bar in a tavern, screaming at a bunch of barbarians who had just pinched her butt, and the Knights Errant who refused to reprimand them. Sound familiar?

Deciding that there might be some merit in that rant, I expanded it into a scene—what's now known as Chapter Eleven of *The Untold Tale*—and then took some time to think about whether or not there was a novel there. I began writing what happened next, what happened first, trying to figure out where in the story this soapbox moment would work, or if it had to be scrapped entirely, and whose POV this portal fantasy should be told from. *Howl's Moving Castle* remains, to this day, my favorite example of the genre. So I took a page from Diana Wynne Jones's book and decided to tell the tale, and deconstruct the tropes, from the inside. Not five minutes later, Forsyth Turn walked into my brain, sat down in a very nice Turn-russet leather club chair, perched one ankle on the other knee, and said, "Well now—are you listening? Very good. Take up your pen and let us begin."

But it wasn't a series. It wasn't planned to be one, and I hadn't left any room in the narrative to create one—I didn't think. As you can tell from the fact that you are now holding book four of the trilogy (yes, I know how that sounds), we can assume that I finally figured it out. Not without a lot of ink on my whiteboard office wall, calls to friends, and bottles of Valpolicella. And not without a lot of rewriting of those plans as each major work in the series was completed; the next one always needed tweaking, revising, or straight-up raze-and-rebuild of what was originally planned based on what had just been written.

And I had to do it while pretending to be a different author entirely.

Authors like to write stories about writing. Stephen

King did it. John Scalzi did it. Jodi Picoult did it. Jim C. Hines did it. Cornelia Funke did it. Jane Austen did it. When I started *The Untold Tale*, I knew it would be about fans, and community, and cosplay, and Mary Sues, and all the things I loved about fanfiction and conventions. But I didn't realize so much of the books would be about writing, and writers, and the burden/joy of creating a novel.

Through the writer character in this series, I had the unique pleasure to not only talk about writing, but show my audience what it meant to be a creator. I hope you like Elgar Reed and his creations: Kintyre and Forsyth Turn, Sir Bevel Dom, the world he envisioned. And when you next read a book—not just my books, but every book—I hope you also have a better understanding of just how much of each of us goes into the work we write. And what had to go into basically writing the series twice.

Every scene, every reaction, every moment where something had to happen, I had to envision through three different lenses. Like the eye-testing thingy at the optometrist's, I had to first isolate from the novel as a whole each scene, or moment, or decision on the part of a character. I had to view them with—let's call it a Viewing Tube in this analogy.

Then, I had to add another disk of glass: the Lens of What Needs to Happen. In every moment of a novel, a character needs to agree, or disagree, or take action, or fail to take action. This is a pretty clear lens; no issues. But then things got fuzzy, because that motivation had to be informed by how the character was *created* to behave, not how I (or even they) *wanted* them to behave. This is the Lens of How Elgar Would Write It. I had to decide how it would happen, then figure out how a completely *different* author would write it. And then I needed a third lens, to counteract the fuzzy Elgar one—the Lens of Characters Gaining Sentience and Agency—where they fought their own Written-in instinct to behave how they wanted to. And just for funzies, a fourth lens was added—let's call this one a colored lens, the Lens of J.M. Frey is Actually in Control Here Guys, where I actually had to *write* the darned thing.

Remembering, of course, that Elgar Erasmus Reed isn't actually real and I made him up, too. (This is why writers talk about their characters as if they're real people, folks. Because how else are we supposed to keep track of the little buggers?)

And it's been fun. I love this series. I love these people. I love this world.

But I'm also ready to let it go.

Are there more stories I could tell here? Sure! But I think these are the important ones. These are the ones I *had* to tell. Everything else, my beautiful Readers, I leave to you to imagine.

So yes, it's been a lot of work. Certainly more thinking than I've had to do since my MA thesis. As well as writing and editing hours that count well into the multiples of thousands. You'll get a glimpse of those processes in this collection, as each chapter will feature another mini-intro from me, sharing more information about why and how I wrote each of the stories between these covers. It's been fun to be able to go back and figure out where I was when I wrote each piece, and what I was thinking.

It's been exhausting, true, but it has also been wonderful, and enriching, and so, so worth it.

And I am delighted, and verklempt, and honored to share this story with you, my dearling, darling Readers. This whole world has grown out of Pip's little soapbox moment on the steps of a tavern, lost in a fantasy world not Written for People Like Us, and into one where, I hope, everyone who picks up these books and falls into them in their own ways, knows in their hearts that they are always, and forever, well come.

Happy reading. And thank you for coming with me to Hain one last time.

Jessica Marie Frey
On a beautifully sunny Summer Solstice, 2018
Toronto, Ontario

TOLD

THE COMPLETE COLLECTED TALES OF KINTYRE TURN

✴

Funnily enough, this was one of the first things I wrote after completing the first draft of *The Untold Tale*. I had decided to go back inside the novel and really punch up this idea that the characters have a genesis myth. And that this myth makes it clear that they're at least a little aware of the fact they're works of fiction. (Lucky I did, too. It ended up becoming one of the most important plot points of the series—though this was years before I was even thinking of it as a series.)

I realized that, like any good world-builder, if I was going to invent a God, and a Pantheon, and a Religion, I better make sure I write a Bible, as well; I needed to make sure I kept the details straight. So I spent a weekend reading Golden Era sci-fi and fantasy book covers and reviews to get the right vibe, and then a week writing a detailed set of notes about the eight-book story arc for a series that doesn't actually exist, and never will.

Below is the most coherent part of that pile of scribbles, the "back cover copy" for all eight of *The Tales of Kintyre Turn* novels, and its "collection of shorts" follow-up.

The Hand of the Foesmiter

Kintyre Turn, eldest son of House Turn and heir to the estates of Lysse, dreads the day his father will make him take up his destined role as Lordling of the Chipping. There's nothing less interesting to him than ledgers, books, and accounts. Even the formal dinners and balls are boring. Desperate for adventure, Kintyre sneaks away from his own birthday party, intent on joining the wandering mercenaries hired to battle the mounting skirmishes at the Urlish border.

Along the way, Kintyre befriends a young squire by the name of Bevel Dom. The seventh son of a seventh son, Bevel's chances of making a living in his family's trade are close to nothing. Equally unenthralled with their lots in life, Kintyre and Bevel become fast friends, and are ready to take on the world.

What neither of them know, however, is that a darkness waits for them at the border, a darkness that threatens to devour whole the Kingdom of Hain. The only thing that can stop it is a legendary sword known as the Foesmiter. The problem? It's been missing so long, no one actually knows where it is.

Thus begins the epic saga of adventure, romance, and a pair of heroic partners.

The Dire Dragon of Drebbin

Sir Kintyre Turn, hero of Hain and wielder of the legendary sword Foesmiter, has spent the last four years bouncing between King Carvel's court at Kingskeep and adventure after adventure. With his friend and squire, Bevel Dom, he has slain monsters, navigated labyrinths, and rescued many *grateful* damsels. But now, Kintyre wants a break. Holidaying in the seaside town of Drebbin, known throughout the kingdom for its excellent whiskey, seems like the perfect escape for a Hero Made Good.

But something is afoot in Drebbin, and the townspeople refuse to talk about it. Something lives high in the mountains above the town. And at night, that same something comes down to snatch up a virgin for its dinner.

Soon, there is only one maiden left: the beautiful and modest Gwinnaten. Kintyre cannot deny his attraction, and he vows that the creature will not have her for its supper—though Kintyre himself just *might*. With the town in an uproar, and a creature stalking his footsteps, Kintyre must navigate the rough waters of attraction, heroism, and modesty... all while trying to convince the stubborn Gwinnaten that the best way to get herself off the creature's menu is to get herself into *his* bed.

The Dark Elf of Erlenmeyer

Sir Kintyre Turn, along with his friend, the newly knighted Sir Bevel Dom, has traveled to Sniwl Chipping at the behest of Lord Span. Located in the furthest reaches of the Kingdom of Hain, far to the north of fertile and fecund Lysse, where Kintyre grew up, it is a world of ice and darkness.

There, the intrepid adventurers discover that Span's daughter, the sultry beauty known as Cassiopith, has been betrothed against her father's will to a Dark Elf of the Erlenmeyer Forest. Tricked into the betrothal as revenge against House Span for a wrong so far in the past that it is out of human memory, Cassiopith has only the span of the next full moon to win her freedom, or become the elf's dark bride... *forever*.

Short on time and long on lust, will Kintyre be able to

win Cassiopith free of this horrible fate? And if he does, will he be able to deny his own attraction to the mystical lady? Or will his days of adventuring be traded for a life of domesticity at last?

The Shadow Hand of Hain

When his father's death calls Sir Kintyre Turn—wielder of the legendary sword Foesmiter—back to Lysse Chipping, he can't help but notice that something seems off about his childhood home. With the title of Lordling formally turned over to his book-mouse little brother, Kintyre is free to turn his attention to the source of the unrest.

Melinda, a humble woman from the far south of Hain, has come to stay in Turnshire with her uncle, Sheriff Lewko Pointe. And she hasn't come alone. Melinda, it seems, has a secret, and a ghostly pursuer. Everyone in town has fallen in love with the Sheriff's gentle, quiet, kind-hearted niece—even, it appears, the dead! Could the slight silhouette of the man Kintyre and his trusted sidekick, Bevel Dom, witnessed sneaking into Melinda's rooms *really* be a barrow wraith? And if he is, how is a hero meant to dissuade a man bent on courting when he won't stay *dead*?

Saving the damsel this time leads to unexpected discoveries of a sordid sort, however. And armed with this newfound knowledge, Kintyre and Bevel manage to unmask the mastermind behind the strange, seemingly random acts of evil that have plagued the kingdom for the last decade: a villain known only as the Viceroy.

A villain who isn't keen on his identity being revealed, and who will stop at nothing to see the world rid of the Great Hero of Hain.

The Siren of the Sunsong Sea

After the tragic death of Sheriff Lewko Pointe, the Viceroy, master villain of Hain, got away. But this time, Sir Kintyre Turn and Sir Bevel Dom intend to beat him at his own game. Hard on the Viceroy's trail, they join the crew of *The Salty Queen* as she sails along the western coast. But *The Salty Queen* harbors her own villains... and secrets. For the Captain is not the strong and stalwart man Kintyre met in the harbor. In fact, the Captain isn't a man at all.

Pirate Queen Isobin is in charge of *The Salty Queen* now, and she has a bone to pick with Kintyre Turn. Before they next set foot on land, she's determined to get her revenge on Kintyre for the treasure she lost in Drebbin... by claiming the one treasure no maid has yet achieved—marriage to the Great Hero of Hain.

But while Kintyre battles against forced domestication and aggressive feminine charms, Bevel Dom has bigger problems in mind. The Viceroy seems to have developed a strange, disgusting fascination for him. And for the first time, Kintyre must wonder: is there more than meets the eye to this blacksmith's son, to Kintyre Turn's most trusted companion? What secrets lurk in the shadows of his past that make him the object of the Viceroy's obsession?

The Request of the King

After escaping an ill-fated marriage proposal and yet another defeat at the hands of the Viceroy, Sir Kintyre Turn and Sir Bevel Dom are exhausted. Following in the footsteps of a troupe of wandering players, they look only for a night's entertainment, and perhaps somewhere to lay their heads in return for a few days of handiwork for the actors. What they didn't expect to find was a play so fantastical that the creatures described in the prose seem to be coming to life—and killing members of the audience, one by one, night after night.

Larissa of Rotham is a woman masquerading as a man. With her hair cut short and her breast bound flat, Larissa works as an actor by day, a fortune teller by night. Her colleagues fear she is a witch, but are too scared of the creatures she summons from the pages of their scripts to give her up to the local constabulary.

Lucky for them, Sir Kintyre Turn and Sir Bevel Dom have dealt with spiteful women and vengeful witches before. And an easy victory is just the sort of thing these battle-worn heroes need.

The Serpent of the Sleeping Vale

They say that the appetites of the Prince of the Naga are dark, twisted, and bottomless. And that his depraved lusts are matched in intensity only by his desire for vengeance against the Viceroy. So when the two villains team up to wreak havoc on the Kingdom of Hain, what else can King Carvel do but summon Sir Kintyre Turn, wielder of the legendary sword Foesmiter and the only man who seems to be the Viceroy's match?

But before Kintyre can track them down, he will have to rescue his best friend and travel partner from the clutches of the Viceroy's henchman, a twisted torturer known only as Bootknife. Torn between saving Bevel and obeying the command of the king, Kintyre is wrapped up in a quandary so powerful, so painful, that he fears for his very sanity.

With time running out, Kintyre must decide: is he willing to sacrifice his most trusted friend to save the lives of an entire kingdom? Or is he willing to let the kingdom burn for the sake of just one man?

The Bane of the Viceroy

King Carvel of Hain has declared that the Viceroy must be destroyed. All over the kingdom, great libraries and collections of books, scriptoriums, schools, and scroll-shops have been robbed, raided, and razed. Nobody knows what the Viceroy looks for, or why he destroys everything in his wake when he moves on to the next pile of paper.

Summoned one last time to the aid of Hain, Kintyre and Bevel will not face their archenemy alone. This time, the great knights of the kingdom will rise up to fight alongside the Great Hero of Hain and his legendary sword, Foesmiter. But Kintyre fears they might not be enough. As preparations to make war against the Viceroy's army of dark creatures and vile men commence, Kintyre desperately seeks to uncover the identity of the king's spymaster, the Shadow Hand that aided them in Lysse. They need the Shadow Hand's expertise to find a way behind enemy lines, but how do they locate a man who doesn't want to be found?

As the battle draws ever closer, Kintyre begins to grow ill. By what magic or spell, Bevel cannot decipher, but one thing is clear: if Kintyre Turn leads the knights into battle, despite Bevel's begging that he remain behind, this might be the great hero's last fight. And if it is, the entire kingdom will have to pray he has both the strength of arm and the strength of heart to take the Viceroy with him.

True Tales Told in a Tavern

A collection of short stories and novellas set in the world of *The Tales of Kintyre Turn*. Many of these shorts first appeared in gift charity auctions, or in such venerable institutions as Locus, Asimov's, and Playboy. Features the Hugo-award winning fan-favorite story "Seventh Son of a Seventh Son," and the entirety of the five-issue comic miniseries adaptation of *The Hand of the Foesmiter.*

IVY

This started as a fun picture I commissioned from K.B. Fesmire (a.k.a. AnotherWellKeptSecret on Tumblr) of my four heroes. As we chatted, it occured to me that I enjoyed the heck out of her webcomics, and that webcomics would be a great way to tell a missing part of the story. This is a series about breaking mediums and tropes, about adaptation and adoption, after all.

So I worked with Kelley to script—from Pip's POV, this time—the events that happened just prior to the opening of *The Untold Tale*. Some of the dialogue you'll recognize from the book, and some is new to fill in the gaps that witnessing this part of Pip's journey from Forsyth's POV created.

My only regret is that this is a black-and-white printing, and you can't see the gorgeous glowing green of the vines on Pip's back in this version, as well as the wonderful, subtle foreshadowing Ms. Fesmire created with the green throughout.

You'll have to head to her Tumblr for that.

WRITTEN BY   ILLUSTRATED BY

J. M. FREY   K. B. FESMIRE

I was about to do my PhD defense.
It's the public kind, where people can come and ask you questions. No pressure, right?
Right.
So of course I'm panicking and re-reading all the books that I dissected for my PhD.
That's me. Little Miss Type A.
The Bane of the Viceroy
Holy hell. What's--

Where am I?
How did I...?
How?
He-Hello? Is anyone...?
I think I've...I don't know what happened.

No.
I don't...I don't remember.
You fell.
No, he's...
This isn't right.
No. I expect not.
Oh! I know...your costume? Sorry, sorry, did I interrupt a cover shoot?
Why would you think that?
He's too perfect.

Well, you're Drew Mayfair, aren't you? And you're all got up in your costume, so...
Oh, but I don't remember walking into... Dammit, what happened? How did I get here?
This place...it even smells right.
Damp. Musty. Sour.
I brought you here. You fell.
No, I don't think so.
Who am I? Name me.
Drew Mayfair.
His breath...honey and poison.

No.
You're Drew Mayfair, the cover model from all the books. I know you.
No. Name me.
Do hallucinations have rank breath?
No. No, I won't. This isn't possible.
No!
No, no!
I have called you down, you will do my bidding! Name me!
It can't be real!
This is a photo shoot, you're just in character, you're trying to prank me. This isn't real. Stop it, you're scaring me!

Name me.
Name me!
Stop it, you're hurting me!
Name me!
Let me go!
The Viceroy!
Yes.
This can't be... it can't be happening. Reality doesn't work like this.

It just doesn't!
And him?

Oh god. Not him. Of all of The Viceroy's lackeys, not him. Please.
...Bootknife?
Very good. Bootknife, our new friend is hurt. Bind her wounds, please.
Please. Please no!
Wake up! Stop it! You can stop it if you just wake up!
Aaaaaa! No!
Wake up now! Wake up!
No, no no no noooo.

You know about me. About all of us.

I brought you here because I want to know what you know. Tell me.

I...what?

Whatever this guy wants cannot be good. If he is real, then I can't... I can't...

You're a Reader. Tell me about what you read.

Absolutely not. If you're really him, I can't help you. Never. This may be a hallucination but even here I could never--

Tell me the name of our book!

Don't try to lie. Just say nothing.

I'm
disappointed
that I didn't
expect that
from him.

Asshole.

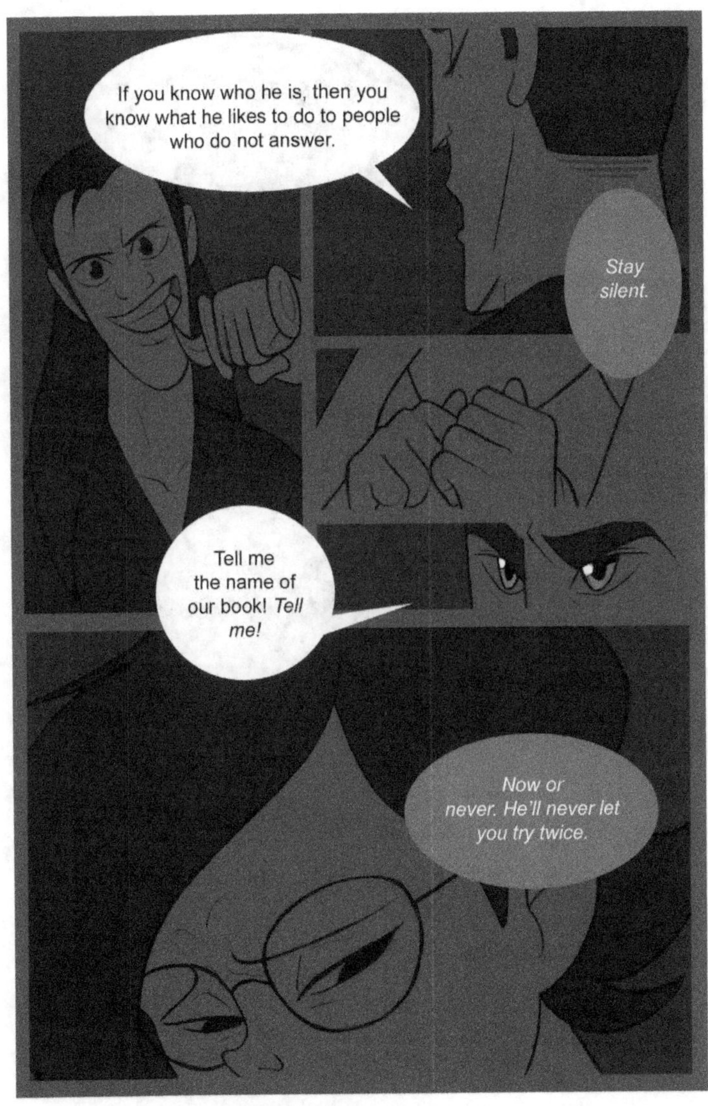

If you know who he is, then you know what he likes to do to people who do not answer.
Stay silent.
Tell me the name of our book! Tell me!
Now or never. He'll never let you try twice.

Now!
HA HA HA HA
Don't let go!
HA HA HA
He is laughing. The lunatic is actually suffocating and laughing.
And now... Now what?
Be brave.
I'll throttle you! I'll save Kintyre the trouble!

I was so close.
I'll carve you a new smile if you don't let go.
Don't stop.
You'll carve me anyway if I do. Might as well do your world a public service and take this son of a bitch with me.
Can I do it? Can I kill...?

No.
Coward.
No.
Not coward.
I hope you're done trying to prove your little point!
cough
Tell me the name of the book!
cough
Hero.
In your own small way.
Oh, so that is how it is going to be? Very well. Your choice.

Bootknife, darling...upstairs. The Rose Room, I think, don't you?
Be brave, Pip. Be brave.
Oh, this is going to be fun! I'm going to carve you so pretty!
Be brave!
I'm so scared.

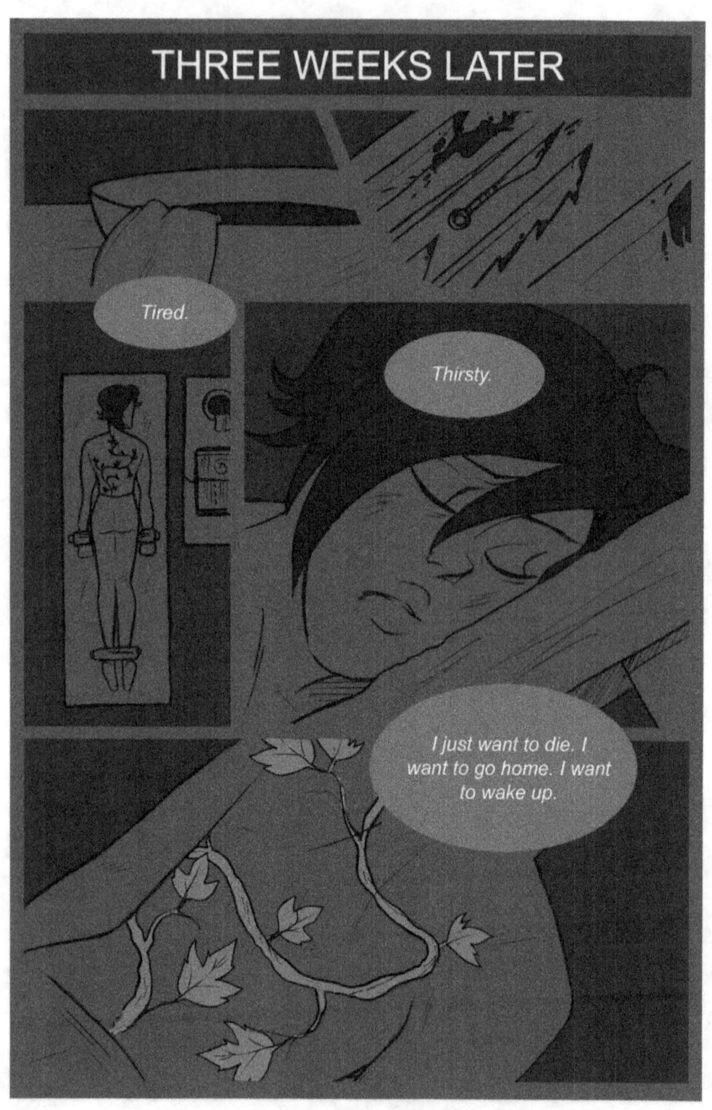
THREE WEEKS LATER
Tired.
Thirsty.
I just want to die. I want to go home. I want to wake up.

Check this room! Take all the books you find!
And do it quickly before the Viceroy and his toady come back and fry us all. Hurry, we need to--augh!
Dear Writer. Miss? Are you alive? Miss?
What did you find?
Another of Bootknife's pretty carvings.
Help me.
Quick, cut her free. We need to take her to the Shadow Hand. We'll stop for the healer on the way.
I didn't tell him anything. I didn't tell. I won. I won.

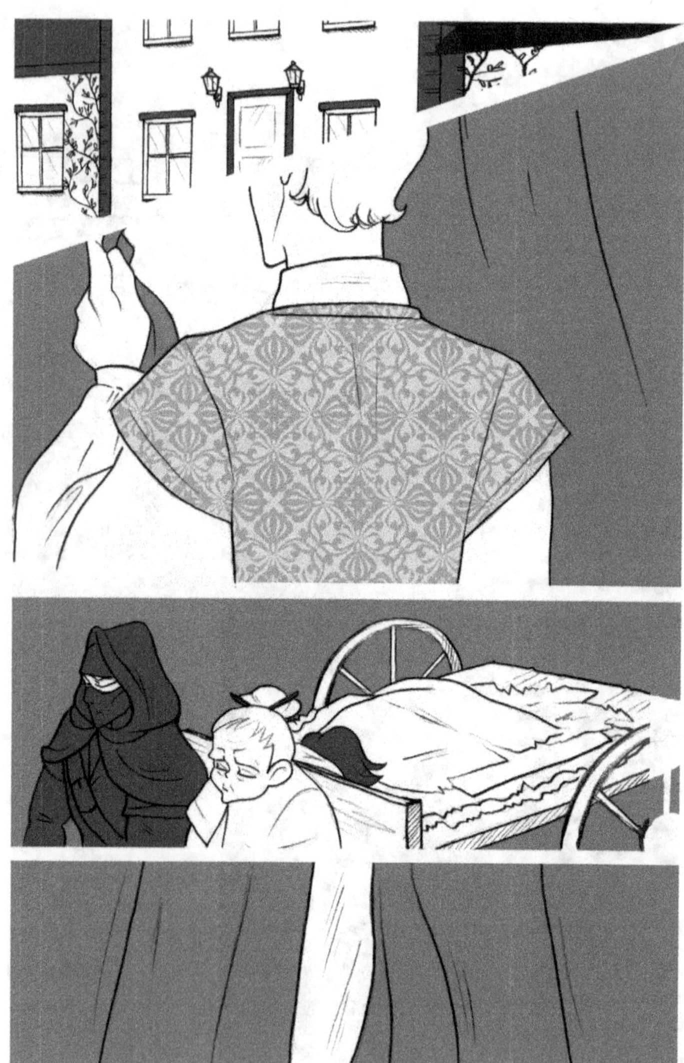

By the Writer. That's *Bootknife's* handiwork.
I don't detect any curses on the wounds.
Does she live?
Barely.
That is enough. Get her upstairs. Velshi!
Sir?
Have mother's old rooms opened up.
Sir.

Oh.
It's you.

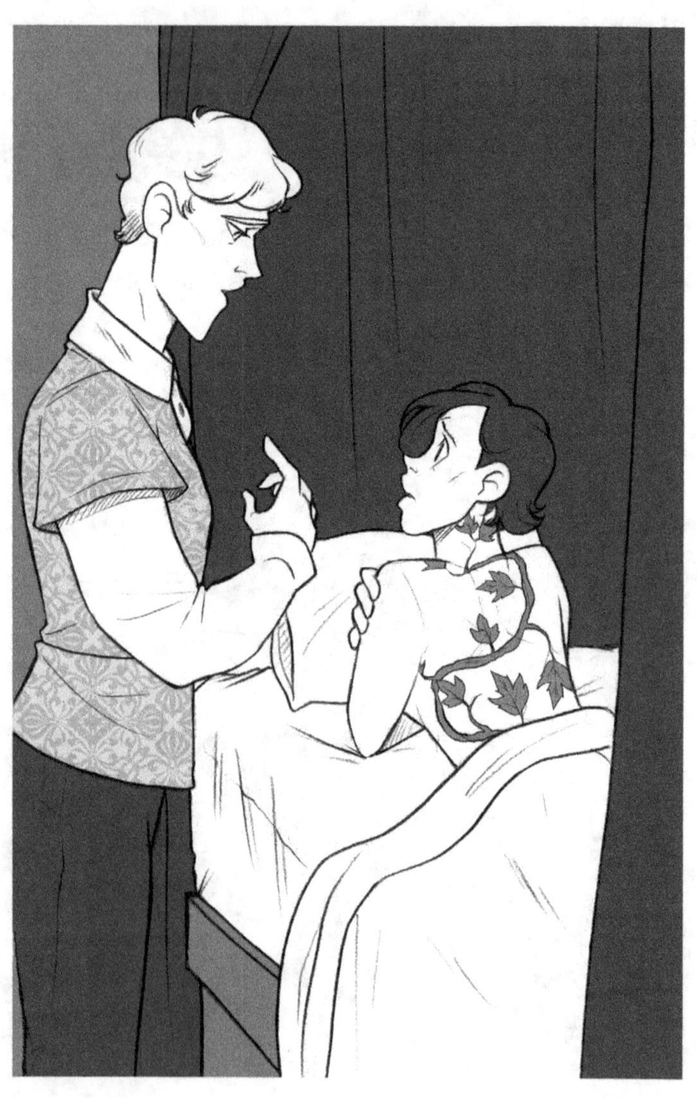

GHOSTS

There were many incarnations of *The Untold Tale* that never came to fruition. At first, it was going to be told from Pip's point of view. Then, I considered a version where the POV would alternate between Forsyth and Kintyre. In one version, the POV was even meant to peel off after Kintyre and Bevel storm away in a huff in act one of the book, with the next part of the story taken up by Bevel as he struggled to come to terms with the fact that he's madly in love with Kintyre and had never allowed himself to acknowledge it before—or rather, that the constraints of how he was Written wouldn't allow for it.

Ultimately, I decided that the story was strongest told from a single character's point of view. *Ghosts*, however, grew out of those few scenes I had written from Bevel's perspective, and then cut. They haunted me, especially since I was seesawing between whether or not I should write the story of "How Kin and Bev Got Together" in the first book.

In the end, the answer was "not," as it didn't work for the way the novel—and then, later, the series—was structured. But I still had those scenes, and I decided that I would in fact write another story featuring Bev and Kin. It wavered for a while between full-length novel and novella; romance, or angst; before, during, or after *The*

Untold Tale. This one story required more thinking and planning than almost the whole rest of the series combined.

Eventually, I decided a prequel would work best, and that, while I still wanted to write "How Kin and Bev Got Together," it is sometimes more fun for everyone to let Readers imagine how the big moments happen than it is to actually see them on the page. So, like *Ivy*, *Ghosts* is set shortly before *The Untold Tale*, and the fateful summons to Turn Hall that finally forced them to admit to first themselves, and then one another, how they felt.

PART ONE

✴

The messenger hawk is only odd because it wears
a band of Turn-russet around one leg. I'm more used
to seeing Carvel-green, or, if Mum can scrape together
enough to cover the expense of a hawk and the emergen-
cy is dire enough, Dom-amethyst.

It lands first on a branch close to Kintyre's head,
overhanging the stream where Kin is grumpily scrubbing
our travel pots out with sand. As he always does, Kin
ignores the ruddy thing. The hawk chirrups in disdain
and hops down to the ground. It bobbles over to me like
a grouchy pigeon, sidestepping the still smoking ashes
of my morning cookfire. I was in the middle of packing
away our leftovers, so I've got some jerky in my hand. I
offer it up, and the hawk snips at it daintily, careful of my
fingers. The beast is probably the politest of the three of
us. Kin and I don't work too hard on our table manners
when we're out-of-doors.

"Never know why you lot always go to Kin first," I
say, wiping jerky grease on my trousers and then shaking a
finger at the hawk. "I'm the one that feeds ya."

As a kind of answer, the hawk fluffs up in the sunlight, resettling its feathers after what has probably been
a long flight. I've always liked how sleek the creatures are,
how deadly, and at the same time, how much they look
like a curious cuddle toy. The hawk lets me scritch along
the crest between its eyes, crooning. I smooth back the

small plume of white that marks this bird as a messenger, as one of the breed clever enough to recognize different human faces and follow simple verbal commands. Dead useful things, these birds.

Appeased, the hawk lifts its foot and I untie its burden. Covering a yawn—didn't sleep so well last night—I wonder if there's enough heat in the embers of our fire to kick it back up and boil another kettle of tea. It's not like Kin and I have anywhere else to be, and the thought of a long, lazy morning fishing and napping is suddenly delicious. Yeah. Could do lots with a day of nothing.

I'm also missing the warmth of the last lassie we left behind, if I'm honest about it. And that of her father's hayloft as well. But we're one day's walk from Estagonnish, and there's no bloody inns between here and the next sprout of farms. Just sparse forest interspersed with wildflower meadows, and the curving sweep of a balls-cold stream.

Good for catching rabbit and eel. Bad for a good night's rest. And after all the adventures we've been on—and enemies we've made—I'm not too keen on sleeping out in the open. Or, really, anywhere that's lacking a roof and walls, a door that can be booby-trapped, and a window that makes noise when it's broken. Sleeping out under the stars sounds heroic when I write that sort of drivel, but in reality, it fills me with wary paranoia. And it's bloody chilly to boot. 'Cause unless there's a pair of tits between us, Kintyre's not too keen on sharing body heat.

Shame, that.

Of course, this bone-weariness knifing through me doesn't just stem from bad sleep. Not even really from our most recent quest, or from the bloody great sword-fight it took to vanquish the Dark Elf. No. It's from the many, many houses filled with so many grieving people.

I am wrung out from comforting so many husbands

and wives, parents, children, and lovers while returning the jars of eyes stolen and collected by the elf. Their grief is like a greasy smear against my skin. I feel a hundred years old, pulled loose and weak by the weight of it.

Sadness always makes me absolutely *bagged*.

I yawn again and try to cover my mouth, then wince, juggling the hawk's note into my off hand.

Writer's nutsack, that aches.

In my morning haze, I forgot that I wrenched my wrist in the fight. I'm going to have to rewrap it soon. Or maybe I should go shove my arm into the stream for a bit, see if the cold won't do some of its own magic on the swelling.

The bird, freed from duty, pops up onto a nearby branch and preens its wings. It's trained to wait for a return message, if I want to send one. But more likely it's waiting for more jerky. I could send it away, back to Turn Hall, with the hand gesture that means "go home." It would go, empty-pouched and immediately, but... nah. Maybe, like me, the damned thing deserves a rest after its long task. Maybe it could use a lazy afternoon on the riverbank, too. I could feed it fish guts, if it wanted them.

Or maybe the hawk might appreciate a mug of reviving tea. That brings up the image of a hawk with its whole head jammed into one of our metal cups and I grin. Then I stand, wiping soot on the thighs of my leather trousers.

"Kin," I chortle. "Post!"

"Who's it from?" Kin asks, standing. He leaves the pots by the shore—hopefully somewhere where they won't wash away again, or I'll put my boot up his arse and make him go for a swim to fetch them back—and saunters his way back to the campsite, in no rush this fine morning. Kin squints at the hawk's leg-band. That wrinkle appears between his eyebrows, the one that I still haven't been able to describe correctly when I write about it. "Not actually Turn Hall?"

"Why not Turn Hall?"

"Most likely the sheriff," Kintyre says, dismissing my question and the assumption that it could be his younger brother all at the same time. "Sneaking Forssy's things again."

"You know, your brother is actually quite generous," I point out. "Never lets us leave Turn Hall without full ration packets and wineskins. 'Course, he'd never admit it."

"He's a pretentious twat."

"I won't argue with that. I'm just saying he's a *generous* pretentious twat. Pointe wouldn't've had to sneak anything, is all I'm saying." I hold out the message, but Kintyre folds his arms and glowers. His stupid rivalry with his brother now apparently includes him not even stooping to open his more-superior-than-thou brother's letters. "Come on," I cajole.

Kintyre's only answer is a huff and rolled eyes.

"Fine," I say, and untie the leather lace keeping the message rolled. "Huh. It really is him."

"It is?"

"It is."

Kin tries not to look interested, but I can tell that he is. He's trying to peer over my shoulder out the side of his eyes. "What's the book-mouse want?"

I suck air in between my teeth, unsure of how to say this without setting Kintyre off. I'm sure as the Writer's calluses not going to actually *read* the message out loud. That's just asking for an hour of pacing and ranting. "You, apparently. We're being summoned."

"He can't summon *me*." Kintyre bristles, and I barely manage to clamp down on my own eye roll. "I'm the eldest."

"But he's the Lordling of Lysse," I remind him. "And he summons us."

Kin grumbles, but asks, "What for?" He leans over my shoulder, taking up all my space, like usual, and sucking all the air out of the world. He peers at the parchment, a tongue of corn-silk hair brushing against the skin just under my ear.

The shiver it causes is entirely involuntary, and I squeeze my eyes closed, and swallow hard.

Bastard. I try very hard not to wonder if he's doing it on purpose. If he knows.

Of course he doesn't know.

When I've got myself composed again, I turn my face up to him and grin, ignoring the way his mouth is just right there and I could—*auhg*.

Bastard.

"An adventure," I say, and the grin I force across my face has the perfect partner on Kintyre's. Without even looking, Kin smugly waves the hawk back to Turn Hall, message-less.

The way to Lysse leads us back through Miliway Chipping, and the road spears through the prairie lands that provide Hain with our staple grains. Farmers don't mind travelers camping on the side of the road, but are understandably wary of grass fires. This means that in the breadbasket of Hain, no traveler is allowed to light a campfire. And *that* means no nighttime cooking, and no nighttime heat.

It's still spring this far north, and the nights are still just this side of too chilly to sleep without a fire, or alone. I'm now *really* missing that last lassie, and I wonder blithely if it isn't too late to backtrack to Estagonnish and invite her to Turn Hall with us. Of course, what to do with her when we get there is a problem I don't want to deal with. 'Cause I sure as the Writer's ink-stained fingers don't want to marry that one.

Mum wouldn't approve at all—the lass was all bosoms and no brains. Good for a while, but not good for a wife. And nobody I would trust to leave behind with the resulting sprogs while I go adventuring. She might set the thatch on fire if she tried to cook. Besides, I wouldn't want to Pair up with someone I couldn't take along on the road, anyway, so that excludes pretty much anyone at all.

Except...

Aw, ruddy bollocks. Now I'm back to thinking about how Kin and I will have to lay side by side in our bedrolls to stay warm. I scrub my eyes, trying to will the ridiculous domestic fantasy out of my head and pay attention to where I'm walking.

I must be getting old, like my brother Dargan teased the last time I was home. He said the older you get, the less willing you become to dither about things that are important. At first I laughed it off, but it's been two months since I last stopped in Bynnebakker and his warning has been eating at me ever since. Prat.

My wrist throbs again, as if agreeing with Dargan's bit of pithy wit. I'm getting old. I'm getting slow. I barely blocked that blow from the Dark Elf's sword, and damn near broke my wrist for the trouble. I don't have the protection of an enchanted blade, or the skills taught to a lord's son, like Kintyre. I've just got forge-earned muscles, a good piece of dwarf-crafted weaponry, and all the wily tricks that come with being the youngest of seven boys. And lately, they're all starting to seem like not quite enough.

I suck on my lips for a moment, thoughtful. Maybe I was hasty in dismissing the idea of a wife. Sitting by the fire, playing with dogs and babies while someone cooks for me for once sounds like a kind of paradise right now.

If only it could include my best friend.

Ugh, and there is that damned domestic fantasy crap again. I need a distraction. Fine. I start cataloging what I can remember of our travel stores, and the result makes me groan loudly enough that Kintyre looks back over his shoulder and grunts, questioning.

"We're gonna need to stop before we get to the grasslands."

Kintyre grimaces. "Aw hells, cold rations. I forgot."

"Yeah. For at least three days." I kick at a stone in the path to keep from having to look up at his ridiculous face when I make the suggestion I'm about to make, knowing he isn't going to like it. "We could rent horses? It would go faster."

Kintyre grunts, but otherwise doesn't reply. Kin hasn't been fond of horses since Stormbearer, the horse Kin's father gave him, was slain in the Battle of the Walking Woods. I hadn't been all that attached to my own horse, a fussy old nag named Hey You who had also felt Stormbearer's death keenly. I'd left Hey You with my older brother Vulej just a little over two years ago.

Vulej's wee ones apparently love the wretch, and whenever I pick up post from my pa's forge, there's always shaky pencil smudges on the edges that my sister-in-law assures me are drawings of Hey You giving the twins rides to the Hay Market. I keep them all in a well-oiled leather fold at the bottom of my pack. I have very little in this world aside from Kintyre and my family, so I try to keep both of them as close as possible.

It's sentimental, sure, but a man's gotta have something worth fighting for, something a little more tangible than reputation, and glory, and the fleeting bliss of a lassie's charms.

"Right then, no horses." I sigh, and keep marching. "Arse."

It's just past midday when we reach the first of the farms. Out flung houses surrounded by gleaming acreages of lively, growing green things always mean there's a center of commerce and civilization nearby. If I remember correctly, this particular center had a goodly number of taverns and markets last time we were through.

And good company, too. Blonde, I think she was, but in truth they all sort of blur together in my memory. It's really only Kin that stands out in my... *recollections.*

Mind clearly wandering the same paths as mine, Kin finally slows his damnable long-shanks striding and falls back to match pace with me. "Do you think we'll meet someone in town? We've got time for it, right? You can find us one."

My knee-jerk reaction is to stick my tongue out at him like one of my nephews. Or to flick a rude gesture at his back. Or to say: "Aren't I enough for you?" Or sometimes: "If you do, don't involve me. I want nothing to do with it anymore." Or sometimes: "Enough, I'm done with you. I'm going home to work in my pa's forge and forget you." Or sometimes: "I love you."

Writer's bollocks, sometimes I want to say nothing. I want to just grab Kintyre's ears, wrap my fingers behind the tender pink shells and pull him down for a soft, wet, sleepy kiss, full of all the dopey affection I can't seem to rid myself of. Sometimes I want to get my calf in behind Kintyre's knees, give a shove of my hips and sprawl the arrogant prick on his ass, get a fist into the laces of his trousers and slurp down his—

Bastard.

He doesn't even understand all the ways he's killing me. The ways I'm torturing myself, because it's ridiculous. We're Paired, but not like that. And it will never be like that, and damn Dargan to all the hells of the Writer's imagination for planting this stupid bloody seed of thought in my chest anyway. I'm going to kick my brother in the nutsack the next time I see him, and damn what his wife has to say about that.

"We've got time," is all I let myself answer from between my clenched teeth.

I shove my hands in my pockets, annoyed by my own cowardice. "We're not to be in Turnshire for a fortnight, and it will only take a few more days to reach Lysse." I heroically don't add that, perhaps, if this is the village with the blonde, we should move on immediately after resupplying. It's entirely possible that either of us may be confronted with the harvest we sowed on our last trip through.

Kintyre doesn't answer, as usual, so I let my mind wander down the path the thought of kids has begun to lay. I always thought there would be children in my life. I actually want to be a father. Being an uncle is wonderful, even though I only see the little pests infrequently. I love the squirts, and it's great to see how much they've grown, all that they've learned, the ways their personalities and preferences develop between each visit. The youngest of the horde seems to think that "poop" is the funniest damned word the Writer ever Wrote.

I want their chubby, sticky fingers locked around my neck, the sweet kisses, the cuddles, the little feet racing through the hallways shouting, "Pa's back! Pa's here!" There's something more, something magic in the way they say that to their fathers, different to the way they shout "Uncle!" when I surprise one of my six brothers at home. Almost like "Pa" is a Word, instead of just a word, and one that I want to mean *me*. I would like a home to go back to, I think. A place where it's warm, and I can sit by the fire and be adored by everyone around me because I adore them back.

That had always been the plan, anyway.

Grow up, work with Pa in the forge, marry a farmer's daughter, build a croft, raise a brood, and spend the rest of my life shoeing horses and being loved.

But then a handsome lord's son came along, and that was the end of those dreams. I could have a wife, a home, the children, if I wanted. But that would mean no Kintyre.

A sudden thought drops into my stomach like a fire-warmed stone: *I'm tired.*

This is not the grief-born weariness I felt this morning. This is something else, something deeper, something that has soaked into my skin and settled in the dark marrow of my bones. This is something that is etched on the very fiber of my muscles, the pull of my tendons, the lining of my stomach. This is something born of Dargan's careless teasing, yeah, but also the contemplation that his words have caused over the weeks since I was in that tavern with him, both of us a little too far into the keg.

I am tired.

I am tired of walking, tired of traveling, tired of having nowhere to call home, no place to call my own, no pillow and bed waiting at the end of the day, no surety of the next meal. I am tired of following after Kintyre Turn and wanting. I am tired of not having.

I am tired, and I want to stop.

I could pay for somewhere to call my own, true; I'm not much for banks and moneylenders, but I've squirreled away the reward purses I didn't give over to Mum over the years. I don't need to build a croft now—I've got more than enough clink to buy a cottage, a few acres, some pigs. Probably a calf. Or five. Or ten, really. Right, so there's actually probably enough to buy a title and the estate that goes with it.

Hells, King Carvel has offered me one often enough. Maybe I could just write to him and tardily accept. Though what on the Writer's hairy backside I'd do with the trappings and responsibilities of a lord, I don't know. I wasn't raised to it. I'd have to hire someone to do all the actual work, and the life of an idle gentleperson is not even close to appealing.

The only thing I *am* certain about is this: Kin would never live with me.

Even if Kintyre Turn did finally settle down, turn in his sword for a ledger or a plowshare or a guardsman's cap, it would be with a buxom woman who could gift him with little Turnlings. More likely, it would be with some nobleman's daughter or simpering princess, and it would be on the coin of a king, or the late Algar Turn's estate, where his brother Forsyth would maintain the responsibilities of Master while Kin enjoyed the luxuries with which he'd been raised.

If Kin stopped, that would be it. There would be no room in Kintyre Turn's life for a Bevel Dom, his questing partner, sword-mate, and dogsbody. And a life for Bevel Dom with no Kintyre Turn in it is a life I'm afraid I might not actually have the strength to live.

I know with the surety of a man who has been in love for half his life with someone who will never be aware of it that I will die of heartbreak, or maybe by my own hand, the day Kin marries someone else.

And Writer, that sounds melodramatic as bloody anything. More fit for my scrolls than my thoughts, but there it is. I jam my fists down harder in my pockets and hunch, chewing on my bottom lip to keep from scowling.

And the bastard is *still* walking, just a few paces ahead, like his long legs can't be bothered to shorten his stride for the sake of anything as banal as a short companion. Fine.

So I do as I have always done: I put one foot in front of the other. I shove the weariness away, raise my chin, squint to keep the sun out of my eyes, and follow after Kintyre Turn.

The tiredness can be ignored.

He's unpleasant from the moment he dismounts, is how I introduced Kintyre Turn in the epic scroll-series that documents our adventures. But that's a much kinder way to think of it than how I really felt.

"What an elfcock," was what actually came out of my mouth. The twat had wanted me to drop what I was doing to replace a thrown shoe on Stormbearer, which was both arrogant and entitled. And he hadn't even been willing to pay extra for the inconvenience.

Now, watching the way Kin's swagger increases the closer to the village we get, the same sentiment rolls between my ears.

Though I'm not annoyed enough to admit that the thought of finding a nice warm bed with a nice warm woman does sound appealing, but for reasons different to Kin's. I torture myself with it, I know, the thought of finding a way for it to be acceptable to reach out, to touch, to stroke... damn Dargan anyway!

All the same, my own swagger is probably just as pronounced, so I say nothing about it. The view from a few paces behind Kin is a nice one, after all. Kin's customary leather trousers seem to be especially tight today, and his Sheil-purple jerkin leaves very little to the imagination.

I catch myself licking the road-dust from my lips and decide to be optimistic. A bed tonight, shared sleep rolls for the next three, and six days on the road with just Kin for company, except for the taverns or inns we'll stay at. No battle stress, no strategies, no deadlines nor swords looming over our throats. No insidious plots, no villains to roust, no blood.

Just nice, calm, congenial conversation, honestly earned sweat, and at the end of all that, Turn Hall with its feather mattresses, large copper tubs, and fresh baked bread waiting for us. Even the adventure Forsyth proposed in his missive seems more like a walking holiday than a quest—escort damsel in distress from Turn Hall to her far-off home? Easy!

Maybe there'll be some bandits en route, which will keep my sword arm from getting too rusty. Maybe there'll be some fancy politics and fast talking when we get the damsel in question to where she's meant to be, just to make it clear that we weren't the ones who took her in the first place—that will keep my wits from atrophying. But most likely it will be boring, easy, and finish in a feast. We'll have forged yet one more ally, have one more community in which we'll be welcome, maybe even one more castle from which we can draw supplies.

And, if the damsel in question is amenable, the nights of the journey will be warm for other reasons. I like the adventures like that.

Either Kin will try to seduce her first, or I will, but neither of us leaves the other out. Hard to, when you're on the road and there are no walls between you. I do like that about traveling with Kintyre—everything we have, we share. The burdens, the battles, the packs, the blood, the joys, the feasts, the wine, the women, and sometimes, though we never talk of it, the nightmares. *That* is something I will never grow tired of. The sharing. Not the nightmares. Those can just go right back on whatever Shelf the Writer pulled them off of.

By mid-afternoon, we've reached the outskirts of a small market village. The sign by the side of the road depicts a festival of sorts, something with fire and foliage, as well as the place's name.

"Gwillfifeshire," Kin reads, carefully parsing out each of the tangled syllables.

"Gilsher," I correct, the side of my mouth quirking up at his gaffe.

"But there's—"

"It's pronounced gil-sher, Kin," I insist.

Kintyre points indignantly at the sign.

"Yeah, I see it," I say mildly, determined to hold on to my self-imposed good mood. I hook my thumbs into my belt and nod. "But that's how they pronounce things 'round this area."

The wind goes out of Kin's sails when I refuse to rise to the verbal spar and his shoulders slump. Instead, Kintyre readjusts his pack, head high and fingers curled lightly on Foesmiter's pommel, and leads the way toward the small square as if he actually remembers being here before. He doesn't. I know he doesn't, because he never does.

The square is the only open space amid the cramped, close buildings of the village. There are three or four layers of buildings separated by cobbled streets spreading back from the square, which get progressively smaller, made of more wood than stone, and finally give way to an open meadow. In the distance there's a knoll, and atop the knoll is something gray and crumbling, probably an old monument, or the remains of a castle. Many of the house walls are made of that same gray stone, so it was probably dismantled for building materials a century or two ago.

There isn't much use in statues and monuments, I guess, when there are houses and barns to build and hewn bricks already on hand. I approve of the sensible repurposing, but Kin, who grew up in a manor house with a wing to himself rather than amid a pile of brothers in a three-room cottage, is always vaguely upset that the beautiful architecture and statues have been pulled down.

He'd never own to it, of course, but Kin is secretly a great admirer of the arts. The deep well of his affection for anything creative always raises froth and waves when something beautiful is destroyed—more so if it was vandalized or dismantled so long ago that there's no way to even know what the original art looked like.

Kin is predictably glowering at the top of the knoll, huffing in indignation. He gets that wrinkle between his eyes, and he fingers the small whittling knife he carries in its own leather sheath alongside Foesmiter, and chews on the outside corner of his mouth. He looks like a drakeling. It's hilarious.

Just once, I gave in to the urge to reach out and press my thumb against that swollen, abused lip, but Kin didn't meet my eyes, didn't look up, didn't lean forward, so I've never done it again. Doesn't mean I don't want to, though. Resisting the urge, I say, "Draw it for me. The way you think it looked." He usually does, when I ask him, and it makes him feel at least a little better about it all.

In the seventeen years we've been traveling together, Kintyre has acquired a sword, a questing partner, maidenheads and titles, prize purses and scars. But I firmly believe that the most important thing Kin ever picked up in all that time was a pencil. He's always so much calmer, so much more content when he's had the time and tools to draw. There is no better way to distract Kin out of his agitation and worry than to put him in front of a blank piece of parchment.

Maybe tonight, we'll forget finding someone to seduce and go out to that knoll with a torch and our stationery cases. Kintyre will sketch the statue as it once was, and I can lean back against him, spine to spine, our ribs pressing together warmly with each of Kin's inhalations, sharing support and warmth as I compose the tale of *The Eerie Eyes of Estagonnish.*

The scene I create in my mind fills me with a hot swell of yearning, as appealing as my little domestic fantasies from earlier, and no less ridiculous. I can almost feel the cool night breeze on my cheeks, the backs of my hands, the hollows of my wrists—along with the ache in the small of my back from carrying this ruddy pack all day and the pain in the bottom of my feet from the walking. I'm north of forty now, and yeah, the Doms are long-lived—Pa is going on seventy soon—but that doesn't keep us from feeling our age. Still, I can almost smell the pine pitch, the grass, and the special butter soap that I hoard and only dole out in small shaved curls for scrubbing away road-dust when we can hire a proper tub. There would be graphite and stone, and the crisp spring of grass under us. If I close my eyes, block out the harsh sun and the reek of the open gutters, I can just feel warm skin, a wet mouth as we both lay aside our tools, a hot push against my stomach, and...

Stop, I snarl at myself, and open my eyes. Kin is nearly around the next bend, all but lost to sight. I've been dawdling as I daydreamed and rush to catch up, moving as fleetly as possible to hide that I was ever gone. Secret. Shamed.

As the fantasy ebbs, I feel both empty with want, starving for touch, and at the same time, strangely at peace. I can't deny that I desire what I do: the small domestic instants, the quiet, the stars. Dargan was right: things that didn't seem important fifteen years ago, ten years ago— Writer, even three years ago—seem as vital as water and bread now. But these small, stolen moments will have to feed me. I consume them greedily, stockpile them carefully, and turn them over and over in my mind on days when things are bad.

And if I'm honest with myself—I should be, it's the least I owe me—if I'm really, truly *honest*, I *know* that this is all I'll ever have. The small moments, and the hoarded memories, and the oblivious companionship of Kintyre Turn. I will never have more.

At least until we're old enough to stop adventuring and settle in one place. If we settle together at all. I think back to that croft, that cottage, that estate I've been building in my imagination, but instead of a hearth with a rocking chair, surrounded by puppies and babies, a wife in the chair opposite me placidly cross-stitching, I conjure up Kintyre with his pencil and sketching book. Maybe Forsyth will take pity on a graying old adventurer and let me live out my retirement in Turn Hall. No babies. Maybe puppies.

And wouldn't that be a sight: three old bachelors, sniping at each other until we die, heirless and cranky, surrounded by slobbering dogs.

If we *live* to retire, of course.

I rub my wrenched wrist and frown. I may fantasize about the domestic life, but I also have no illusions about the sort of life I lead. I stretch out my arm, circling my left hand under its bandages.

A few paces ahead of me, Kintyre stops so abruptly that, lost in my wool-gathering, I nearly run nose-first into his pack. He's peering up at a painted sign, hanging above a large, clean window of lead-mullioned glass cut in the shape of diamonds.

"What about this one?" he asks. His gaze drops to the window, and he smirks, then throws a smug look over his shoulder at me. "Seems perfect to me."

"The taproom?" I ask with a chuckle. "Or the truly spectacular tits behind the bar?"

PART TWO

The tavern is called *Pern*, probably after someone's beloved nag or something just as sentimental, but it's the cleanest one on the thoroughfare. Even better, it lets beds above the taproom. Good enough for me. The perfect tits behind the bar turn out to belong to our landlady, and she brings them over to the booth we settle in to take our request for food, ale, and rooms.

Kin is scratching idly at a wood block, scraping away a careful layer of shavings into a tidy pile on the tavern table. It's a terrible habit. But I'm sick to the teeth of asking him not to do his carving over our dinners. I've lost that battle for seventeen years running. I have no illusions that I'll be winning it today.

Instead, I crane my neck and try to figure out what the picture is supposed to be.

"What's that, then?" I ask around a mouthful of a really, *really* tasty savory game pie. I'm going to have to ask the Goodwoman what herbs she used. There's an unexpected, spicy sweetness clouding up the back of my nose, and I love it. Spices make all the difference when foraging on the road. They can make each meal taste like something else, something new and interesting, especially if you have to keep using the same boring old road rations. And they absolutely make up for the fact that I currently have to eat with the wrong hand.

Kintyre holds up the block, and I can make out the

beginnings of a reversed image—Foesmiter, and some sort of craggy outline that could be either a cliff or the beginnings of a forest. I cast my mind back over what I saw Kin smudging into a piece of vellum a couple of nights ago, right before we went into the Dark Elf's cave. Ah, yeah. It's the maw of an entrance, and the beginnings of figures that are probably supposed to be us standing in front of it. He always draws me too short, the twat.

"Oh, ah, that's for the eyes story?" I ask, sitting back.

Kin nods. "If you decide to write it up."

"Of course I'll decide to write it up," I say. "You're already illustrating it. I have to now, don't I?" I shrug, trying to sound jovial about it. It's not like I wasn't already working on it anyway.

Kin grunts, his mouth twisting into an aggravated line, and he sets down the block with a *thunk* that rattles my fork against the metal tureen. He picks up his own fork and stabs at the center of his pie, rich brown gravy oozing from the wound.

"Oh, come on, Kin, I didn't mean it like that—" I cut myself off when Kintyre just shovels a steaming heap of lunch into his mouth and turns his blue, blue eyes out the dirt-streaked window. "Fine then, be a snit," I say, and reapply myself to my own pie. "Not like you can't actually see that I've been writing."

Kintyre grunts and holds out his hand. I would like a "please," but I know I'm never going to get one, any more than I will ever get him to stop flicking curls of wood shavings into my cooking. I gave up on that a while ago, too.

I hand over the scrap of paper I've been scratching at between bites.

I've also long since stopped being precious about my writing. When I first met Kin, I was as illiterate as every other title-less peasant in my Chipping; he'd taught me to read and to write. He'd helped me craft letters back home, letters that my mum still needed to pay a scholar to read to her, and to reply for her. But I had kept my first, colt-ish forays into fiction—a sort of sensational journal of our adventures—to myself. I never liked to share anything but my best work when I was a blacksmith's apprentice; I had felt the same about my writing. But Kin found the first of the story scrolls and had sat with me, patient, for many long nights as he taught me story structure and punctuation, and coaxed description and depth of narra-tive out of me. I'd been ashamed of my work, but he had likened it to smithery. I had the tools, he said, now that I could read and write. I just needed to work on the skills, the little tricks and shortcuts that masters knew, the mus-cle memory of the thing. I just needed practice.

Kin drops his eyes to the parchment and reads, chew-ing thoughtfully. His praise made me a writer, and his diligent generosity made me a *great* writer, and that is as close to divinity as worn-out, tired old Bevel Dom is ever going to get. So I can't help but watch his expression, my stomach twisted into knots, as he reads.

My work is recited in salons all over the world, and every one of the royal libraries has leather-bound, gilt-edged copies on display. I never pay for drinks in taverns and public houses where I read my scrolls. And I always have company to bed when I'm done.

But it's different when the subject of your stories is reading your descriptions of their own adventures. I want Kin to like it so much. I study every eyebrow twitch, ev-ery swallow, every motion of the left corner of Kintyre's mouth, seeking out the approval that the crinkles in the corners of his eyes signal, or the confusion that comes from the corner of his lip. It all *means* something—bore-dom, amusement, that he thinks the prose is too purple, or that he's found an error in the way I wrote the events.

It's torture, and now that I'm published and out of his tutelage, he rarely says anything beyond "s'good" when he's done.

For all that Kin has a deep and intense love of the arts, he keeps his opinions held close to his heart, and doesn't like to speak out against errors or interpretations. I've always guessed that it's because of the way his father believed that real warriors had to leave the feminine pursuit of artistic knowledge to women. Patient enough to teach me but dismissive in praise, Kintyre is a study in juxtaposition when it comes to his father's beliefs, and how they clash with his own passions.

Kin is a man imprisoned by the expectations of a mean drunk ten years in his grave. I sometimes wish that I'd broken Algar Turn's nose when I had the opportunity. It's too late now, unless I want to spend an hour shoveling first.

Instead, I settle on reading the parchment upside down, my eyes following my own messy first-draft scrawl along with Kin:

THE CAVERN REEKED OF MOLD AND LEAF-ROT, AND THE FAINT TANG OF WHATEVER LIQUID WAS IN THE PRESERVING BOTTLES AROUND US. THE AIR WAS BOTH HUMID, CLOSE, AND YET ODDLY STALE. THE COBWEBS IN THE HIGH CORNERS SURGED AND BOBBED AS AIR PASSED THROUGH THE TUNNEL, LIKE A GIANT'S FAINT SNORE WAS DISTURBING THEM. THEY WERE TATTERED AND COLLECTED DUST, SILVERY IN THE HALF-LIGHT OF OUR LANTERNS, HANGING LIKE A FOP'S SILVER-LACED CUFFS SPILLING FROM HIS COURT-ROBE SLEEVE.

AND THE SHELVES, OH, THE SHELVES. GLEAMING CLEAN, THEY WERE, NOT A SPECK OF DUST ALLOWED TO FALL AND REMAIN ON THIS BELOVED, MORBID COLLECTION.

WE KEPT ALONG SILENTLY, KINTYRE TURN AND I, AND AS WE DID, I RUMINATED ON WHY IT IS THAT THE TERRIBLE, MOST POSSESSIVE, AND

CREEPY PRACTITIONERS OF THE DARK MAGICKS PREFER, ABOVE ALL OTHER THINGS, THE EYES OF A PERSON.

SOMETIMES IT'S LITERAL, LIKE WHEN THEY TRY TO CLAW YOU IN A FIGHT. I WOULD PASS JUDGMENT AND CALL IT UNSPORTING, BUT WHEN IT IS A CONTEST OF LIFE AND DEATH, THEN ALL THE RULES HANG.

HEED ME IN THIS: THERE IS NO SUCH THING AS UNMANLY FIGHTING. THERE IS WINNING, AND THERE IS DEAD. AND I TELL YOU, MY LISTENER, THAT THE GOLDEN HERO AND I BOTH AGREE AS TO WHICH SIDE OF THAT COIN WE'D RATHER BE ON.

BUT MORE OFTEN THAN NOT, IT IS ONE'S EYES THAT THEY, IN THE MOST PHYSICAL AND LITERAL SENSE, WISH TO OWN. PERHAPS IT IS BECAUSE EYES ARE THE DOORWAYS TO THE SOUL? POSSESS THE EYES AND YOU OWN THE SOUL?

IN THE STALE CHILL CLOSING IN AROUND ME, FETID AND FOUL, I SHUDDER, FOR I CANNOT HELP THE SURGE OF DISGUST AT THE THOUGHT OF MY OWN SOUL CRADLED IN THE FOUL, SOILED HANDS OF THE VICEROY.

With Kintyre's attention on the parchment, I think about the lines I *hadn't* written down, the confession that had been on the tip of my pencil, but had seemed too personal to invite the rest of the world to read. I grind the heel of my hand against my right cheek, doing my level best to dispel the ghost-memory of Bootknife's blade sliding clean and neat along the wrinkle of my bottom eyelid. There's a scar there, just a small one, and it has mostly become lost in the folds of skin I've seemed to acquire with age. It goes unseen by any who don't already know to look for it, and that's as small a mercy as I can hope for, really.

I'm not vain. I know I'm sort of bland, and short, and going gray, especially compared to Kin. But I'd feel ten kinds of ashamed if I knew Kin was looking at my face and seeing only the scar. I don't want him to remember my fear and pain. Or to only see the blood, and sweat, and— yeah, I'm not too proud to admit it—the tears that my terror had wrung out of me when I thought, when I *realized*, that Bootknife was going to cut out my eyes.

Kintyre grunts and stops reading when he catches me scrubbing at my face. He looks up, his fork suspended between tureen and lips, and dammit, I haven't been subtle enough. He is looking at the ruddy scar now.

At least he's still got enough of his Turnish manners not to mention it, though. He taps the parchment with the butt-end of his fork, slopping a bit of gravy on the edge—*twat*—and says, "I've never understood why you write like this. You never sound like *you*. Sometimes, it's like someone else's got control of your quill."

"It's called having an artistic voice, Kin," I sneer back, gamely.

"'S weird." He taps the parchment again. But he doesn't add anything else.

The strange antagonism from earlier flares back up, making my shoulders tight and my belly burn. I take back my scrap and swipe away the gravy. Bugger him, then, if he doesn't like it. I don't write for him, do I?

We pass the next long moments saying nothing to one another, too used to each other's tempers to know that speaking right now would just make it worse. I have enough manners to not lick the tureen clean, at least, unlike the lord's son sitting across from me, and after the Goodwoman clears our table, I sit back and pack my pipe with the sticky herbal mash I learned to make on the decks of *The Salty Queen*. I light it with a long match and suck in a white, fragrant mouthful, reveling in the heady, soft taste.

It floods my lungs, burning at first and then becoming prickly, soothing, and I blow it out my nostrils, feeling playful and dragonish. I like the way it makes my nose hairs singe.

"That's a disgusting habit," Kin says with a grunt.

"You pick your teeth," I point out, jabbing at the air in front of his face with the stem of my pipe. I take another deep puff in defiance.

"But it doesn't make me smell like the ass end of a tannery when I'm done."

I clench the stem of my pipe between my teeth, hard enough to make the bone mouthpiece creak. "It's an orange-blossom hash. How is it even remotely like boiling urine?"

The Goodwoman laughs behind her apron as she delivers another round of her excellent ale and says, "You sound just like my parents. You must be very much in love."

Kintyre snorts and says nothing, eyes turned out the window, and I work very, very hard to beat down a blush. *Bloody buggering hells. Is the whole of Hain determined to see Kintyre and I Paired and rogering each other stupid?*

"We're not," I blurt. "Trothed, I mean."

"But I am in love," remains unsaid.

The Goodwoman cuts a glance between the two of us, and a quick, short look of pity flickers in her gaze when she turns it back to me.

"Well," she says, and I'm grateful to hear that her tone has turned formal and brisk, backing away from the uncomfortable topic. Good. She should feel bad. "Perhaps at the festival, then."

"Festival?" Kin asks, reaching for his ale and turning his light eyes to the Goodwoman. She wears a marriage bob in her ear, but that doesn't stop him from turning on the charm. His smile is warm and luminous, and my stomach twists, my heart lurching to the side.

Bastard.

"Oh, aye," the Goodwoman says with an actual, honest-to-Writer *titter*. "The Fire Flower Festival? It's why you're here, isn't it?"

"Just passing through, actually." Kin smiles wider. "We stopped for provisions—and lucky we did, for *Pern* has the most delicious ale and pie we've had the honor of tasting, and we've supped at the table of King Carvel himself, haven't we, Bev?"

I nod as the Goodwoman giggles, and do my best not to roll my eyes. Maybe Kin should have been a theatre-player instead of a hero. He certainly seems to come by his ridiculous charm naturally. Writer, he's laying it on thick. Is he really so desperate for a warm body between us tonight that he'll pounce on the first woman who flutters her eyelashes at him?

Well, she does have really perfect tits. It seems a shame not to even try for them, I suppose.

"But now that we know it's a festival night, we'll have to stay," Kin says, as if we weren't planning to do exactly that anyway. Writer.

I don't protest, though, because Kin seems to be making strides.

The Goodwoman's cheeks flush and she says, "Aye, well, then why don't you and your, um, friend, join my family's fire circle tonight? Wouldn't do to have you outside a circle. And in the meantime, why don't I fetch you both a bit of sweet cheese?"

"That's very thoughtful of you, thank you," Kin says, and I scoff and grin down into my ale, because of course the only time Kintyre Turn remembers his "pleases" and "thank yous" is when he's playacting the gallant. And he only playacts the gallant when he wants to get a leg over. Arse.

The Goodwoman bustles back to the bar, and I level

an unimpressed look at my friend. "She's married. Look, she's got a little boy behind the bar wiping the mugs."

"I see no spouse," is all Kin says.

"Writer preserve me," I sigh.

"Speaking of," Kintyre says, reaching across the table to pull my hand toward him. He turns it over slowly, unwinding the bandage that wraps around my wrist. His touch is dry, and warm, and absolutely does not send lightning skittering up my skin. Kintyre bares my swollen joint to the air and I gasp at the light touch of his fingertips against the very sensitive underside of my wrist. "How is this? Do you need some of the pain tea?"

"Not mixed with my ale, I don't," I say. All the same, I let Kin massage my arm gently, soothingly, discovering all the places where the pain lingers, inspecting the ligaments and the bones.

I should pull back. I should keep my distance. I should bloody well stop *torturing* myself with this.

Kill, I am going to kill Dargan. It will be violent. I will *enjoy* it.

"Not broken," Kintyre murmurs, golden head bent over his task. The tail of his hair brushes into the pile of wood chippings and some tangle into the ends like cockleburrs. It shouldn't be endearing. It is.

"No," I agree. "Barely even sore anymore. I'll be pure as unicorn piss come Turnshire."

Kintyre chuckles at my crassness and grins up at me. His eyes are crinkled around the corners in new ways, ways that speak of our long years of friendship, of the sun and the wind and the salt spray we've both endured, of the cold and the heat, of the pain and the laughter. There are small white hairs in his eyebrows and at his temples, but luckily his hair is light enough to disguise them. Kin looks simultaneously aged and ageless, still like the brash young man I first met, swinging his well-formed thighs across Stormbearer's back to dismount before my pa's forge. And yet he also looks like a man who is well into his middle life, the way I know we both are. His eyes have not changed, though. They still sparkle like northern ice cliffs in his mirth.

It's not fair.

I look my age, scarred and weather-rough, hair sprinkled with a dirty white, the corners of my eyes crinkled like a lady's badly-closed court fan. Blast and bugger Kintyre Turn for remaining gorgeous while I age. Bastard. Twat. Arse.

Kin sits back, and I leave my wrist unwrapped. I tap the ash out of my pipe and repack it. The Goodwoman returns with another tureen, and this one is fragrant with the scent of baked apples, onions, and cinnamon. Kintyre perks up and sends her another one of his beaming smiles, and, deciding that I like his plan, I offer up a grin of my own, reaching out slowly to brush the backs of my fingers against the edge of her apron, just casually enough for it to look like an accident. Her eyes follow my hand, and I curl my fingers up, close to the apex of her thigh, suggestive without being too lewd.

"Sorry," I say, but I wink to show her that I'm not, not really. Her ears flush pink, very sweetly.

If I can get her into bed, then I can touch Kintyre, kiss him, *have* him, and then maybe get this madness out of my blood, strangle the weed that Dargan planted behind my ribs.

The Goodwoman, flustered, thumps the tureen onto the table, slaps the plate of cinnamon-infused flatbread down beside it, and scuttles away. Kintyre meets my eyes with a pleased smirk. I lift the lid off a pot of melted goat's cheese mixed with stewed apples and onions, and file away the flavor combination to try in one of my own dishes when we're on the road later.

We take our time with the sweet cheese. Kintyre returns to his carving, and I scribble some more of the story, enjoying the fragrant smoke that curls around my head, and we have several more tankards of ale. We both flirt and charm the Goodwoman whenever she returns to the table, arousal slow and syrupy in my limbs, and she blushes but doesn't avoid us, or scold us. To my mind, this is as good as a "yes." Lovely.

In this drowsy, golden-sweet way, the afternoon passes.

We have nowhere pressing to be. We bought all our cold rations for Miliway, and it seems as if we're attending a festival tonight. Two festivals, if things with the maybe-not-really-married Goodwoman goes our way.

When the dinner crowd begins trickling into the tap-room, the Goodwoman comes back.

"Your rooms are ready," she says. "Were you wanting dinner, or did you want to go up?"

"Up," I say. I'm tempted to add, "*And will you join us?*" But it's too soon for that. Don't want to tip my hand just yet. "And if we're off to your festival tonight, then perhaps we should bathe as well. Can you ask your husband to bring up your tub for us?"

"Husband!" The Goodwoman snorts. "I reckon not. The hall boy took it up an hour ago. Figured you'd want it as soon as I caught a whiff of you both. My son will fill it now, if you like."

"No husband, then?" Kintyre asks, and under the table, I step down hard on his foot, warning him not to be so obvious so soon.

The Goodwoman snorts again and crosses her arms under her breasts, which makes them even more plump and... yeah, I can't wait to bury my face between them. Writer at His desk, they look so *soft*.

"No husband, nor wife, neither," she says. "Not no

more." And she nods once, firm, and leaves it at that. "Now, up the stairs with you both. You're stinking out my regulars."

Kintyre and I laugh and go. She's not wrong, is the thing. Our last bath was in Estagonnish—we do reek. Splashing around in a river will never replace what hot water and good soap can do.

"There's only the one tub," the Goodwoman says as a parting shot, and then seems to think better of it and hesitates. Kin waves her concern away.

"We've shared before," he says.

The Goodwoman smiles, nods, and then cuts another curious glance at me. I resolve then and there to ask her what she meant by, *"Perhaps at the Festival."*

Thinking about sex, and thinking about domesticity, and thinking about murdering Dargan, has led me to thinking about marriage. Never a good place for my imagination to go, especially lately. All the same, sitting in this room and watching Kintyre disrobe, I figure that if I were to exchange promise tokens with Kin, I'd like the tokens to be clothing.

Swords and weaponry are traditional for soldiering Pairs pledging a troth, but Kin has Foesmiter, and I've got my compact bow and my own sword, and after seventeen years, we don't really need any other weapons. Our kit is already perfected, comfortable. It would make no sense to change it. Likewise, we already buy each other pipes and quills, carving tool wallets, boots and tack. We've always bought each other the kind of gifts trothing Pairs do, not to show our dedication, but because, inevitably, somebody's money purse will get left behind in the middle of the night, or accidentally slide down some monster's gullet, or get stolen by a conquest. And then we'll have to share coinage until we have the chance at another reward, or can swing through Turnshire or Kingskeep for more. Because of that, anything else we'd buy (or craft) one another wouldn't be, well, as meaningful.

But clothing, clothing would be good. Neither of us can make clothing, so the purchase would mean something. And frankly, I hate that Kintyre still wears the color of his mother's House, as if everyone doesn't know he's a Turn. Seventeen years ago, when Kin was running away from home to join the border guard, it made sense. Now it just seems forgetful, and gives him the air of being ashamed of his family.

True, the only time I met Algar Turn, he was a drunk-flushed, boil-covered, pus-weeping elfcock. And Forsyth is bossy and skittish and annoying. But the Turns have done great things in their history. It's a grand legacy that Kintyre has augmented honorably, and he should be proud of his lineage. He should be wearing Turn-russet, even if only to make it clear that he is a member of a Seated House when we're on the road. Preferential treatment is nothing to be frowned at. It's dead useful if you've been in a fight with some horrible monster and the master of the estate has a beautiful, grateful daughter.

And of course, I wouldn't mind being able to wear Turn-russet myself, to declare myself part of that same great House, that same honorable lineage, to tell the world that I love and am loved... to be a part of Kin's *family*.

Uhg. I'm so sentimental I'm making myself sick.

And, yeah, I can admit that I'm a possessive little bastard. I'd like to see Kintyre wearing the same Color as me, to be clad in the same shade, so that when we walk into a room together, it's obvious that Kin is taken. And that I'm the one that took him.

But the thought is fleeting, even though it's complex,

and drops right out of my head the moment Kintyre finishes unlacing said Sheil-purple jerkin and drops it onto the end of his bed. The flex of Kin's shoulders through his thin, much-abused shirt is momentarily distracting, and I have to swallow hard to banish the dryness in my mouth.

By the Writer's left nutsack, this is torture.

Two bloody decades of torture, and still I can't seem to walk away, or put myself out of my misery. My fingers twitch with the desire to touch. Instead, I hook them into the laces of my own shirt and turn my eyes away.

The Goodwoman's son comes into the room, without knocking first, to dump another kettle of boiled water into the travel tub. I'm suddenly grateful that I didn't give in to my urges. That would have given the boy more of a show than I think he would ever want. It's the fifth kettle of hot water, and the boy is dawdling so much I figure the whole lot will be cold before Kin and I ever get the chance to get into the tub.

A flutter of fabric in the corner of my eye catches my attention again, and I turn to watch as Kin strips his shirt off over his head. It is yellow with sweat and grime. Once we're done with the bathwater, I'm going to throw our clothes in it for a good scrub. I'd ask Kin to do it, but he's never got the hang of scrubbing laundry. He grew up with maids to do it for him, and had no desire to learn on the road because he always knew I would get annoyed enough to just grab it out of his hands and do it for him. I'm a fool, and I've spoiled the great lump.

We've both got spare trousers and shirts in our packs, so I slip out after the Goodwoman's son and pop back over to my own room to fetch mine. I come back to Kin's room, where we both plan to bathe so the Goodwoman doesn't have to move the tub, and spread it out on the drying rack. I have a vague hope that the lavender-scented steam might help pull out the wrinkles and give the cloth the illusion of freshness. When Kin doesn't seem to catch the hint, I grumble and rummage through his pack to lay his spare shirt and trousers beside mine.

Half naked, and in no rush to strip any further, Kin stands by the window, watching the procession of villagers as they head down the main road with garlands and wreaths and bouquets. He lounges against the sill in just his leather trousers. His skin, though scarred, still glows gold from years of living under the sun, his shoulders broad as a ship's masthead, tapering to battle-trim hips and an arse that fills out his trousers like a ripe peach. He looks appetizing, and he knows it. It's probably for the benefit of the lovely lasses on the street below. Or the Goodwoman. Or both.

The sight of his bare feet against the wooden floor nearly does in my self-control. I distract myself by stripping out of my own short-robe jerkin. Writer, my shirt's in no better state than Kin's.

The boy lingers in the doorway, gawking at Kin instead of heading back down to the kitchen for another kettle. The Goodwoman comes up the hallway with a tray of ales we didn't ask for. I'm chuffed to see them all the same. My mouth is horribly dry. The Goodwoman shifts the tray so she can swat the back of her son's head with a free hand.

"Layabout!" she snaps, but her tone holds affection and exasperation. This isn't a blow from an abusive parent, but one merely at the end of her tether. I've seen innumerable swats delivered by my own sisters-in-law to my abundant nieces and nephews in just the same way. "Stop staring and go."

"But Ma—"

"But nothing," she cuts him off.

"But it's *Kintyre Turn*," the boy interrupts in reply.

Ah, so that's the problem.

Hearing his name spoken in that tone of awestruck worship, Kin stops being outwardly annoyed by the delay and instead turns and offers the boy a dazzling, white-toothed grin.

"Let the boy—" he starts, but then the Goodwoman is glaring at him, too.

"I've already told my son that he can pester you *after* his chores are complete. Don't undermine me, Master Turn," she says.

Kintyre blinks, startled by her forthrightness and his complete failure to charm her into obedience. Her twit-terpated blushes from downstairs are no match for moth-erly chagrin. I snicker, amused by this reversal.

"As for you," she says, rounding on the boy, finger poking his nose playfully. "You finish your chores, or no festival for you."

"Aw, Ma, no!" the boy whines.

"Aw, son, yes," the Goodwoman replies. "Get on, now, or I'll have you off to the ghost!"

The boy's whole posture goes rigid, his face turning white as milk, and he flees down the hall with the empty bath kettle at speeds I'd say he normally saves for running toward sweets.

"A ghost?" I ask, as the Goodwoman hands out the ales. There's a nice sharp bite of condensation against my palms as I take the offered tankard. "Surely not a real ghost."

"Oh, aye," she says, setting the tray down on the hearth and fussing with the towel rack until it is close enough to warm the bath sheets, but not so much so that they'll singe.

"A real ghost?" Kin asks, attention well and truly caught finally. I can tell because Kin's looking the Good-woman in the face, and not elsewhere. "And you use this as a threat for good behavior?"

"Why not?" the Goodwoman says, hands on her hips as she leans over to peer up the flue, opening the hatch a bit more to allow the fire a little extra air. Her perfect tits sway perfectly. "A mother uses what weapons are in her arsenal. You'll learn that when you have sprogs of your own, Master Turn."

"But a *real* ghost," I say, and meet Kin's ice-blue eyes over the Goodwoman's head. We conduct the same sort of silent conversation we've had a hundred times before through grimaces and waggling eyebrows.

This could be a problem, I communicate.

Kin's tiny head-jerk means he agrees. *We should look into it, see if we can rid the town of this monster.*

A sniff and a nose wiggle: *Agreed. I'm especially concerned that she doesn't seem concerned about it at all.*

Me too, from a seemingly idly scratched cheek.

"So, where would we find this ghost?" I ask, voice a study in nonchalant interest. I hook my thumb into my belt and rock back on my heels, as if I were no more than a curious farmer passing a lazy afternoon in idle chatter, then sip my ale.

The Goodwoman laughs over her shoulder, eyes crinkling in what appears to be genuine joy, which makes my guts clench with horror.

"In the old well, o' course. Where else would a ghost be?" She jerks her head vaguely south.

"Of course," I murmur, and shake my head when Kin opens his mouth to ask for more details.

Don't get her suspicions up, I communicate with a tug of my trousers. *Ask the boy,* I mouth, because we haven't devised a signal for that one.

"Your, er, your son, will he be back up soon?" Kin asks.

"Oh, aye, he ought. We have two kettles we swap

around. You'll get your warm bath, Master Turn, no worries. Fear o' goin' to the ghost is a good motivator for boys like 'im. Sometimes it takes the children," the Goodwoman says, smoothing her hands down her skirt and fetching the empty tray up. She sighs; it fluffs the locks of hair that have escaped from under her mop cap. "But only when they're naughty. If that's all, gentlemen?" And then she has the chilling gall to smile at us, as if all was still level with the world.

"No, no, that's... thank you," I say, too stunned to say any more. The Goodwoman bustles out. She seems so *blasé*. And about a ghost that takes away naughty children, presumably back to the old well where it... well, in my experience, it probably drowns them. Possibly in punishment; possibly because it's lonely and looking for ghostly playmates, and thinks murdering village children is the best way to gain them.

Kin and I have twin expressions of carefully contained horror aimed at the now empty doorway.

"Bloody buggering hells. That was creepy as all get out," I breathe, breaking the silence. I shiver despite the hot steam curling through the air, making the tips of my hair limp and sag. Everything smells of lavender and butter soap, and I think I might never be able to smell the combination ever again without feeling sick to my stomach.

"Do you suppose they've been bespelled to be so calm about it?" Kin asks, voice low in case someone's in the hall.

"Possibly." I run my hand through my hair, scrubbing the goose pimples away. "Writer, if Tallah ever spoke that way about the twins—"

Kin presses one square palm against the nape of my neck, reassuring. He loves those boys too. He sends them little drawings in my return letters, and carved them wee swords from willow switches last time we were through Bynnebakker.

They're children. Children are meant to be loved. Cherished.

Protected.

We perch on the end of the bed, lost in mutual contemplation of what it will take to slay a ghost. I rotate my wrist, testing it, becoming familiar with the stiffness, the burning pull, stretching it where I dare. Kin whispers Words of Healing under his breath, and slowly the soreness fades. The Words always help, but their magic's never strong enough to heal a hurt entirely and immediately, more's the pity.

In silence, we prepare. In silence, we make careful ready. We exchange head jerks and long stares, plotting, planning, and all the while keeping the air free of whispers that can be overheard. We're well practiced at this, too.

When the boy comes back with the kettle, Kin leans down to meet his wide brown eyes. "My boy, I have a proposition for you."

"You do?" the boy asks, readjusting his grip. Kin takes the heavy kettle from him and passes it off to me. Not wanting to waste the bathwater, I dump the kettle into the tub, but keep my attention on the conversation. I pour the water out slowly and from a height, causing splashes to muffle Kin's voice from any eavesdroppers. My wrist twinges, but I ignore it.

"I do," Kin says. "How about, after you finish all your chores and we finish our baths, the three of us go on an adventure?"

The boy's eyes and mouth become comically round. "Yes, sir, Master Turn, sir. Yes, please!"

"Excellent," Kin says, straightening and rubbing his huge paw against the top of the boy's head, scruffing up his dark curls into a disarrayed nest. "Meet us back here at sundown. Wear sturdy boots."

PART THREE

We take turns bathing, and dressing, and then fill the idle time between that and sundown with more writing and carving. My teeth are clenched tight around the stem of my pipe, but for once Kin isn't bitching about the smell. He's seated by the window, which has been opened enough for my smoke and his whittlings to get out, and the noise and conversations of Gwillfifeshire to get in. Both of us are silent, ears attuned to the chatter of the festival-goers walking past the inn, listening for any other tidbits about the ghost which might give us an advantage. So far, no luck.

I'm only half-heartedly scratching at the story, to be honest. My blood is singing with the possibility of adventure and danger, and it's making me fidget. I always get squirrely when we're forced into inaction, knowing that a fight is just on the horizon. Kintyre is the fussy one in daily life, but when it comes to camping out and waiting, he has the ability to sit still and quiet for long periods. His little brother is the same. I've never asked, but I get the feeling it has something to do with their arsehole father.

I praise the Writer again for being born into a family where I didn't have to be scared of my own pa, where I didn't feel the need to be still in an effort to be over-looked. Brain cramping with the futile wish to sock Algar

Turn in the nose again, I force myself to focus, to pay attention to the pencil and parchment under my hands.

It feels as if the shelves of crystal decanters are watching us as my companion and I slip past, I write. Luckily, the eyes—all shaded between teal and emerald, grass and old copper—can't actually see us. Or, at least I pray strongly that they cannot.

A few paces ahead of me, Kintyre pauses. He raises the Wisp lantern slightly, throwing rainbows of illumination against the cavern wall as the light reflects from the facets of the decanters. They splinter against the rough rock ceiling and glisten in the moldering deadfall. It occurs to me just then to wonder how the leaf-rot got into this cavern, for there are no trees in this subterranean hell to drop them.

"What is it?" I ask, my voice ratcheted down to a harsh, hushed whisper, palms sweating on the leather-wrapped pommel of my sword. I want nothing more than to sheathe my blade and wipe my hand on my short-robe, but I know better than to put away my weapon now. Seventeen years of adventuring, and I've learned this lesson above all others—the moment you put away your sword is the minute you're going to wish you hadn't.

"This decanter is different," Kintyre says, and his powerful voice is a soft boom against the barren stone rocks. "Different color."

"Liquid?"

"Eyes."

Before I am certain of his next action, he has plucked that decanter from amid its shelf-mates, and has tucked the neck of the bottle under his wide leather belt. The angle at which the shadow of his arm now falls across the bottle means that I cannot make out what, exactly, is singular about it. "Maybe it's a favorite. Could be

LEVERAGE."

I SUPPRESS A SHUDDER, AND INSTEAD OF SHAKING MY SHOULDERS, IT CRAWLS DOWN MY SPINE LIKE A DROP OF COLD SWEAT.

"Kintyre?" I ask, voice a hush, and he hums to show he's heard me. I read the last few paragraphs to him. "What did you say then?"

Kintyre looks up at me from his carving and grins with that wicked boyishness that always makes my heart lurch. That same damnable grin that made me trot after him when I was done shoeing Stormbearer all those years ago, a witless blacksmith's son trailing like a tugboat in the wake of a lad determined to make a name for himself outside of his great House, and with enough arrogance and charm to get whatever he wanted.

"Ah, I think what I said was, 'The Dark Elf can suck my cock. Let's just kill the creepy bastard and be done with it.' Then I suggested we smash a few decanters to see if that would bring him running, but you reminded me that we promised to give them back to the families."

I snort, swallowing down a chuckle. "Kin," I admonish in a whisper, grinning back, "I can't put that."

"Well, then I don't know why you asked me," he says. "Make up something."

"I don't know what," I say. I can't help the frustrated sigh. "Maybe I won't write this after all."

Kin frowns, holding up his woodcutting, and I nod.

"I know, Kin, but I just... the eyes." I touch my scar. My eyelid twitches and jumps at the memory, my eyes suddenly watering, and I squeeze them shut, hard.

"Oh," Kin whispers. "I didn't think about... huh. Well. I mean, if you don't want to..."

I shake my head, bare my teeth once, and then run my free hand across the back of my neck to banish the goose pimples. "Right. Blast. Right. I just... I'm really, really not comfortable here, my friend."

"I know."

"The Viceroy—"

"I *know*." Kin lays a comforting hand along the back of my neck, filling the space mine has left, and it almost feels as if we're holding hands, our fingers deliberately tangled instead of by accident. I ache with the want of him.

I push the story aside and stand, shrugging Kin off before I can do or say something that I'll regret later—or worse, that *he* might regret.

Luckily, that's when the boy knocks on the door.

Our shirts are still slightly damp from the steam, but there's no time to let them toast by the fire any longer. We throw them on, and I open the door for the lad. The sun has set, and Kintyre has been muttering about the Witches' Hour since the twilight slipped from orange to soft gray. If we're going to confront this ghost, we both know that it will have to be before midnight, when the monster's power would be at its apex.

The only blessing of the damp is that the shirts no longer cloud the air with the reek of long travel. Instead, the scent of lavender-soap and hearthfire curls under my nose, and I do my best not to be revolted. I wasn't jesting when I thought I'd never be able to stomach the herb ever again. I've already packed my hip satchel with all manner of potions and talismans. Some are tricks and trinkets I've picked up over the last two decades of adventuring, some are from a standard set I replenish through Mother Mouth with each return trip to Turnshire. I rummage in it now, pulling out my small brocade bag of healing unguents. I swipe some lemon cream along my upper lip to mask the smell of lavender.

We lace up our jerkins before the fire, sealing in the

last of the warm air. The boy is wearing sturdy boots, as instructed, but only a pair of black trousers and a thin, wine-colored shirt that his mother clearly chose for him to wear to this Fire Flower Festival. His wee waistcoat is furled with intricate embroidery picked out in brightly sparking copper thread, and I make him take it off and leave the fine and flashy garment behind. It will attract too much attention. Instead, I have the boy don my own short-robe of Dom-amethyst, so travel-grimed now that it's practically mud brown, just so he won't freeze. It's not horrifically cold outside, but cold enough that, with the window open, Kin and I had been able to see our breath.

As we finish kitting up, the boy gleefully introduces himself as Thoma, and then proceeds to tell Kin all about the adventures he has with the other children of Gwillfifeshire while pretending to act out the tales in my scrolls. He has a small sword, made of two sticks tied together with twine, shoved into his belt and, beside that, a more sensible kitchen knife. I'm torn between taking the knife from him so he doesn't accidentally cut his own leg and leaving it so that the boy has some sort of protection, just in case this little adventure gets out of hand. I don't intend to leave the boy in any sort of situation where he'll need the knife, of course, but sometimes plans don't work out as they are, well, planned.

Better to let him keep it. He seems sensible enough not to cut himself, and it's always better to have a weapon when none is needed than to *not* have one when it *is*.

It's easy enough to slip down the stairs and out the back of the building. Thoma is an excellent guide, having grown up in the *Pern*; he knows all her secrets—like the servant's hall tucked away in the shadows, and which treads on the delivery stairway squeak. He thinks all the skulking and sliding is great fun, and he turns a bright grin to us each time we round another corner. Kin and

I let him continue to have his glee—there's no point in frightening him now, not when we need him as a guide.

There will be time to make him understand how deadly serious we are later.

Thoma leads us to the back kitchen door, and out through a small cobbled courtyard where the laundry is hanging and raised boxes cradle his mother's herb garden. On the way back, once we've dealt with this creature, I fully intend to indulge myself in cataloging everything she's growing.

A bustling festival mood has gripped the main street, where villagers in what appear to be their celebration best travel in pairs and family groups toward the ruin on the hill. It covers the sound of our footfalls as we slink down the alley between the *Pern*'s small stable and the neighboring row of shops. In the distance, over the wooden roofs of Gwillfifeshire, I can see that they've lit a bonfire at the apex of the knoll, and as we slide past yet more revelers on our way around a corner, I realize that each household seems to be carrying with them an unlit torch wreathed in fresh meadow flowers.

Fire Flower Festival, I remind myself. *For whatever it is that means.*

We take more back alleys and squeeze through fence slats, following a circuitous route that only makes sense to the boy. Finally, we arrive in an older, crumbling part of town where the houses lean against one another like limping beggars and the square is frosted with the refuse of what appears to be a butcher's market. The breeze gifts us with the odors of old meat and blood, spilt marrow and bowels. Mixed with the lavender of my shirt, it's bile-inducing. I clamp my mouth shut against the taste of it, absurdly glad for the lemon cream.

If Kin is nauseated, I can't tell. Dammit, I should have offered him some of the unguent. Thoma doesn't seem to even notice the smell. Kin scans the square, but all the houses appear empty. The festival has pulled away all the residents. Hmph. That's an unexpected blessing.

In the center of the square, bathed in auspicious and melodramatic moonlight is an ancient yew tree. Its circumference is at least twice the span of Kin's arms, and the light from above filters through its creaking branches, casting the well tucked into the lee of the thick trunk in ominous shadow. The wall is crumbling, lopsided, and rough. It would come to Thoma's waist if he was standing beside it, and it seems the roots of the tree have crowded it so bad that the ground around the yellowed stones has buckled and heaved, shoving the well into a motley array. A small pulley-rack is planted into the ground beside the wall, a fresh rope threaded over the wooden block and attached to a slim, clean bucket.

"Of course it's right out in the open," Kin grumbles.

We stop in the last patch of shadow afforded by a narrow alleyway before the exposed air of the square. Kin leans against the wall of the building and scratches the back of his head, thinking. I settle in beside him, watching the well warily while Kin is distracted, as I always do. Someone has to remain alert and ready.

"She's in there," Thoma says, rather pointlessly, as that much is already obvious. He steps out of the slice of shadow and thrusts his finger at the well.

"Yes," I hiss, and drag him back. "Thank you, Thoma. You should head home now."

"What?" the boy yelps, eyes large and wounded. Writer, I don't want to wrestle with a child having a tantrum right now.

"You've been very helpful," I say quietly, crouching down to meet the boy's eyes. "And we thank you. But things are about to get dangerous, and I think your mother would be happier if you were not here with us when they do."

Thoma's brow wrinkles, and he frowns fit to resemble the arches of Kingskeep's gates. "Dangerous?" he repeats, incredulous.

"There's a ghost about," Kin says, and he speaks with a tone that makes it clear he thinks Thoma a stupid child. Thoma is grown-up enough to take umbrage with being spoken to in that way, though, and puffs out his chest.

"I ain't afraid," he insists. "She ain't scary."

Kin makes a sound at the back of his throat that I know is muffled disbelief, and then covers it with a cough. "All the same, young Master Thoma," Kin says, without turning to the boy, "you'll go now."

"No, I won't!" Thoma brandishes his twig sword. "I'm a *hero*, and I ain't scared of nothing!" He waves the toy in a wide arc and I have to duck to avoid its swing.

It's stupidity and bravery like this that gets people killed, and I'll be damned if I'm going to watch it happen to a *child*. It's dangerous work, adventuring. And it's not for the innocent, the uninitiated, the small, and the weak. I have stood beside too many graves and attended too many wakes, mourned for more of our companions than I can count on both hands. I will *not* attend one more.

As the boy flails, chest thrust out and chin forward, I grab his wrist. It's harsher than I should have been, but I'm annoyed. The boy yelps and drops his wooden sword. It clatters against the cracked flags and both Kin and I suck in a breath at the volume of the sound.

The world goes quiet. Thoma whimpers. Kin and I scan the area, ears open, eyes darting. When nothing jumps out at us, I uncurl my fingers one by one, slowly enough not to startle the boy. As soon as he's free, Thoma yanks his arm out of my reach and cradles it against his chest. The skin's red, but there's no bruising. He looks betrayed.

"You're mean," Thoma hisses, whispering because Kin has raised a finger to his own lips. "You're not nice, or smart, or courageous, or anything like the stories. You're terrible, and you're stupid, and I want you to go away."

"We'll go when the ghost is destroyed," Kin hisses.

Thoma gasps, eyes bulging, and takes a step back so swiftly that his narrow shoulders slam into the brick wall behind him with a muffled slap.

"No!" he says.

The word is freighted with such horror that I whip around to spot whatever is coming up behind Kin. But I find only empty air over Kin's shoulder, and turn back to look at the boy, wondering if it's something only he can see. That's when I realize that his gaze isn't trained on some invisible creature, but on Kin himself.

Thoma sees a monster. But it isn't the ghost.

"No," Thoma says again, and this time he takes a step forward, glaring. "I won't let you!"

"*Let* me?" Kin snorts. He looks as if he's about to palm the boy's forehead, to hold him away and out of punching range like a schoolyard bully. I shoot Kin a warning look and Kin heaves a sigh, crossing his arms over the pommel of Foesmiter instead. We share another conversation of facial twitches and almost-gestures and agree that whatever spell this ghost has cast upon the Goodwoman of *Pern*, it must also have cast it on her son.

Monsters often enchant their human slaves into loving them. Love means that the slave will sacrifice themselves to save the creature, or betray the people who have come to rescue them. And that means Thoma can't be here.

"Go home, Thoma," I say. "Please."

Thoma crosses his arms in deliberate imitation of Kin, mulish. "No. I *like* Mandikin, and I won't let you hurt her."

A sharp blast of grave-cold air rushes through the alley. I groan. Kin runs his hand through his hair, puffing out an irritated sigh.

"Perfect," I mutter. "You said her name."

Another chill blast rushes past, and this time the origin direction is clear. Kintyre spins around and faces the well, Foesmiter leaping into his hand. I press my back to my partner's, feeling the slide and bunch of muscle, reading Kin's readiness and wariness in the shift of balance and the heat of his skin. Kin will watch my back as I try to drum some damned sense into Thoma and get the little brat to hide.

"Thoma," I hiss through the rising wind, pushing the strands of hair flapping into my eyes out of the way. It stings. "You should never name a ghost so close to its grave, or midnight."

"It summons them. I *know*," Thoma says, and peers at me as if *I'm* the one who's the idiot. When he realizes how worried I am, Thoma's grin grows wide and his eyebrows pull down into the eternal expression of a child willfully about to throw himself into mischief.

It is so like one of Kintyre's expressions that I'm momentarily poleaxed. I raise my hand, to silence, to muffle, but my surprise makes me too slow.

"Mandikin, Mandikin, MandikinMaaaaaandikiiiiin!" Thoma calls. "Mandik—*umunf!*"

I slap my palm over the boy's mouth. But it's useless. The wind, pulsing with half-hearted blasts, grows steadily stronger, and cold enough that my next exhale hangs in front of my mouth like a specter itself. Thoma digs his fingernails into the back of my hand, whining high and shrill between my fingers, but I grit my teeth and hold on.

The alley is no longer a defensible position. Too many shadows. Too many walls that a creature of air could corner us against, with too few handholds for climbing away.

Without me even needing to say it, Kin gallops forward into the open air of the square. I wrap my free arm around Thoma's shoulders and drag the gagged brat into the square behind Kin, once more taking up my position at Kin's back, facing out, waiting.

The boy kicks my shins and swears under his breath, but I hold on. The last thing I'm going to do is let the boy wriggle away and run. He'll be cut down by the creature. Or worse, join it and turn himself into a hostage, leverage, a shield and a distraction.

The breeze is freezing. It grows into a gale, and my fringe cuts at my eyes. I squint, unwilling to let go of Thoma until I know which direction is safe to push the boy toward. The freezing wind turns the lingering dampness of my shirt into an icy punishment.

And then the gale stops. Just like that, our clothing and hair drop limp, the night air suddenly unmoving. It's like those summer nights when it's so hot that even the breeze can't bear to stir, but it's *chill*. Wrong, in every and all ways.

Goosebumps march up my spine, and I take a deep breath, forcing myself to ignore the eeriness around me and focus. I narrow my eyes, watching the debris and mist kicked up by the wind as it slides slow and molasses-like through the butter-thick air. It coalesces, dancing like dust motes in a library sunbeam that's cold, so cold.

"There," Kin says, but doesn't point. Doesn't need to. Didn't even really need to speak, except that our world is too quiet, all of a sudden. It needed shattering.

Thoma goes still. I spare him a glance, worried that the boy will be limp or statue-like, eyes glowing, mouth parted in a grimace, or any of the other horrid things I have seen humans become while under spells of compulsion or Words of Obedience. But the boy seems fine. Irritated, fuming, but otherwise fine.

Carefully, I release him, my free hand curled, ready to shoot out and nab the kid by the back of the collar if I need to. Thoma shuffles a few steps away, but doesn't seem inclined to throw himself at the ghost, or on Kin's sword, or at me. He only glares mutinously, tiny jaw thrust out, thin arms crossed over a skinny chest. He seems to have totally forgotten that he has a kitchen knife threaded into his belt, and for that, I'm grateful. I don't need a child flashing around a blade on top of everything else. I should have taken it away at the inn. Fool.

I risk looking away from Thoma and at the monster.

It's a woman, or at least, it's woman-shaped. I get the sense of white, white, and white—long hair, long scarf, full-length sleeping gown, all of it trailing into frosty mist, flakes of the ghost breaking off and falling like a never-ending drift of sparkling snow, but never piling up at her feet. Fingers of ice crawl out along the paving stones toward us. The wall of the well grows rimed with ghost-frost.

It seems, at first, as if the ghost cannot, or does not see us adults. Kin's grip on Foesmiter shifts as two tendrils of frosty mist reach out toward Thoma. They don't grab, they just... reach. Invite. It's not seductive, or dangerous. It's... maternal. Parental.

Terrifying.

My stomach tries to crawl up my throat, and I swallow hard, my heart fluttering. The pose is the exact same one my brother takes when he's beckoning the twins over for cuddling. And nothing *dead* should look so *inviting*.

"Back, wretch!" Kin snarls, rocking up on the balls of his feet, Foesmiter held at its most menacing angle. Starlight tumbles down Foesmiter's keen edge, a threat and a promise both. The ghost startles, straightening a bit and scowling. It beckons again, agitated. Thoma inhales, obvious and indicative. I dig my fingers into the back of Thoma's coat seconds before the boy tries to break into a run.

"Mandikin!" he squawks, when it's clear that I have no intention of letting him go.

Only then does the ghost straighten fully. She scowls harder, fierce and furious, hair lifting, scarf and nightdress whipping about in a hurricane wind that neither I nor Kin can feel. She reaches for the boy, arms out and issuing ghostly tendrils that remind me of the menacing tentacles of a kraken.

They writhe and reach. Foesmiter cuts, but the mist only parts like pipe smoke, coalescing again as soon as Kin's blade has passed, unharmed.

"The phials! Bevel, the Words!" Kin prompts, but I don't have enough hands to hold Thoma, my sword, and root into my pouch.

"Writer's calluses!" I snarl, and shove Thoma down hard, hoping the daft brat will have the presence of mind, or at least the willpower, to stay where he's put. The boy cries out, a sharp yelp that seems disproportionate to the mild pain of landing arse-first on cobblestones, and I belatedly remember the knife.

If the kid's been hurt... no, worry about the ghost first, I scold myself.

Sword up, I keep an eye on the ghost and Kin, and get Thoma flipped onto his hands and knees with one foot, putting enough weight on the wriggling little brat's back to keep him pinned in place. The ghost hisses in displeasure, probably annoyed that I keep manhandling its slave instead of letting the boy go to her, and I duck quickly to tug the knife out of the boy's belt.

I lift it by the pommel, point down, looking for blood.

There isn't any on the blade, and neither Thoma's clothing nor flesh looks slashed. There's no dark stain on his trousers, thank the Writer. I take my boot off the kid.

And that is when the ghost *howls*. It points a finger that's slowly growing sharp at my face, at the knife. The sweet, womanish face transforms into twin black pits and a sucking, terrifying wound of a mouth.

"I'm fine, Mandikin!" Thoma yells from the ground. "I'm fine, see?" He kneels up and holds out his palms. They're scratched and dirty, but there's no blood.

The sharp finger, the accusatory point aimed at me, curls into claws and suddenly, immediately, I *understand*.

Mandikin's not trying to hurt Thoma. She's trying to *protect* him.

Protect him from Kin and me.

I look down at the knife in my hand, at the boy, then up at the ghost.

"Oh *hells*," I mutter, and fling the knife away. "Kin, stop!" I yell, but it's too late. Kintyre is already lunging at the thing, muttering Words of Repellence. He's rat-arsed rubbish at Speaking Words, always has been. The ghost wavers and shifts a bit back toward the well, but is otherwise unaffected.

"Get the boy to safety!" Kin shouts over his shoulder, lunging again. Is he really trying to make himself a human shield between me and the specter? Apparently, he is. It would be so easy for the ghost to cut through him, to *step* through him—hells, to even just step *around* him—and I'm reminded very suddenly why I'm often the one who has to do the planning in this partnership.

"Kintyre!" I call again, but Mandikin's howling has risen to such a pitch that I doubt Kin can hear me. "Kin, stop it!" I lunge forward, sheathing my sword and grabbing on to Kin's bicep, only to be shrugged off as Kin whips Foesmiter through the ghost's non-existent skull.

"Kin, stop! Writer, for once, will you *listen* to me?"

Just as I guessed she would, the ghost smokes through the gaps in our bodies and reforms behind us. Thoma stands and smiles, but Mandikin doesn't go to him. Instead, she turns to the hill outside of town and rushes away along the cobbles, down the main thorough-fare. Her hair is whipping around behind her, loose and flapping with the trail of her scarf, the fluttering hem of the modest, incorporeal nightdress diffusing like smoke rings against the starry sky.

"Follow!" Kin growls and, being the faster of the two of us, pelts after it. As always, I follow. And if I fall behind, I'll follow Kin's footprints.

"No, wait!" Thoma cries, and I can hear the clatter of the boy's boots fall away behind me. Thoma is a smart boy—smarter than me, it seems—he'll catch up.

I shoulder through the rough, narrow gap between two wattle-and-daub houses, and suddenly I'm in a muddy field. The sky bursts into full radiance above me, deep indigo and black splattered with a cornucopia of constellations and, in the distance, capping the hill, the firefly wink of torches.

The Fire Flower Festival, I realize. *Mandikin's not running from Kin. She's going for help!*

The ghost flees up the hill, and I catch up to Kintyre just as he begins to climb it, Foesmiter slashing wildly and stupidly at her trailing scarf. We're perhaps a giant's stride behind when the ghost stops. She is standing beside someone, female, but beyond that, the finery of the lady's festival attire makes her difficult to recognize.

"Ma!" Thoma cries from somewhere behind us, voice sharp and loud for such a small pair of lungs, and the woman beside Mandikin turns to its source. The ghost points at Kin and me, steaming up the hillside, Foesmiter naked in the starlight.

"Mandikin? What are you—good gracious! Thoma!" the Goodwoman of *Pern* hollers. "Master Turn, Master Dom! What*ever* are you doing?"

"Back!" Kin roars, skidding to a halt and menacing his already-proven-to-be-useless blade in the ghost's face like the dumb lump he is. "Stay back, away from that thing!"

"Kin, wait—" I try again, reaching out to grab for my partner's bicep a second time. Kin actually smacks my hand away and I dance back, both my knuckles and my pride smarting.

Kin again mouths Words, and a fission of terror shivers down my spine. Words of Banishment, and, with Foesmiter so tuned to the ghost... no wonder Kin was cutting through the fog. He wasn't trying to hack at a specter, he was aligning Foesmiter to the ghost's energies.

"Writer, Kin, stop!" I shout.

Then Thoma barrels past both of us. At first, it seems as if the boy is heading to bury himself in his mother's skirts, but he swerves and throws himself at the ghost instead.

Mandikin is just solid enough for the boy to puff against, like diving into an overfilled feather pillow. Her skirts flare and curl around his shoulders and head like protective fingers.

Kin stutters to a halt, tongue tripping over the final Words of the destructive phrase, and the world goes horribly, breath-stealingly silent. Foesmiter glows gold in the starlight, lit from within by the Words it waits to cut at their foe.

"Move," Kin hisses at the boy.

"No!" Thoma spits back. "I won't let you hurt Mandikin!"

"Hurt Mandikin?" another voice roars, and a man with mutton chops and a sash stretched across his rotund belly shoulders his way to the front of the increasingly horrified-looking crowd that has begun to condense around us. The town's lord, I'd guess, and then I dismiss him to focus on my stubborn friend.

"No one's hurting anyone!" I shout, but my voice is lost under the sudden wave of protests and noise from the people of Gwillfifeshire. Bodies shove forward, getting too close to Kin's blade, and I wriggle myself between them. Kin's broad hand lands on my back, using me to shepherd the incensed bystanders back, like I'm better for nothing but acting as his shield. Humph. Arse.

Shouting rakes against my ears, pierced by Mandikin's ghastly wails. I want to clap my hands over them, but instead, I shove my arms out to the side, taking on the role of human barricade that Kin has foisted on me.

Thoma is crying now, clutching at Mandikin, and other children have begun to wail as well, one little girl screaming over and over, "Don't kill her! Don't kill her! Don't make her go away like Daddy!" The town's lord is trying to bully his way to Kin, and Mandikin is no help—the more the children cry, the more she screams.

"Enough!" I roar. This is my battlefield voice. "By the Writer's left nutsack, that is *enough!*"

The expletive is harsh, but it works. Everyone on the hill falls silent all at once, the adults blushing and glowering furiously, the children muffling sobs or giggles behind their hands. Mandikin offers me an expression so poisonous I wonder vaguely if I'm now cursed to die at dawn, or something. She primly lays partially opaque hands over Thoma's ears.

"Finally!" Kin bawls, puffing up his chest like he's just killed a dwarven pimp.

I spin on my heel, duck under Foesmiter with extremely practiced ease, and stab my finger against Kin's sternum. "I was talking to *you,* you thick-skulled tit!"

Kin gapes at me, blinking rapidly, Foesmiter wilting

in his grasp. The Goodwoman of *Pern* applauds slowly, loudly. No other sound except the crackle of the nearby bonfire shreds the quiet.

"Now, what is this about harming Mandikin?" the lord blusters, and, Writer, he sounds like a satire of a lord, all jowly vowels and burring consonants puffing out from behind his soup-strainer moustache, like something from a play.

"It was a misunderstanding," I say, taking a step back from Kin and waiting until my partner has caught up enough to sheathe Foesmiter. Then I make a very humble, very simple, but very low bow to the official. Not my court bow, not the one I save for King Carvel, but the one I really mean. "We apologize most humbly."

"They were going to hurt Mandikin!" Thoma snarls, wiping tears from his flushed cheeks with the cuff of my short-robe.

The lord puffs up his own impressive girth to match Kin's and rocks forward on his feet, ready to have a fight.

"We were, it's true," I jump in, hands up and placating, before Kin can open his mouth and doom us to another night on the road. Or to a lynch mob. "But you must understand, sir, that with our, um, extensive experience with malevolent spirits, we might have, ah, made some hasty assumptions. We now stand corrected and offer no ill will to, ah... Miss Mandikin. Or Gwillfifeshire."

"Extensive experience?" the lord asks, eyes narrowed in suspicion.

The Goodwoman leans over and hisses, in a deliberate stage whisper, "That's Kintyre Turn and Bevel Dom, Lord Gallvig."

A ripple of murmurs and suddenly craning heads spreads back over the crowd.

Oh, thank the Writer, I think as I feel the last of the tension that had crackled in the air break and crumble away amid the buoyancy of the town realizing that they have heroes in their midst. Write a few dozen scrolls, and suddenly you can do no wrong. I try not to take too much advantage of our fame (Kin's head is big enough without drinking and getting favors from brothels for free), but sometimes, just sometimes, it's welcome.

"And you were after the ghost?" another woman calls out, startled.

A man raises his arm and makes a sort of panicky hand gesture over the heads of the crowd. "But Mandikin is the town babysitter. You can't banish her!"

"We need her!" says another. "She's one of us!" More voices join in, a chorus of parents as desperate not to lose Mandikin as the children.

That deflates Kin a bit. "We apologized," he mutters.

"I apologized," I correct, under my breath, just enough for Kin to hear. Kin ducks his head and nods once. My friend is stupid sometimes, but he can learn, too.

"I am deeply sorry for my mistake," Kintyre says, using his Eldest Son of Turnshire voice and executing the matching bow. It's a bit showier than mine was, as befits his station and fame, but it's not his peacockish court bow, either.

Good. At least he's taking the apology seriously.

Kin turns to Mandikin, taking a deep breath for another formal apology. Thoma puffs out his chest in defiance of the hero's attention on his friend. Kin is wounded by the boy's lost worship. It manifests as a small twitch in the corner of Kin's mouth, but only I see it because I know him so well. Gutted, Kin swallows back the flowery words I know he would have said and simply bows again. Mandikin nods solemnly, slowly, just once.

When she raises her head, it is wreathed in smiles, and the chill of ghost-breath seems to have warmed into a summer breeze, rather than the sharp snap of winter. A spill of children push past and around us. They all crowd around her, and their parents seem happy to let them go.

"Well then, back to it, back to it!" Lord Gallvig roars, belly shaking with the force of the laugh that follows as he ushers people back toward the bonfire and the food stalls pitched haphazardly against the walls of the ruin.

Mistress *Pern* sidles close enough to pluck my short-robe off her son. She shakes out a bundle of fabric that proves to be the waistcoat we'd left behind in our rooms, wraps it around him, and then sends him off after Mandikin and the other children. She pats down my short-robe, a motherly gesture that I've seen women everywhere perform, and then hands it to me.

"Thank you," I say.

"Thank *you* for wanting to protect him," she replies. "Even if it was misguided."

I scratch the back of my neck and fight the flush I can feel trying to crawl up my cheekbones. Usually I'm the one making other people blush, and it's a nice change. It's also a nice change to come out the other end of an adventure unhurt, unbloody, and unbruised for once. I nod to the Goodwoman, feigning humbleness at her gratitude, and she cants a hip at me. Oh, she's *flirting*. With me. That's lovely.

That is very good, indeed.

Kin cuts a look between us, and his eyes widen fractionally. Realization is followed by a small smirk of anticipation and triumph. Oh. He expects me to share.

After all this? After everything that could have been avoided if Kin had just *listened* to me? Not bloody likely.

"Thoma left one of your cooking knives in the square," Kin says, abruptly charming again. "I'll fetch it back to the tavern." He jogs down the hill to give me space in which to work, dodging around a group of pretty young women and men trying to get his attention. Followers of my scrolls, most likely. Adoring youths like these are always pie-eyed in Kin's presence, cooing and making offers they're all too young to really understand.

I take a deep breath, taking a moment to watch Kin go, giving myself time for my face to cool.

"So," I venture, playing at harmless and polite. I reseat my sword in its sheath to give myself an excuse not to meet the Goodwoman's gaze. Acting a bit nervous makes women want to coddle and protect, which are feelings that are more easily translated into "taking care of me in bed" than those engendered by approaching them with overconfident arrogance. I duck my head, look up at the Goodwoman through my lashes, and fiddle with my pouch, rearranging things so they're all laying correctly. "A ghost?"

"That's both supremely unsubtle and a fair bit more narrow-minded than I expected from one as well traveled as you," the Goodwoman replies with an unladylike snort. Startled at having my ruse caught out, I look back up. And I only now notice that her mop cap has been replaced with a crown of intricately braided golden hair and wildflowers. The smile lines beside her eyes deepen as she grins at me. "You'll not be charming me with your wiles and your false coyness. I know you, Master Dom. And I know your habits. If you want the story, just ask. Your scrolls say you've consorted with nixies and sirens, nagas and ogres. You should know better than to assume. You've taken dinner with wolves."

I snort and resist the urge to shove my hands in my pockets like a truant child who's been caught out. For I absolutely have been caught out. Instead, I shrug on my short-robe and roll my eyes theatrically, willing to banter. It seems I should focus on a more forthright, mature approach with the Goodwoman. Fine by me. I prefer it when no one needs to be persuaded. "It was bloody."

"It was still dinner."

"True." I look over at the ghost thoughtfully. "She's sweet with them," I decide. I'd trust her with the twins.

"She was in life, also," the Goodwoman says softly, taking the whispered confession as an excuse to step closer, to brush the tips of her fingers against the inner curve of my elbow. "She wanted nothing more than to be a mother."

I obligingly tip my head down toward her. "How did she... if it's not impertinent to ask?"

"Childbirth."

I nod grimly. "The babe?"

"Gone to rest on whatever shelf the Writer places our books when our story is over. Or not quite begun."

I nod again, brushing my nose against the shell of her ear, the one that earlier today had a marriage bob. Which is now missing. "And the father?"

The Goodwoman grimaces slightly. "You know as well as I that fauns don't mate for longer than a season."

Oh. *Oh.* I sigh slowly. All the excitement of the adventure drains out of me, leaving only hollow, empathetic sorrow. That poor woman. "So, he's likely forgotten her name by now."

"If he ever knew it," the Goodwoman agrees. "It was a good love, though. A solid love. And Mandikin had no illusions, no imaginings that what she had was other than what it was: just a season."

"You knew her well, then?"

"My grandmother was her sister. I know her better than most, but not from firsthand experience."

"Still a treasure," I say. I reach into my pouch for a pencil and some scrap parchment, and then pause. "Before I... do you mind? I mean, do you think the gh—Mandikin would mind if I wrote her story down?"

The Goodwoman's eyes shine. "Mandikin's tale told by Kintyre Turn's bard? I think all of Gwillfifeshire would be quite, quite honored, Master Dom. So long as you tell it honestly."

I chuckle as I retrieve my writing tools. "So, making a fool of Kin and myself, am I?"

"Aye, Master Dom, that you will be. Come, I haven't forgotten that I offered you two a place in my family circle." The Goodwoman pulls me off to the side of the festival fairway, where people have begun to clump and cluster on the grass. There is a blanket there, and Thoma has already deposited his stiff, formal waistcoat in a crumpled heap on the knitted wool. The Goodwoman sighs fondly, scoops it up and refolds it, and then seats herself. I sit beside her, deliberately pressing my side against hers. She doesn't move back. Progress. Excellent. I lay the scrap of parchment against my knee.

"Very well. Go ahead, please," I say.

The Goodwoman's tale enchants me, and I take every opportunity to encourage her to rest her cheek against my shoulder and whisper it into my ear. I turn my face only a few times, when I want clarification, and make it seem as if brushing my lips against her nose or chin is an accident. If she wants to kiss me, she will—I'll let her initiate that.

I don't know how long it is before my notes have filled up both sides of the sheet, and she's placing her hand on my shoulder and saying, "Ah, Master Turn has returned."

I twist to look. Kin is climbing the hill slowly. He's still wearing Foesmiter, but he's carrying my writing box under his arm. As he passes stragglers carrying torches, the light gilds his hair and the embroidery on his jerkin with gold. Writer, Kin looks edible—flushed from the earlier adventure, windblown and confident. And better than all of that, my pipe is in that writing box. Now that is a true hero.

"He's handsome," the Goodwoman admits, clearly admiring the view as much as I am.

I feel my guts twist with the small jealousy that always curls there when someone else openly admires Kintyre the way I can't.

"He is," I say carefully. The last thing I want to do is reveal the extent of my wounded heart to a woman who is, by virtue of her occupation, probably the proud spider at the center of Gwillfifeshire's gossip web.

"You're a lucky man," the Goodwoman says guilelessly, and it takes a second for me to remember what she said in the taproom. She thinks Kin is my lover. We're not wearing the same Colors, so it's clear we're not trothed, which means she must think... Writer, what a scandal that would be, if Kin and I were carrying on like that, the eldest son of a lord and a blacksmith's boy.

Yet, we're both knighted, both men of titles and wealth now. Both men of renown, and to be frank, the bedsport we engage in with women is already extremely close to actually making love.

I feel my cheeks go hot. I lower my face, making a show of putting my notes away in my pouch to avoid having to answer. The Goodwoman clears her throat expectantly, and I have just enough time to murmur, "He doesn't love me," before Kintyre reaches us.

Her face slips into an expression of shock, which, for his sake, she quickly shutters. Then she stands, and my whole side feels suddenly cold. I try not to take that as some sort of portent.

The Goodwoman is formal and polite when she offers Kin a seat on a second blanket that she shakes out next to her own; the flirting and the geniality has stopped. She is still kind and warm while the three of us chat idly, and I realize that she was never really flirting with me.

She was just trying to see if she could get a rise out of Kin, see if he and I might... might what? Put on a show? Reveal ourselves?

As lovers? As trothed? Maybe goad me into pledging my troth now, before the whole village, in a romantic gesture inspired by battle and burning flowers? The Goodwoman must be one of those faithful readers who seems sure there is more happening between me and Kintyre than I put in my scrolls. Of course.

What an absolute minx. I'm supposed to be the charming one who talks people into things they didn't realize they were agreeing to.

I refrain from pinching the bridge of my nose and dig through my writing box for my pipe. I clench it between my teeth and try not to hiss as I pack the bowl; adrenaline spent, my wrist is throbbing again. Kin has edged closer to the Goodwoman, mistaking her warmth for genuine interest, the same way I did. When his hand edges up the pool of fabric that is her gown to brush one questing knuckle along the Goodwoman's ankle, I take a breath to stop him. Before I can, the Goodwoman shoots to her feet and crosses her arms under her bosom, taking a step back.

"Shame on you, Kintyre Turn," she says, glaring first at Kin, and then shooting a meaningful, sympathetic glance at me.

What, does she think he's going to take that as an opening for a love confession? Absolutely not. I take a puff of my pipe and blow out a ring, trying to figure out how to command my brain to say any sentence that doesn't start with, *"Come back to the inn with me, Kin. Just us."*

Uhg! I'm a stupid, foolish, desperate, hopeless sop, and it's really starting to infuriate me. *Murder. Death. Killing Dargan. Killing him slow.*

"Where's she going?" Kin asks, eyes trailing after her like a puppy left tied up in the yard. There is actual petulance in his tone. "I thought that you—"

"No," I interrupt.

"But she—"

"No!" I can feel the rage rising from the knot in my chest, sliding up my face like mercury in a thermometer. "And to be quite frank, Kin, I'm not really in the mood tonight."

"But you said—"

"Well, that was before you made a fool of us in front of a whole town, wasn't it?"

Kin splutters and his face crumples into that calculatingly adorable look of surprised hurt. "Before *I* made a—"

"Oh, Writer, just *stop!*" I slam my pipe down hard enough against the ground that the embers scatter all over the dew-damp grass and splutter out. I toss my pipe into my writing box and stand. I haul Kintyre to his feet, and this time, Kin goes with me when I grab him by the bicep and drag him far past the back of the festival stalls, out of the ring of firelight, to where the din of the people will cover the shouting match we're about to have.

I wouldn't want to sully Kintyre's reputation by screaming at him in public, after all.

"How is any of this—? Where is *this* coming from?" Kintyre asks with a pouting mutter. "What's wrong with you?"

"Wrong with *me?*" I snarl. "My problem is that you never bloody well listen to me!"

"There's no need to be womanish about it!"

"Did you really just... ?" I gawp. "Womanish? Really? When you know Captain Isobin, and Cassiopith and... by the Writer's balls, Kin! You don't really think like that, do you?"

"Like what?" Every line of his body screams defensive and deliberate ignorance.

I throw up my hands. "*This*, Kin. This right here is why I'm mad at you! You pretend to be so stupid; you don't think, you just *react!* You just wave Foesmiter at something, and you think it will fix everything! Either one or the other of your swords needs to be unsheathed and that's it, isn't it! That will solve all the problems! Never mind Bevel Dom. It's not like you trust *his* judgment, or advice, or his Writer-be-damned friendship!"

Kintyre does exactly what he always does when I try to confront him, to pin him down, to stake him to the spot and force him to absorb truths: he deflects. "Well, I wasn't wrong. It was a ghost, and it sounded like it was—"

I rock back on my heels, mouth hanging open in stunned fury. "Do you even hear yourself?"

"It's not our fault that—what did they expect, a hero hearing about a ghost? They should have *told* us..."

I stab a finger against Kin's sternum. "It's easy to be a hero when you're born to all the advantages, Kin. Wealth enough for a good horse, and fine gear. Wealth enough to have grown strong on good food, to have training masters hone your body, and scholars to teach you the paths and secrets of the world. But have you stopped to consider what it *means* to be a hero? What it means to be the idol of that little boy? Thoma looks up to you. The twins worship you. Even Forsyth looks to you for clues on how to live his life. We must cast our names carefully, Kin. We must think before we act. And we can no longer be unaware of how our actions read. Whom we shun, whom we throw our support behind, this *matters*."

"It was a mistake!" Kin shouts again. "It wasn't our fault!"

"It's entirely our fault!" And I'm sick of it, just sick of it. Kin just can't be wrong, can he?

"We weren't to know—"

"We could have *asked*!" I snarl.

"You never asked either!" Kin bawls back.

"More the fool, me!" I shout. "Why, *why* do I never learn? Why do I always, *always* go along with you? Why do I always follow, unquestioningly, *unthinkingly*, like a stupid spaniel? And why am I always surprised when you kick?"

"I don't kick you!" Kin says, and every line of his body, every blink, every breath is suddenly desperate. His entire demeanor changes, becoming contrite and needy. He fists the shoulders of my short-robe in his hands, scrunches down to meet my eyes, blue to blue. "Bev, no, I don't hurt you. I never want to hurt you."

"But you do! Writer, Kin, you do!"

"I don't mean to—"

"That's not the *point*! I am tired, Kintyre. Tired!" I roar. The truth that has weighed on me since yesterday comes falling out of my mouth like a cannonball, crushing the air out of my lungs. I gasp for another breath. "I'm sick of the road, and I'm sick of the travel, and I'm sick of fighting, always *fighting*. If I'm not fighting monsters, then I'm fighting with *you*. I'm sick of waking up sore and cold. I'm sick of having nothing, and I'm sick of you not..." I trail off and stop, biting down hard on the tip of my tongue to keep the words trapped behind my teeth.

I can't say it. *I can't say it.*

It would ruin everything.

He would never agree. He will never say yes. If I say it, he will leave, and it will all be over. And I would rather be tired, and sore, and cold, and be fighting monsters and bickering with my truest friend than be *without*

Kintyre Turn.

Kin blinks, icy eyes wounded, chin tucked in shame. "Sick of me?" His voice is so small.

I sigh lustily, a gusting burst of irritation drawn from my very guts. "That's not what I meant."

"You said—"

"I know what I—Kin, please, you don't... you don't understand."

Kin lets go of my robe. His hands slide upward, palms skimming over leather to cup the thin flesh of my throat. His thumbs circle, just once, along the edge of my jaw, calluses rough against my larynx. I swallow hard. His hands are warm in the chill spring air. My flesh tingles.

I want either to grab his hands and kiss him, or punch him. I ball my hands into fists and rest them on my belt, refusing to allow myself to do any of those things. I can't... Kintyre has to make the first move. He has to do it first. He has to *want* it.

I feel my own eyes growing wide, and I can't seem to stop them, can't blink. I don't dare look away.

"Kintyre?" I ask, and I can't seem to get my voice to go louder than a croak. I want. I'm *shivering* with want, and Kintyre has to say yes, doesn't he? This is a yes. It *has* to be a yes. I just might die if this isn't a yes.

Kin licks his lips, tongue sliding against the bottom first, corner to corner, and then the top, disappearing again and leaving a shimmer of wetness, and, Writer, how desperate I am to chase it back into Kintyre's mouth with my own. We exhale as one, inhale, and we are so close to-gether that our chests bump as they inflate. The moment stretches, stretches.

And then it snaps.

I surge forward and throw myself on Kin's mouth.

It's probably the stupidest thing I've ever done. But I can't, I absolutely cannot *stand* it anymore. I can't *not* be kissing Kintyre Turn.

I dig my fingers into the hair behind Kin's ears and yank him down. He's such an infuriatingly tall bastard. I mash our mouths together, biting, devouring, taking first one of Kin's lips, and then the other between my own; wet, hot, wonderful. Breath puffs against my cheek, a surprised snort, and Kin grunts. I toss my arms around his neck, hold on, and think dazedly that breathing? Breathing is for suckers.

"Let me show you. Writer—" I pant against Kin's mouth, peppering words between kisses. "I—what I—for so long."

And then there are hands on my shoulders, and Kin is holding me, massaging, pushing... pushing?

Pushing.

I freeze. Shame splashes down my spine. Ardor turns to ice in my veins.

"Bevel," Kintyre whispers. His breath is hot on my ear, and still it turns my limbs to frost and snow and isolation.

With one word, Kintyre the basilisk turns me to stone.

"You beautiful, beautiful idiot," I moan, and my voice crackles over each word like a winter pond crumbling beneath my feet. I hope Kintyre thinks I'm talking about myself.

I turn away, press my hands against my face and scrub. Because if my cheeks are flushed from chaffing at them, then Kin can't possibly believe it's from the way I'm desperately, desperately swallowing back tears.

"Bevel," Kintyre says again, and I both do and don't want to turn, to see which expression his face has twisted to house. Disgust? Pity? Fear?

Never love. It will never be love, and hope, and joy, and affection, and if it can never be those, then I don't want to see it.

"Look, I didn't mean it," I say, softly. I offer it up, just like that—an escape route for Kin. "I'm feeling... I'm just tired, you know? I'm muddled. Just... go back to the blanket. I'll... I need a walk. I'll clear my head. Then I'll meet you back there."

"I'll buy us some ale?" Kin whispers. His voice is tremulous, low, and I don't allow myself to believe that it's because Kin is as affected as I am. It didn't mean a thing to him. It was just weird, something strange, just Bevel Dom having one of his breakdowns. Something to get drunk over and laugh about, and then forget. Like always. "Something to... I can get you, I don't know... do you want some honeycomb?"

"Sure, Kin," I sigh. *If you think I'm some simpering maiden whose good humor can be bought with treats and booze and gewgaws... oh, Kin, how are we getting this so wrong?* "I'll be along soon."

"As you wish," Kintyre says. "Just... follow me soon?"

I make no response. I just keep my head down, my hands firmly at my sides until I hear Kintyre's boots on the grass shuffling away, out of hearing.

Only then do I raise my face to the moon and wrap my arms around myself. "I'll follow. I will always follow you. And that's the real problem, Kintyre Turn. I was made to follow you. And I'm so sick of walking one step behind."

PART FOUR

✴

I'm *gasping* for a few moments of quiet time with my pipe. Without Kin. Just to drown this buzzing, itching desire and the horrific shame that flares under my skin, in the base of my spine, lingering on the back of my tongue. To numb all the places and patches where Kin has touched me before, where I want him to touch me again. But my pipe is in my writing box, and that's on the blanket with the Goodwoman of *Pern*, and I don't have the guts to look her in the face right now. Not yet. So instead, I walk the perimeter of the festival.

It makes me feel better, one eye on the people, one eye on the darkness beyond, like I'm patrolling. It makes me feel like I have a purpose.

On the far side of the massive bonfire from the Goodwoman's blanket—and presumably Kin—Lord Gallvig is standing on a small, knocked-together wooden platform, accepting strips of cloth from a line of people. Some of the cloth looks new, some worn, and some even looks like it was torn from wedding finery or funeral shrouds. I lean against the pole of a pastry tent and watch the lord wrap the cloth around and around a long length of pine, until the end is absolutely bulbous. Some children offer up string to tie it all in place, fussing over their knots and bows, tongues poking out and eyes squinting in their concentration.

When it's done, the lord walks twelve circles around

the fire with the cloth-stick held aloft. Every time he passes the ruins side, the children squeal with delight and shout the name of a month. When a whole year's worth of laughter has been counted out, a woman who must be the lord's wife wreathes the head of the torch with a garland of dried flowers and fruits, herbs and winter wheat.

Together, her cheek resting on his shoulder, fingers intertwined, they touch the ball of fabric to the flames. It catches slowly, sweetly. Deep beneath the layers of cloth there must be pitch. The torch, once lit, doesn't smolder or flicker out.

The lord plants the torch into a hole bored into the side of the ruin wall. The scent of sage and clary, rosemary and golden roses, weeping martins and forget-me-nots perfumes the clearing as the fire licks at the wreath. It is the bouquet of mourning and remembrance, of filial love and neighborly admiration, of gratitude.

I breathe deeply and am filled with shame.

Judging by the fall of the moon, over an hour passes as I wander the stalls and impromptu dances that have erupted wherever someone has thought to plant themselves with an instrument. In that time, I have drunk more than one tankard of ale that was pressed into my hands, and swung about two fair young lasses and a youth just old enough to know what he likes and how to ask for it with the coy tilt of a chin and a look up through his fanning lashes.

But it is not his company I want tonight.

There is only one man, one person I want to talk to and touch, to smell and laugh with, and even though my heart is a little more broken tonight than it was when I rose from my bedroll this morning, Kintyre Turn is still the man I want to spend the rest of my life with.

My miserable, masochistic, foolish life.

In whatever way Kintyre dictates, I am his.

So I find the Goodwoman's knitted throw among the throngs of families picnicking on the grass. Kintyre sits alone on one corner of it, slightly removed, contemplative looking. There is a small basket with a packet wrapped in oilcloth by his knee.

"Hello," I say, and drop down beside him on the ground, sprawling as if I don't have a care in the world. The posture is very carefully put on, and it makes Kin look all the more tense and nervous, sitting upright with his legs folded under him.

Kin blinks, and then looks as if he's screwing up his courage. I lick my lips again, a quick flicker, and draw in a breath. I can't stand it. If Kintyre tries to explain, or deflect, or blame away, I'll scream. So instead of letting him talk, I pull back the oilcloth on the basket and inhale.

"Oh, a spinach and cheese roll. My favorite."

"I know," Kin says, deflating. He reaches into the basket and pulls out two of the steaming buns.

I take mine graciously, prop myself on one elbow, and go about the very important business of not talking about it. I nibble and people-watch, quiet and companionable. Slowly, the tension bleeds out of Kin's posture. As the buns vanish, the silence becomes comfortable and familiar again, and just like that, the storm is over.

Thank the Writer, it's over. And Kintyre is still my friend.

When I've licked the last of the crumbs from my fingers, I retrieve my pipe, my wallet of sweet herbs, and matches from my box of writing tools on the blanket beside us. Kintyre takes one of the matches from my hand, strikes it against his own belt buckle, and holds it out for me. The gesture is intimate, as Kin brings the small sliver of wood to his crotch, and then offers it toward my mouth.

I nearly forget to inhale. Just before the flames can lick the tips of Kin's fingers, I remember that I'm meant to be lighting my pipe.

Kin's breath, when he leans in close to cup the bowl, betrays that he has somehow acquired mead or honeyed ale. When he withdraws, he tugs a dark drinking skin off his belt and takes a swallow. He offers the skin to me, fingers loose around the neck as he brings the rim to my lips. I hold the stem of my pipe to the side to accept the sip without needing my hands.

It's silly, but I'm suddenly in a silly mood: giddy with relief, skin starved, both of us wanting to reassure ourselves that we are still the most important person in all of Hain to the other. Even if we aren't... that. When he lowers the skin, Kin turns and leans back-to-back against me, as if we are about to do battle. Close, without being intimate. He pushes a bit, playful, and I shoulder him back and take a deep, soothing draw of sweet herb.

It tastes and feels like forgiveness. Or at least a desire to return to the way things were three hours ago, over dinner in the *Pern*. Which is close enough.

Kin is warm. Kin is always warm. It's one of the things I like best about him, unless we're in the hotter climes. Then Kin is clammy and sticky, and clings like an octopus when he's irritable and uncomfortable, which just makes me irritated in turn. But now, in the cool night breeze, with the fire at our front and Kin mapped against the constellations of my spine—stars of shoulder and muscle, bone and cloth, the dips and swells—I'm comfortable. I'm content. It is not all that I've ever wanted, but it is close enough. Close enough. I can live with this.

I'll have to.

I tap a finger over the bowl of my pipe and relish the sweet smoke that sifts up my sinuses. A deep breath in clears the smoke from my head, and brings me a hint of my friend.

Kin smells of sweat, and the faint hint of butter soap and lavender water. He smells of man. He smells of Foe-smiter's whetstone and polishing oil, petrichor and musk, leather and road-dust, horse and hard work. Kin.

I turn my face to the flames, resting my cheek on Kin's broad shoulder. In return, Kin sighs and arches his neck, settling the vulnerable curve of his skull against my cheekbone.

All around us are families, most sitting on woven throws of every dye color, embroidered with flames and flowers and bursts of glittering metallic thread that could be Urlish Fire-rockets or the cold glitter of the full moon reflecting on the Sunsong Sea, or the distant twinkle of the Sky Lights above Erlenmeyer. Flasks are passed among the adults, wineskins and steaming glass bottles of what appears to be hot chocolate and tea. Chil-dren's mittened hands reach up to snatch, sliding on the smooth sides, fingers wiggling unseen beneath patterned yarn. Some of the skins are held up to cupid's bows and sticky mouths, and the adults laugh when the children make horrified faces as the wash of whiskey or tart wine dribbles against their lips and they realize the adults aren't drinking anything desirable after all.

Beside the old ruin, the ghost of Mandikin crouches low, her skirts dissolving into the night-cool grass like dew mist. Her fingers fly as she tells a tale to the rapt audience of toddlers that have piled around her like sleepy puppies. Her eyes shine silver; her smile is wide. She is happy. She must feel my gaze on her, because she raises her head to me and winks, charming the children around her into a crescendo of high, sweet giggles.

Over the crackle of the bonfire, I can hear some sort of fiddle being brought into tune. There are tin pipes in the muddle, too, and the deep strum of what might be a harp or a large guitar, but the players are on the far side of the flames from us, and I can't see through. A tinkling chime rings out, and then suddenly everyone's attention is on the half dozen couples who are mingling between the families and the fire.

Pairings, I realize. Yeah, they must be.

Standing stiffly, closest to the flame, is a career military man. The fellow to his left, with a matching bearing, must be his new shield-partner. Next to him, a shy couple very obviously in love blush and flutter at one another, only their pinky fingers entwined. He has bright red flowers woven into his dark beard, and she has the same woven into braids hanging from her temples.

Next to her, a woman about the same age as my oldest sister-in-law is grinning slyly up at a tall, slim, nude fae creature, all onyx eyes and ebony skin, and an unashamedly bare phallus.

The Pair next to them consists of two sweet young girls who keep kissing and giggling, tucking each other's hair behind their ears, righting ribbons, only to fall back into each other's orbits, to grab and kiss again as if their lips were iron and magnets. And beside them stand another pair of young lovers, this time both young men. One is talking incessantly, his hands flying, and the other cradles his cheek close to his own collar, indulgent and attentive.

And lastly, slightly off to one side, is a sturdy couple. They are a man and a woman, clearly farmers, and are surrounded by nearly adult children with two very different hair colors, eager to finally be one family.

Each pair carries a broom, the birch-twig skirt of it woven with pitch-soaked ribbons, the handles carved smooth and intricate with a hundred little knots and whorls, chains and images, symbols that must speak of love, fidelity, promise, and those little moments and secrets meant only for the Pair. I wish I could get a closer look at the brooms. What stories they must tell.

Kin sits up and I shift, strike another match and tamp the bowl of my pipe as I wait. Another ringing skirl of string and pipe and, one by one, the partners join hands on the broom handles, fingers twined. A third flourish of music, and they turn their backs to us and touch the tips of the brooms to the flames. The pitch catches, the birch twigs crackle, and a flash of magic flares, containing the fire to the broom head, sealing the flames away from the handle. A fourth and final skirl, and the partners plant the ends of the brooms into low stone pockets that hold the flame just high enough off the grass that they won't sputter out, but not so high that when the Pairs entwine their elbows, brush back their beards, ratchet up their skirts, and leap over the flame, someone catches fire.

One of the young girls, one of the kissing ones, shrieks in surprise as a trailing ribbon from her hair sparks up, but Mandikin is there quickly. She douses the flame with her wet hand, and the girl's yelp trails off into embarrassed laughter before I've even really registered the cry. Mandikin scolds the girl, and then kisses first her forehead, and then her new trothed's, fond and a little sad. The ghost probably minded both girls when they were young.

Kin's hands are on his thighs, curling and flexing in a way that says he clearly wishes there was enough light to sketch by. Instead, he swigs more mead, and I wonder if he intends to get drunk tonight. Not that a nice little festival isn't worth celebrating, but it's me who'll have to haul him back to the inn, who will have to strip him out of his clothes, have to dunk his head in a cold basin and dry his hair, have to tuck him in and... I shift, suddenly glad that the firelight is low enough that Kin can't sketch. Because, if he had enough light to draw by, he'd also have enough light to see the tent I'm pitching.

Bloody hells.

Instead of doing anything about it—it'll go down on its own, and I'm not feeling particularly inclined to handle it any other way—I tap out the ashes of my pipe on the heel of my boot, repack the bowl, and relight the herb. We watch the revelers in companionable silence.

Kin is lax in the aftermath of adventure and a few good swigs from his skin, not to mention an argument forgiven. Pliant and nonverbal, this is my favorite version of my friend. This Kin lets me touch, lets me run my fingers through gold-threaded locks, lets me rest my palm on his wide thigh, lets me wrap around him in our bedrolls, lets me bury my nose behind an ear.

I take a breath to speak, lick my lips, and then abruptly freeze, my brain tripping to a stunned halt at the question my tongue was just about to push from between my teeth.

No. I can't say that out loud. Can I? No. *No.* Kin wouldn't... *I* can't. Could I? Can I?

"What?" Kin grunts. "Just say it."

I release my breath in a rueful chuckle, forcing my spine to unfuse, my shoulders to lower. I should be startled that Kin knew I was building up to something, but... seventeen years. We know each other well.

Well enough that Kin knows when I'm biting down words. Well enough that my request might actually go unmocked.

I'm a brave man. I've faced down dark elves, Bootknife's blade, hungry sirens, and vengeful barrow wights. And yet, I can't directly say it. Instead, I decide to take the flank, to test Kin's shields and how drunk he is, how... amenable.

"Looks fun," I venture, slipping the stem of my pipe out from between my teeth and pointing it at the Trothed

Pairs now dancing around the Fire Flower torches.

"Mmm," Kin grumbles, which isn't an agreement. It's not an evasion either, though.

I lick my lips again, tasting mead and smoke, herb and possibility. "We could do that."

Kin swigs, seeming to be processing what I suggest. "Dance?" he asks, half in jest. "Set you on fire?"

I'm feeling loose-jointed and warm, and ever so slightly drunk myself after those few ales and the honey mead. I screw up my courage and blurt: "Jump a broom."

The guffaw is half out of Kintyre's mouth before he seems to realize he's even laughing. He doesn't even bother to raise his hand to cover his mouth.

I can feel my face going cold, all of Kin's lovely warmth pulling away as he curls over the mead skin and giggles. Shame surges in its absence.

Stupid. I'm not sure who that's directed at. Both of us, maybe.

"Forget it," I snap, climbing to my feet, shaking the ash out of my pipe with a hard swing that smacks against my thigh and is nowhere near as satisfying as, say, punching Kin in the nose would be.

"Aw, no, Bev!" Kin chortles and paws at my arm. "Come back, you daft bastard, come back."

"Let go," I snarl, feeling more embarrassed and angry with myself than I think the situation warrants. It's not like I'd even *wanted* it particularly badly. It's not like anyone else overheard my awkward, awful proposition.

"Hey now," Kin says, sitting up and looking instantly sober. Whether or not he really is, I can't say. Despite seventeen years of companionship, Kin can still keep things from me when he wants to. "What's this?"

"I said forget it. It's nothing." I turn my face back toward the center of town, toward the Pern and the bed that's waiting for me—probably clean, but definitely cold.

Writer, I'm a stupid, *stupid* fool.

Kin squints, tugs the hem of my short-robe, and says, "Bev. We don't need to jump a broom together."

"Yeah, right, sure," I say and tug my robe out of his grip.

Kin scrambles to his feet. "Bev, stop, I mean it. We don't need to jump a broom together."

"Why, because we're already Paired?" I sneer. I jam my pipe into my pouch before I end up snapping the stem in my rage—a pipe Kin had given me, sure, but not as a Pairing gift. Kin's never, even after everything I've done, even *thought* about me like that.

Yeah, he'll lick, and touch, and kiss—when there's a woman with us. Sometimes he'll even sheathe himself in me, or allow me to sheathe in him when we are out of our minds with passion. But to declare it, to even admit to it... no. Never. Not in front of my brothers and sisters-in-law, never in front of the children, the people of Bynnebakker. Never where Forsyth Turn, Lordling of Lysse, or Sheriff Pointe, or anyone from Turnshire could hear. Never even in front of his damned horse.

Never even when it was just the two of us, alone in a shared berth or bed, on the hundred and one nights where we were jammed together for warmth, or because the room was too small, or because we were imprisoned together, or because the makeshift lean-to or snow-hutch we'd constructed had been too narrow. Never when we were sharing breath, and spit, and tears, and blood. Never once has Kin even acknowledged the humid air between our mouths, the way the whorls of our fingertips lock together, the flutter of eyelashes, the scrape of stubble, the peaked nipples, the stained smallclothes.

Never.

Except tonight. And only then to push me away.

And that is not a Pair. That is not what it *means*.

Kin rocks back on his heels and goes absolutely still, absolutely silent. It takes a moment for me to register through the harsh hiss of my own breath slithering through my clenched teeth, to hear the silence for what it is. For what it *isn't*.

Finally, when I have ahold of my temper, when I've managed to unclench my fists and wiggle my toes in my boots, I look up. Kin's face is a well-carved expression of carefully considered blankness.

"Aren't we?" Kin asks, and his voice is low, barely audible above the crackle of the great bonfire, the giggles and shouts of laughter, the yelling children, the cheering adults, the music on the far side of the flames. His shoulders are a straight, unreadable line against the bright aura of firelight, his arms loose at his sides—neither tense nor prepared to fight, nor actually as relaxed as he's trying to appear.

He is so tense, so prepared to be hurt, so ready to just take this blow on his stupid, perfect cleft chin that I can't... I can't. I crumble.

"We are," I lie, hating myself for every syllable of it. "Of course we are."

Kintyre relaxes, happy, oblivious, satisfied. I take the mead skin and drink heavily.

As we depart Gwillfifeshire the next morning, packs weighted down with supplies enough to see us through Miliway, my heart is as heavy as my load, my feet plodding. I can't tell if the regret I'm carrying is from what I did last night, and what I said... or from what I didn't have the stones to say.

But Kin looks like he's carrying air, the great prick. He raises his face to the sky and grins. He folds his hands on the back of his neck, mischievous. It makes him look so young again, so carefree, that my heart lurches. And my head throbs; I've got one troll of a hangover.

As I work to unstick my fuzzy tongue from the roof of my mouth, Kin offers me a drink—the last of the mead. It must be stale by now, and certainly warm, but the best cure for a bite is the hair of the dog that bit you, so I accept it with both a grimace and a small nod of gratitude.

There's just one mouthful left when I pass it back.

"Do you suppose there'll be time to find someone in Lysse?" Kin asks, eyes bright as he fists the flask. He tilts his chin up to glug, but his eyes remain on mine. It's not a challenge, not really, so much as a silent plea to keep things as they have always been.

Change nothing, that look begs. *Leave things as they are.*

And I, living in terror that each day will be the one where Kintyre Turn realizes the true depth of my affection for him and departs in a cloud of offense and disgust, give him the closest thing to a nod I can muster.

"Possibly," I answer. "We may have time. We're headed straight there, and Bossy Forssy didn't want us for a fortnight yet. I'd say that's plenty of time."

Kintyre lowers the flask, licking syrupy golden liquor from his lips, and claps me on the back. "Good lad! You'll find me someone good, eh? Maybe this maiden in distress we're meant to be rescuing will be grateful!"

"We can hope," I allow. I swallow hard. It tastes like ash, but I arrange my face into a mask of pleasant blandness all the same. I check our direction by the sun, squinting to spare my eyes. And my throbbing head. I wish something could spare the agonizing squeeze of this damned seedling Dargan planted behind my ribs. I wish I could yank the weed out of my heart.

"Well, to Lysse and Turnshire, then?" Kin asks, twisting the cap of the flask back into place and running his wrist along the underside of his cleft chin to catch any fleeing droplets.

"To Turnshire," I agree, and do as I have always done. As I will always do.

I put one foot in front of the other. I walk.

And I follow Kintyre Turn.

LOVE LETTER

This piece is in response to a companion short that was originally published on a blog. The host had asked us to create love letters from our characters to their spouses or special someones. Pip lives in a very digital world, so of course her love letter was always going to be an email, and it was always going to be peppered with raunchy GIFs. While I can't recreate the experience of reading the letter with the graphics intact, I can give you an idea of what it was like by writing up Forsyth's reply (previously unpublished and only a few years late).

This love letter challenge was, and is, important to me, as it gave me the opportunity to talk a bit more about what happened between Pip and Forsyth, and their relationship, in the immediate aftermath of their arrival in the Overrealm. For the sake of Plot in *The Untold Tale*—and, later, *The Forgotten Tale*—I didn't get the opportunity to dwell on Pip's recovery from her trauma, or the way that Pip and Forsyth had to start their relationship all over again, slowly, the way I would have liked. So I took the opportunity to hint at it here, to make a point of highlighting the truth that visceral, violating trauma of the kind Pip experienced is not something that you just "get over." It takes time, and work, and Pip will probably be in therapy for the rest of her life to ensure she remains healthy and happy.

The following is a love letter between Forsyth and Pip, but it is also my love letter to those who work so diligently to help others recover themselves from such traumas. Thank you, on behalf of all of us in the Over-realm.

From: Syth Piper <forsyth.turn@gmail.com>

To: Lucy Piper <l.piper@uvic.ca>
Sent: Sunday, Feb 14, 2016 11:17 AM
Subject: Re: Another New Thing – It's a Holiday!

>>...*or, Your Wife Finally Explains The Weird Red Hearts Popping Up Everywhere.*

I do so enjoy it when you take the time to send me these emails, my dear. Thank you. I followed your links, which led me to further study of this St. Valentine, which led me to Lupercalia, which in turn has reminded me of just how many cultures and civilizations have gone into creating the one I live in now—and how singular mine was, for being only ever what it was Written to be, of one source and one understanding.

Sometimes, I am vastly unprepared to be reminded that I am fiction. But then, it could be worse—I could be slapping your arm with raw meat, apparently?

My dear, what were the humans of this realm thinking?

>> *So, this is really your second Valentine's Day, but we were all feeling a little shell shocked and raw for the last one, and I decided not to dump yet another New*

Thing on you.

For which, I am still grateful. Those first few months were terrible, and I did not like feeling so separated from you. Yet, I did not know how welcome I was, and at the same time, how welcoming I desired to be.

I remember lying awake on that horrid old sofa, a spring digging into my cheek, wondering if I had made the biggest error I could have possibly made in accepting your invitation to follow you here. Silly, small Forsyth Turn, so blind and naive that he'd followed what he thought was love into a realm where he knew no one, had nothing of his own, and could depend only on a woman who, in the end of all things, was really still just a stranger. All of what we'd shared had been false, and horrible, and all of what we were then was timid, and scared, and tentative.

>>*It is now February, however, and the proof of our love is pretty determined to kill any romance we might have even hoped to wish for this time around.*

Oh, how quickly the wheel of time turns. Said "proof" is currently curled in my arms, clutching that lion stuffie that came with the ridiculous zoo set from the bookstore. She has decided that she shall cleave to it, and thus, I have named the wretched thing Library the Lion, which I think shall amuse you.

We both miss you terribly though, bao bei, and wish you home with us as soon as possible. Please do hurry back from setting up your curriculum and office. We are quite proud that Alis's ma is to be a professor, but also glad that your tenure does not begin until the new year.

>>So I guess our second Valentine's Day is gonna blow a little, too. (Though, hey, that's not a bad idea, is it?)

Goodness, wife. Whatever could that GIF of a woman blowing up a balloon be implying?

>>So, seeing as you're all Master of the Internet now (god, I never imagined what it would be like to be married to a human knowledge-sponge), I thought I would send you a super-romantic Valentine's email.

I am endeavoring to find a compliment in amid the romance.

>>Which brings us to the first question that Lucy Turn Piper must always answer for Syth Turn Piper when we come to a New Thing: WHY???

Does that need quite so many redundant question marks?

>>What is Valentine's Day?

It took some further research, but I now understand the significance of the GIFs of hearts and chocolates, and candle-lit dinners. I believe Alis and I may spend part of this afternoon watching Hallmark films together—though the parenting chat boards reliably inform me that many reinforce negative stereotypes of romance and a healthy relationship. Nevertheless, I would like to watch some and compare them to the courting of my youth. And, of course, with the teachings of our therapist.

(Speaking of which, she called to verify our first

post-baby session for next week. She'd like to meet Alis, if we're comfortable with it. I am, if you are, my dear. It seems only appropriate, as she's been there to help us sort through our anxieties about every other stage of our relationship. And if, as you say, we're going to "ruin the kid," we might as well get her used to healthy coping methods early, yes?)

>>And so, in the spirit of the holiday, I have picked up an ever so romantic Easy-Curry kit for us to have at dinner, bought the second-cheapest bottle of red wine that you have deemed palatable (you're worth it, bao bei!) and have lots of wicked plans for after the baby is asleep.

How bold. Though I suggest that, in addition to the GIF of the woman eating a hot dog, you should also add a man eating a taco. All is fair, I have learned they say here, in both love and war.

>>What, you think your creative wife has taught you everything there is to know in the bedroom, my sweet little virgin-before-I-got-to-you? Nuh-uh, bao bei. I still have tons of awesome tricks up my sleeve, and I learn more every day. I read fanfic.

I am shocked and horrified, truly I am. Ignore my smile. It is not as if I have ever read any of the multitudes of pornographic stories available on the internet—nor, indeed, the very interesting and educational sites, as well (have you read any of Oh Joy Sex Toy? I find it delightful).

You may be creative, my wife, but I am a thorough study and never do anything by half measures.

>>But in all honesty, I want to write you my very first love letter. Yes, it's yours. My love letters will always and only be yours, Forsyth Turn, Lordling of Lysse. So here goes.

Oh, Pip. I don't regret that my first love note was to Melinda, but I promise you that this is my second, and you will always only ever be the recipient of my own love letters, until my tale is Shelved.

>>Thank You

>>First, I wanted to say thank you. Thank you for coming with me. Thank you for choosing me. Thank you for saving me. Thank you for letting me save you.

Thank you for inviting me to come along. Thank you for choosing me in return. Thank you for saving me, and thank you for teaching me that I am allowed to save myself in that same way that you let me help you save your own self.

>>Thank you for your patience. Thank you for sleeping on the sofa when we got back here, so I could have my space and the time to get my head back on straight, so I could process the fact that you were used to hurt me so much. Thank you for understanding when I said I needed you to come to therapy with me, and thank you for being up for it, even if you didn't completely understand what it was for.

Thank you for letting me go slow, as well, to relearn myself with you. Thank you for letting me come to terms with the fact that my body was used as a weapon to harm you, a device to torture you, and that I, too, had no say in that matter. Thank you for letting me be hurt alongside you, rather than telling me that I have no right to be in pain, as I was not the one harmed. Thank you for acknowledging that I was, in fact, harmed, and that I wasn't aware of it at the time. And thank you for being open to working through our mutual hurt together.

>>Thank you for taking things slowly. Thank you for being game. Thank you for stopping when I asked you to stop, and for touching me when I beg you for it.

Thank you for teaching me that I needn't fear or be ashamed of my own desires, and that I may love and lust as freely as I like, for teaching me the best practices of consent. Thank you for finding me sexy. Thank you for teaching me that I am sexy, that I may be content and satisfied in my own skin, and that no matter what I look like—even with my newfound pouch—you find me attractive.

>>Thank you for holding me when I cried, and for soothing me when I was freaking out, and for going away when I asked you to go away. And for coming back when I needed you.

Thank you for running your hands through my thinning hair, and also for waking me up when I have a nightmare, and leaving me alone when I need you to, as well. Thank you for being patient when I flinch, when you come up behind me soundlessly and I jump, for when you raise your hand and I cringe. Thank you for understanding that it's not you I fear, but the memory of a man who is long dead, and thank you for helping me wash that all away with each loving touch, overwriting every place he ever did me harm with your kiss.

>>*Thank you for never holding it against me - or blaming me for - the traumas that were inflicted on me, and the way they made me react to you. Thank you for teaching me about the right to desire.*

Thank you for understanding my right to desire, and thank you for desiring me in return.

>>*Thank you for being enthusiastic when I needed you to be, and thank you for being Generous, Giving, and Game in bed - that's been especially fun.*

My goodness, Pip! Thank you for teaching me things I never could have imagined in my world! I never knew one could laugh so in bed, nor love so, nor give pleasure so. I never knew bedplay could be such good play.

>>*Thank you for the privilege of letting me fall in love with you a second time. Thank you for letting it be on my terms.*

Thank you for letting me fall for you, the real you. On both our terms.

>>*And thank you for yelling at me for being a selfish prick about it, sometimes.*

Seconded.

>>*Thank you for the awesome kid we made.*

SECONDED.

>>*Thank you for being there for me while I suffered through making that awesome kid.*

My fingers still click strangely when I make a fist sometimes. I am certain now that you actually did break one, though I find I do not mind.

>>*I Love You*

And I, you.

>>*And now, for all the reasons I love you. I love it when you look at me like this:*

I was never half so charming as the man in that GIF, but if you like, I can try that eyebrow waggle. I don't think it will look half so charming on me, though.

>>*I love it when you grab me under the arms and haul me out of my office and away from grading papers when it's past midnight. I love it when it's for sleep. I love it when it's not for sleep.*

Yes, about your hours, Pip. You were a TA while you were pregnant, but now, as a full professor, I find I may have to sneak into your office at the university to drag you away from your desk. (Or, I suppose, on top of it, if your office door has a lock.)

>>*I love the way you look at our daughter.*

How do I look at her? As though she be the stars in my sky? For she is.

>>*I love the way you dance with me when no one is watching.*

I love the feel of your heartbeat up against mine.

>>*I love the way you're scared of the phone, still. It's adorable. Please never stop being afraid of the phone.*

Begone, woman.

>>*I love the way you are so not even into the toxic masculinity bullshit of this realm and make funny faces at MRA doofuses.*

I will not lie: it is quite fun. But I have learned it all from you, my darling Pip. I have learned how to unlearn what I have been taught. The least I can do is help others to unlearn it where they are willing to. I always did want to follow in my brother's footsteps and become a slayer of trolls.

>>*I love watching you practice fencing with Smoke (hot damn).*

I am learning more about your proclivities than I anticipated, my dear. Do we need to watch Lord of the Rings again some afternoon when we have the house to ourselves?

>>*I love that you loved me more than you loved magic. I mean, honestly, magic is pretty cool. I sometimes wonder why you gave up the ability to Speak Words for me.*

What is the point of magic when one lives in a world

where one has no worth? I don't say that to sound maudlin—the Pointes and my staff must miss me a little, at least—but beyond that, I was a secondary character in my brother's life, and a shade in my own. Who needs magic when one may have, instead, a sense of self?

>>*I love how patient you are with wai po, and how earnest you are with your Mandarin lessons because it's important to her.*
>>*I love that you let me love you. Even if it is some-*

我正竭尽全力。这是你的一部分，因此它是我的一部分，因为它永远是我们女儿的一部分。

times not as much as you deserve. Even if it is sometimes unfairly reluctant or tentative. Even if it took me a long time to get where we are now. Even if I sometimes wonder if it was selfish and rash to invite you to come here with me. Even if it was selfish and rash. I love that you let me love you.

I love that you let me love you, too. Even if it is sometimes not as much as you deserve. Even if it is sometimes unfairly reluctant or tentative. Even if it took me a long time to get where we are now. Even if I sometimes wonder if it was selfish and rash to accept your invitation to come here with you. Even if it was selfish and rash. I love that you let me love you, in return.

>>I love you.

I love you.
--Your Pip

>>*我那么爱你*

Lucy Piper
Associate Professor
Department of Sociology (Pop Culture)
University of Victoria

--Your earnest and devoted Forsyth,
Lordling of Lysse Chipping,
House Turn,
Delighted, devoted father…

…who has just been spat up on.

HOME

s I was writing, there were several places where I wanted to take the time to explain a little bit more what happened between the novels, to show some of the daily life and routine of the Piper family. But there wasn't always a way to do that within the narrative of the novels themselves. Thankfully, I was asked to write some shorts to debut exclusively on Wattpad. This is the first of those stories.

For these, I settled on a fun, quirky second-person-POV stream-of-consciousness kind of ramble that mimicked the sorts of dialogues I've watched my friends have with their infants. Forsyth would definitely be the kind of father who narrates everything for his baby, especially after he's read all the articles about early exposure to vocabulary and communication. (We all know he read the whole parenting internet before she arrived.)

This story, therefore, is set just a few short days after Alis Mei Turn Piper was born.

Hush, hush, sweeting. No, no, no, don't cry. All is well. Your... well, no, I shan't have you calling me *father*, as if I were that miserable old bastard. Papa? No?

Oh! Such wails, sweeting. Such lungs! You are all dry, and your wee tum is filled with sweet milk, so what you must want is a story. Yes, a story, sweeting. Shall your silly old da tell you a story? That's a girl.

Very well... hmmm...

Ah! Do you see that there? Hmm? The banner hung above your cradle? It's quite pretty, isn't it, sweeting? Yes, that's right, follow Da's finger. That's my girl. Yes, you may have that finger if you like. Though I can't imagine it tastes of anything delectable.

Let me tell you about how you and that banner finally made your silly old da feel like he was home.

You see, once upon a time—I like this phrase; don't you, dearest? I'd never heard it before I came here—*once upon a time*, there was a great knight and his steadfast sidekick. This story, however, is not about them. This story is about the knight's little brother, a scholar who es-caped the world he was Written for and came to a strange land I shall call... hmmm... what do you say, sweeting? The Overrealm?

Yes, I thought you'd like that. The Overrealm it is.

The scholar journeyed to the Overrealm with the damsel who had rescued him. It was difficult for him at first; he was so used to being sure of his place, you see, to being master of all knowledge. It grated on him terribly to feel so stupid. To not know the things everyone else did. To have to question, constantly, everything around him, and to beg for explanations like an ignorant farm boy.

He was homesick, you see. Terribly so.

He barely slept, and barely ate for his first few weeks in the Overrealm.

It was made harder, of course, by the fact that the ties of love which bound the scholar and the damsel were still fragile and new. They loved each other, but they hadn't yet understood how deeply, nor how tightly. A tragedy had befallen them both, you see, and while the damsel was helping the scholar adjust to the strangeness of the Overrealm—oh, the smells, my sweeting, you cannot guess!—she herself was suffering with the memory of all that had befallen her.

Luckily, there are things here called *therapists*, a sort of doctor for the mind and spirit. The scholar is ever so pleased that the damsel began to see one, and is more pleased still that he has since been invited along so that they may all talk and work hard together. Mental health is as important as physical health, after all—that is what is believed in the Overrealm.

Eventually, the scholar and the damsel were able to reconcile the bad that had happened and build upon the good. And when you find your own love, sweeting, you will see that the building together part is the most important.

And then, my sweeting, good news! The scholar and his damsel were to be blessed with a child! Ah, a lovely and clever guess, my sweet girl, yes! That child was you!

Of course, yes, how *clever* you are. The scholar is indeed your da, and the damsel your ma. Quite sharp of you to pick that out.

Well then, let me see... what happened next? Well, there were forged IDs, and paperwork, and a wedding, and the scholar—I mean, your da—he figured out that the way the Writer had Written him was still in effect, even here in the Overrealm. His charm, his air of trustworthiness, his ability to read body language prevailed, and very shortly, the scholar and the damsel were set up with employment, a home in a city named for a queen, and all the privileges which those expecting an heir are accorded by this world.

Though, did you know, my sweeting, that there are machines in this realm that allow a person to see a babe inside a woman's belly? It's rather horrifying.

But I shan't bore you with the details of your birth, sweeting, as you were there. Instead, I would like to linger on the month just before you decided to come out and join us.

You see, that was the month I went to my first science fiction and fantasy convention. Many important things happened there, though I think perhaps I will save those revelations for another few decades.

For you see, after arriving at FantaCon28, after being mistaken for a cosplay of myself, after literally meeting my maker and telling my untold tale, after the Artist's Alley and the woman who mistook costumes for consent, your da could not help but be intensely interested in fan culture.

You shall grow up a geek, sweeting, and for that I am pleased, but you must understand that there is *nothing*, absolutely nothing like this back in the Kingdom of Hain.

Well, there is the Sowing Celebration, but that's more about inversion, and celebration, and pushing Brother Sun back into orbit by tempting Sister Moon into sleeping later and later in the bed of Harvest than it is about actually pretending to be the Great Constellations. And besides, that really is more of a fae holiday than a human one.

The point is, my sweeting, that for all that meeting Elgar Reed left a faintly bitter taste behind my teeth, I *adored* the rest of my weekend in Toronto. The crowds were overwhelming, true; I needed to retreat to a rest area often. Your mother calls it social anxiety, dearest, and we both hope that you do not inherit that particular Turnish trait. I had never felt so *observed* before in my life. Your da is very used to being either masked and shadow-cloaked or totally ignored. But beyond the discomfort of being in such a large crowd, I had... well, I had rather a lot of *fun*, didn't I?

Oh, I must tell you about the Klingon Karaoke. I know what a Klingon is now, my sweet, and someday, so shall you—and perhaps you will eventually share in my disappointment that the people dressed as Klingons didn't sing in the language invented for the species. I wanted to learn more of it. But watching my eight-months pregnant wife take the microphone and give an incredibly rousing and humorous rendition of "Shake It Off" was so entertaining that the Vulcan at the table over pointed at me and shouted to the waitress, "I'll have whatever he's having!"

Perhaps your ma will sing it for you tomorrow. Would you like that, sweeting? Ah-ah—ah, such a big yawn! Are you ready to lay back down and—ah, oops, I suppose not. Okay, shhh, shush, sweeting. It's all right. I will tell you more about FantaCon.

Let me see...

Ah, there was the Cosplay Masquerade. Your mother had to drag me away from several of the contestants afterward; I insisted on monopolizing their attention to learn just how they had made such accurate and impressive armor out of *foam*.

There was a pub event where the bar served themed cocktails based on the Guest of Honor's books, such as the *Kintyre*, some pale ale-based monstrosity named for your uncle; the Bevel, a sweet vermouth cocktail that spoke softly but carried a big punch, named for your other uncle; and the *Viceroy*, a mixture of red wine and cola that made its drinkers prone to gagging and screwed up faces even as they ordered another. I thought it perverse that one would name a drink after that monster.

My favorite was *The Foesmiter*, a purplish drink made of spiced dark whiskey, sour plum wine, ginger ale, and a muddle of ginger roots and fresh plums. It reminded me of the dragon whiskey of Drebbinshire. Your ma says that I spent the whole evening with a terribly fond grin on my face, but I think she is teasing me. Your da is a spy-master and entirely in control of his own expressions.

What else was there? Ah, yes. During the day, there was the Dealer's Room, and you will forgive your da for sounding a little daft when I explain this, but you must understand that I have never been to a market larger than the one in Faversquare, on the eastern side of Lysse Chipping, and that the Dealer's Room exceeded its size threefold at least. Though, with your ma's enormous belly parting the crowd before her like a majestic elf queen before an army, we were able to get up close enough to peruse each hawker's wares. That's right, you had the best view of the show, sweeting.

Working in the University Library, as I did then, I was well aware that the number of fictional worlds like my own numbered in the thousands upon the shelves of this Overrealm. What I didn't realize was that the library's selection of science fiction and fantasy titles was humble. Nearly *miniscule* compared to the great bounty of selection available from the merchants of comic books, films, television programs, novels, and audio dramas.

I was overwhelmed by the sheer number of stories, sweeting. There were more, perhaps, than even the Lost Library could hold! I had to sit down outside, in the sunshine, to process it while your ma fetched us hot dogs from a food cart in the park opposite the convention center.

And that night at the hotel, your ma shared with me a manga she had bought. She taught me the trick to reading the novel backward, of flicking one's eyes in the opposite direction and turning what feels to be the wrong pages. It is *fascinating*. There are, of course, no graphic novels in Hain. There were woodblock-printed illustrations in the copies of Bevel's adventure tales, of course, created by some illustrator I did not know and copied by librarians for the nobility who could afford the leather-bound tomes. But that was as close to comics as Hain produced.

Did you know, sweeting, that I have only recently begun to read Pip's trade paperback comics? My favorites are *Fables*, for I feel a deep kinship with the characters of Fabletown and The Farm, and *Hawkeye*, for I like reading about the life of a man like me: average in all ways, and yet striving to live up to the legends all around him. But this manga had an entirely different sort of narrative structure, different visual conventions, different ways of portraying emotion and thoughts, and it was wonderful, incredible, fascinating. Your da lost most of his night's sleep reading and rereading that book.

And then.

And *then.*

And then, there was the Artist's Alley.

But, oh, my sweeting, before I tell you about that, there is a history you should know. Backstory, if you will. Exposition. An info-dump? Yes, I know, fascinating.

Let me tell you a bit about your uncle, the hero. He is a very good man, with very good morals, but he is also brash. He prefers to brawl rather than apologize. He is selfish, and he takes up too much air in the room. But in this one, rare thing, your da and your uncle are alike. We both hold a deep, abiding respect for *artists.*

Our father discouraged it, of course. He wanted his sons to be proud, broad, rough-and-tumble *men.* But of course, the surest way to guarantee a child will do exactly the opposite of what you want them to do is to forbid it. Before I became lordling and inherited Turn Hall, there was a woefully small collection of books about art and artists in the family library. Your uncle Kintyre and I must have devoured them all several times over, sneaking about with candles in the dead of night, thrilling at the illicit nature of our clandestine artistic education. And we both thought it quite the injustice that only the young girl-children of nobility were given drawing lessons.

Of course, when your grandfather discovered our forbidden reading, he burned all the books.

I was seven, my brother fourteen. And after that, I dared not defy Father in this. By the time that old bastard—please do not tell your ma that I used that word—had done me and everyone in Lysse Chipping a favor by breaking his own fool neck via a drunken fall down the foyer stairs, I thought myself too old and too busy to try to learn painting.

But this is a new realm, my sweeting, and I find myself aching to reinvent myself here. I think, perhaps, I have finally found a vocation in this world that will please me as much as the one I had in the last—no, it is a surprise, sweeting. I shan't tell you yet. I have a wife, a home, a daughter. Why should I not also have painting lessons? They offer them in the community center. Perhaps we can go together. What do you say, sweeting? Shall we play with paints, the two of us curious Turns?

When you are older, then.

I do so love art. Did you know, I made a point of becoming patron to several promising young students of the Free School I funded in Turnshire? I even paid for one lad to go to Kingskeep to study under one of the Grand Masters. The youth sent me his first painting in gratitude, a beautiful landscape that immortalized the view of Turn Hall from the Field Road. It is still in Turn Hall, hanging above the fireplace in my study. Your mother covered it over with her Excel.

Ah, you are right, my darling, my dear, my sweeting, I have strayed from the purpose of my story. Yes, your canopy. *Well*, there, in Artist's Alley were *hundreds* of people, of all genders, and sexualities, and creeds, and ethnicities, and ages, creating art of all kinds. I have never seen such a great variety of humans before, my sweeting. I quite enjoy being a minority.

I am not too ashamed to say that I nearly wept at the glory of it. Your ma and I spent the majority of our final day at the convention lingering over each table's offerings, exclaiming over the exquisite jewelry and the humorous dolls, the painstakingly rendered chainmail and knitted goods, the gorgeous paintings and sketches, the sparkling glass and the wrought leather.

And better than the talent the artisans displayed was the love that went into each creation. Here were people who were not just passively consuming the tales they enjoyed, but using them as inspiration! Here were the fans so passionate, so dedicated, so clever, so willing to build communities and celebrate that which brought them to-gether that they *had* to find ways to express it through art.

Ah, yes. That's what it was—what I had been missing, you see, sweeting.

I felt, for the first time since stepping through into the Overrealm, a tight and intense sense of *community* that had been lacking in my life. For all that I was at a special event, in a different city, in a different *realm*, it felt, just enough, like *home*.

And for the first time since coming into this world, I was grateful that Pip and I are not wealthy. That we'd spent our dragonet's tears on buying a home. For I could easily have depleted the entirety of our coffers on those incredible, wonderful works of art. But no, that would have been irresponsible. I was to be a father soon, as you well know, sweeting.

And so, I limited myself to just one purchase.

Your mother told me it was a good choice when I picked it out. And when we left, she helped me pack it very carefully into our one shared suitcase.

And now, here we are, my wee sweeting.

Three weeks, two days, fifteen hours of labor, and one hospital overnight stay later.

What do you think? Another mighty yawn! Excellent answer. Up, up, and in you go.

And now, Alis Mei Turn Piper, I shall lay you down in your crib for the very first time, glowingly pleased that my daughter sleeps under this hand-embroidered banner of the symbol of House Turn. Do you see? The key lancing the lock? Embroidered in russet and orange, and all the shades of the leaves in autumn on a field of doe-eye brown. I am told your wee eyes can't focus on that yet, but you'll see it soon enough. See it and love it, as I did at your age.

In this world, there is a blossom called *Forsythia*. Your ma and I painted the walls of your new nursery the same color as its petals. Do you like its glowing yellow? Doesn't the banner look beautiful against it?

Your canopy looks exactly like the one my own mother, Alis Sheil Turn, made and hung above my cradle, so many years and a literal world away. And, like that banner, the love, the passion, the adoration that went into the creation of this replacement can almost, if one closes one's eyes and opens up all their senses, be detected.

Can you feel it? There is no magic here, sweeting, but I can smell it in the air all the same. Cinnamon and apples, and the scent of the breeze off the fallow fields. Can you smell it? The banner radiates a peaceful, glowing sense of *belonging*.

We are home, my dearest. *Home.*

REMEMBERED

ARRIVALS

So here's me angsting—again—over whether or not I should write the story of "How Kin and Bev Got Together." It occurred to me after we put out the first novella that if I was going to have three novels in this series (and to properly call it a series), then I was going to have to have three novellas to go with it. If Forsyth got three tales, then it was only fair to give the same to Kintyre!

For this second installment, I really did consider going back and writing the scene where Bev and Kin profess their love and become a Pair, an actual account of how-it-all-went-down. But the more I thought about it, the more I didn't want to tread on the imaginations of Readers who had already come up with their own headcanons.

Instead, I decided I wanted to deal with what happens after Happily Ever After. I knew we'd be seeing that with Forsyth and Pip in *The Forgotten Tale*, and I wanted to address it with Kin and Bev, too. They'd been friends for so many years that I think the expectation was that they'd be instant and perfect lovers, but that kind of friendship doesn't automatically mean they'd make a perfect couple; it doesn't mean they'd have no problems to work out. So I took this opportunity to show what it would be like for them in the aftermath, when the battle had been fought, and the dust had settled, and a life of retirement was all that waited. We all long for retirement, but is it all it's actually cracked up to be?

Besides, I'd been given the opportunity to show these two big dumb dorks in love. How could I not relish the idea of showing the softer side of the Great Hero of Hain and his partner?

PART ONE

✴

It's too late to climb down a bloody mountain. Even with the skies clear and the night's first stars starting to peek out. Instead, without asking whether Kintyre agrees with me or not—I'm not going to be the one who has to wrap up his ankle when he twists the ruddy thing because we can't see where we're walking—I hunker down by the small ring of stones we used to make a campfire last night and get to the business of making another.

Writer's nutsack. Just last night, Kin and I had been sitting close, trying to see how much play we could get away with while Bossy Forssy and Pip sulked in the shadow of the Rookery wall. And now they're... it feels a lot longer than just a day, what with all the fighting, the shouting, the tears, and the goodbyes. My shoulders are stiff, and I shrug and roll them out as I poke through the ash for some charred charcoal to prop up the kindling.

"Staying, are we?" Kin asks, when he realizes what I'm doing, and then, without me having to ask, he trots up the granite stairs. His silhouette is distinctive and, yeah, *heroic* against the lingering orange of the setting sun. I watch him collect dried scrub and fallen branches, and pause every once in a while to scan the horizon.

The chirrup and caw of birds slowly swells as the gloaming becomes complete. The riddling ravens have returned to the Eyrie with the Deal-Maker and the Viceroy gone. Up on the ridge, Kin makes sure that nothing and no one can sneak up on us in the night by sharing our travel crackers with them.

Down in the basin, waiting for Kin to get back, I rest against the Desk that Never Rots, my pipe clenched between my teeth, and decide it's worth using up one of our precious few matches for a smoke. I'm gasping for a bit of time to myself and a bowl of my orange-blossom and molasses hash, and Kin's not here to whine at me about the smell. I'll use Pip's trick of chewing dried peppermint after, so the taste will be out of my mouth before he can come back and kiss me.

A ridiculous, childish grin curls at the corner of my mouth, and I can't help licking my bottom lip in anticipation. Kissing Kin is one of my favorite ways to pass the time. Lucky for me, it's one of his favorites, too.

Dinner—dinner can probably wait until I've got my burly barbarian nice and kiss-fuddled. I'm feeling lazy, too; I can make a meal of the scraps we have left. We'll hunt down in the Stoat Forest tomorrow, so we can afford to finish it all up today. Besides, I'm not keen on dragging everything back down the mountain after dragging it all up the damn thing in the first place.

"Here," Kin grunts when he drops an armload of logs and brush by the cold fire pit. I tap out my pipe, return it to my pouch, pop some peppermint into my mouth, and make my way back to start laying the fire.

One of the nice things about having been on quests with Kintyre Turn for the last seventeen years is that I no longer have to nag the oaf to chop the wood instead of just dumping it on the ground. He's already got the small axe out of his saddlebag. Good. Before he applies himself to breaking up some of the bigger bits, he strips out of his Turn-russet jerkin and sweat-stained canvas shirt.

Ah, *yes.* Excellent.

Right. So, there's *one* thing that's changed about our

quests. Now, when Kin parades around shirtless in the reaching dusk and flattering firelight, I can *look*.

Not that I didn't look before. I'd have to be blind, a eunuch, and cursed by the Writer before I'd have been able to ignore a shirtless Kintyre Turn. But now, I can look *openly*.

Because Kintyre is *mine*.

The possessive curl deep in my guts flares warm and syrupy, and when Kin bends over slowly to pick up the first log, arranging it over another one for chopping, I know the cheeky bastard has caught my smirk. He's doing it on purpose. And *that*, Writer-be-blessed, is a *damn* good show.

As the seventh son of a seventh son, I had to make do a lot as a kid. Mum had taught all us boys the art of cookery, as she'd had no daughters to chain to the hearth. She'd taught us how to stretch the bread and water the soup so there was something for all the little bellies. I'd resented being tied to my mum's apron-strings when I was a snot-nosed little goblin-turd, wanting always to be at the forge with Pa. Besides, I was going to get a wife who would take care of all the woman's work for me, wasn't I?

But when I followed Kintyre Turn out into the world—him still a narcissistic lordling fleeing his responsibilities with an enchanted sword he'd just found and didn't yet understand—I was happy for the cooking lessons. And the sewing, too, turns out. 'Cause I've done my share of repairing battle-rent clothes and stitching torn skin out in the wilds of Hain.

Kin's always harassing me to add a tome of roadside recipes to my legacy of adventure scrolls, but the idea is even less appealing these days than it usually is. Mostly because I've been failing pretty spectacularly as a cook since Kintyre Turn became my lover. I have burnt, over-seasoned, and boiled-dry more of our meals in the last three months than I ever did in the first year of our adventures. And every single incident was Kintyre's fault. Because the rat-bastard keeps doing things like *this*.

He keeps on chopping, long after there's enough wood piled up by the fire, long after I've got the grub on the go. Because I'm watching. Right, fine then—I was going to wait until after we'd eaten, but if he's keen for our usual post-battle celebration now, who am I to deny the Lord of Lysse his whims?

I snort at my own fanciful thinking.

This time, at least, I have enough blood in my brain to take the potatoes out of the embers and cover the stew pot before I go chasing down my shirtless, sweaty ruffian. And, hells, it feels good to be able to. To not have to second-guess myself or try to gauge how my advances will be received, or to wonder if I will be forever ruining our friendship. It's easy.

It's so good, and it's so *easy*.

A little while later, the sun has set and I'm filled with a dusky kind of glow all my own. Sweat cools on my skin, and I feel the pleasant soreness of exertion well-earned, the burn of an over-extended stretch. Kintyre is finishing the last of the stew right out of the pot, intent on his spoon, starved in a way that only fighting, followed by a good bout of bedplay, can make him.

I've eaten, and have something else to preoccupy me. Firelight dances over the planes and elevations of the Shadow's Mask. I turn it over in my hands again, and again, and again, silently reciting the Word Forssy whispered in my ear with each turn.

That's it. Just one Word, one gesture, one *moment*, and... and I could be the most powerful man in Hain. Forget the king; I'd know all of his secrets, too. I know most of them anyway, but with the mask, with Dauntless, with the cloak, and with... well, Forsyth took Smoke into that strange place that is the home of the Writer, but I'm sure I can commission a replacement. One with a bit more heft to it, something a man can really *swing*. And once I have that, once I have all the trappings, I'd be the Shadow Hand of Hain.

Me. Scrappy, sassy, small little Bevel Dom, who's never had a thing to call his own that couldn't fit in a saddle-bag before, and never minded a bit, besides.

It's bloody *terrifying*.

I've stared down dragons, and kraken, and fought off flesh-eating sirens, and Iridium-mad Night Elves. At sixteen, I ran away from home to chase after a boy I'd fallen in love with at first sight, though I didn't realize it until ten years later. I've abandoned my sleepy town, my sure place at my pa's side and in his forge, to travel the world and shiver in the open and cold, to never know where my next meal is coming from, to face starvation, and dehydration, and hypothermia, and dying of exposure, or infected wounds, or poison from politicos whose schemes I've thwarted.

I've looked Kintyre Turn in the face and told him (my voice and hands shaking, my face burning with shame and hope) that Lucy Piper was right, that I *did* desire him, that I *do* love him, all the while bracing for the punch in the mouth and the shouted vow that Kintyre renounced our friendship and never wanted to see me again. A punch and a vow and a shout that, thank the bloody Writer, never came. (What had come instead was fists in my collar, and chapped lips on mine, and a kiss that was desperate, and wonderful, and *just right*, and terrifying in its desperate wonderful just-right-ness).

But *nothing* has scared me the way this does. This Shadow's Mask, and all that it means... I don't even really know what it all means. The responsibilities, and the knowledge, and the way that, if the mask doesn't like me, it could *melt off my face.* The acrid smell of burning flesh and the memory of the way goopy strings of Boot-knife's skin came away on the metal makes me shudder. I could very easily lose not only my face, but possibly my life to the mask if I do this wrong. Or even, really, if I do this right, and everything *else* is wrong.

And the most terrifying thing of all: if I do this, there's no going back.

Writer's hairy left nutsack.

While I'm busy being horrified by the thing I'm holding, Kin plucks it out of my hands. His fingers are still smeared with grease from the last of the jerky, and he leaves cloudy prints on the silver, which seems just *rude.* Without wiping them away, he tucks the mask into its black velvet bag, then into the saddlebag by his knee.

"Kin, you shouldn't—" I start, but the ruddy oaf pulls me tight under his arm, my head on his chest. The rest of my scold crumbles in my mouth as I listen to his heartbeat, smell the sweat and the sulfur of our fight, the blood and the leather of his jerkin, the musky aftermath of our bit of bedsport, the stew on his breath. I inhale deeply, close my eyes, and hold on.

We are both shaking, but it's not from cold.

With our habitual post-fight celebration done, our meal eaten, and the last distraction set aside, we now have time to... to let the truth sink into our skin.

We did it. It's over.

The Viceroy is gone for good. The relief leaves me feeling giddy and lightheaded, like I've had too much pipeweed or just that one ale too many. It's joyful. It's *freeing.*

The villain is gone forever. I have my hero, and he has all his limbs and all his wits. We are hale, and hearty, and we are lovers now. I close my eyes, wrap my arms around his waist, and squeeze. Kin grunts, but squeezes my shoulders back.

In every and all senses of the word: we won.

The trek back down the Eyrie takes all of the next day. I kick Kin awake at sunrise, and we shuffle through breaking camp before the sky is really blue. We have a lot of practice erasing our presence in the landscape. After all, someone with ill intentions may use it to track us.

Though, I do wish we had brought the kettle up the mountain. Bugger all, tea will just have to wait until we're back in the Stoat.

Of course, by the time we hit the foothills, it's not tea I want anymore, but a good slug of dragon whiskey and a bitter ale to chase it down my gullet. It's near supper by the time we get back to the clearing where we left Karlurban and Dauntless, and my belly is rumbling loud enough to scare off any creature that might be licking its chops as it watches us. There are no such creatures around the horses, of course. Though there's some blood on Dauntless's left forehoof that hadn't been there before. The Shadow's Horse is shod with dwarvish steel, so I'm not too surprised when Kintyre, distracted by his own rumbling belly, steps right in the smashed mess of a goblin scout's skull.

"Oh, yuck!" Kintyre bawls, and wipes his foot on the grass like a prissish miss. Dauntless wickers like he's laughing at Kin, and I can't help but join in. "We're not staying the night here."

"No, best not to," I agree, pointing at the red pulp in the grass. "They might wonder what happened to that one. Saddle up."

Kintyre's stomach growls again. It's loud enough that Dauntless's ears flick back. Then the horse—clever bastard—looks over his shoulder for his master.

"He's not coming," Kintyre tells the horse softly, and I'm startled to hear how shaky and damp his voice sounds. He reaches up and runs his hands over Dauntless's neck, swallowing and blinking hard.

I'm just flat-footed enough by Kintyre's emotional confession that I decide to leave him to it, alone, to not call attention to it. Because if I did, I would have to say something, and I have no idea what it would be. Instead, I check on Karlurban, and review the supplies we left with the horses in the lean-to of pine boughs. We've got four people's worth of gear to juggle between us now, since Forssy buggered off. I'm very tempted to leave some of it behind, but good gear is good gear, and a waste is a waste.

Hells, we can sell the extras and doubles if we need to, anyway. No point leaving it to rust or rot out here when we could turn some coin on it. Never know when you're going to need an extra bit of clink. Lysse is awful far away by messenger hawk, and there's no lordling there anymore to send us a loan if we're desperate.

A hot ball of grief lumps up in my throat and I swallow hard, blinking against the burning in my eyes.

Bloody hells. Forsyth isn't *dead*, he's just... *gone*. Unreachable. Forever. I shake my head, annoyed with myself.

He's got his Happily Ever After, don't he? No need to weep like a milkmaid over that.

Annoyed, I force my attention back to the gear. Everything is still where it should be, at least. Though it looks like some small rodent has chewed its way into one of the spare packs and made off with a satchel of nuts. Little beggar.

There's still another package, though. I toss the nuts to Kin and take some apple chips for myself. They won't silence the beasts in our bellies entirely, but it'll do us until we're situated somewhere less filled with the pungent reek of dead monster.

We skirt the outer edge of the Stoat. The forest isn't dangerous, really, but with goblins a possibility, it's always best to stay along the foothills, where we have a clear sight-line. The horses, restless from their several-days' boredom, filled with grass and tender shoots and skittish energy, are as ready to be far away from any potential violence as we are. They bolt into a canter that takes us well toward the Valley of the Tombs by the time night has fully fallen.

We make camp on the edge of the forest. Kin and I are too hungry to do more than set snares, finish the dry rations from the saddlebags, and curl up together like a knot of naga. Ah, yes, body warmth is a lovely thing, even when there's nothing else salacious about it. Waking up next to Kin, with his big rough hand on my hip, cradling me close like I'm more precious than Foesmiter? That's nice, too.

There are rabbits in the snares when we wake. Kintyre cleans them while I harvest tubers and the last of the autumn berries from the shrubs at the growth line. Now that we're clear of goblin territory, there's no rush. It's always good when we have the opportunity of a leisurely start. We roast one rabbit to break our fast, splitting the berries between us. The skins we clean, rinsing the fur free of blood, to sell to a tanner in the next town. The rest of the meat goes into a stew with the tubers and a few pinches of the precious spices I hoard in the small metal cylinders adorning my belt.

Next to our string of coins, the spices are our most precious commodity—not for the wealth they represent, but because of how dire road-food can be without them. They go everywhere with me, even into battle. You never know when you'll need cinnamon or turmeric.

Once the stew is reasonably thick, I clamp the lid on

the pot, hang it from Karl's saddle where it won't burn the horse, and break camp. It's noon by the time we're back on the road, and with our bellies full, we have time to contemplate other things.

"It's strange to think he won't be there," Kin says as we trot toward the Valley of the Tombs. I don't have to ask who, or where, because I was thinking the same thing.

His thoughts are on Forssy, and Turn Hall. Mine are on Forssy, too—not on the legacy he's left behind for me to uphold, but a task. A position. A *promise*, maybe. Maybe a threat, too.

The Shadow's Mask is back in my hand (the one not holding the reins), and I can't help but run my thumb along the inside of it, stroking back and forth over metal made smooth by the brows and cheeks of a hundred men who have had the same choice thrust upon them as me.

"Yeah," I say.

"No fussy Bossy Forssy to yelp and cringe about his whiskey. No dire looks over the state of our boots in his grand foyer... our grand foyer," Kintyre corrects himself. And then, quietly, he adds in a crumbly voice: "*My* grand foyer. Blast."

"Kin," I say softly, just loud enough to be heard over hooves, but I don't know what to add to it, so I just look back down at the mask.

"Put that thing away," he says. "Stop panicking."

"I wasn't—"

"You are." He levels a knowing look at me—the one that says, very clearly: *I know you. You can't fool me.*

I put the mask away.

It takes several days longer than it could to reach the tomb of King Chailin, because Kin and I are reluctant to speed our journey. We both know we are headed toward...

something. The end of something. The start of something else. A *change*. And so little has changed between us in seventeen years—even when we became lovers, admitted our feelings for one another and pledged our Pairing, nothing really changed.

We shared one bedroll instead of using two. We bought each other new jerkins in Turn-russet, putting away our purples. We kissed, and swived, and didn't need a woman between us to touch each other, didn't need the lie anymore. But we traveled, and ate, and bickered, and fought villainy all the same. Things got simpler in a way I never thought they would, actually. That change was a good one. There's no telling that the next one will be. And so, we're reluctant to race toward it.

A thought's been tumbling over and over in my brain these last few days, jolted with every step of the horses, scrabbling when I try to sleep: *we're fiction.*

I didn't remember right away, what with the battle finished and the joy over the Viceroy's final defeat, the unexpected and surprising grief over the loss of Forssy. I'd never liked the pompous, self-important arse, but these last few weeks of questing with him had shown me a side I think I could have befriended properly if he'd stuck around.

And all of this because the Writer and Readers are real. We're all fictional characters in a story-scroll. Takes a bit to get your head around it. And if we're Written, then in this world devoid of the Viceroy, who are Kintyre Turn and Bevel Dom? What do they strive for? How do they spend their time? What awaits them at Turn Hall, and all that it houses, all that it represents?

I'll be the first person to admit that I'm not the most profound of blokes. I don't overthink things much, though I know I've got the better head for strategy and planning between my lover and me.

But dwelling on the idea that, in some strange way, I'm not *real?* Nah. That makes me nauseous.

So, what's waiting for us at Turn Hall, then? Concrete things. *Real* things. Real beds, and fresh bread daily, and meals I don't have to cook if I don't want to, and a steady stream of clean clothing, and warmth and comfort. A life—new and different, and safe.

But also responsibility, and permanency, and being tied to a place and a people. How are we ever going to live up to Forsyth Turn, beloved by his tenants, patron of a Free School and friend of the Sheriff?

I fight the temptation, daily, to suggest we just… run away. Run off into the wilds, like we always do when the battle is over and the damsel safe at home, when we've been feasted and fattened and tupped and thanked. Run off before we can be pressed, or tricked, or cornered into titles, or marriages, or duties. Run off to where responsibility can't catch us.

Run off so that it's just the two of us.

It's only a small temptation, though, because we promised Forssy. And a Writer-be-damned last promise *means* something. If a man isn't good to his promises, what good is he to the world, anyway? That's what my pa used to say.

The chill of the Valley is a welcome distraction from our wordless worries. We make camp on Chailin's front porch, in the same place we had less than a fortnight ago, when our pursuit of Bootknife had led us to the unlike-liest of adventurers and changed everything about how we saw Forsyth Turn. And his damsel. And the world we inhabit.

While Kintyre builds the night's fire, I pay a visit to the unmarked, still-fresh grave of that bastard Boot-knife. Just to be sure, you see, that the monster is still underground, where he belongs. Kintyre didn't bury him deep, so it only takes a few minutes to uncover his face and chest. They've both begun to sink, and a gruesome pleasure fills me to see that the worms have already eaten through one of his cheeks and out an eyeball. I take great joy in driving one of my arrows through his heart before I close up the grave again. Petty, yeah. But a stake through the heart is a cure for more than just vampire troubles, and it's always better to be safe than sorry.

When I come back, I stop to wash my hands in the cold stream that bisects the valley, and Kintyre doesn't ask why they were dirty in the first place. He doesn't need to.

Once the sun has set, and we're both wrapped up warm against the chill of the night, we take the time to clean and hone the dagger Kintyre's been carrying at his waist for over a decade. When the blade is sparkling and sharp, the few remaining gems shining once more in the firelight, we take a torch into Chailin's tomb and return the fallen king's dagger to him. I say a few Words of Peace, and Gratitude, and Good Rest as Kintyre slips the blade back into its moldering leather-and-gold sheath. We carefully push the lid of the sarcophagus closed, and reseal the edges with the pot of pitch we usually save for kindling fires.

We sleep poorly and light that night, starting at every sound and shivering with every gust of wind. You never know what might accidentally wake the dead. If it wasn't stealing a beloved symbolic dagger, then it might be re-turning it.

All the corpses stay where they should, though, and our luck holds for at least one more night.

In the misty, watery-weak light of day, we decide to cross the Cinch Mountains to the west via some of the dwarvish tunnels we know, and take the opportunity to resupply in Chasmshine. From there, we can cut through North Urland to the Salt Crystal Caverns to give back the Cup that Never Runs Dry, and then double back into fertile Miliway and head to the Lost Library to return the Parchment that Never Fills. Winter is nearly upon us, and crossing the Cinch even a few weeks later than we are now would be foolhardy. There are no dwarf cities in North Urland, and we would have to go *over* the mountains there, instead of under them. No, better to cross now, and head back south to Miliway Chipping later, save the easier road for the harsher weather.

Chasmshine is another two day's ride. Queen Andvari Stoneborn welcomes us to her halls, as I knew she would, and promises us a quiet night to recuperate and bathe, a day's restocking and catching up with her—her way of saying "gossip about the world of the humanfolk"—tomorrow, followed by a feast to see us off. It takes a day, at least, to put together a proper dwarvish feast, but we don't mind the wait, really. It's always worth it.

As soon as we're in our rooms (human-sized, for those out-sized guests who need to visit the dwarf kingdom occasionally), Kintyre strips to his skin and streaks with unashamed eagerness to the attached bathing chamber. The stone basin is sunk into the floor and filled with steaming hot spring water from the heart of the mountains. Massive prismatic diamond windows line the chamber and look out onto the underground portion of the Northwash River that eventually flows over the waterfall of the Crystal Caverns much further north of us. Kintyre flops into the water like an ungraceful selkie toddler and, as I'm hot on his heels, splashes the mineral water in my face.

"Oh, that's the way of it, is it?" I shout with a grin, and jump on his shoulders.

What follows is probably the most ridiculous battle in the history of heroics. In the interest of never sullying our good reputation as questing adventurers and knights,

I vow never to write it down, even as I yank on my lover's hair and spit water in his face. Once we've had our rumpus, I steal back into the sleeping chamber in naught but my towel. I'm looking for the wine the dwarves always keep by their bedsides and, finding that, come across a tray of broken cold cheeses, rolls, and pickled root vegetables that some poor chambermaid must have delivered while we were carousing. I wonder what sort of tales are already circulating among the serving staff about the clumsy, oafish, too-large and too-loud humans. Doesn't matter, really. We *are* too-large and too-loud for dwarvish tastes. And Andvari will squash any whispers that get too prejudiced or hateful.

While I've been gone, Kintyre's mopped up the worst of the splashes, and created a rolled pile of towels around one end of the basin so we can lay our heads back on the edge and just turn to soup. I put the tray on the floor beside this, and Kintyre cuddles close as soon as I've slipped back into the water. For my kisses, I had hoped, but he just snatches the wine bottle out of my hand, the magpie, and swigs off the first swallow.

"Brute," I complain, but he holds the bottle out for me, and tips it against my lips sweetly, so I suppose I forgive him.

"I'm the brute?" he asks, after taking another swig and turning onto his stomach to pick at the tray of savories. "Look at this. No meat."

I smack one of the plump arse cheeks bobbing out of the water, and he yelps. "You know dwarves eat no meat. Don't be an elfcock," I say, and smack his other cheek for symmetry.

"Wouldn't hurt them to be hospitable," Kintyre mutters with a scowl, and then grabs my wrist before I can land another playful blow on his rump and starts another scuffle which sends splashes of water flying from our elbows and feet.

"Elfcock," I repeat, and then use his distraction to snatch the wine bottle out of his hand.

"This is nice," Kin says, when he's got me pinned to the side of the tub so he can monopolize the wine. "I feel so weightless."

"I like big baths like this, too." I wrap my legs around his waist to demonstrate.

"No, I mean... yeah, the bath, too. But... no Viceroy. I never realized how much I... I *worried* about him. And Bootknife. Never realized how much I *thought* about them, all the time, in the back of my mind, you know?" he says, eyes going squinty as he tries to figure out how to say what he means. "It was like a mosquito in my ear. I used to think about him a few times a day, wonder where he was, what he was up to, what he was plotting next. I would check on you, when that happened. Wake up from sleep or look over on the road. Make sure you were still there."

"You would?" I ask, pleasantly startled by this revelation. "Yeah?"

"Yeah," Kin says, and kisses my neck, and each of my eyelids, and the tiny scar under my eye from Bootknife's blade.

"And now?"

"Now I just look at you because I like what I see," Kin says with a wicked grin, and grinds closer against my hips. "And every time I think about the Viceroy, it's like a... a surprise, you know? But a good one. Because I get to remember all over again that he's gone. And it's like my whole body relaxes, and I get giddy because... because I don't have to worry anymore. I never have to fear..." He doesn't admit what he feared, but he kisses the scar under my eye again, and I can guess. He feared having to face me across the battlefield the same way Forsyth was forced to face a green-glowing Pip across the lavender-gray expanse of the Rookery.

We nibble and roll about in the water for another hour, until a messenger knocks on the door and politely informs us that if we're quite finished ruining the floors, Queen Andvari would like us to join her in her private parlor for a nightcap. Kin and I each quickly scrub soap through our hair and make ourselves as presentable as we can with the clothes from our packs. They're wrinkled, but they don't reek of the road and horses, so that's something at least. What we were wearing when we arrived has already been carted away to the royal laundry, thank the Writer.

Hair still damp and sheepish grins on our faces, we make our way to the queen's suite. We are greeted at the door by the queen's second spouse, Nyrath. The Princess Consort is plump-cheeked and glowing, her tightly curled black beard adorned with Rose Quartz and Malachite.

"Writer's balls, you're pregnant!" I hear myself saying before I can shut down my stupid mouth when I parse what the stone-language message means.

Nyrath giggles coyly and ducks her head, and from behind her, Andvari's distinctive braying laughter rings across the stone ceiling. "And you, Bevel Dom, have changed not a bit."

"Well, maybe a bit," I call back as Nyrath leads us over to her wife. I hold my hands out, showing off my Turn-russet short robe.

The queen's eyes widen, then narrow shrewdly and jump between Kintyre—who is also wearing Turn-russet—and me.

"Writer's balls," she echoes, jumping up from her wingback chair by the fire. "*Finally.*"

Dwarves, as a rule, are about four feet tall, but Andvari stands at nearly five. There's mixed blood in the

Stoneborn line, some say, while others whisper that the Stoneborns are larger than most because they are filled with the destiny of their people. Andvari once confessed to me that it was just a family trait, and meant nothing whatsoever. Andvari is also thick with muscle, where her wife is plump and her husband slender.

Sviur was a bard and poet who charmed the crown princess while he toured the dwarvish courts, and she had asked for his hand as her first spouse just before we first met her. I'll never forget the headache of trying to help her unravel the political bellyaching that occurred because she'd chosen a commoner as First Spouse while also trying to keep Kintyre from rushing off to the Urlish wars with no idea of what being a common soldier was really like.

Wars that caused the death of Andvari's father and her ascent to the throne. In retrospect, it's a good thing we did stay, because if Sviur had never got an eyeful of Foesmiter, Kin would never have known that his weapon was one of the Ten Magical Swords of Legend, nor how to work in harmony with the blade's magics.

To appease the courts, Andvari had next married Nyrath, the daughter of a neighboring kingdom—a shy, sweet girl raised to be some other ruler's wife and knowing from a very young age that she would be sent away from her homeland and all she loved dear for political gain. Instead of growing petulant and resentful at her lot, Nyrath had determined to chart her own destiny, hold her own power in her future spouse's court. She had studied the art of treaties and warfare, bargaining and trading, politics and backroom deals. On the surface, sweet-faced and sunny Nyrath was nothing more than a pretty, biddable girl. But under that, she was a shrewd and sneaky chess-master. Andvari was luckier than she had ever thought she would be in her choice. Andvari's genuine admiration for Nyath's political prowess had made the marriage smoother and, eventually, a love worth treasuring had grown between them.

As soon as I get close enough, Andvari grabs my hand and pumps it energetically, her grin sharkish behind her fire-red beard. Her hair is down for the night, the braids of rulership now loose, waist-length waves that swing around when she turns to punch Kintyre in the kidneys.

"About time, you clueless granite-skull!" she bawls joyfully.

Kintyre doubles over, not expecting the blow, and Sviur rises from where he and their son Virfur—by the Writer, how he's grown!—were practice-strumming his lute. Sviur's lost none of the grace his dancing days instilled in him, and he offers both of us a polite greeting. We shake hands, clasping at the elbows to check for concealed daggers in the dwarvish way. Sviur's golden fall of hair is loose, too, as it must be because of his common birth, but now it's threaded with white. The braid at his chin is almost entirely colorless. Much more so than I was expecting. Virfur comes to stand beside Sviur, shy in the way young children are. He's probably just on the brink of ten years old, but that's still young for a dwarf—closer to our two or three. When we saw him last, though, he was still a babe in arms.

Some small secret part of me pangs with hurt. I was hoping to hold the baby again. How silly of me to have forgotten that the world below the Cinch wouldn't just freeze like winter ice and wait for us to come back. Ridiculous.

"Sit, sit," Nyrath admonishes. She bustles us onto cushions on the floor, which is what we prefer in order to be eye-level with the dwarves when we're in casual company. Sviur passes us both cut-crystal glasses of the clear root-vegetable liquor the dwarves specialize in. Kintyre downs his immediately, in one gulp. I shoot Sviur a look of apology, but the dwarf shakes his head. He's used to Kintyre's manners by now, and just refills the glass without comment. Kintyre sips this second one, at least.

Virfur, curiosity overcoming his shyness, crawls immediately into Kintyre's legs and stretches up to stroke his naked chin with wonder. Kintyre clamps down on his grimace, picks the toddler up from under the armpits, and deposits him on my lap. I hastily set aside my glass, putting it up on a side table and out of the child's reach. His parents laugh.

"Not one for children, Kintyre?" Andvari asks in that rumbling contralto of hers.

Nyrath narrows her eyes at my lover, but says nothing. Neither does Kintyre.

"It's not that Kin dislikes children," I say, and I'm reminded, sharply, of when Pip had once called me *Kintyre's walking apology*. At the time, it hadn't annoyed me, or even really registered as an insult, because that was part of my relationship with the man who had been first my master, then my friend, and then my brother-in-arms. But now, sitting beside him on the floor of a queen's salon, holding the heir presumptive, Kin's Paired and supposedly now equal in rank to Kin, I'm still making excuses for his poor behavior, enabling his entitled assumption that I would smooth things over, that I will hold what Kintyre doesn't want to, that I will fetch and carry and cook and bow my whims to his.

Bloody aggravating.

"Then why?" Nyrath asks, forcing me to continue the lame half-explanation, half-veiled request for forgiveness for the insult of passing off a prince like he was a sack of rotten meat.

"He just... doesn't really know what to do with them

until they're old enough for him to roughhouse with," I say lamely. "He likes my gaggle of nieces and nephews, to be sure enough, but more so now that they're all walking and talking on their own."

The dwarves seem to take this at face value, and attention turns back to conversation. In my lap, Virfur wobbles his way upright. The boy doesn't seem to mind whose lap he's in, as long as he can explore the oddity of a smooth face. Kin and I indulged in a shave with hot water and proper lotions before we answered the queen's bidding, and it feels fantastic to finally be scruff-less, after so long on the road. Must be odd to the boy, though.

Oh, that will be one of the advantages of our return to Turn Hall, to be sure. A daily shave, with proper tools. Sublime.

But Pip's words are circling in my mind now, distracting me from what's being said, taking on a sharper and sharper tone with each repetition. *Kintyre's walking apology. Aren't you sick of it, Bevel?* Something querulous and cranky lodges in my guts, something shapeless but quickly solidifying, something unspoken but pushing against the hollow of my throat.

Something... *something...*

I'm the only one in my immediate family who is unmarried and childless. While Kin and I are officially Paired, we haven't made it known that we are a Romantic Pair by pledging our Troth. It hadn't seemed important before, when all I wanted was a visual acknowledgment that Kin was mine. Let others see our shared Colors and assume we were only pledged as brothers-in-arms, if they prefer. What does it matter to me if their assumption is wrong?

But now, watching Andvari pull her pregnant wife in beside her on the wingback chaise, the pleased curl of their mouths and the striking picture of their very different skin tones mixing together as they clasp hands, seeing the way Sviur joins us on the cushions so he can lean back against his wives' legs, the way they are all so content and unashamed and casually public in their displays of affection... I'm struck, suddenly and hard, with a kind of envy I never thought I would experience.

Married.

I want... I want to... I *want*. But I don't know what it is I want, exactly.

It's not skin, or warmth, or sex. I have those. It's not even affection, because Kin gives that freely, too, gifts it like a lord bestowing bags of grain to the pathetic, needy, starving peasants he has *made* pathetic and needy and starving by his own blind and selfish nobility.

No, it's something else that I want.

Kintyre is too busy chatting, already sharing news of our latest quest—how we had fled Turn Hall in our individual rages, how we had separated and come back together, how we had confessed and hashed out our relationship, how we had scented Bootknife's trail when we stopped in Nevand to commission our Colors, how we had followed him down to the Valley of the Tombs—to see the upset on my face.

I feel it growing out of my guts, infecting my expression, my posture, and I'm... I'm *angry*, and I can't... I *can't...*

Virfur catches it, and babbles something sweetly soothing at me in the secret language of the dwarves, one that I'll never have the privilege to learn.

If you put on the Shadow's Mask, you would know it. The thought jars against my wallowing self-pity so quickly that the room spins. *You would understand the boy if you put on the mask. You would understand everything.*

"And what about you, Sir Dom?" Sviur asks, and I blink, hard, trying to wrench my brain around to the question he asked.

"What?"

"I asked you how you felt the morning of your Pairing. I had a stomach filled with bubbling sulfur the whole week before Andvari and I got married." He flashes a brilliant smile at his first wife, and she threads her free hand through his hair, affectionate. "What were you like before your wedding?"

Resentment boils up faster than I can contain it. "Yeah, well, we're not really married, are we though?" I say, and then click my teeth shut hard enough that the whole room can hear it.

By the Writer's left nutsack, is *that* what's been brewing in the cauldron of my frustration?

"We're Paired, though, Bev," Kintyre says affably, like all the hurt in what I just spoke has passed him by completely. "And it's not like two blokes can get married among the humanfolk anyway. Not *married*, married."

"And since when have we ever cared about what humanfolk normally do?" I say, and in my arms, Virfur plops down on my knees, making me wince. He reaches for the lute and strums the strings in a discordant twang, looking up at me with the expectation of praise and a grin that matches his father's. Instead, I hand the boy off to his mother. I cannot *bear* to have a child in my arms right now. A child that's not... that's *not*... but there never will be, never could be a child that's...

Andvari gathers Virfur up, and he hides under her beard, both of them startled by the abrupt arrival of my foul mood. I swallow hard, trying to pull this strange, roiling ball of emotion and confession back down into my chest. But I've repressed my discontent for so long it seems like now the cork has been popped from the bottle, I can't just jam it back in.

"I... thank you for the invitation, and the drink," I say,

waving at my untouched glass. "But I'm tired."

"Bevel—" Andvari and Kintyre say at the same time, but I'm already on my feet.

"Goodnight, Your Majesty, Your Highnesses," I say with a curt bow, and then I run away with my tail between my legs.

"Why are you so pissy?" Kintyre grumbles at me when he crawls into bed a few hours later. I wasn't asleep, lucky for Kin. I would have walloped him if he'd woke me up from a comfortable sleep on a real feather tick, especially after so many sleepless nights on the hard ground with only a travel-worn bedroll. His breath smells like liquor, and his hands are too warm. Likely he and Andvari have been playing that palm-slap game that rock-headed dwarves and thick-skinned human heroes seem to love in equal measure.

"I'm not pissy!" I snarl, which just proves how much I'm lying.

Those warm hands land on my shoulder and suddenly I'm on my back. Kin knows how much I hate it when he uses his size against me. I kick him in the jewels and he curls in on himself and falls off to the side of the mattress, gasping in pain and looking at me with big, stupid, betrayed eyes that are just so damned blue I want to scream.

"What..." he gasps. "That was dirty! What did I do to deserve that?"

And it was dirty. It's awful, the pain of being sacked, and I have no idea why I did it, how I could do it, to my lover, let alone to a part of him I enjoy so much. Only that maybe it's the symbol, the center of everything that's annoying me and I'm a warrior, rough and brutish, and I attack those things I can't control, that annoy me, that make me angry.

And how's that for insight? Forssy would be so proud! Ha!

But at the same time, I'm still angry. I'm utterly filled with a tickling, twitching, zinging energy, and it's not arousal, or hunger, or hatred. I don't know what it is, except that it's *awful.*

Kin gingerly levers himself onto the bed. I shove the blankets back and clamber up onto his torso, pinning his arms against his sides, controlling, the one in charge for once, and kiss him hard enough that I taste blood.

"What? Bevel, stop, ow, off—" Kintyre mutters, words smeared into my mouth, and with a fancy bit of calisthenics, he has our position reversed again.

"No!" I snarl, shoving hard at his shoulders, kicking his knee out from under him and squirming off the bed in a display of pretty impressive calisthenics myself. "*No!*"

"No, what?" Kintyre says, kneeling, hands out, palms up as if he expects to have to plead for his life. And I don't know; in the mood I'm in, maybe he will. "I don't understand what's going on here!"

"Neither do I!" I snap, and the words froth and boil in my mouth. Words that I don't understand, that I'm scared of saying because I don't know what they're going to be.

"Then what in the name of the Writer's blue balls has gotten into you?" Kin snarls back.

"I can't do it anymore!" I shout, and it's loud enough that the sound of my voice rings across the high stone ceiling of our chambers. Probably loud enough that the guard in the hall heard it. Probably loud enough that Andvari and her spouses heard it in their own bedchamber.

"Do what?" Kintyre shouts back, though at half the volume. "You're not making any sense!"

"Anything! All of it!" And I fist my hands in my hair because I can't find the words. Oh, the blessed unbelievable irony of it! Bevel Dom, scribe to the Great Hero of Hain, the man who single-handedly turned the bumbling adventures of a stupid, selfish man-child into a thing of gorgeous poetic eddas: speechless. "I can't... I can't be... I can't do..." I pace in a circle, scrubbing, tugging, and the pain in my scalp matches the pain itching, itching on the underside of my skin, the writhing, wrathful thing in my belly.

Kintyre slowly shuffles to the edge of the bed, reaches out to wrap soothing arms around me, shushing me as if I was his Writer-be-damned horse, and I duck away. I don't want to be shushed, and soothed, and petted like I'm some stupid fretting maiden.

I want... I *want*...

"It's not fair!" I finally bawl, the dark, writhing thing inside me vomiting up out of my mouth. "Why didn't the Writer make it so that two human men could have children?"

"What?" Kintyre asks, and he looks exactly how I feel—utterly *poleaxed* by what I've just said.

But the puking confession isn't over, apparently. Even though I back up, press myself against the wall, turn my face away, screw my eyes shut, smash my fists back against the ornately carved stone, I can't seem to shut up.

"It's not fair!" my mouth says again. "Dwarven women can get children on their wives, why not human men?"

"That's what all this is about? A baby?" Kintyre asks, that frown I know so well furrowing down between his eyebrows.

"No!" I say, then, with a grunt of frustration, "Yes!" Then: "No! I don't know! It's... it's... it's the way you hand everything off to me, Kin! I'm not your tag-along, or your squire, but you dump the gear on me! You toss the baby at me! You think a Pairing is enough, and I'm somehow, someway, always... always... *always*..."

"Always what?" Kin asks warily.

"*Less!*" I snarl. I turn my back to him and punch the wall again. It smarts, and my knuckles make a sharp cracking sound. The scent of blood fills my nose, but I pull back my arm for a third strike.

Kin's big hands grab both of my elbows before the blow can land, and he pulls me backward, hauls me off my feet in exactly the way I don't appreciate, entitled and pushy and *bigger than me*. We tumble back again onto the bed, him on his back, me on his chest, and he wraps his giant thighs around my waist and his giant biceps around my upper arms. He makes me feel small, and it's hateful.

"Peace, Bevel, peace," Kintyre says as I squirm and struggle.

"No, no, let go!" I snarl. I gnash at the air, and I'm certain that if the stupid oaf tries to cover my mouth with his hand, I will bite the officious bastard. "I hate this! I hate it when you do this! I hate you!"

"You don't hate me, Bev," Kin says, but his voice is tinged with a desperate, gulping hurt I haven't heard in it since the night we fought and raged and confessed our love. "You're just tired. You—"

"Don't you condescend to me, Kintyre bloody Turn, lord's son and Chosen One!" I hiss. "Don't you *dare*."

"Is that what this is?" Kintyre asks. "Going back to Turn Hall and—"

"No! Yes! All of it!"

"All of what?" Kintyre thunders. "Speak!"

"I can't... I can't *do* it," I say again, and there's some stopper in my throat, something that is keeping the right words from escaping me. "The... going back. Being just your Paired, being the lord's... *bum-boy*. The arrogant little goblin-snot from a nothing village on the forgotten border, always one step behind, the seventh son of the seventh son, unmarried and childless, the scribe with no more stories to tell, *useless*."

And there. There it is.

There it *all* is.

The anger and fear and fury fly from me so suddenly that I feel like a zombie whose necromancer has been abruptly slain—I flop back against my lover's wide chest, all tension gone, stringless and boneless. Tears form behind my eyes in a hot, burning lump, and they are equally tears of relief, and shame, and embarrassment at what I've confessed, how I've behaved. I turn into Kin's shoulder, and he loosens his hold enough to allow me to turn over and bury my flushed face in his neck.

"What if Forssy made a mistake?" I whisper, because I can't talk about the rest of it. I can't say it again. I can't even admit that I just said it. "What if I'm not good enough for the mask? I'm no hero, Kin. I'm just the sidekick."

"Oh, oh, Bevel," Kintyre says, petting my hair, and it doesn't feel condescending now, only comforting and kind. "Oh, Bevel, how can you not know? It doesn't matter what the rest of the world thinks about you. You're *my* hero."

Kintyre's insistence that I'm his hero is all well and good, and our make-up sex is as spectacular as it always is. But in the morning, I'm still left feeling agitated and hollow. Itchy and frustrated, dazed as a bloody mooncalf, and useless as tits on a bull. Being Kin's hero doesn't solve any of my other problems, or lay to rest any of my other fears.

We stay in bed late. My sleep is heavy and hard, and I wake like a punch. When I open my bleary eyes, it's clear that someone's been in the room. A dwarven servant cleaned up the mess, and replaced last night's clothes with the freshly laundered and repaired set, stealing yesterday's away for the same treatment. There's tea, strong and thick with honey, waiting for us on the hearthstone, staying warm. There's also a fresh bath drawn.

Thank the bloody Writer for that. I feel like I've stepped into a jousting arena with a Writer-be-damned rock golem. My hand is throbbing and swollen, punishment for being enough of a fool to throw a punch at a stone wall. I deserve it.

I stumble out of bed, weaving like I'm punchdrunk, bleary-eyed from my misery, head aching from my confession, mouth dry. I feel hungover, though I only had a few sips of the dwarven liquor last night. My hair is sweaty, and matted, and there's seed dried to the hair on my belly.

Without even waiting for Kin, I sink into the bath and

rinse my mouth. I clean the cuts on my knuckles, wincing, and curse myself for being an idiot. Kintyre slides in beside me a few minutes later, looking just as rough as I feel. Though he has an *actual* hangover. There's a bright blue bruise on his inner thigh, and I wince as he gingerly sits in the tub.

"Sorry 'bout the sacking," I say. He grunts, nods, and sips the tea he's got with him, then hands the mug to me wordlessly to share. Apology accepted, then.

When we emerge from the bath, wrinkly, steamed, and silent, there's a tray of sweet rolls, fruit preserves, and more cheese on the foot of the freshly made bed. The second cup of tea is still hot, so we share that between us, too.

It's not tension that fills the air between Kin and me. Not really. But there's... the acknowledgment and memory of my confessions. And a big fuzzy gap where both of us are still searching out the meaning of what I said, how it affects the us that we've forged, and what—if anything— we can change. Or at least, try to change.

Bugger all and blast it, besides.

Me and my big mouth. It was good before, wasn't it? I had Kin, and I had the road, and soon I was going to have fresh bread and regular baths, daily shaves and warm feather beds, and I would get to grow old with Kintyre. Beside Kintyre.

One step slightly behind and to the left of Kintyre.
Blast it.

Normally, when we have an afternoon with no villains to roust, no road to travel, no armies to drill, no plans to hatch, no supplies to collect, no schemes to unravel, no horrors to fear, Kintyre and I sit in companionable silence in a tea room, or tavern, or inn, and work on our artistic pursuits. Kintyre will scratch away at his charcoal illustrations, or painstakingly transfer the images to a wood block he carves and whittles into a stamp. And I, in our early days, would practice my hard-earned skill of reading, or writing. Once I'd mastered that, my practice grew into chronicling our adventures in a collection of journals. Which, one drunken night, I let a desperate printmaker convince me to allow him to print. Which then put me in the position of turning bard, writing everything out in scrolls peppered with Kin's woodcut illustrations. Which then, somehow, brought us fame across the four kingdoms, and enough clink to keep us in travel rations.

The same Kingskeep printmaker has been made a very wealthy man on my scrolls and Kin's stamps. He's also sent three messenger hawks in as many months asking after another tale for his shop. Except I have none to give him. None that I feel I could share, at any rate. At least, not without some heavy fibbing, and some fabrications, and...

Oh, hells, I'm going to write it, aren't I? I can't even fool myself. I've never been a good liar.

But, no, not *all* of it. Forsyth and Pip and the Readers of Legend... no. That's not something I can tell the whole world. Especially without proof. That is a secret Kin and I will have to take to our graves. Bugger all.

So, with nothing to write until I figure out just how much of this adventure I *can* share, and nothing to illustrate on Kin's part till I've written a bloody thing, we pass the afternoon in uncomfortable but companionable silence. We take a wordless luncheon on the balcony that overlooks the foothills of the Cinch, one of the few places where Chasmshine opens onto the outside world. I smoke more hash than I probably should, and Kintyre, upwind of me, doesn't scold for once. When the afternoon light grows longer, I repack my bags with the supplies the servants have dropped off for us, and catch myself reaching for Kin's pack before I realize I'm doing it. I straighten abruptly, dropping Kin's bag by the hearth—nearly on his foot—and say, "Actually, no. Do it for yourself."

There's more venom in the order than I intended. I can feel the blush crawling up my cheeks, settling in my ears, when I realize how it sounded. Kin stares at me with wide, startled eyes, and I mutter a curse and flee to the stables. How embarrassing. How *childish*. Writer, why does Kin even put up with me?

Deciding that, while I'm hiding, I might as well see to Karl and Dauntless, I check their hooves, comb out and then re-braid their manes, and spoil them with a pair of apples stolen from our lunch. Kin should be here. Normally, he's good with doing his share of work with the horses. He enjoys pampering the beasts, but he's still smarting a little from the death of Stormbearer. And yeah, my little blow-up just now wouldn't encourage him to follow me.

Horses have their own personalities. Stormbearer was a swagger-er, just like the man who rode him. Karl is excitable, keen to be in the middle of everything. But Dauntless—Dauntless was the product of both the dam and sire of Stormbearer, a little brother in all ways. That should have given the stallion an excitable temper and a passionate drive. Instead, Dauntless is... sweet. For all that he is the Shadow's Horse—would be *my* horse, if I put on the mask—he's a polite gentleman. His primness re-minds me again of Forsyth, and that spot in my heart that had once been the placeholder for the rough, big-broth-er-bully sort of affection I'd held for the simpering lad throbs a little.

Forsyth is gone, and it will take two of us to fill his shoes. One to be lord. One to be Shadow Hand. And how in all seven of the hells are we going to survive the transition?

The dwarvish feast is as raucous and filled with spirits and illicit kisses behind beards as they usually are. Before it disintegrates into the normal end-of-night orgy, Kin and I skulk back to our rooms, eager to be out of the fine lawn shirts and velvet waistcoats that we only wear to these kinds of official functions. Otherwise, they stay jammed in the bottom of our saddlebags, padding for the pots and pans.

As little as a few months ago, we would have stayed for the orgy. But I know I've lost all desire for sport of this kind with anyone except Kin. I'm relieved, I think, maybe more than is fair to my lover, that he seems to feel the same way about me. It soothes some of the hurt in me to know that the only one Kin wants to swive with is me.

And as little as four or five years ago, we might have snuck out of the mountain that night. The officious and boring seeing-off ceremony the morning we left was always a chore, and more than once we've repaid Andvari's hospitality poorly by dashing out under the secret cover of darkness. But we are old adventurers now, well into middle age. We—or, at least, I've—since learned the importance of diplomacy. That, and also that the luxury of a feather mattress for another night is too good to give up.

Writer, I've turned into my Pa. He used to groan for just another five minutes in bed, too, and hoard all the feathers from the plucked chickens for pillows to cradle his forge-weary shoulders.

So, in the morning, we pointedly don't tease the hungover dwarves peppered with love-bites, hair still in disarray, as they stand on the gates of Chasmshine and solemnly wish us well on the remainder of our quest.

Then I mount Dauntless (Dauntless and I should grow familiar with each other if I decide to... well, if I decide), and Kintyre mounts Karlurban. We spend the rest of the day in silence, except for the horse hooves striking the slate of the underground highway. The quiet is less tense than it was the day before, though. It's more contemplative. I'm not sure if it's me or Kin who's thinking the most. Maybe it's both of us. Maybe we're just both frantically thinking about *not* thinking. Writer, it'd be funny if I wasn't so preoccupied.

A few times, I take a breath to say something, open my mouth, then shut the damned thing again when I see Kin's shoulders tense like he's preparing to take a blow. We sleep in the underground way station, and emerge the next day at dusk on the northern coast of Urland. Say what you will about how dismal and claustrophobic dwarvish highways can be, the magic that allows you to traverse a whole kingdom in just a few hours is still wondrous. Kin and I are lucky we've befriended the dwarvish nobility, otherwise we'd never get access to the tunnels.

The horses are happy to be out in the fresh air again, and, yeah, to be honest, so am I. They canter a little showily through the broad scrub plains of Urland. This part of the world is sometimes called the Giant's Graveyard because of the way the rough, age-pocked stone swells up, bone white, out of the hard-scrabble vegetation. It curves like ribs in some places, exists in dome-like skulls in others, with succulents and marrowbrush growing in the weather-carved gullies and little crevasses between. Some rocks are straight, and jagged at their tip, like a femur that was snapped, the leg left to rot under the sky. The Graveyard eventually levels out into the flat plain of grassland that abuts the Cinch, a thin strip that had once been at the bottom of a lake, when a river had ushered a torrent of ice melt and rainwater into the now-dry floodplains of Urland, lifetimes before Kin and I were ever born. Or Written into existence.

The reality of everything we've learned and heard and done over the last few weeks—last few *months*, really—hits me all at once. I feel lightheaded. The bright sunshine isn't helping matters, but I swallow hard and shake my head, force myself to *pay attention* to my seat, lest I lose it.

Generations of history in our world, and it's really only a few decades old. Written to seem ancient, but fresh as bad wine.

I have no idea if the stones are real giant bones, but the *mask might know.* Again, I am startled by the suddenness of the thought. So persuasive and calm, and sounding a hells of a lot more like Forsyth than I think I'm ready to admit to myself. Kin scouts the curve in the road ahead, searching for a good gully in which to make camp. I pull the mask out of the pouch in the side of my saddlebags, and hold it out ahead of me, an arm's length away so a sudden jarring of Dauntless beneath me won't accidentally fumble it toward my face. Through the eye holes, the Giant's Graveyard looks just the same. Would it still if I said the Word? If I pressed the cool silver against my cheeks and—

A shiver runs through me, and I let the arm holding the mask drop.

Seductive, that's what this is.

On its own? Was it part of the enchantment on the mask, that it works on the person who holds it until they give in? A spell that ensures there will always be a Shadow Hand? Is it a sort of semi-sentient parasite that needs a body and a brain to host it?

Or is it just my own inclination? My own curiosity and... and my own desperate desire to be needed in a way that isn't auxiliary of or appended to Kintyre? To have something of my own. *Just mine.* In a way that nothing—not even my own body, really—has been mine since I was sixteen and watched a gorgeous blond git ride up to the forge and dunk his head in my smithy's cooling trough before even saying so much as a "hello" or "may I?"

The sound of Karl's hooves coming closer warns me in time to tuck the mask away before Kintyre turns the corner. I'm not ashamed, or hiding the mask, really. It's just... it's a conversation that I'm not sure I'm ready to have. Not after how the last one went. Not when we're both still smarting from that. Kin more than me, though, judging by the way he's sort of holding himself up from his saddle by the stirrups. Writer, his calves must be killing him.

"There's a culvert over here," Kin says, and his voice is a bit hoarse from the fact that neither of us has said much in the last two days. "Doesn't look like rain, so we should be sheltered without getting soaked."

I nod, and direct Dauntless to follow him. *Culvert* is a bit of a fancy word for what Kin leads us to—it's more like a shallow depression between rolling hills, padded with the squashy moss that lives on the stone. But it'll do for a night. We've slept in worse places.

Before I can get to unpacking anything, Kin's taken over getting the saddlebags off the horses and brushing them down. Bemused by his sudden desire to take charge, I turn my attention to dinner, only to have him tell me that he wants to look after the fire and rehydrating the travel rations, too.

"Shall I collect brush for firewood, then?" I ask, hands on my hips as I watch him make a hash of it all already.

"Naw," Kin says. "You just sit and smoke your pipe."

"Sit and smoke my pipe," I repeat, jamming a cork in the ire that's threatening to bubble up again. "Like some useless maiden?"

Kin, who had been crouched over the pile of rocks he'd been arranging in a circle, looks up, jaw dropped and eyes wide, aghast. "What? Bev, *no.*"

"Then why don't you want me to do my part?"

"It's not that... I don't want you to not do... Bev, I'm trying to be nice."

"By implying that I can't do anything for myself."

"No!" Kin straightens. "No, of course not! I just thought that it would be... I want to... Writer's balls, Bev, come on. You're not making this easy for me!"

"Making what easy?" I ask, but the genuineness of his dismay has my ire flickering out already, the cold splash of his worry dowsing my embers.

Kintyre gestures around him and makes a frustrated noise. "You say you don't want to be lesser-than, that you're sick of having to do things for me, and I'm *trying*, Bev. I'm trying to show you that I... I don't take you for granted... that *you...*"

"All right," I say, letting him off the lure. The dangling has been amusing—once I realized what he was on about—but it's not fair to let the fish suffer. I crowd up to him, grab his ears, and pull him down to catch his mouth.

"Don't like it when you pull my ears," he mutters into our kiss, but doesn't shake off my hold.

"Your fault for being so damnably tall," I say, but I say it with a smile. "And thank you."

Kin grunts again and goes back to making dinner. I sit and smoke a pipe, and only occasionally shout suggestions as he over-boils the water, burns the last of the travel stew, and somehow makes mush out of what ought to have been a perfectly serviceable bowl of round-grain.

"It's wretched," he complains as we plow our way through the meal.

"Yeah," I agree with a mischievous grin, and a wink

that's a peace offering. "But I appreciate not having to make it. I'll take care of breakfast, though."

In the bright, cold chill of a late autumn morning, I stand in the Northwash River. In front of me, the waterfall crashes on, oblivious to my shivering discomfort and the way my arms are starting to quiver and burn from holding the chalice aloft. Kintyre might have been more enticing bait for the sylph, but I'm more devoted to my love. I've loved Kintyre longer than he's loved me. It's more deeply entrenched in my spirit and heart, so I won't be easily turned. It has to be me who does this.

Not that I doubt my Pair's adoration for me, or the depth of his affection. It's just that my love is older. It's harder to get grappling hooks into and pull apart. It's been tempered by sorrow, and self-recrimination, and anger, and jealousy. It's been buttressed with heroics, and sacrifices, honesty, and care. It's strong. Today, I believe it. If the sylph does to me as she did to Forsyth, if she tries to bespell me and tempt me into her grasp, I'm confident that I won't give in.

"Bevel, it's not working," Kintyre calls to me. "Come out of the water before you turn into an iceberg."

"Just a little longer," I call back. "I can stand it. It will work."

"Are you sure?"

"Yeah."

I have to be.

"Daft arsehole!" my lover calls.

Kin stomps back to tend the fire he started when I insisted that it would go better if we let the sylph come to us rather than invade her home. He wants to be ready to help me dry off and warm up. It's a bit sweet, really. Berk.

My patience is rewarded. After waiting in the frigid

river for over an hour, the Cup that Never Runs Dry held toward the waterfall, standing unarmed and unarmored, the curtain of the water parts and the sylph steps out.

"What's this?" she asks, licking her black-toothed chops, her voice a siren song of silver bells over the thunder of the cascades. "A silly little man who—oh." She stops on the jumble of granite and lavender crystal talus accumulated under the crest of the falls. "My cup."

"He said he'd return it to you, after the adventure was over," I call back. My voice doesn't carry like hers does, doesn't have the magic of the water to amplify it, and it's shaking with my chattering teeth, besides. "He wasn't able to keep that promise, so we offered to return it in his stead."

"Is he dead, then? The skinny one?" the sylph asks. She's got one hand raised, as if she doesn't believe that the cup is right there, before her, and also as if she expects me to suddenly whisk it back away again.

Kin makes a sort of gasping, choked sound at the insinuation that his baby brother is dead. In a way, he is, and we both know it. Dead to us, at least. Dead to this world. We know. It's just jarring to hear someone else say it, and so flippantly, at that.

"Yeah," I lie. If the sylph knows it's a lie, she says nothing about it.

"Set the chalice in the water and begone, oath-keeper," she says, chin thrust out and head held high like she expects me to argue with her.

"It'll wash away!" I say.

"These are my waters," she rejoins sharply. "It will not."

Feeling my joints creak with the cold, I carefully release the chalice into the water. It floats serenely in place, as if the current around it wasn't strong enough to nearly knock me over every time I adjust my footing.

"Right, then," Kintyre calls. "Ah, thanks for letting us borrow it! Um... farewell?"

The sylph snorts and makes no reply.

Kintyre sloshes into the river, grabs me under the armpits, and hauls me to the bank. Normally, I'd fuss and complain at him for using his height against me, but this time, I don't mind. Without even checking to see if the sylph is gone, he's got me skinned out of my soaking clothes in a heartbeat. I'm too stiff—my fingers and toes and, I assume, my lips too blue to resist.

"My, my! What a thoughtful showing!" the sylph calls, the valley filling with her seductive laughter.

"Oh, piss off!" Kintyre calls back.

Over his shoulder—he's kneeling to wrestle my boots off—I watch as the sylph makes a cutting gesture at the river. A spout flies off the surface of the water and smacks Kintyre in the back of the head. He splutters, surprised, and then, with another waterspout, the sylph calls the cup to her and vanishes back behind the falls.

"S-Serves you ri-right," I chatter at him.

Kintyre looks up the length of my body with a glare, and then smirks mischievously. He shakes his head, and his wet, blond hair slaps against my goose-pimpled stomach.

"Hey!" I protest, but don't have the opportunity to say anything more, because then we're tussling and kissing, and he's rubbing my shivering limbs with his palms, and I'm being wrapped up in all of our blankets and bedrolls and being plopped like a sack of grain beside the fire. Kintyre cuddles close, feeds me sips of hot broth and wine, even though I'm perfectly capable of holding the cup myself by now. And it feels, a bit, like understanding. And a lot like forgiveness.

There are inns on the road south between the Salt Crystal Caverns and the Lost Library, and except for one night in Miliway where we can light no fires, we spend the next week pampering ourselves with daily shaves, nightly feather mattresses, and hot meals cooked by someone else. Kintyre is very careful not to cut me out of conversations, to ask my opinion, and to leave me space to speak for myself, which I appreciate, even if the tentative conscientiousness does start to get a little aggravating. He doesn't need my opinion on *everything*; he *can* make up his mind for himself if he wants. But I remind myself that he's trying. Trying to make it clear, in his ham-fisted and knuckleheaded way, that I'm more to him than just his sidekick.

We don't talk about my apparent desire for marriage and children, though. And what would be the point of that? We're two men. We can't have either. A Trothing, like we saw in Gwillfifeshire, that we could do... but I can't even begin to imagine Kintyre agreeing to something as full of spectacle and ceremony as jumping a flaming broom. Too common for him... too *obvious*.

We send the second to last quest item to Kingskeep by care of messenger hawk, now that we're back in Hain. We talk briefly about going to Kingskeep ourselves, to put the Quill that Never Dulls into Lordling Gyre's hands personally, but frankly, I can't stand that little prick. And if we show our faces in Kingskeep, we'll have to deal with King Carvel's questions on Forsyth's whereabouts, and the gaping absence of a Lord in Lysse Chipping, and the mysterious and sudden disappearance of Hain's worst antagonist, along with his sadistic conspirator.

And, Writer's balls, there will be feasts. *More* feasts. I think Kintyre and I are feasted out. We just want to go back to Turn Hall, enjoy the silence of the country, eat simple fare, and sleep for a week.

So we send a hawk to Gyre with a curt note of thanks and the quill wrapped in canvas. It's signed by the Shadow Hand with his secret sigil, (or at least the best version of it I can accomplish from my hazy memory of the complicated squiggle the Shadow Hand uses. Lordling Gyre, at least, won't know the difference.)

A second hawk goes to Carvel with a letter explaining the barest details of our adventure. If nothing else, he should be informed that the Lost Library has been recovered, and that its defenses have been made passive. I urge the king to send along some scholars and wizards versed in preservation magic to begin the restoration. We also tell him that Kintyre will be assuming the seat of Lysse, that we are retiring as questing heroes. And, oh, yes, the Viceroy is dead, so feel free to ransack the Ivory Tower. We make no mention of Forsyth for the present, still uncertain of how to tell people where he's gone. Especially the people who knew he was the Shadow Hand.

It feels strange to write of our retirement in the letter. So final. And yet, so *right*. So permanent. So starkly true.

We receive nothing back from Gyre, as expected. From the king we get a long, long letter which we read, chuckle over—his use of exclamation points is excessive, even to a poet like me—and use for kindling. The king can beg all he likes. Our retirement is happening.

And each night, after Kintyre has dropped off to sleep, I settle before whichever hearth or fire or window is available with my pipe and the mask. I practice the Word in my head, turn the mask over and over in the fire- or candle- or starlight, and try not to think of Bootknife's face. He'd been unworthy. Forsyth has given me the secret of the mask, but ultimately, it seems to me that it's the mask who chooses whether to bow to the whim of the intended successor.

And, yeah, beyond my fears of being a good Shadow

Hand, I fear being a *worthy enough man.*

I'm a champion of good, but I have had no problem getting there through nefarious, devious, and sometimes bloody means. I have killed. I have shed blood. I have hated. I have loved where it's sometimes not encouraged to love. I have throttled the man who is now the closest thing to a brother-in-law a Pairing allows for, bullied and teased him when he was younger, and I have threatened a Reader. I drove a stake through the heart of a corpse, mutilated the body of a fallen enemy simply to quench my thirst for revenge. I have lied to my king. I have lied to women to bed them. I have lied to my best friend in order to just be able to touch him, before he was my lover. I have lied to myself. Constantly. Daily. For *years.*

Am I a good man? Am I a worthy man?

This question keeps the mask in my hands, and in my saddlebag, and away from my face. I'm not vain—I have scars enough on my face and arms, and one particularly nasty one that bisects my torso and was nearly my end at the Battle of the Walking Woods, where we lost Stormbearer. And I wear all my scars proudly, proof of my valor and, yeah, my pigheaded foolishness. But I don't think I could honorably bear the scar of melted flesh on my face if the mask rejected me. Not at all.

Returning the final quest item, the Parchment that Never Fills, is easier than we feared it would be. With the enchantment broken on the Lost Library, the main gates have remained open, and the vines shiver and strain to get a good look at us, but don't attack or entangle.

This time, Kintyre insists on being the one to stick his neck out. So I wait at the bottom of the spiral stairway that leads to the balcony and the pedestal from which Pip snatched the paper, my sword at the ready. But no great guardian creature ambushes us from the dusty shadows of the stacks, and we are back out of the sneeze-inducing tomb of cobwebs and decaying paper faster than a lad having his first go at a nymph. It's not even midmorning by the time we emerge. We're sheathing our swords and chatting about whether we'd rather spend the night at the Library or try for Gwillfifeshire and the *Pern* before sundown when we both realize that something has changed in the courtyard.

It takes a moment to realize that the problem is with the horses. The buggers have somehow multiplied. Well, not the horses themselves, no, but there's some other four-legged creature with them. Big as a horse—bigger than Stormbearer was, and he was huge—and the color of sandstone. It's sitting beside Dauntless, who doesn't seem to mind that it's grooming the horse's mane with a massive great tongue.

"S'at a lion?" Kintyre asks, thumbs hooked into his belt as we both pause on the portico.

The horses are on the far side of the wide, also-sandstone courtyard, so it's a bit hard to tell. I squint and blink, and I'm not sure if it's the distance, or how exhausted I still am from all this travel, but, yeah, it kinda looks like a lion. The body isn't quite right, though. Strange proportions, like an artist drew it based on a description of lions, never having seen one themselves. But it's not eating the horses. Just licking. Grooming.

"I think so," I say, scratching my nose. "Funny ears, though."

Kin drops his palm to Foesmiter's pommel and runs his hand over the ornate gemstone butt. "Think we ought to...?"

"The horses aren't spooked," I say, resettling my satchel so it won't unbalance me if we do need to fight, or flee. I put my hand on my own sword. "Let's go slow?"

Kin grunts his agreement, and we pick our way across the jumble of flagstones and debris.

Dauntless sees us first. He whickers a welcome, and steps away from the creature grooming his mane. It lets him go, so we stop a few lengths away and let Dauntless nose at Kintyre's shoulder. Karlurban doesn't seem any more perturbed than Dauntless, though he doesn't move either toward or away from the predator beside him. And then the great cat bounds away, quicker than I expected. I lose track of the lion-thing long enough for it to sneak up around my unguarded left flank.

I catch its open mouth in my peripheral vision and shout, startled, and prepared for pain. Foesmiter leaps into Kintyre's hand, and I reel back, away from the creature's—

"*Oh!* Uhg!" I say, as a sandpaper tongue laps over my shoulder, up along my bare neck, and across my skull. I can *feel* the globs of spittle in my hair.

Kin, the arse, just laughs.

"Suppose this is Pip's Library Lion, then," I say, and it's not really a question. I shove the damned cat away as it tries to nuzzle into me. It's strong enough to knock me forward a few steps. "Oi! Shoo, you!"

It's not that I don't like cats; the feral cats that used to hang about my pa's forge and beg for scraps of my dinner were nice enough, but I'm already feeling prickly about my height right now, and others' assumptions about my place at Kin's side because of it. The last thing I want to contend with is an oversized fluff-ball that will make me look even *more* impish.

The creature flops onto its back on the weedy flagstones and looks up at me, enticingly, an expanse of temptingly fluffy tummy the size of a bedroll on offer. I have known too many barn cats to fall for that ploy, however.

I clamber onto Dauntless and scrub at the back of my head. "Come on, Kin. Let's go."

Kintyre snorts at me, but mounts. "What, scared of the kitty?"

"No, I just... we're done here, aren't we?" I cluck Dauntless into motion, and Karl lurches to follow, never liking to be left behind. "No point in lingering. I have half my mind on the Goodwoman Pern's game pie already, and if we want to make it by sundown, we have to—"

The cat bounds in front of the gates, blocking our horses with a yowl that sounds like a rusty pulley and recrimination.

"Oh, go on with you. Shoo!" I say to the Library Lion. "I'm not Pip, to coddle you!"

Kintyre pulls up behind me. "It's sort of—"

I swing around in my saddle and point a sharp finger at my lover. "Don't you dare say it, Kintyre Turn."

Kin grins at me, all cheek. "*Cute.*"

"No."

"I bet it's lonely, stuck here with only the books for company. Forsyth said it followed them halfway to the—"

"*No.*"

Kintyre grins wider. "Imagine what a sight we'll make when we return to Turnshire with such a creature at our command."

"No!"

"Imagine how respected we'll be as lords if we have such a pet!"

"I said no, Kin," I say, but I can already see that my protests are in vain. The cat has come around to purr and nuzzle against Kintyre's leg, and subsequently Karl's whole flank, as if it knows where its oversized dish of cream is going to come from. Kintyre is running his hand over its velvety ears, entranced by the texture.

Oh, my silly, narcissistic blockhead. What a soft touch

the great lunk is. Kintyre reaches down and scruffles the cat's ruff gently, and its purring increases in volume. I can see it there, in Kin's eyes, the desire to be surrounded by the loyal and unquestioning adoration of an animal— Algar Turn never let his sons have any pets, aside from fiercely trained bloodhounds, which were no good for playing with.

Yeah, he grew up with wealth and comfort, but really, Kintyre had so very little. He ran away from home so that he could *live*. And I, who grew up in a household forever on the teetering brink of poverty, had a childhood that was warm and full of love, and laughter, family, and the adoration of my parents and siblings. I had everything, in that respect. And Kin, nothing.

"Fine," I say, heaving a great sigh so my lover understands just how much of a burden I find capitulation to be. "But we're bypassing Gwillfifeshire, and it won't be me that cleans up its droppings in the foyer, or hires a whole new hall boy to keep the fur off the tapestries."

Kintyre just grins at me, the beaming smile of a thrilled little boy in the adventure-weary face of a man, because of *course* I'll be the one doing those things.

The first snowfall catches us with our dicks out. We're on the road just outside of Lysse when the first flakes start catching on our eyelashes and hair. Kintyre's always been a bit of a woman about the cold. It's a good thing we're already headed for Turnshire, 'cause he'd have us running back here for Forssy's best whiskey and the Hall hearths faster'n a rabbit that had scented blackberry jam.

"We're nearly there," I say as Kin tries to turn Karl off the main road and toward the small border town with the inn that has mulled wine I've immortalized in scrolls. "Plow through, and we'll be home by nightfall."

"Home," Kin snorts. He pulls his shoulders back, flicks the tail of his hair back over his shoulder, and sits up straight like a lord. But the magnanimous expression on his face is strained. The smile is thin and fractured. He's worried, Writer, he's *worried*.

About what's ahead? Yeah, well. Me, too.

To cover it, Kin whinges. Kintyre whines more than the Library Lion, who, as we've learned, dislikes being left alone for any reason, and firmly believes that it has every right to curl around us as we sleep like a furry, protective pillow. At first, it was nice to have the cat's extra body heat and the warmth of its fur to keep away the chill, late-fall air. But in the weeks we've been making our way northward, the cat hasn't left us alone to sleep *once*.

And this has made Kintyre and me cranky. Very, very cranky. Yeah, I refuse to engage in any sort of bedsport with the Library Lion watching.

Kintyre was right, though. I gotta give him that. We do make one hells of a sight riding the Market Road up to Turnshire with a massive lion-bear-thing gamboling behind us like a winsome kitten. We cut through the squashed central square and continue on to Turn Hall, but slow as we approach, our pace turning positively slug-gish the closer we get. I think this is maybe the first time I've ever come up to Turn Hall the front way. And it's definitely the first time I've been filled to the eyeballs with reluctance and uncertainty. I've always had the swaggering assurance that I was coming as a guest of the lordling—then, later, the lord—and would be welcome.

Oh, there will be a warm welcome, yeah. But after that, what?

Forssy let Cook have the run of the kitchen garden, and he'd let the rigid and regimented back gardens go a little bit wild and woolly after Algar Turn drank himself into a back-stair tumble. I never got the full story, but the fall had something to do with why Forssy rarely employed pretty young misses in the house—too much temptation for the ill-behaved, he'd said once. Too much temptation for his father when the late Lord Turn had been in his cups, anyway.

In the back of Turn Hall, the ivy has grown willy-nilly over the red brick facade of the hall's rear wall, and the covey forest that abuts the edge of the eastern wall is boarded with seedling trees encroaching on a manicured lawn spotted with clover, buttercups, and a galaxy of twinkling starflowers like a negligent and particularly colorful pox. Creeping vines that flower blush pink in the spring and wine-red in the summer flow in verdant curlicues around the base of the back courtyard fountain, and the fishpond in the midst of the lawn on the west approach is thick with bulrushes and lily pads that delight frogs, fairies, and the hungry trout alike. Even the low stone wall that separates the lord's lawn from the tenant's fields is dusted with lichen and the gossamer nests of Kiss-Me Frogs' eggs, made from the hair stolen from maiden hair brushes.

But the front approach of Turn Hall? That is the exact opposite. Algar's penchant for rigid control still stands here. Forsyth was always too afraid to change anything, afraid of not being able to be what he thought his people wanted, afraid to step out of the box his father had built around him and his role as lordling.

And now, Kin and I are faced with an austere and frigid facade of cream-colored marble threaded with russet and gold veins. The wall is blank and without personality, save for the heavily, overly ornate gold-leaf cornices and sills. Geometric bushes are attended to meticulously, and separate a white stone drive from a ruthlessly rich-green carpet of even grass, dusted now with snow.

In short, Turn Hall is the exact portrait of the last

lordling who held power at this seat, who had ruled Lysse for a decade: staid, boring, and predictable on the public face, disguising a wonderfully complex, colorful, and gently passionate secret life.

In the first coat of snowfall, the oxymoronic, bland ostentation of the front drive is muted. Dauntless cuts through the untouched snow primly, with Karl doing his best to stay in his hoof-holes, far as I can tell with the way the younger horse is jerking and sidestepping under Kin. But the Library Lion leaves no paw-prints on the drive at all.

Writer's calluses, that's eerie.

The front door opens as soon as we gain the front portico. We haven't even dismounted yet. Writer's calluses, *that's* eerie. A groom shoots down the stairs to take the reins of our horses, and the butler meets us on the top step, studiously not looking at the great cat who seems torn between following the horses or following us.

"Go on," Kintyre shoos the beast. "Go with Dauntless and Karl. There's room enough in the stable for you." The cat meeps in protest. "I'll come visit you once we're settled, you silly creature. Off with you." The cat goes.

I will never stop being amazed and annoyed that the Library Lion both understands and obeys my lover. But not me. Brat.

"Master Kintyre," the butler says, flicking his eyes behind us and down the drive tellingly. "Well come."

"Ah, thank you..."

"Velshi," I whisper to Kin, annoyed that I have to remind him of his own damned butler's name.

"Velshi," Kintyre repeats without missing a beat. "Good to be home."

"If you and Sir Dom will come in, we can, ah, send up a bath and a hot meal?"

Kintyre takes the not-so-subtle hint in stride, and we

are both relieved to leave the chill air and the soft, gentle snowfall behind us. But Velshi doesn't close the door. He doesn't even come back inside.

"Pardon me, sir, but... is, ah, is Master Forsyth behind you?" The butler asks it in a small voice. Tremulous. Like he's waiting for us to impart the news of the lordling's death. In a way, I think, we are.

Kintyre sways on the spot, knees weak. He grabs the doorframe in a white-knuckled grip. If he were a maiden, I'd call it a near-swoon. With his free hand, he gropes out for my hand, and I let him bury my fingers in his broader palm as he turns to face his Head of Staff.

"Ah. No, Velshi," he says softly. Velshi sucks in a horrified gasp, his face immediately draining of all color. He takes a reeling step backward. Kintyre rushes to add: "But not for the reasons you think. He lives, believe me. He lives. I... close the door, Velshi. And assemble the staff in the, uh..."

"In Forsyth's study," I suggest softly.

"Yes, the study," he says, nodding slowly. "Assemble the staff in the... in *my* study. We have something to tell you."

PART THREE

✹

Turn Hall has more employees than I thought. In our past sojourns here, I only ever saw the valet and the butler. Sometimes the cook. Yeah, and once a chambermaid and a hall boy each. Even with Forsyth's reduced complement—he always felt conspicuous having too many people wait on him when he was a bachelor alone—I'm counting near to twenty folks, both inside staff and out. There're gardeners, and a little scullery maid, and footmen, and cleaners, and grooms, and the Writer only knows what else the rest of these poor sods do to earn their bread and beds.

It's a lot more people dependent on this estate than I thought. And a lot more people to share our roof, our lives, and our privacy with than I was expecting. By the Writer, it'll be almost like being back in Bynnebakker for Solsticetide, except that all of these people won't be jammed into one room every night. There won't be gleeful shouting, and pinching, and screaming with laughter, and dancing, and making cutting remarks about the last letter I sent home or the most recent adventure to be disseminated by my printer.

Unless Kin and I fill the house with deliberate rowdiness, it will be... quiet. Eerie. Stuffed-full, but silent. That's one of the reasons I never liked spending too much time here. Forssy liked things too tidy, too sedate, too... boring. Writer's calluses, how am I going to put up with this quiet and boredom for the rest of my life?

Be the Shadow Hand, says that seductive voice I'm still not convinced is mine. *Lots to keep you occupied, then.*

Now is not the time for that, though. Our... *Kin's* employees are waiting for an explanation.

The lie we tell them is this: Forsyth succeeded in his quest to reunite Pip with her family. But having got there, he realized his love was too profound, and Forsyth couldn't leave. He has given up his place as Lordling of Lysse to remain with Pip's family and wed his lady love. Forsyth has thus charged Kintyre to do right by their people. Humbled by his brother's loyalty to his maiden fair, Kintyre has vowed to give up the life of an adventurer and come home to serve his people and his lineage.

The first lie is that Kintyre has, of course, never been humble about a Writer-be-damned thing in his whole blasted life. The second is that Kintyre has no intentions, whatsoever, of doing anything about his lineage. Or at least, none that he's shared with me. (Though that does beg the question, then, of from where will—with Forsyth absent and Kintyre Paired with a man—the next Lordling Turn spring forth? Bugger and blast.)

There are very few dry eyes when we've finished weaving our fib. I am, after all, a well-practiced master storyteller. And Kintyre is genuinely shook up about the fact that he has said his farewells to his little brother for the last time. That lends credence to the tale. He is dealing with it silently, and slowly, though, as is his way. Kintyre is a bit like an old cow—he chews and chews on things until they sit just right in his stomach.

The serving staff thanks us, we shake hands and buss cheeks, and slowly they all file out, back to their duties and off to their celebrations or mourning, depending on their moods. Kintyre stops Velshi as the butler is closing the study door behind the staff, and suggests gently that perhaps he would like to select a few bottles of something fine to toast Forsyth's happiness with downstairs.

When my lover turns back to me, my surprise at his foresight and compassion must be on my face. He snorts and points at my expression. "Don't need to look *so* surprised, Sir Dom," he teases, dimpling cheekily. "I might have left this all behind, but I was trained up to it for eighteen years. The paperwork will take some study, but I do remember how to make sure the servants don't poison your tea. Or quit by droves."

I snort in echo, crossing my arms and leaning back against Forsyth's desk. Or is that Kintyre's desk? Or... thinking of all the times I saw Forsyth in quiet conversation in this very room with men in black I assumed were merchants or scholars... perhaps this is my desk, now. The Shadow Hand's desk.

I circle the imposing hunk of glorified firewood and sit slowly in the plush velvet-and-leather chair. Forsyth was taller than me, that's for sure. Though, annoyingly, most men are. I'll need a footstool. Or to saw a few inches off the desk legs. I run my hands over the arms, rest my elbows in the worn patches on each, and place my hands, palm down, respectfully, on the forest green blotter.

Dust hasn't been allowed to settle in this room, though it seems like none of Forsyth's things have been moved otherwise. There's a partially written missive in the top corner of the desk: just a list of items to discuss with the mayor, it looks like. Beside that, in a shaky, uneven hand that I don't recognize, is a list of items needed for going out on an adventure. Pip's packing list? Yeah, probably. Handkerchiefs is written in large letters and underlined twice. To the side of that is a letter addressed simply to "Pointe." It takes me a second to remember that this is the sheriff.

"Oh, hells, Forsyth wrote a goodbye note," I say, pointing to the letter. Kin picks it up. It's already sealed with the rusty-red wax Forsyth preferred. "We're going to have to deliver it."

Kintyre makes a face. "He's making us say all his goodbyes for him. Lazy brat."

I'm going to have to tell King Carvel myself, in person, I realize. I can't just send a letter off and let him know that the Shadow Hand is gone and that the new one is... is...

I rattle a locked desk drawer, and wonder if this is where Forsyth kept his Spymaster letterhead, his Carvel-green bottle of ink, the purse of bribes and rewards for his spies. Or is that too obvious, the one locked drawer in the desk?

Put on the mask, then you'll know where he hid it. And where every Shadow Hand before him hid their supplies, too.

The thought of all that knowledge, all those people's memories, their intimate thoughts just... shoved into my head; to have them swirl in through the mask, like water down a drain, and *be there*, forever; to know that my own thoughts and memories and knowledge would be passed on to my own successor, that putting on the mask means that I'll have no privacy in death, that I will be getting an intimate look into Forssy's thoughts... it's overwhelming. My head hurts suddenly, and I haven't even put the mask on yet.

If I even choose to.

I have to. Don't I? *Do* I?

Forssy left it to me. He *trusted* me to do right by it, even though I'd never been kind to him a day in my life. Shame floods my guts, and I groan, slumping forehead-down on the desk. This lordling-and-Shadow-Hand lark is harder than it looks.

I had noticed the stream of people in and out of this study and hadn't known what it meant. I just thought Forssy was a fussy, overworked, overly diligent lordling. I thought he was overwrought with the minutia of running the Chipping and not engaged enough with the freedoms and entitled pleasures of his seat. Even I, Bevel Dom, chronicler of the hero Kintyre Turn and supposedly a bright, observant bloke, *didn't understand* what was happening right under my nose.

I saw it all, and saw *nothing*.

Writer's calluses, how am I supposed to do this? How could Forsyth possibly think I was equal to this? Writing, sure, I can do that. And bashing about with my sword. And firing arrows, and seducing maidens and warriors alike, fine. Adventuring, map reading, all of it. I can do that. Yeah.

But *politics*? Subtlety? Presenting the right words at the right time, like even Kintyre manages to do here in Turn Hall? When he wants to, that is, even though it's been decades since he has chosen to be subtle, and magnanimous, and anything but the demanding eldest son coming in, taking what he wants as his due, and leaving again. And oh, I can see how inadequate I've been all this time, how much *better* at it Kin is. How can I be equal to that?

How can I... rise to the challenge that Forsyth Turn has laid at my feet? With his stupid knowing grin and his stupid clever brain and his... Forsyth-ness. Being Shadow Hand, that was what he had been Written for. But me? The rough-and-tumble, uncouth, blacksmith's boy? The overeager lad who foolishly followed a hero into battle, and who was lucky to come out the other side of it alive? The man more at home under the stars than under a roof, with a bow in his fist, or a travel-work pencil instead of a fine quill and Carvel-green ink?

What am I thinking, accepting this?

All of it. Not just the mask.

Worse still, what am I thinking, second-guessing it?

My brain throbs against the sides of my skull, and I wish I could just stop thinking, like blowing out a candle or shutting a door. Just... *put it away* for a while. But I can't seem to do that.

Writer, is this what it's like to be Forsyth all the time? Or Pip?

Uhg. *Exhausting.*

Kintyre doesn't ask what's plaguing me, just chivvies me up from the desk. With a mischievous grin, he hoists me up over his shoulder like a saddlebag.

"Oi!" I snarl, kicking him dead in the sternum. He grunts and stumbles, but doesn't let go. I wrap my hands around his belt, the dumb oaf, and he sneaks us to the back laundry room through a secret passage behind the bookshelf and some narrow, dusty servant's hallway. I only bump my head twice—that's something, at least— but we're both covered in cobwebs by the time we get to the laundry. And I'm laughing too hard by the time he puts me down, my stomach bouncing on Kin's broad shoulder, to really be angry about the manhandling.

We steal a hot bath in one of the soaking tubs instead of making the staff bring the copper one up to Kin's apartments. After that is a quick hot meal that we fetch ourselves from the kitchen, much to Cook's horror, and a visit out to the stables to make sure the Library Lion is behaving itself. It's asleep in a stall piled with fresh hay. The groom's lad is ecstatic with glee and utterly *covered* in sandy-golden fur and spittle. And then it's to bed.

For the first time in Turn Hall, though, I don't bother with the pretense of needing my own room. Not that it was really pretense before—we always slept apart when we weren't on the road or bedding some willing slattern. But now...

At any rate, Keriens, the valet, has put my travel bag in the guest room a few doors down from Kintyre's. He's not wrong; that's the one I usually use. Feeling bold and remembering Forsyth's advice that a gentleman should begin how he means to continue (though, probably, he wasn't talking about *this*), I grab the bag and the personals the staff have laid out for me, and hike them down the expanse of the family wing's hallway. A footman watches with wide eyes from the top of the stair, clearly startled, and I offer him a smug nod as I shoulder into Kin's room. Then I dump my kit right beside Kintyre's bags.

My lover is already seated by the fire in one of two massive wingback chairs, the spindly table between them laid with two glasses and a decanter of that Brystalian wine I like, even though Kin prefers ales. His hair is still damp, combed but left loose to stain the velvet of his Turn-russet house robe, which is just *barely* done up.

The glorious tart. Expecting me. I like that.

"You don't have to try so hard," I say, picking up the decanter and pouring for us. "I forgive you."

"Nope," Kintyre says, grinning as I hand him one of the glasses and then crawl right into his lap. My knees are jammed against the sides of the chair, probably pinching his broad thighs. "Nope. This is something I'm never going to stop doing."

"What?"

"Making you smile."

I lean forward and bite his earlobe.

"Yow!"

"Softie," I say, and soothe the hurt with my tongue. Under me, Kintyre shudders from top to tail, and then glugs off the wine.

"One of these days, Kin, I'm going to have to teach

you to appreciate a fine drink in a way that doesn't resemble a duck."

"I can appreciate a fine drink," he protests, and sets his glass down. "I just wanted my hands free to do *this*."

This is enough to make me quaff off my wine, too, despite how jammy and lovely the vintage is, so that I can get my own hands free in return.

As much as I fantasized about sleeping for a week once we arrived in Turn Hall, there are duties too long left unattended by any Lord of Lysse to let that dream come true. Once it gets around that Kintyre is in and Forsyth is out, there's all but an actual queue at the servant's entrance. Kintyre and I only get one decent lie-in before we're inundated with every merchant and scholar demanding their time in front of their lord, and gathering gossip about their former lordling to take home in the bargain.

Our second morning, I wake to find the scullery standing at the foot of the bed, charcoal bucket in hand, staring at us with her mouth gaping open. Over a decade ago, on my first visit to Turn Hall, I traumatized the first maid I'd ever met. Well, what else was I meant to think, finding a strange girl in my bedroom, crouched in front of the hearth, where I'd also, consequently, left my gear? Of *course*, I accused her of being a thief. And loudly, too. She'd quit the very next morning, and I've always felt vaguely guilty about that. This time, I just flick a hand at the girl and croak, "Go on, s'fine. Lay the fire. Ignore us."

She drops a curtsey. "I was told you would already be up, Sir Dom... uh... m'lord... uh... consort?" she adds vaguely, head tilted with confusion like a dog's.

"No," Kin grumbles and rolls over, half on top of

me, flashing the lassie a goodly view of his naked chest, then his naked back, and finally his plush bottom liberally sprinkled with bruises left behind by my fingers and hips.

She squeaks and turns her face away. "It's only that there's... uh, the schoolmaster's here already, and so's the marketers' representative. And Cook's had your tray warm for an hour."

"What time did Forsyth get up?" I mumble, more to myself than to the girl. I pull the blankets up to my chin, muffling Kin's entire head in the process. My lover chuckles, and his breath is warm across my own bare skin.

"Seven of the clock, every day, sir," the scullery says, obediently.

A glance out the window tells me it's at least nine.

"Blast," I swear. "No way on the Writer's good green backside am I getting up every day at seven, not when there's no dawn to get in my eyes and no monsters trying to kill us."

"It's a lord's life," Kin says, and he sounds almost cheery, the cruel bastard. He flings back the blanket, making the scullery squeak again and turn completely around, back to us. Kin covers up with a loosely tied house robe of Turn-russet, which he'd left on the foot of the bed the night before. My house robe is still in the wardrobe. In my *old* room. Hells.

"Pop downstairs and tell Cook we're ready for our trays," Kintyre says, and the girl leaves the drop cloth, pan, broom, and bucket on the hearth and dashes out at a speed I would almost find insulting if I wasn't so put out.

"I'm not getting up at *seven* every morning," I repeat, abandoning the warm softness of the bed for the wardrobe. In there, I find an old shirt in Dom-amethyst. It just barely covers my pride, but cover me it does. Our branch of the family might have been a little more hard-up than our distant cousins, but we were once noble enough to still have a House Color. All the same, I grimace at the tattered thing. It's not even nice enough that the servants put it in my borrowed guest room down the hall—they just left it to rot in the back of Kin's barely used wardrobe, where it couldn't offend any of Forsyth's other guests.

I have nothing else to wear, though, so I put it on and sit in the chair that Kin and I so thoroughly despoiled the night before. Kintyre frowns at my shirt, too, and I can already see him plotting against it. Good. I want to be wearing Turn-russet.

We've both wasted too many years in shades of purple.

"So, what do you suppose the gossip is like in the servants' hall this morning?" I grumble, wishing the tea was already here. Maybe I can convince this newly mindful Kintyre Turn to always ring the bell *before* he wakes me up in the morning, so I won't have to wait so long for it to arrive?

Or I could also just not be a pampered, lazy arse and walk down to the kitchen like I used to. The servants never liked it, but as a younger man with something to prove about his place at the Great Hero of Hain's side, I'd wanted to make a point of not getting high and mighty. I'm not high and mighty now—at least, I don't think I am. I'm just old. The thought of the trip through the narrow, stone servants' passage down to the kitchens at this time of morning, in the early winter chill, without any tea in my belly, is horrid. It seems, at this exact moment, more an insurmountable obstacle than the white cliffs of the Astrolabe promontory.

Writer's hairy balls, I've really turned into my pa in my old age.

At least some blessed servant left a blanket by the fire last night, folded neatly over a wooden stand to toast, and there's just enough heat left in the fading embers when I yank the thing over my lap and burrow under it like a disgruntled rabbit.

Oh, Writer's nutsack, I'm not going to turn into one of those gouty, cranky, creaky old adventurers who drones on about past battles and amorous conquests while muttering and shuffling and contending with stiff joints and always-creaking bones, am I? I don't want to spend the rest of my life in an eternal, unwinnable war against the cold.

The mask, the voice comes to me again. *Get out, see the country. Spy on it. Know it. Stay in the saddle in some small way. Stay in the business of saving the world.*

"The gossip is hysterical," says a voice from the doorway, the same time as a knock. "And it seems to be entirely true, my lords." A young man, maybe around twenty-three or -four, steps into the room bearing a tea service with a pot that is, blessedly, steaming.

This is Keriens, Forsyth's valet—I suppose he is now our valet, unless one of us wants to hire another of our own. But why in the world would we want two people fussing and poking at us? Without permission, Keriens swaggers into the room as if it's his due.

"Do you normally deliver the trays?" Kintyre asks, frowning at the livery the valet is wearing.

"No, sir," the lad says with a grin. "I don't. But your regular footman, Recce, has no head for details at all. That's why the staff nominated me to deliver it this morning. I'm very good at reconstructing a scene."

I groan and cover my face with the blanket as Keriens sets the tray down on the spindly table. "I'm not looking forward to being the private entertainment of everyone who works at Turn Hall," I moan.

Keriens, the cheeky blighter, pats my shoulder con- solingly. "You should have thought of that before you

Paired with our lord," he says, but there's a warmth in his voice that surprises me into looking up at the young man. He is smiling puckishly, but his eyes hold a gladness I didn't expect. "Though there's a few of us who say it's about time, sir."

"Mind your manners," Kin says gruffly, dropping into his own seat, but he's grinning, too, dimpling outrageously. Everyone is entirely too pleased about this whole thing for my pre-tea state, so I pour myself a cup and fix it to my liking. Dash Kin. He can fix his own.

He does, chuckling at my pettiness, and Keriens watches us both carefully, no doubt memorizing how we prefer to take our tea for the future. Eerie.

"If there's nothing else, sirs, I'll hie myself to the wardrobe and see what I can scrounge up for today? There's plenty around, between what you've left here, your father's old clothes, and what Master Forsyth abandoned. Though I daresay I'll have to take up a few things," he adds with a wink at me. I scowl back, but wink as well, letting him know that I don't mind his teasing. Much better than the bowing and scraping I had feared.

If I have to share a house with dozens of folks I'm not related to and don't know well, I would much rather be teased and laughed with, than mocked behind my back and treated with stony proprietary to my face.

Kintyre is spirited away as soon as he's properly dressed, still cramming sweet rolls into his mouth.

I have a more leisurely breakfast, then wave off Keriens when he tries to help me dress, because I'm bloody well an adult and can dress myself. The clothes he's unearthed are from some mothball-strewn trunk, judging by the smell that clings to the trousers and the house shoes, and it occurs to me that at some point, if

I'm going to live with Kin as the lord's… what was the word that scullery used? *Consort.* Then I'm going to have to get house-clothes. Waistcoats, and lawn shirts, and neckcloths, and soft-soled slippers, and those weird sort of knee-length house-robes Forsyth preferred to the boxy, structured dinner coats. I won't be able to wear my jerkins and leather trousers and knee-high boots in the house anymore. Will I?

Writer spare me. I *hate* being fussed over by tailors and valets. That's why I only have one good shirt, and I keep it in the bottom of my travel pack.

With nothing better to do, I spend the day reacquainting myself with Turn Hall. It's funny to realize that I know the secret back ways better than I know the halls a lord might travel. Kintyre hates being accosted and rerouted and ordered about, so we always used the secret passages to move between his room, the stables, the kitchens, and the wine cellar, as much to avoid the attention of Algar Turn as to avoid the staff. I suppose I can't keep doing that anymore. Well, at least not as often.

One of the places I *do* remember how to get to easily is the ballroom. Forssy'd turned the space into a sparring gymnasium, and for once, I have to agree with his choice. With the centuries-old great hall for feasting and dancing, why did some daft Turn ancestor or another decide to append a second, wooden spring-floor ballroom as well? Sure, it's the fashion in old stone houses to put in solariums and terraces and rooms so porous with doors and windows that they're really little more than roofs held up on ornamental toothpicks. But at what expense, fashion? I could have built my parents a new house twice over with the material that went into this superfluous ballroom.

Though I suppose the windows make it cool during summer fetes, the room is useless otherwise. My guess is

that it was Kintyre's grandfather who put this room in—
from what Kin's said, he was the foppish, dandyish type
who cared very much about showing off the wealth of
Turn Hall to the other noble Houses, and to the Chipping. Some aunt or other of Kintyre's had been married
high into the Houses of Kingskeep, but I'd never known
which one; Kin'd never introduced me to her while we
were visiting the court. At any rate, his grandfather'd
had ambition. And an ornamental but useless space like
this is the perfect example of that kind of conspicuous
spending, no matter how sensible it would have been to
put the money into the upkeep of the tenant cottages
instead.

I push back the door to the ballroom-gymnasium,
thinking about the last time I was here. Kintyre said it'd
be funny to interrupt the sparring match with a well-
aimed dagger. And it had been—the look of startled fear
on Forssy's face had been hilarious.

And there had been a pretty maiden reclining on
a daybed, watching the two men flash their steel at
one another with wide, round eyes, parted lips, and an
enchanted expression that had immediately stirred up all
the competitive ego I possess. There was just something
so aggravating and funny about *Forsyth* being the center
of attention for a girl that I'd *had* to get between them.
Even if I didn't actually want her.

The memory of that curdles in my guts. Shameful. What an elfcock I was. And for what? Because I'd
thought Forssy a bossy, limp rag. And I was wrong about
that. But even if I hadn't been, even if he was a bossy,
limp rag, I shouldn't have deliberately sabotaged his
chances for romance. I knew well enough what it felt like
to want and never get.

The room is barren of those ghosts, though, when
I enter. The smell of floor polish is ripe in my nose, and

the winter sun is watery, filtered through a light drifting
of snow that has been falling steadily, like pollen fluff,
since we woke. Frost flowers have already started to
grow along the edges of the windows, rimming the glass
with tendrils of ice that resemble ferns and blossoms.
Beautiful, yeah. But, uhg, shoddy insulation; that's what
that means. I might have to pull apart one of the sills
and see what kind of work was done on the installation.
Or... hire someone to do it? Is that what a lord does? Or
a lord's... whatever I am?

As I step around the overlarge door and let it fall
closed behind me, I realize that the ballroom isn't entirely devoid of ghosts. In the middle of the room, standing
in a puddle of sunlight, shaking the snow off the shoulders of his riding cloak, is a man dressed entirely in gray.

"Forsyth," he says happily, as he turns at the sound
of the door closing behind me. He has straight white
teeth in a tanned face, with a kind of charming male
beauty that I can admire in the abstract. He's handsome,
but he's not Kin. There are comely laughter lines around
his mouth and eyes that lend him character, scruff
peppering his jaw in shades of gray rapidly falling into
silver, and a thick head of hair to match. He is robust
with good exercise and good purpose, for this is Sheriff
Rupin Pointe, the Sword of Turnshire.

"Oh!" he says, startled when he realizes that I'm
not the Lordling Turn. He sweeps a quick bow, rough
in form but honest, and then resumes his grin when he
straightens. "Well come, Sir Dom. When did you arrive?"

"Kin and I returned two nights ago," I say, twisting
my hands behind my back because, oh Writer's balls,
Pointe hasn't *heard*. He doesn't know. And I'm going to
have to tell him. Now.

I'm not ready for this.

"With Forsyth?" Pointe asks. "I heard the lord was

returned—the grandmothers of Turnshire will gossip. I should have waited for an invitation," he says, hands out, sheepish, "but you know Forsyth. He gets his head buried in things and forgets social niceties, like invitations, and replying to letters, and, uh, sleeping. Where is the blighter?"

I groan, I can't help it, and rub my forehead. It seems like all I've done for the past seventeen years is be the deliverer of bad news to good and kind people.

"You'd better come into the study with me, Sheriff," I say.

"Why?"

"That's where the whiskey is."

The man's face falls so fast, grows ashen so quick, that I wonder for a moment if I'm going to have to have Mother Mouth sent for. He nods abruptly, just once, ducks his head as if he's preparing to shoulder through a mass of cutting brambles, and follows me out the door.

We're both silent as we cross the foyer to the formal library and into the private study beyond it. Sometime since Kin and I were last here to deliver this same bad news, someone has come in and cleaned off the desk, reshelved the haphazard pile of books that had been left by the reading chair, and refilled the decanter on the sideboard. I pour a measure for both of us, and wish fervently that I had my pipe with me, so I'd have something to fiddle with.

Pointe, when I turn to give him the glass, looks ghastly.

"He's alive," I say gently. No use prolonging the torture.

Pointe crumples into the reading chair and sucks back his drink. He coughs hard when it's gone, his face flushing and a curl of black smoke escaping one nostril. Ah, the Drebbinshire Whiskey, then. I take a sip of my own to confirm it, and then cross the room to pour Pointe another measure. He nods his thanks, otherwise silent. Waiting.

I'm tempted to just hand over the letter addressed to him—where did... ah, there it is, propped against the inkwell—but I don't know what Forsyth might have put in it. For all I know, he had assumed he would die on his quest, and it's a goodbye. No, I'll let Pointe read the letter, but not until after I've told him what *actually* happened. I wish Kintyre were here. He's blunt, and he can sometimes be a bit mean when he explains these things, but at least he gets it over with quickly.

Pointe takes another sip, and then clears his throat. "So, when the village said that the lord had returned, they meant... ?"

"Kin, yeah," I say, leaning back against the desk.

"They really meant the lord," Pointe mutters. "I had thought I'd just misheard. And Sir Turn is... here to stay?" He looks up at me then, silver eyes narrowed, taking in my clothing shrewdly.

I'm wearing soft black trousers and house shoes instead of my normal leathers, though I'd found the fine cream lawn shirt Keriens had set out for me too tickly. I'm wearing one of my normal sturdy cotton shirts, with the short-robe of Turn-russet that Kin had commissioned shortly after our Pairing to replace the ragged, faded one of Dom-amethyst that I used to wear around Turn Hall. I hate waistcoats, so I don't have any. The same with neckcloths, which had filled Keriens with theatrical despair. In short, I look nothing like myself.

"Paired up then, are you?" Pointe asks, jerking his chin at my chest.

"Yeah," I say.

"Soldiers' Pairing, or... ?" He lets the question linger, and it's the first time someone's asked us outright if Kin and I are sharing our bodies. I can't believe it, but I feel myself flush up like a milkmaid. I never thought I'd find the direct question so... embarrassing. "S'pose that's answer enough," Pointe grunts. "Trothed?"

"No," I say, and take a burning gulp of my own whiskey to drown anything that might try to follow that confession.

Pointe wisely doesn't ask anything else about that, and I'm starting to understand what Forsyth saw in him as a friend. Aw, hells. I reach around behind me and fetch the letter, holding it up for him to see. "He left this for you, but I want to tell you what happened before you read it. Forssy's melodramatic, yeah?"

Pointe nods again, the flush from the whiskey draining away. He sips and settles back into the chair, waiting. But his jaw is clenched, and his fingers are laced together, hard, around the glass, his shoulders tense. He looks like he's waiting for me to punch him in the face.

And the Writer knows I don't know how much better this kind of a blow is going to be. I might be doing the poor sod a kindness by simply knocking out a few of his teeth and bloodying his lip.

I take a deep breath and, both of us braced and primed with whiskey, tell him. All of it. Even the Shadow Hand parts. The only thing I leave out is the stuff about Readers and Writers. As far as I know, Pointe thinks Pip was just kidnapped and used against Forsyth because the Viceroy thought she'd make a biddable puppet, an intriguing mystery for Forsyth because of her, even now, mysterious parentage.

"And... what *was* her parentage?" Pointe asks, when my voice is hoarse and my throat is dry, the decanter half-empty, and I have run out of things to say.

I refill our glasses again, and the room sways a bit under my feet as I do so. Oh well, it's just in keeping with the picture of a wastrel lordling, isn't it? To be knackered in the middle of the afternoon? Might as well own to it.

"All human," I lie. "S'all I know. Just a unique blend of bloodlines, I guess."

"Those green eyes," Pointe muses.

"Yeah, no, brown actually," I correct. "That was the Viceroy."

Pointe looks down into his tumbler, glassy-eyed and despondent. Finally, I hold out the letter for him. I'm curious about what's in it, and I actually hope he'll open it now, let me read it too, but he just tucks it into the pocket on the inside of his jerkin. Of course. Yes. He has every right to read it in private.

"So," I say, after the silence has begun to grow heavy, like a thick humidity warning of an oncoming summer storm. "What had you rushing over here in the first place?"

"Oh," Pointe says, blinking hard and looking up at me, looking me in the face for the first time since I began my story. "I... I had good news," he says, absolutely forlorn.

"You can share it with me," I say, squirming at how earnest that sounds. Writer, I sound like a... like a schoolmaster. "I mean, if you want."

"Oh, I... I found an apprentice. While Forsyth was... while you were all away. Good lad. Menkin's his name. Strong arm, and a good heart. Absolutely a—I... I'm sorry, S-Sir Dom, I need to—" He stands abruptly, and paces over to the fire, knuckles white around his tumbler. He drinks it off and puts the glass on the mantle, then scrubs his hands through his hair. He turns to me, eyes wide and dry, but growing redder. "You're not lying to me, are you?"

"About what?"

Pointe looks me in the eye and scowls. "Is Forsyth

Turn dead?"

"What?" I squawk, and stand up, setting my own glass on the desk. "Absolutely not! Do you think I'd lie to you, of all people, about *that*?"

Pointe rubs his eyes and puffs out his cheeks, groaning. "I don't know. I don't know! He loved being Shadow Hand! He loved Lysse! I just... I can't believe *Forsyth* would just... just... leave."

"He would have made time for his farewells, if he'd had it," I say.

"But why didn't he have it? Why did he have to stay with Miss Piper? Why not come back, and then go? I don't understand!" He points a finger at me, and it's not a sword, but it's still a threat. "There's something you're not telling me about this whole business, and I don't like it."

I hold up my hands, empty. "There is, I'll admit it. There is. But Forsyth wouldn't have wanted you to worry."

"I'm worrying now," he snarls. "The lordling vanishes with a strange damsel, and his arrogant, oafish brother returns, claiming that Forsyth has found his Happily Ever After elsewhere. The greatest villain Hain has ever known is defeated, and now the useless lunk is going to take up the position he has derided and avoided for decades? And conveniently, it also plays out that my best mate has just turned over the Shadow's Mask to you? The hedgehoggy, lolloping strumpet pimp whom Forsyth resented hugely for his place as his brother's best friend? You? Yes! I'm worried!"

"Oi!" I shout, the accusations landing hard. "Hold up now——"

"I can't fathom it!" Pointe snarls. "Why you?"

"Because I was *there*!" I snarl back, advancing on Pointe. He stumbles backward, shocked by my rocking anger, tripping on the hearth. He catches himself on the mantle. "You think I'm not asking myself the exact same thing? *Why me?* Why pick Bevel Dom, when there are a thousand more worthy men in Hain? And the only answer I can come up with is that it was because he was leaving, and there was no one *else.*"

Pointe glares, face hard. "You really expect me to believe that, in a series of fortuitous events precipitating from the bizarre arrival of one maiden, you and Kintyre became a Romantic Pair, Forsyth found his Happily Ever After, the brothers Turn reconciled, Bootknife was killed, the Viceroy vanquished, Kintyre was convinced that resuming his place as Lord of Lysse was a good idea, and you inherited the mantle of Shadow Hand?"

"Yes," I say, mulishly.

Pointe puffs out a noise which I realize is meant to be a chuckle. He's trying very hard to have a sense of humor about this. "That's a hells of a lot of coincidence in one place," he snorts.

I throw out my arms, exasperated. "Just like the rest of my life! Well come!"

"And you're bringing all that *coincidence* here to Lysse," Pointe says again, huffing another chuckle. "I'm suddenly worried that I'm going to have a lot more teachable opportunities for Menkin than I thought I would."

"Trouble does seem to follow Kintyre Turn," I admit, ire cooling. I feel a kinship with Pointe, now that we've finished our shouting.

We're both exasperated by my Paired. We both miss Forsyth. We are both wary of luck and coincidence. Surely this can be the start of at least a neighborly truce? The lord and the sheriff have to work in such close tandem, it would be good to make a friend of Pointe. Even if only in honor of Forsyth.

"I just... it's just a lot to swallow, all at once," Pointe says eventually, voice low. "Forsyth gone, and Hain safe from that madman, and... oh. Oh, Writer's calluses," Pointe groans, and the color drains from his face so fast I think he's actually swooning. He has to hold on to the mantle to keep from crumpling onto the rugs. He looks up at me with pleading, watery eyes. "It wasn't Forsyth this whole time, was it? He wasn't the Viceroy, was he?"

"Hells no!" I say. "No, don't you worry about that. Forsyth was a good man—is a good man," I stubbornly correct myself. He's not dead. He's just... *gone.*

Pointe rights himself, smoothes down his clothes and corrects his hair, takes a few deep breaths, and composes himself. "Yes," he agrees at length, patting the inner pocket of his jerkin, where his letter waits for him. "Yes, he was."

PART FOUR

Kintyre looks in on us soon after that, having finally been released by Velshi and the endless stream of gossip-mongers from the village. Together, we walk Pointe back to the stables, where he's left his horse and, it turns out, his son.

Lewko Pointe is an absolute picture of childish adorableness, and like all children, he gloms immediately onto Kintyre. Kin grimaces, peels the mucky toddler off his boots, and hands him to me. I give Kin my best *"we talked about this"* glare, and I'm satisfied with my Pair's wince when he realizes what he's done.

"Hullo, Master Pointe," I say, hoisting Lewko onto my hip.

"Hello, Sir Dom," the boy says, and he's holding himself stiff. Ah, I guess he still remembers how I treated Forsyth at the last dinner we took together. Children can be very loyal for a stubbornly long time. I'll have to earn Lewko's respect if I want it. And I find, I think, that I do.

It's not like there's going to be any other children to dote on in Turn Hall, not unless one of my brothers comes to stay with their brood and... no, I shudder to think what Vulej's twin hellions might do to the precious Turn Hall tapestries. Though, it can't be much worse than what I'm holding now. Lewko is absolutely covered in Library Lion slobber.

"What is—?" Pointe asks, trying to whisk a glob of

it out of his son's hair. He's interrupted by a rumbling purr deep enough to shake the snow off the eaves of the stables. He whirls around, draws his sword, steps between the Library Lion and me, and yells, "What is *that*?"

The great cat yawns and flops over onto its back in the snow, brushing its tail through a bank and sending flakes flying into our faces. Pointe splutters and wipes at his eyes. Lewko giggles, and Kintyre, the fool, bends over to scrub at the Library Lion's tummy. The cat seizes Kintyre in its forepaws, claws sheathed, and tussles with him.

"Me too, me too!" Lewko shouts and wriggles down from my arms. I don't think Kin will let anything happen to the kid, so I let him go. Lewko rushes past his father and throws himself into the fray, much to the Library Lion's apparent delight.

"No, wait," Pointe says, stepping forward, but then stops to watch the cat at play. "Well, I'll be damned to all seven of the hells," he says wonderingly.

At length, the groom appears with Pointe's horse and a smaller pony which is clearly saddled for Lewko.

"C'mon, sprog!" Pointe says. "It's cold out. Time to go home."

"Awww, Da!" the boy protests.

"It's fine. He can—" Kin starts to say, but stops when Pointe holds up his hand.

"Sprog," he says warningly.

"But if Master Turn says that I can—"

"Nuh-uh," Pointe interrupts his son. "Master Turn isn't your father. And your father says it's time to go. Come on. I'm freezing here, and your mum will have seed cakes cooling on the rack by now."

Lewko scrambles off the Lion's nose and onto the snow-covered flagstones of the stable courtyard, clearly torn between cat and cakes.

"You can come back another time to play with him," I say to the boy. Though I don't specify if I'm talking about the Lion or the big blond lunk still perched on the creature's back.

"All right," the boy says, and lets Pointe help him mount the pony. "Bye, Capplederry!"

As they ride off into the light dusting of snow, Kintyre looks down at me and asks, "Who's Capplederry?"

Cook wants to serve us a full dinner in the great hall that night, but Velshi comes to our rescue as soon as he sees the look of panic cross Kin's face.

"Master Forsyth felt the same way," he confides to us. "He set up a small table in, ah, he called it the nook. Perhaps a more intimate setting would be appreciated?"

"It will, yes," Kintyre says, blinking and following after the butler like a toy boat being pulled across a puddle by a string. "Forssy did this?"

The space is between the kitchen and the great hall, in a little pocket that I know in other great households is usually a sort of pantry where the serving staff keep things like seltzers and spare candelabras and extra fussy napkins. I know this because they are also usually marvelous curtained spaces where a little bit of harmless loveplay can happen between, say, a visiting knight of the realm and a particularly enthusiastic serving wench. Or two.

"Master Forsyth felt keenly the... solitude of his household," Velshi says, and the hesitation is the closest thing to a criticism of Kintyre that I've ever heard from the normally staid and steady servant. "It suited him better to be close to the kitchen, so he could engage in conversation with the staff."

"Why not just eat with you lot, then?"

The gaze Velshi turns on Kintyre as he pulls out his master's chair for him is one I can only describe as *withering*. Kintyre winces.

"Hardly appropriate, wouldn't you say, *sir*?" Velshi intones gravely.

"Right. Yes. Entirely," Kintyre mumbles to the tabletop. I drop into my own seat, before Velshi can hand me into it like a fainting maiden.

"I'll inform Cook that you're ready for the first course, then, sir?"

"Yes, Velshi. And, uh, from here on out, you can tell Cook that we don't need, um, *courses*," Kintyre adds lamely.

Velshi nods once, as if Kintyre has done something he approves of. "Master Forsyth had it the same way." And then he's vanished back behind the curtains and into the warm cave of good smells and fine edible things.

Kintyre slumps back in his plain wooden chair and crosses his arms. "I'm really starting to tire of everyone comparing me to my brother."

"He held the reins for near on a decade, Kin," I say, reaching out to squeeze his thigh. "It'll take folks time to get used to you."

"I thought I would be different from Forssy," Kin admits. "He was so proper, you know? So *upright*, I thought. Forssy must have a full staff on hand, and he must eat off the good silver and the china trenchers in the great hall every night, and he must have a ball every season, and he must have his skinny old nose poked right into the curriculum of his Free School, and his fingers wrapped tight around the taxes, and..."

"And?" I prompt, sitting forward and resting my elbows on the table in a show of manners so abysmal that even my own mum would come after me with a wooden spoon if she caught me.

"I'm confused," Kin admits. "Forsyth wasn't like that at all. Bossy Forssy was... generous. D'you know he hasn't raised taxes in three years? Says the Chipping's doing well enough on what it makes, didn't need more. And he just *gave* all of the neighboring estate over to the sheriff? Doesn't charge them rent or anything. It's in the name of the Sword of Turnshire in perpetuity. That means *forever*, Bev."

"I know what 'in perpetuity' means," I tease.

"Forsyth wasn't... wasn't what I thought," Kin says again, musingly.

"I think we were both pretty surprised by him," I admit. "Lordling and Shadow Hand, and no spouse to help him with either."

Kintyre throws up his hands. "He had wealth and a title—he could have had any girl he wanted from the Chipping. Probably even could have had his pick of the nobles' second daughters if he wanted. If he'd spent any time at all at court. I thought he would have been there as often as possible, fawning over Carvel, playing the foppish courtier, but he just... stayed home, and worked diligently in his study, and walked the farms once in a season in a ridiculous floppy hat that Keriens showed me. Can you imagine that? He walked *every single farm* on the estate. Once a quarter! Pointe went with him, *and* Healer Waylin. It took them a week to have tea or luncheon or supper with every single farming family. I just..." He trails off, helpless under his confusion.

"I know," I say, reaching over to wrap my arm around his waist, pulling him close for a little kiss. "I know. My conversation with the sheriff knocked me flat, too. But we'll adjust. And I believe that you can be as good a lord as he was."

Kintyre snorts. "As good," he echoes. "I thought I

would be better already."

"Ah, there's that famous Turn modesty I adore so well," I laugh, and try to banish his sulk with another little peck.

Cook comes in then, bearing two platters covered with domes, but fragrant with the scent of rabbit pie. Excellent. We don't spring apart like missish maidens caught making our gowns green, but we do separate enough for Cook to set the platters down. She gives Kintyre's cheek a pinch.

"Happy to see you back, laddie," she says indulgently. "I've got a batch of them ginger biscuits you love so dear in the ovens now. You just nip on in behind the curtains when you're ready for them."

Kintyre's eyes grow wide with delight, and he grabs Cook's hand and kisses her knuckles gallantly and earnestly.

"And you," she says to me. "You tell me what you like, lad, and I'll be sure to keep a tin of 'em for you."

No one's called me *lad* since I was knighted. But I find that when a woman like Cook promises me biscuits and pinches Kin's cheek, making him flush up with joy, I don't half mind.

"I like the ones with raisins and oats in," I say, and Kintyre groans, because he hates raisins, says they look like dried-up bugs.

"I'll start on 'em in the morning," Cook promises. "Eat up, boys, while it's warm." And then she bustles off.

"Boys," I echo with a snort, and then tuck in. For all that I haven't walked for hours, or sparred, or beaten back monsters, or even bent my head over a scroll today, I am both exhausted and famished. Emotional turmoil is almost as good as a battle for the appetite, it seems.

When we've both licked our plates clean, Kintyre executes a perfect skirmish on the kitchen's biscuit jar.

While we're munching away, I take better stock of the nook. The table and chairs are plain, wooden, the kind of thing I've seen before in peasant houses—sturdy, well-made and well-polished, but not ornate. The stone walls are unadorned, save for the twin swags of green velvet separating the nook from both the kitchen and the great hall. There's one single skinny window, and under that a narrow credenza against one wall, like every other room in Turn Hall.

"Think I could stash some things in this sideboard?" I ask, reaching behind me to open it. It's stocked on one side with those seltzers and napkins and things, as expected, but on the other with a small coin purse, an inkpot and some quills, and a ream of fresh parchment. Clearly Forsyth wasn't above working over his breakfast. "It'd be nice to have my pipe here for after dinner."

Kintyre scowls at me. "That window doesn't open. I hope you don't make the drapes stink of stale smoke."

I roll my eyes. "How about I promise to take it into the back courtyard when the weather is fine?"

"Very well, then," he grumps. Though we both know the weather is not fine, not right now. "S'funny."

"What is?"

"You and me, sitting here, talking like... like we're staying." He scrubs at the furrow between his eyebrows, uncomfortable.

"Aren't we?" I ask, sitting up and regarding him carefully. Kintyre can't be regretting this great Lord Turn adventure already, can he?

"Well, yeah," he says. "I just... with the meetings and... and the clothes, and all of it. We're... planning. Planning ahead, you know? S'odd."

"Sure is," I agree. "But... I think I like it."

Kintyre smiles at me, and I reach out to brush crumbs out of his late-evening stubble. "Yeah?" he asks.

"Yeah," I say. "It's nice to think that I'm going to wake up every morning in that ridiculous big bed of yours, beside you, for the rest of our lives."

Kintyre's eyes get wide, his pupils blowing open, and he grabs me by the hand. I laugh the whole way as he drags me up the back stairs to our room.

Deciding that it's an open secret that Kin and I are Paired and already sharing a bed, we go about rearranging the rooms after dinner (and after *after*-dinner). Maybe it's our way of proving to ourselves that we really do mean to stay, that we're really going to do this.

I'm not comfortable at all with someone else sleeping in a room adjoined to ours, so the valet's room has to go. Luckily, Keriens is good-natured, and doesn't mind moving into one of the private rooms up in the servants' hall. Forsyth's kept the staff so thin, each person's got a room of their own already, with a few to spare even, so no one has to share yet.

Kintyre and I are grateful for the opportunity for some good old-fashioned physical labor after a day of just sitting around and talking. So we help Keriens pack up his bureau, and then shift both that and his bed up to his new room for him. We move the cot that was in the room originally up to the lumber room in the attic, and fetch down a simple desk, chair, and set of shelves to make the valet's room into a study. (To think, the boy who once had to share a bed with three brothers now lives in a house grand enough to have a whole room dedicated to storing furniture no longer fashionable enough to use and call it *lumber*.)

Kintyre's got it in his head that he'll keep using the estate agent's office as his own—apparently, Forsyth was his own agent as well. Maybe my vision of Forsyth as a micromanaging glutton for insanity and sleepless nights wasn't all that far off the target after all. The agent's office is out the back of the Hall, where the folk of the Chipping can access it without bothering the family, so this new study off our bedroom will be mine for... Shadow Business. By unspoken agreement, we have decided to keep Forsyth's library study as... not a *shrine*, that's not the right word. But that study is *Forsyth*'s, and it feels wrong to... well, it just feels wrong. Feels final in a way that is false, because Forsyth Turn *isn't dead.*

I will only use the library study when I need to entertain spies I don't want traipsing through my bedroom. It's not like either Kin or I are going to spend much time in the library, anyway. Kintyre only reads books when they're about him, and I prefer getting out for a ride or a spar over crumpling myself up into a chair and not moving for hours.

Although, I wonder if once—if—*once* I put on the mask, that will change. Will something of the scholars who came before me leak into my personality? Will I start craving solitude and lamplight and a tome? Or will reading become even more abhorrent because I'll be able to recall every book the Shadow Hands who came before me read?

I know the knowledge of being Shadow Hand is passed on: the locations of secret passages, the rites of spells, the secret Words that aren't freely taught, the rules of magic, the languages of the four kingdoms. But must the physical things, like sword fighting, be learned by each inheritor? To be sure, I'll probably gain the memory of how to perform the flourishing moves of court fencing I'd never bothered with before, but I'll have no muscle memory from practice, no automatic reaction based on them. I'd have to work at that if I wanted the skills. Not sure I'd need them, really, but if I wanted, I could.

But what else is transferred? Will I have to parse a hundred different men's tastes in wine? Will I suddenly come to despise apples? Will I dream other men's nightmares and experience another man's heartbreak if I walk into a graveyard where his wife is a century dead and buried?

Not for the first time, I wish Forsyth had bloody well stuck around, at least long enough to explain.

Put on the mask, and you'll know, that damnable seductive voice in my head says, and it's overlaid with Kintyre calling from the next room: "You're not going to spend all night in there shuffling things around, are you, Bev? I said we'd fetch your books up out of the library in the morning. What else are you—oh."

I look up at him, and he's in the doorway, staring at my hands. Why my hands? I look down at them and... oh. I'm holding the Shadow's Mask again.

I don't remember picking it up. I was unpacking my saddlebags, laying out my writing box, and then... right, yes, I picked up the black velvet bag and... and then...

The candle on the corner of my new desk is half the height I last remember it being.

Writer's calluses.

I shake myself all over, fear like a cold splash up my spine, and jam the mask back into its bag. Then I bury it in the farthest corner of this room's credenza.

"Shit, Kin," I whisper softly. "That thing is..."

"Have you put it on?"

I shake my head. "But I think it wants me to."

"Come to bed, dearest," he says, and the pet name startles me so much that I sway away from the mask and into his arms.

"I'm not a dragonet that needs soothing," I scold him gently. "*Dearest.*"

Kintyre smooths his large hands down my back

anyway. "You're *my* dragon. Huff, huff, burn, burn. Little dragonet with such sharp teeth."

I pinch his waist in revenge, and Kintyre squirms.

"I know you're feeling full of flame, but it's just magic. We know magic well enough. And this is good magic."

"Is it?" I ask, and I'm *shaking*. I'm shaking, and it's not because the fire in my new office hasn't been lit and the world outside its windows is white with an evening blizzard. "I hope so."

Kin kisses me then; sweet, and gentle, and reassuring. "I know it's good. But there's no rush, Bev. Take all the time you need."

I nod, comforted by his rock-steady certainty, and let him take me off to bed. I lose myself in his body in order to drown my cowardice.

Our fourth day of our new life in Turn Hall brings a messenger hawk, and a whole host of problems that Kintyre and I had never even remotely considered when we began planning our little domestic adventure here.

"Marriage?" I repeat, my pipe hanging off my bottom lip. True to my word, I'm indulging in a smoke in the kitchen garden after lunch. It's here that Kintyre found me. He has the messenger hawk perched on one outstretched arm, a letter written in Gyre-blue thrust under my nose, and a look of panicked horror on his face.

"They're offering me their daughter. Like... like she was a cask of wine!"

"Marriage?" I repeat, scanning the letter. "But if news that you're back in the seat of the Chipping has already gotten all the way to Kingskeep, surely the news that we're Paired must have—"

"Babies! The letter talks about how handsome our sons would be. Bev!" he wails.

"Well, you do need an heir," I say musingly, taking the letter from his shaking hands so I can read it properly. The sky is an endless, cloudless blue, the same color as his eyes. The snow that fell in great drifts last night is already burning off in the warm sunshine; Kin's shaking is not from cold.

"Bevel!" my lover gasps, scandalized. "I don't want a wife!"

This admission does something to my insides, makes them all warm and melty, unwinds a knot of fear I didn't even realize had been twisting up behind my sternum. For all that we *are* Paired, it's not the same as pledging a Troth—the closest thing to marriage two men can achieve. And Pairs can be broken, or remain Platonic. It doesn't surprise me at all that Lord Gyre is willfully misunderstanding our Pairing to be a soldierly one.

"What reply do I send him?" Kintyre begs me. "You're the clever one, the thinking one. Tell me what to say to him to put him off."

"Put them *all* off, you mean," I say.

"All?" he gasps in dread.

"Kintyre," I say, tapping the ashes out of my pipe on my boot heel and stuffing it into my pocket. "You are the eldest son of House Turn, with no lordling in the wings. You are wealthy, you are titled, you are of noble birth, you are knighted and a bit of a folk hero. Even if you didn't have the seat of Lysse, I think the moment you settled down, these letters would have begun arriving."

"But I don't want these men's daughters!" he complains.

"Writer, am I glad we got ourselves sorted *before* we retired," I say, brushing the messenger hawk off him so I can pull Kin down into a sweet kiss. The bird circles us, and then alights on the edge of the garden wall, waiting for our return message or its command to return empty-clawed. "I don't think I could have stood it, watching all these women throw themselves at your feet, trying to trip you into marriage, when I wanted you so badly for myself."

"Yes, that is one blessing from Pip, at least," he says, leaning into the kiss. We reassure one another with lips and tongues until the cold begins to wrack us.

"Into the stable with you," I tell the hawk when we part. "I'll have a letter for you soonish."

The hawk chirrups and goes.

"'All these women,'" Kintyre says as I usher him into the warm kitchen and fuss at him until he sits by the bread oven. At least I had been wearing my house robe when I went out for my smoke—Kin's just in his shirt-sleeves, and his fingernails have turned blue. "Writer, I hope not."

"Hope all you like, Kin," I say, brushing his hair back from his face. "But they're coming, mark my words. And the only way to stop it is to marry."

Kintyre hooks his fingers into the pockets of my house robe and draws me close. And that's all we say on that subject—for the moment, at least.

Though I've augured no signs, my prediction proves depressingly accurate. Days five, six, and seven bring five more messenger hawks between them, and Toflan the groom is getting annoyed with the amount of hawk shit collecting in one corner of the stable; Kin hasn't let me send back replies yet.

"Not until we've come up with a plan that will stop all of them, all at once, once and for all," he begs me.

"Coward," I reiterate.

"Politics," he corrects.

We're seated in another one of those seemingly

useless rooms in Turn Hall, a salon on the ground floor filled with squashy furniture that Velshi called the ladies' parlour, but which has the nicest view of the back lawn and the snowfall that is persistently filling in the gaps the mild thaw left in the carpet of white. It never snowed this much in Bynnebakker at Solsticetide, never mind this early in the season. I think it's enchanting.

"Still cowardly," I reply.

"I can't seem to be favoring one offer or another, so I have to answer them all at once. I remember this, at least, from when I was eighteen. My father hired someone to handle the matchmaking."

I startle and blink at my lover, turning from where we're leaning against each other on a sofa, watching the wintery sunset. There's mulled wine keeping warm on the hearth, and empty goblets in our hands. "Kintyre Turn, are you telling me you were betrothed when I met you?"

Kintyre shrugs. "If I was, nobody told me."

"And nobody's said anything about it all the times we've been back?"

"Nope."

"Huh," I say, and look back out. The messenger hawks are chasing each other across the sky, playful in their boredom. "I guess there was no one, then."

"Why do you say that?"

"Because Forsyth would have bullied you into at least meeting her, if the matchmaking had been completed."

Kintyre makes a humming noise and rises to get us both refills.

The next evening isn't as blissfully domestic, because around noon we are inundated with the first of our guests.

The Gyre girl comes just before lunch, and Kintyre and I have to abandon our plans to eat over the maps of the estate farms, forced to eat with her in the family dining room instead. It's paneled in wood that matches the ballroom, and was probably added to the labyrinthine Turn Hall around the same time. It's smaller than the grand hall, but that's not saying much, because the table is still large enough to seat at least twelve adults comfortably, and the walls are absolutely jammed with a century's worth of disapproving Turn ancestors rendered in oil paint. Kin explains that they'd break their fasts here as a family when he was little, and points out a scratch in the table from a tussle he and Forsyth had over some plate of sweets or another.

The Gyre girl—I say girl, but she's probably twenty-five, already a desperate spinster—is pretty enough if you like them emaciated and doe-eyed. I used to be a connoisseur of woman-flesh, or at least the kind that Kin preferred. But now that I haven't lain with a woman in months, and I have all that I want in Kintyre, I find that I'm not attracted to her at all. I don't know what to hope with Kin, though; he's never said no to an easy tumble, and I find myself nervously picking at the impressive meal Cook managed to pull out of thin air, fairy dust, and a last-minute warning.

When I mention that it's my first time at this table, the Gyre girl smirks, as if this being mutually our first meal in the cold, formal room puts us on some kind of level playing field.

Ha! When I've taken so many meals in Kin's rooms? In Kin's *bed*? I find myself irresistibly tempted to tell the silly little bitch so to her face. But what good would that do? It's clear now from the tone of the letters that everyone knows we're Paired platonically, and probably also romantically, too. But that doesn't stop the correspondents from pointing out that the scion of a Great House needs children, and for that, he needs a wife. And they're not wrong, that's the wretched part of it.

Writer's nutsack, all these fathers are expecting to sell their daughters to House Turn, *knowing* that they'll all be second to me? Or do they assume their daughter's charms could usurp me? And these women are content with being breeding stock? I mean, well-kept *breeding* stock, sure, but breeding stock all the same. And then what? Are this wife and I meant to compete for Kin's affection? Share it? Share each other? Or is the assumption that she won't be part of our lives at all, except for the nights when she lays with my Paired?

No. I have no problem with dwarvish marriages, even among humanfolk, but I'm a jealous man. I don't share. I *won't* share. Not my Kintyre. Not after everything it's taken to pin the ruddy bastard down.

The Gyre girl—she has a name, I'm sure she does, but I don't give a fig what it is—flirts and flutters and flushes her way through lunch, and I can't look at Kintyre. I can't. When the plates have all been cleared away, I beg my excuses and flee the dining room as fast as I can. I probably shouldn't leave Kin alone in there with that... that *harpy*, but if he is going to change his mind, if having a flesh and blood woman right there, available, *eager* even, stirs his blood even a little bit, then I don't want to see it. I can't.

And the worst part of all of it is that it would be the right thing to do.

Kintyre Turn *should* marry some nobleman's daughter. He should produce heirs. He should live a proper, laced-up, traditional life with a woman to head the household and manage the staff and host the banquets. He should be attending court, and presenting his children. And I should be... I should be back in Bynnebakker, sweating my life away at the forge and having dalliances with whatever passing soldiers fancy a tupping from a little hedgehoggy powerhouse like me. Maybe have a wife and children of my own, just so I won't be lonely, and be miserable in it, anyway.

Why did the Writer ever create men like me, men who prefer the bodies and company and pleasure of other human men, but who also long for the children a union of two men can never produce? How cruel, this Writer! I wish Pip was here so I could yell at her in proxy. Or demand an explanation.

I'm halfway down the hall and so lost in my own mind and misery that I don't hear Kintyre coming up behind me. I don't even know he's been chasing after me until he grabs my elbow and drags me to a halt.

"What in the seven hells was that?" Kintyre snarls at me, anger and betrayal in every line of his handsome face. "I thought you were on my side, here!"

"Your side?"

"Or have you changed your mind?" Kintyre asks, searching my face, suddenly scared. "Do you not like it here? Do you want to leave me?"

"What?" I ask, stunned, and reach up to cup his jaw in my palm. I run my thumb across the small white scar under his left ear, a souvenir from a Sunsong siren. "Of course not. What makes you think that?"

"You just sat there, Bev! You let her flirt with me, and you didn't... you never snapped at her, you never teased, you never... you usually chase them off. I was... why didn't you try to chase her off?" He sounds like a child when he whines like that, and I shouldn't find it adorable, but I do. Oh, I'm so sunk in this man it's appalling.

"I..." I say, and then trail off, uncertain of what I actually want to say. "I suppose because it's your house? And I feel that you should be the one defending yourself in it? I mean, you're the lord. I don't want to undermine—"

"It's your house, too!" Kin says. "Yours and mine! We're going to stay here, together, forever! Right?"

The vehemence and desperation for reassurance in his voice reaches into the core of me and shakes it. "Yes, of course, Kin," I say around a growing lump in my throat.

"And it's your House, too," he adds, fingering the lapel of the Turn-russet waistcoat Keriens nagged me into donning when it was announced that we had a guest. "You are a Turn, now. Unless you want me to be a Dom. I could do that. I look good in amethyst."

"And where would we live then?" I tease. "My mother doesn't need an eighth son, and there isn't much room in the loft above the forge."

"Your mother already has an eighth son," Kintyre insists stubbornly, and, Writer, he's not wrong.

"Fine then," I say gently. "I apologize for not defending what's mine."

Kintyre nods, smug. "As well you should. Do better at dinner, will you?"

"If my lord wishes it," I laugh.

"He does."

We kiss again, and make our way back to Kintyre's office, where we lose ourselves in the maps. We're forced to entertain the Gyre girl at dinner, but with Kin's leave to be as vicious as I like, she looks like a woman whose hopes have all been dashed when we part for bed.

Good.

I feel sorry for her, I do, because of her age and the way her father is trying to dispose of her. But Kintyre Turn is *mine*, and Bevel Dom no longer walks one step behind.

PART FIVE

The Gyre girl stays the night, apparently not prepared to give up the field just yet. Or perhaps she's not allowed to go home without a marriage promise. Who knows what a father who'd offer up his daughter like a prize cow might do if she returned to him defeated.

Unfortunately, House Gyre isn't the only one to decide to wave their daughter under Kin's nose like a well-cooked steak, and we are soon inundated with pretty maidens, which works in our favor. Traditionally, the men and womenfolk separate to their own pursuits in the evenings, unless they decide to stay together. And stay, we certainly do not. With one maiden, it would have been rude to abandon her. With many, they have each other for company and we needn't bother.

Besides, between my correspondence with King Carvel sorting out the Lost Library and the Ivory Tower, and the readying for scholars to descend upon both plac-es, my aiding Kintyre in unraveling the nuances of where Forsyth tied up the Turn wealth and patronage in Lysse, and my twice-weekly visits to Law Manor with the Li-brary Lion—whom young Lewko has resolutely renamed Capplederry—to spar with Pointe, coach his apprentice, and learn from them both the finer nuances of keeping the peace in a Chipping, Kintyre and I simply can't seem to find the *time*. There are not enough hours in the day to attend the endless reading circles, winter picnics, skating parties, and card games the noble ladies keep inviting Kintyre (and, grudgingly, *me*) to.

Last I counted, there were six eligible young misses filling up the guest rooms and eating our stores for the winter, and Keriens keeps us fully apprised of the funny bits of competition or drama amongst them while he shaves us each morning. Three of the ladies seem determined to wholly replace me in Kin's affections (as if they ever could!). Two seem content to politely ignore me and share Kin, without admitting to having to do so. And one seems as if she is actively trying to court the both of us simultaneously. An intriguing prospect, and one Kin and I would have jumped at even as little as a year ago, but not now. We don't need a woman to mediate our lovemaking. Not anymore.

And it's funny. But it's also *eating me alive.*

Kin is good at what he does, and what he does is to be honest, good, forthright, brave, strong, and, the Writer bless him, a bit obvious. There are no hidden depths to my lover, no secret scheming, no plots or ploys. He is what he seems.

It's both his greatest weakness and his greatest strength. Every emotion he possesses, every thought that he has, flashes across his face. He is rubbish at games of bluffing and cards. But people trust him, implicitly, for he has no deceit in him.

So he feels sorry for the maidens, and it is genuine. And while I sometimes pity them, I hate them, too.

I feel, suddenly, that I'm not good enough for a man like that. For a man who feels sorry for maidens. I'm not good enough. Not good enough to be the Shadow Hand of Hain. Not good enough to be a Lord Consort.

"Maybe I should be moving back into my own room, Kin," I venture softly, slowly, as we lie in bed together. And maybe my voice is soft with cowardice. Maybe I hope he doesn't hear me at all over the women downstairs, playing whist and drinking their way through Forssy's carefully curated wine cellar. But he has, obviously, because those blue, blue eyes of his open, and stare at me across the shared battleground of our pillows.

The look of them is inscrutable, tinged around the outside with patience, but otherwise, I can't decipher what he's thinking. It's rare, with Kin. I know him so well. But sometimes, just sometimes, he can channel his brother and put on a face that's unreadable.

"Oh?" he prompts when I don't say more.

I chew on my lip—a nervous habit that frustrates me when I catch myself doing it. It's so missish. "Maybe I should move into my own room," I repeat.

"Why?"

"We're not trothed, and—"

"We're Paired."

"That's not the same. It's not... it's not proper the way a trothing is."

"So?"

I roll over and jam my head back against the pillow, annoyed. "Are you being deliberately obtuse? Because it's not cute."

Kin levers himself up on one elbow and peers down through the gloaming of our bedroom at my face, as if everything I haven't been able to make into words the last few months will appear inscribed instead on my forehead. I almost wish it would. It would save me the agony of trying to articulate it.

"Are you feeling stifled?" he asks. "Is that what this is about?"

"What?"

"I dunno—the tapestries and the velvet and the crystal, and all the people, all around us, all the time. Can't seem to ever get to be *alone*, you know? 'M half tempted to bugger off some days, go hide in the glade off the Northward Road and just be alone with the world."

He reaches out and runs his fingers through my hair. What was once a perfectly normal straw-blond has now become so threaded with dull, tarnished gray that I think I'm seeing my pa every time I catch my face in the looking glass. Kin's hair—a gleaming gold—is artfully threaded with a silver that shines. Lucky bastard. Even his wrinkles look charming and distinguished. Mine just make me look *old*.

My hair is also shaggy, clearly not neat enough for Kerien's taste, with the way he keeps hinting at how easy it would be to call the barber up to the Hall. But I don't want a barber *summoned* for me, don't want to fetch people like they're things, like my legs aren't perfectly capable of carrying me into Turnshire on their own. I'm not some stupid invalid or infant who needs things done for him. And what's wrong with a bit of shag? I'll get a haircut when there's a *reason* to get one.

I knock Kin's hand away, frustrated with myself and his gentleness.

This... this *new* Kintyre. This Kintyre with forethought, who works to make me smile; this Kintyre who listens thoughtfully to petitioners, and gives way to his cook; who wears lawn shirts, and lets someone else dress him... I don't know who this man is. And I don't know what part I have to play in his life. In his bed. In his heart.

What's the point of me, when he has *other* people to do things for him? To be his walking apology in my place? To feed him? To watch his back? To tell his stories? To do all the work of being lord while he is the face of it?

"What's the point of me?" I catch myself asking out loud, and immediately wish the words back behind my teeth. I roll over in the bed and bury my face in the pillow, mortified.

"What's the... Bevel!" Kintyre says, and he sounds aghast. "You're not serious—you don't—hey, look at me."

"No," I pout. "Forget I said anything!"

He grabs my shoulder and manhandles me around to face him, and I hate it. I *hate* it when he does that. But he's kneeling back already, one hand hovering over his crotch to protect his stones, and I laugh. And it's a dry, bitter laugh that crawls like dead rats out of my throat. Does he think I'm really that predictable?

"I won't forget, and I'm not letting this go. I know we don't... we don't *talk* about this stuff, Bev, but I've been trying, trying to be everything you want me to be, and I—"

"I don't want to—"

"Then maybe you should move into another room, if all you're going to do is fight in bed!" Kintyre growls, and throws back the blankets. He sits up and cold air rushes over me, my flesh pimpling up so quickly I actually spasm with the shock of it.

"Me?" I snarl, side-swiped by what he's said. "You're putting this on *me*? Don't—"

"I've been trying to be a good lord! To... to think of things so you don't have to tell me! To be—"

"You've got everything that's owed you: a manor, the wealth, the title, the respect. You could have a wife, too, if you—"

"Oh, no! Don't you dare, Bevel Dom!"

"There are any number of nubile, big-bosomed morons downstairs who would just love to be the Lady Turn, to give you little blond Turnlings—"

"I don't want any big-bosomed—"

"You don't *need* me!" I shout. And that shuts him up. He rears back as if I've slapped him in the face. I sit up, wriggle my legs out from under him, and push back against the headboard.

He shakes his head, like a prizefighter recovering from a spectacular right hook, and then his brow furrows, and the corners of his lips turn down, and his cheeks flush, and he is *angry*. "That's complete and utter gryffon shit! Of course I need you!" he roars back. "Why wouldn't I need you?"

"I'm not good enough!" I snarl. "For... for Lysse, and for this—this *life*! Writer's balls, Kin! Pointe thinks I'm a joke, though he doesn't say it. I don't know any of the court fencing rules, did you know that? The blasted cat doesn't even listen to me! And the Writer-be-damned Shadow's Mask—Forsyth made a mistake. You've made a mistake. I made a ridiculous, bloody mistake, and I shouldn't have... I shouldn't have—"

"Shouldn't have what?" Kin rumbles, but there's danger in his tone. Warning. I don't heed it. I'm a fool. I throw myself headlong into my confession, because if I don't say it now, I never will.

"Maybe I shouldn't have told you!" I blurt, and each word feels like ash on my tongue, but it's true. "Maybe I shouldn't have—have ever fallen in love with you! But I couldn't *help* it. I couldn't help it!"

"And what? You're saying you regret it?" Kintyre asks, and I haven't seen grief so profound on his so-readable face since Stormbearer died. And even that annoys me, because I should mean *more* to the bastard than his Writer-be-damned horse.

"Maybe I do!"

Kintyre makes a pained noise, a huffing keen, like he's been stabbed in the lungs from behind. He folds his hands over his chest, and for a second, I fear he really was stabbed. But no blood leaks out between the weave of his strong fingers. The hurt is not physical.

Silence grows between us. It starts small, hangs on the end of our puffing breaths, our wordless fury, but it

grows. It tendrils outward like curious vines, curling between us, thickening as the seconds pass. It feels... terrify-
ingly final.

I don't want it to be final.

I don't want it to solidify. I don't want it to root.

"Kin, I—" I start, not sure, exactly, what I mean
to say next, but Kintyre puts one of his hands over my
mouth. It's not rough, not a slap. Just a cup, like he is trying to catch my words, or my breath. And against my lips,
I can feel him shaking.

He leans forward, slowly, giving me time to pull back
if I want to. I don't want to. He lowers his hand, takes my
bottom lip between both of his, tender and tremulous,
and even this is shaking, this kiss. But it's not the cold. It's
too fine a tremor to be coming from the chill.

"You were Written for me, Bev," Kintyre whispers
into my mouth, smearing the words against my skin. He
pecks a kiss on my jaw, below my ear, on the top of its
shell, on my temple, where the gray hair is starting to
flock like sheep being rounded up by Old Man Time.
"You're my... my conscience. You're my other half. You
plan where I rush in. You're calm when I'm quick to
anger, and you're angry when I'm still trying to figure out
how I should feel about things. You're just. You know
parts of the world I never experienced as a lordling,
showed me compassion and poverty and despair that I
would never have known otherwise. You're perfect for
me."

"As your sidekick," I mutter venomously. But Kin isn't
mad. He just whuffs a chuckle into my hair.

"As my best friend. As my perfect complement."

"I'm not servile, not *made*—"

"Writer, everything is a fight with you. Everything has
always been a Writer-be-damned fight with you."

"Sorry, I don't mean to—"

"I love a good fight," Kintyre says, leaning back, eyes twinkling.

"Good thing. 'Cause that's all we seem to be doing lately," I say, echoing his earlier statement.

"Keeps me on my toes," Kintyre says wryly. "The Writer knows being Lord Turn doesn't."

"Are you bored?"

"Not as bored as you are."

I can't help the chuckle that escapes me. "You're not wrong."

"Being the Shadow Hand would help with that. I know you haven't done it yet, put on the mask," he says softly. "Go on, Bevel. Put on the mask. Then you'll see. You'll believe me. Forsyth didn't make a mistake. I didn't make a mistake. The Writer didn't—the Writer could never..."

I can't help the huffing, snorting laugh that escapes me, even as I paw at my eyes, wipe the embarrassing tears away. "That's not what Pip says."

Kintyre rolls his eyes. "Pip is a Reader. She doesn't understand what it means to be Written. Not like we do."

I look over to my study, where I've hidden the mask behind the box holding my travel pipe and hash. Kintyre carved me that box, to keep my supply safe and dry, when he realized I wouldn't be giving up the habit despite his nagging. He accepted my imperfections and made treasures of them. Including, it sounds like, my stubbornness and tendency to snap and snarl at him.

A dragonet in need of soothing, indeed.

"I don't know if I can, Kin. That's... it's been eating at me since the Rookery. I don't know if I *can* be the Shadow Hand. If I can..." I touch my chest. "If this is *right*."

"Has all of... all of this strife, this thundercloud over your head, has it all been about the mask? Because... because, if you want, I could... I could take it away from you. Do it instead. I mean, I don't know if I'd be any good—"

"No!" I blurt, as a sudden, panicked possessiveness comes over me. Perhaps it's the persuasive magic of the mask, or maybe it's just... just that I realize, suddenly, that if I give this away—if I give this to Kintyre, too—*if I give it up...*

"No, the mask is... mine. Something... something for me. Just me. Something that isn't..."

"In support of me," Kin says, and it's not sad, not really.

"I don't mean it like that. I just mean... I don't know what I mean," I finish lamely, exasperated by my repeated inability to just figure out what in the hells it is I'm feeling and *express* it. Some damned bard I am.

It's now a month out from Solsticetide, and the ladies have determined that since there's no "woman of the house," it's up to them to collectively manage the preparations for the Chipping's annual pilgrimage to Turn Hall for the celebration. Never mind that Cook and Velshi have it well in hand, and have *had* it well in hand for decades. It's not like there's been a woman of the house since Kin's mother died.

When I sneak into the kitchen for raisin biscuits after dinner, the same night the ladies announce their intention, Cook corners me with a wild and desperate look in her eyes.

"Master Bevel," she says, clinging to my lapels. "These women are driving us all mad. *Do* something."

"It's Kin you should be cornering," I say, feeling sorry for her. "He's the one who's too terrified of offending the wrong people to send them off."

"Then, if you can't be rid of them, at least stop all

this Solsticetide nonsense. It's your purview. Don't let them run roughshod over you, my boy!"

"What is?" I ask.

"You're the lord's spouse!" she says. "It's you who's meant to take celebrations like this in hand. Tell them to bugger off!"

"I am?" I say, wondering why no one told me they expected me to head up the event planning—and then the rest of what she said hits home. "Wait, I *am?*"

"Or as good as!" Cook moans. "For the love of the Writer, just troth the fool lad and be done with it! Put us all out of our misery, Master Bevel! Trick him into it if you have to! I'll put a potion in his tea, whatever it takes. Just get these bloody meddlesome women *gone!*"

I make my platitudes to Cook and escape back upstairs to our room with the biscuits and a bottle of wine, and repeat her desperate pleas to Kintyre. Though I keep the part about getting him drunk and tricking him into a trothing to myself, just in case Cook and I decide we're at our wit's end and need to enact just such a plot.

"How did I get it all wrong?" Kin groans, hands covering his face. I try to make him look at me, but he's lost in his head. He's so *lost.* My poor oaf. "How did Forsyth do all of this, and more? How did I... I thought it was going to be easy. Say some speeches, make some rulings, collect some rent money. There's so much... there's the Free School, and judging on petitions, and working with Pointe, and arranging our tenants, and making sure the taxes cover the cost of the road repairs without bankrupting a farmer who's had a bad crop! And the *women!*" He groans, aghast.

"I think that's the first time I've ever heard you say that with despair in your voice," I tease. "Come on, Kin. I think we've tortured the staff long enough for politeness' sake. Time to dismiss the ladies."

"But *how*?" Kintyre moans. "We can't just send them off."

"Sure we can. A trothing will make it stop," I say smugly.

"Ours, you mean?" Kintyre asks, suspiciously.

"Of course."

"What if I need something from one of their fathers? What if I ruin an alliance?"

"Won't choosing just one of them ruin your alliances with the rest, anyway?"

"No, not the way rejecting them all whole-cloth would."

I push Kintyre back into his chair by the fire and climb onto his lap, nibbling one of my biscuits. "I think," I say, after a few moments of thoughtful munching, "that you're failing to see an important aspect of this quag-mire."

"And what's that?" Kintyre asks petulantly, brushing the crumbs off his chest.

"*You* are Kintyre Turn. There's no Great House in the whole of Hain that would dare close its doors to you, or its goodwill. You have saved the kingdom more times than anyone can count. You are a friend of the king, and of many other crowned heads as well. You defeated the Viceroy."

"Lucy Piper defeated the Viceroy," Kintyre corrects, settling his hands on my hips, fingers curled in the soft flesh of my backside.

"Not in the version I'm writing," I say. "Besides, she won't mind a bit of creative rewriting. Or at least, she'll never know the difference, not being here."

"Maybe she'll read it, out there, with Forsyth."

I laugh. "And if she does, so what? She's there, and we're here, and there's nothing she can do. And you, my silly lump, you are a hero. I have worked hard to make you one. And now we can cash in on that fame." I lean in, watching his eyes flutter closed as I draw close enough for us to share breath. I kiss each of his eyelids gently. Cradled in the curve of my lover's body, I pull his mouth to mine and indulge in a languid kiss.

This leads to other things, and by the time the candles have burned low, Kintyre and I are gloriously naked under our sheets and sheened with the good, honest sweat of a perfect swivving. I can't help the smug possessiveness that sweeps through my languor when Kin shifts off his rump and onto his side, wincing a little at the tenderness in his behind.

"Oh, wipe that smirk off your face, Bevel Dom," Kintyre says, his own eyes falling shut.

"Never," I say, and reach out to give that beautiful arse of his a firm squeeze.

He grunts and buries his head further into his pillow, as if to say "*sleeping now!*" I roll onto my side and tuck up against his chest, and he throws one massive arm over my shoulders. I'm just about to drift into sleep when Kintyre says, "All right, all right, stop nagging." As if we were in the midst of a conversation.

I crane my neck and peer up at his face to see if he's talking in his sleep. But his eyes are slitted open, and he is peering back down at me.

"Kin?"

"I agree," Kintyre grumbles, as if he is capitulating under the most hateful and strenuous circumstances. "A-trothing we will go."

"Well, finally," I say, giving in to the urge to kiss him soundly. Kin returns it with enthusiasm, which tells me that he's just as thrilled about this next step as I am. "Why did you make it seem like such a hardship?" I ask. "I mean... if, as you say, trothing is just a different version of Pairing..."

"A more *permanent* version."

"Did you want an escape door?" I ask, and I can't help but feel hurt by that.

"No, but just... tying myself to only one person... and a man... I needed to... I needed time to be sure that I was still me when I was with... you."

"Kintyre Turn! Who you are *with* me?" I ask, indignant. I sit up and take his face in my hands, forcing him to meet my eyes. For good measure, I straddle his chest, so he can't get away. "The more accurate question might be who you are without me? I've been by your side nearly every hour of nearly every day from the moment you turned eighteen years old. I have wanted you for every second of it, and loved you for a good majority of it on top of that. Who are you *without* me, Kintyre Turn? Might as well ask the moon what it is without the sun."

"So you have no big opinion of yourself, then," he says, pinching my stomach playfully, and I jerk and squirm, but don't give in.

"You said it before," I counter. "We were Written for each other. You just as much for me as I am for you. The only thing a trothing will change is how many breakfasts Cook has to send up on trays in the morning, and how many of our guest rooms the maids have to turn out. We'll be the same old thick-headed Kintyre Turn and stubborn Bevel Dom. Except that our house will be free of female vermin."

Kintyre pushes himself up on his elbows and kisses me. "I don't want a big trothing ceremony," he says softly. "I know the Chipping wants it, but... I ran away from all of this because I hate being..."

"Being what?"

"You're gonna laugh," Kin says petulantly, turning away.

"I won't," I promise, and bite down on the inside of

my cheek to make sure I keep it.

Kintyre huffs, and squirms, and pouts a little more. "I hate being the center of attention," he finally mutters.

I'm glad I've got my cheek between my teeth, because only a small giggle escapes me, one that I'm quick to turn into a snort. Not quick enough, though, because Kin scowls.

"I knew you'd laugh."

"'M not laughing, Kin," I say, and stretch my neck to give him a soft, languid kiss, and myself enough time to calm down. "I just... you. You don't like being the center of attention? So, what, all those knighting ceremonies and dinners in great halls where you sat at the head table and were feted and feasted were just torture?"

"*Those* weren't," Kin says, and hooks his top leg around mine, hauling me back onto my side and closer under the blankets so our hips align. I give a little wiggle, to gauge his intentions, but it seems like he's just after the warm comfort of connection right now. Kintyre always prefers to be cuddling when he's making confessions, not that he would call what we're doing by either term. "But stuff like this... when they want to... fete me just because I'm... because of nothing I've *done*..." He squirms some more, and I let him paw at my backside while he chews on his words.

Normally, I'd take pity on the poor lunk. He hates talking about his feelings, and prefers to communicate through bedsport instead. But this is too important to let him off the fishing hook just yet. I shuffle closer, but keep my face away, out of kissing range for now. He grunts and huffs, frustrated when he realizes I'm not going to let him get out of this one just yet.

"Tell me," I say, and run one hand down his side, a teasing reward for trying to figure this out, and a promise for when he's managed this heroic task. "Go on."

Kintyre buries his face in my hair, just over my ear, and blurts: "I don't like being handed things just because of an accident of birth. Because of the blood I happen to have."

"But you've never shied away from demanding things because of who you are," I say, and kiss his neck to encourage him to keep going.

"Things I'm owed because of the things I've done," Kin corrects, his breath humid on the shell of my ear. I shudder, and I can feel his lips curling into that seductive smirk I know oh so well, and adore oh so profoundly. "Give me a knighthood and wealth for performing services to the kingdom, sure. But I hate that Turn Hall and the running of Turnshire, the stewardship of Lysse, and all the wealth and ballyhoo that goes with it, falls on my shoulders just because I'm the offshoot of that old bastard."

Frowning, I push back just enough to meet Kin's blue, blue eyes, but not far enough to give the impression that we're done with our little game.

"Is this you hating your privilege, or hating that your privilege comes from that elfcock arsehole that sired you?"

Kintyre shrugs and bites his bottom lip, looking away. His hand wanders down my belly, down, down, and I let him, flex my hips back to give him room to work, because he can't answer this one, I don't think. Maybe he doesn't know himself. And he'd just get angry and frustrated, and my chances for a second round of sweaty, athletic evening would be ruined in the process.

"No big trothing ceremony?" he breathes into my ear while twisting his wrist, and that is dirty, that is *cheating*, that is *foul play*, because that Writer-be-damned arsehole knows that I will agree to anything he asks when he does it like that.

"F-fine," I stutter out. And then I grab him by those big stupid ears of his and drag his mouth onto mine.

The next morning, Kintyre and I join the ladies in their parlor—the lovely salon with the squashy furniture, which I resent that they've taken control of. They're all thrilled, of course. They fawn, and fetch tea, and the Farnith girl demonstratively bemoans our dearth of instruments, or else she'd play something for Kin. They are all fluttering like a flock of self-important pigeons.

When everyone seems as settled as they can be—Kin on the sofa with five women ringing him in like a hydra, and me by the window with the sweet, small little thing who seems to think her way into Kintyre's bed is through mine—Kin holds out his hands for silence and says, "I have an announcement to make."

A titter washes through the assembly, and I hold back a grimace.

"An announcement about what, Sir Turn?" the Gyre girl flutters, and she's the only one of the gaggle who refers to my Pair by his soldierly title instead of his noble one. I wonder what she thinks that will achieve.

"Well, my marriage, of course," Kin says, flashing that toothy, heroic smile at her that he saves for official ceremonies he despises, and events he wishes he could run away from.

Another titter circles the flock, and this time, I can't hold back my snort.

"With so many fine representatives of the Great Families of Hain here," Kin goes on, and I have to bite my cheek to keep from laughing at the way he's winding them up. Oh, it's cruel, no doubt, but it's also just so damned *funny*. "It makes sense to do it now. Of course, it *was* difficult to come to a decision."

"But you have?" the one who was wanting music asks, the question bursting out of her like an arrow from a mishandled crossbow.

"Indeed," Kintyre says. He takes a deep breath, relishing the way the ladies hang on his every word, and then says, with great pride and pomp: "Bevel and I have decided to be trothed the day before Solsticetide."

Air rushes out of the lungs of all six girls in one long, confused groan. Forget needing instruments in this salon, because that is the most beautiful sound I have ever heard.

Kintyre goes on: "Bevel and I are so humbled that your families chose to send you as representatives for the ceremony, and we're only sorry that we had to make you wait so long for us to decide when to hold it. We're utter rotters," he says with a mischievous twinkle, deliberately pretending to misconstrue the reason the women are here. "But Cook tells me you have Solsticetide well in hand for Turn Hall, so we thought that could free us up to plan the trothing. It's so kind of you to do so!"

There's a sniffle, and the little woman beside me turns her back to the room and covers her eyes with one hand, the other fisted into her stomach. All the glee I had felt at pulling off our prank boils away in my swift and sudden shame.

"If you didn't want us, you should have just said so," she hisses at me damply, when I try to put a comforting hand on her shoulder. She ducks out of the way so she can glare at me full in the face with wet eyes and tear-streaked cheeks. "There was no cause to be cruel."

"We didn't mean to—we didn't invite—"

"You think you're so clever, but you're not," she says. "You're just an entitled elfcock, like every other noble bastard of the blood." And then she *spits* on my boot.

"What—" Kintyre says, standing immediately, but

he doesn't go on when the woman turns on her heel and marches out of the room. The rest of the women hiss and glare, close ranks, and follow after her.

Kin looks at me, helpless.

"I thought it was funny," I say, and Kintyre shrugs.

"Women," he says, dismissing their emotional overreaction with a hand wave.

Four of the six women depart before breakfast the next day, and the remaining two—Gyre and Farnith—remain ostensibly to help us with the trothing ceremony preparations. Of course, they also drop less and less subtle hints about surrogacy, and bloodlines, and heirs each time we are forced into a room with them to discuss flower arrangements and ribbon color schemes.

Still stinging from how badly our early bit of cleverness turned on us, we are very clear and blunt. I explain to these two women that we are entirely aware that an heir needs to be discussed, but that it will *not* be with two relative strangers and in advance of our trothing.

The Farnith girl departs the day after that. But Gisella Gyre, in a moment of resolve that impresses me enough that I decide to learn her name, just thrusts out her chin and says, "Perhaps not now, but eventually, you will need a woman. I have nothing at home, and there are no other prospects for me. I can be patient. And until such a time as you decide you want me to be the mother of your Pair's child—if, indeed, you ever do decide you want me—then I'm resolved to be your friend, Bevel Dom. The Writer knows you will have few enough of those when it becomes clear that House Turn is gamboling happily toward its own extinction. Now, amethyst and russet, of course, in the ribbon arrangement, but what do you think of Sheil-purple, and a bit of white to brighten things up, as well?"

The only thing I can do is nod, dumbfounded and poleaxed.

I didn't expect to find an ally among my enemies.

We hold the trothing the day before Solsticetide, so that the staff needn't decorate twice. The mid-winter evergreens are enough for us, interspersed with some hot-house flowers in amethyst, peach, russet, and deep purple that Gisella sourced from Writer knows where this time of year and wouldn't let us pay for.

"My gift," she said, when I asked her how she'd managed it. "The realities of nobility aside, I've never seen a Pair so revoltingly smitten with one another. That's something worth celebrating with some flowers, no matter how much the cost, wouldn't you say?"

Gisella Gyre is either going to be my most strident opponent or my most vicious supporter one day, and the more time I spend in her calculating, clever company, the more I realize I want her on my side. The coquettish mask she wore while trying to lure Kintyre has completely fallen away, and I find I prefer this thoughtful, blunt, intelligent woman instead. She reminds me of Pip.

I'm not changing my mind about sharing Kintyre with a woman, but if I were to see fit to enter a dwarvish arrangement, I wouldn't mind it with Gisella, I think. Except that there's something about her that is just... so decidedly *unsexual*. I don't desire her in the least, and I don't think Kintyre has even contemplated her in that way. I want to do right by her, yes, but more like a... a mentor than a conquest.

I have a sudden vision of Gisella in the Shadow's Mask, and wonder if I have, perhaps, found my own successor. Of course, to have a successor, I first have to *be* the Shadow Hand, and...

I keep telling myself that it's because I'm busy. There's the trothing to plan, and Solsticetide, and after that, the planting season, and it's just never the right *time*. The mask can wait. There's no hurry.

The Shadow's Mask is still in the back of my cabinet, still shrouded in its black velvet bag, and it would be easy to just... tell Gisella the Word, give her the mask, and... let the responsibility go. Almost as immediately as I think that, my guts curdle. No, I can't betray Forsyth's trust in me like that. I can't just... give it up because it's difficult. Because it *scares* me.

I may not think myself a good man, but I know for certain that I have never been a coward.

And then the trothing day is here. The sun has risen, I have bathed, and Gisella and I are in my study, where she is putting the final touches on my ensemble. Kin and I are both wearing black leather trousers and riding boots. Our shirts are cream silk, and each of us were fitted for brand new waistcoats of Turn-russet picked out in gold-thread stripes and keys, and sashes of Dom-amethyst embroidered with the hammers that are my House Sigil. The flower crowns we'll both be wearing for the ceremony are a secret, though. We wove them ourselves, for one another, and we were allowed to keep them understated—thank the Writer—and void of the girlish trailing ribbons that younger couples usually indulge in. Gisella has been kind to us in that.

I look up at myself in the mirror that Keriens had hauled into my study so that Kintyre and I could get dressed apart. I look as fine as I have ever looked in my life: well-rested, fresh-shaved, my hair trimmed, my clothes neat and new, and a small, ridiculous smile curling in the corner of my mouth.

Would I look so foolishly happy—would I *be* so recklessly, foolishly happy—had I not faced down all those other things that had scared me? The way the mask scares me still?

What if I had not run away to the Urlish wars with Kintyre? What if I had never stayed away, roaming the roads with him? What if I had fled the battlefields, quit the combat lessons, shoved aside the pencil and parchment because I was ashamed of my inability to read, and humiliated by Kintyre's patient attempts to teach me? What if I had given in to Bootknife, or the Viceroy, rather than clenching down on my fear and accepting the pain they doled out as the price for remaining unbroken? What if I had never screwed up my courage and confessed my feelings to Kintyre? Where would I be, now, if I had never done what scared me?

Certainly not here.

So I put aside, forever, thoughts of handing the Shadow's Mask over to Gisella. Instead, I lead her through the servants' passages down to the back courtyard, where the bowl of the fountain has been piled high with brush for tonight's bonfire, and a freshly made broom stands upright in a stone holder, waiting for Kin and I to jump it.

PART SIX

After we have each goggled at the handsome sight of our Pair in our trothing finery, after we have spoken our vows, after we have wreathed the broom with our flower crowns, after we have set the brush of the broom alight, and after we have jumped it, hands clenched together and laughter ringing across the courtyard at the ridiculous spectacle we make of our athleticism, there's a feast. We move inside to the ballroom, which has been reclaimed as an entertaining space for the night. Cook has outdone herself, especially considering that all of Lysse will be descending upon Turn Hall in the morning, and she's been busy preparing for that. The small group of friends and family we've invited early to Turn Hall eat well and dance long into the night.

All six of my brothers, all six of their wives, and all thirteen of my nieces and nephews have made the journey to Lysse, along with my pa and mum. The Dom horde brought along wines and cakes, and food enough for their contributions to the Solsticetide festivities, for they have been invited to stay for those as well, and Cook has accepted the help of my sisters-in-law in the kitchen gamely. From the Turn contingency, we invited all the staff as guests, and made it clear that everyone in the household would have to serve themselves tonight, because no one is to be working. The Pointes attend as well, of course, and Capplederry is the star of the after-dinner entertainment, chasing young Lewko and all the Doms under the age of twelve around the snow-covered lawn. A very select handful of representatives from Turnshire are also in attendance—the mayor and his family, the head of Kin's tenants' group, and the hapless schoolmaster, into whom Gisella digs her claws quite early in the proceedings. The man seems to be happily caught, though, so I don't bother to effect a rescue.

We drink barrels of ale and winter sherry, and dance until our feet ache. Before the clock strikes midnight, I pull my trothed up the servants' stairway, into my study, and from there, into our bedroom. Some cheeky servant or two has put fresh linens on our bed—*white*, as if there was a hymen to break here!—and sprinkled it with amethyst and deep russet petals and leaves, an inviting carpet of foliage that gives off a splendidly intoxicating fragrance when I lever Kintyre up, bodily, and drop him onto that delicious, plump arse of his right on top of it.

"Steady on!" Kintyre slurs, and our entire world is golden and syrupy with drink and happiness.

We have all the time in the world, and our lovemaking is slow and intense. The room is filled with the musk of sweat and sex, and I'm unaccountably grateful for the pitcher of cool water the selfsame cheeky servants left on our bedside table. When Kin and I have curled around one another above the blankets, we recount the day, petting each other's chests and stomachs, reluctant to be out of touch.

"I thought I looked ridiculous with flowers in my hair," Kin says. "But they made you look dashing."

"I'm many things," I tell my trothed, "but dashing will never be one of them."

He harrumphs and kisses my fingertips.

"So, now what?" I ask.

"Well, now we sleep, I think," Kin says, deliberately

misunderstanding what I'm asking. "Unless you've got another one in you."

"Har har," I say. "I mean... Solsticetide, and the New Year."

"We'll take it as it comes," Kin says.

"And the other things?" I ask, my worries eating at me even now. Even in my marriage bed. "What *about* an heir?" I ask into his hair.

"It'll sort itself out," Kintyre says. "We've got lots of time."

"Not too much," I caution. "Or you'll be like poor Pointe—needing to take an apprentice because your own son is too young."

"Apprentice," Kin says thoughtfully. "It's appealing. Wish we could. Just pick some clever orphan lad, one who already knows his sums and his manners."

"A babe," I counter. "One we could raise on stories of his old pa's adventures."

"You sure like them when they're small."

"And you sure don't," I point out.

Kintyre grunts and shifts. "Afraid I'm going to squash them, aren't I?"

I kiss him again, soft and sweet. "Don't worry. I won't let you squash ours."

"Who says we're having one?" Kintyre says, wrapping his arms around my back.

"Kin, you need an heir of your blood," I say reasonably. "And I think, now that we're trothed, I could handle you... sowing your wild oats one final time for a good cause."

"Oh, *would* you?" Kintyre snorts. "How magnanimous of you, dearest."

"You say it like I don't intend to be in the room with you," I say with a sharkish grin.

"Or in the bed."

"To an extent. The child has to be yours, unaccountably. And of course, I'd pick the woman."

"Oh, you *would*, would you?" Kintyre says. He leans back, and runs his hand through my hair. "She'll have to be short. Blonde. Dark blue eyes."

"Why?"

"So the babe looks like you, too," Kintyre says softly.

"Oh, my soft-hearted lump," I whisper against his mouth.

"No, no, use the other word," Kintyre says, pulling back, refusing to kiss me properly until I've given in. "I like that one best."

"My trothed," I say, grinning, and so what if I sound like an infatuated sop? I *am* one.

"Trothed," Kintyre agrees. "Let's just be that for now. The father part of things can happen later. Now, *trothed*, come up here."

It's spring, and love is in the air. Much to Pointe's chagrin. His apprentice Menkin runs off with the kitchen lass as soon as the first blossoms are on the pear trees. Capplederry, too, is in love, though only in the way that cats love doting on young boys. He has abandoned us forever, it seems, to take up residence at Law Manor. I can't say our groom is too put out by this betrayal, though.

Turn Hall is finally void of all maidens, even Gisella. I think she still hoped that after our trothing, we would announce our intention of Kintyre siring a child, and that her proximity would make her an attractive candidate, but she is also a woman who lives without illusions. If we didn't pick her before, we weren't likely to pick her now. She returned to Kingskeep after Solsticetide, but keeps me well furnished in her own brand of dark and sarcastic gossip from the capital.

Besides that, she seems to have taken up a *corre-spondence* with Turnshire's schoolmaster. I have a feeling she'll be telling her noble father to go stuff his head up a gryffon's arse about his nagging her to net herself a noble marriage soon enough. I'd like it if she moved into Turn-shire. I could begin teaching her swordplay, then. Maybe float the idea of teaching her how to translate what she knows about managing household accounts into manag-ing bribe purses—though I suspect this woman might be better at information gathering and informant manage-ment than I may ever be.

And while Kin and I have been batting around the idea of an heir, we both agree that we would never seek a mother from one of the other Great Families. No, that's too complicated. We're thinking of spending the summer getting to know the farmers and tenants around Turn Hall—we'd pick one of those women, sturdy and clever and kind, someone from Lysse, someone who'd have no agenda or desire to pull political strings, but who could be nearby and involved in the babe's life if she so chose. Kintyre, having had his own mother ripped so cruelly from him at such a young age, has no desire to inflict that kind of pain on a young woman doing us the very incred-ible kindness of making us fathers.

But all of these worries are vague and remain mostly in the back of my head. For I find, in the wake of my trothing, that I'm a very, very happy man. I wake with a smile on my face, I go to bed with a smile, and I'm told I smile entirely too much while smoking my pipe after meals, and that it's disturbing one of the footmen.

Kin and I have no trothing tour, though we do travel to Kingskeep a fortnight after Solsticetide for a few days of merrymaking, taking in the galleries, and delivering the highly fibbed version of *The Vicious Vanquish of the Viceroy* to our printer, along with Kin's accompanying woodblock stamp illustrations. Now that we are in Turn Hall permanently, we've decided to use our royalty payments to fund a second Free School on the opposite side of Lysse. Walking to Turnshire is often too daunting for the children who live near Faversquare, and it isn't all that fair.

It feels odd to not take the earnings purse and immediately use it to buy field rations, new tack, or to repair or replace clothing and weaponry. If there was ever a sign that we were no longer wandering adventurers, this is it. Or, no, it's that I no longer wear my sword belt festooned with its tiny metal tubes of precious spices everywhere I go. I have considered turning the tubes over to Cook, but I can't give away *all* my secrets.

One day, Kin and I are going to be nostalgic for something we often ate on the road, and I want to be able to produce it.

As soon as the ground is thawed enough, the focus of the estate shifts from paperwork and catching the lord up on the last two decades' worth of financials and habits, and over to the farms. The tenant cottages are seen to— wattle-and-daub painted, roofs repaired, leaks mended. I'm finally able to spend a few days with a carpenter and a glazier team who teach me how to re-shim and seal windows. I repair Turn Hall's ballroom windows by myself soon after. Yeah, I could have hired those same workmen, but I was itching to dig in and do something for myself. Learn a skill, apply it, and work with my hands.

When the first buds of green appear on the branches of the covey forest, the head of the farmers' group informs Kin of the planting bee date. Though Forsyth never went into the fields to push a plowshare, or sowed seed himself, Kintyre and I have no objection to doing so. All hands are welcome on a farm when there's work to be done, and Kintyre and I are no strangers to hard labor and physical exertion. In fact, after our winter of desk work, we welcome it.

Dauntless and Karlurban appreciate it as well, enjoying the daily rides to and from the far-flung farms, and the opportunity to stretch their legs and try to outpace one another.

Kintyre and I are just home from the last of the season's planting, filthy with field-mud and pleasantly exhausted, when a commotion drags us out of the stables and around to the front drive. There's a racket of shouting, and I catch Pointe's distinctive growl amid the voices, yelling: "Oi! Hold up there!"

The skid of booted feet on gravel comes closer to our side of the house and, still imbued with the instincts of battle, Kin and I bolt in the direction of the sound, ready to intercept. The person fleeing is faster than I thought they'd be. They fly around the corner before we can get there. A black blur slams into Kin's broad chest, staggering back a few steps and giving me a glimpse of a dark, surprised face with a broad nose and whites showing all around jet-black eyes. Human, but unfamiliar.

The man—the lad, I correct myself as I duck down and aim to tackle him to the spring-damp lawn—doesn't waste air on a shout of surprise. He just rolls backward, under my grasping reach, flipping himself neatly over his head and back onto his feet before Kin has really even registered what he knocked into. Pointe comes skidding around the corner, and all four of us size each other up, warily, for a second or two, before Kin surges forward to try to pin the black-clad boy.

He evades by leaping high and *stepping on Kin's shoulder*, flipping over mid-air, landing in another tightly controlled forward roll, and rising straight into a dead run.

"Bloody hell," Pointe pants, watching the lad bolt

toward the stables. "I've never seen anything like that."

"I have," Kin says grimly, and is off after the lad like a bloodhound.

I'm straight on his heels, and we catch up to the boy as he's trying to yank Dauntless's head around. The horse—the Shadow's Horse—has never taken kindly to strangers riding him, and while the lad tries to get a foot in the stirrup, Dauntless gives a rough jolt, body-checking the boy onto the cobbles. Clearly offended by his rough treatment, Dauntless lifts a dwarvish-steel shod hoof. I dash forward and haul the horse sideways by his bridle before he can strike at the terrified lad's face.

Kintyre wrestles the lad upright with a grip under his armpits, and the shock of the attack from the horse shakes loose. The lad comes back to himself quickly. He bends double at the waist, quick as an eel, wraps his legs around Kintyre's neck, and twists, using Kin's own mass to bring him to the ground hard.

Fury bursts in my guts, tainted with a fear that Kintyre is seriously hurt. Kin groans and rolls onto his back, only winded, thank the Writer, though there are vivid red marks on the flesh of his throat. The lad gets his feet under him again, and makes for Karlurban and the stupid groom who's stopped to gawp instead of getting the horses inside and away from the scuffle when it was clear the lad was after a mount.

Pointe has his second wind back, though, and intercepts with a quick punch to the back of the lad's head and a hand in his collar. The boy stumbles, stunned, and Pointe is holding him out far enough that the lad can't swipe his feet out from under him or get his hands on anything but Pointe's wrist.

"Slippery bugger!" Pointe says, whirling the lad around to face us.

I help Kintyre sit up, checking his neck as I do. He is

hacking hard, trying to suck in a breath, and already one of the red marks is purpling up.

"You're lucky you didn't break his neck, you little wretch!" I snarl at the lad. "I'd have ended you where you stand!"

The lad blanches, and I straighten, letting my trothed lean back against my legs as he gets his breath back. We both take a good look at our interloper.

Dangling from Pointe's fist is a boy of about fourteen or fifteen, with the dark skin and cloud of tightly coiled hair of the Gadotian Southerners. Or, if I was to be fanciful about it, the Pirates of the Sunsong Sea. His attire is all black, with a swath of blood-red around his waist holding a curved sword—which he never drew on us, I realize. I wonder how much damage he was really willing to cause to get a horse. And now that I'm thinking of pirates, all I can see in the lad's face is—

"Isobin," Kintyre groans, finishing the thought for me.

The lad's jet-black eyes bug out a little, and I know Kin's scored a hit.

Kintyre levers himself to his feet, twisting his head back and forth and scrunching his shoulders, assessing the damage. He doesn't wince, so that's good. But his eyes are half-lidded with wary anger. He and the pirate queen had not parted on good terms.

"So, you're her, what... brother?" Kin asks.

"Son," the boy says, and all the fight drains out of him. Pointe lets him go slowly, one finger at a time, worried the lad will bolt again if given half a chance. And I honestly think he might.

"And why are you here, at Turn Hall, trying to steal my horses, Prince of Pirates?" Kintyre asks, with a lot less sarcasm than I would have expected from him. Maybe I should have Velshi send for Madam Mouth to check him over, after all.

"Well, where else would tha dumb bitch dump me?" the boy mumbles, and crosses his arms across his chest.

"That's what we're asking," Pointe says.

But the moment he does, I *see* it.

"Writer, Kintyre—he's got... he's got your eyes," I breathe, and the rest of the revelation comes swift on the heels of that realization. I stagger back, toward the nearest bush, and flatten myself into the thick tangle of prickly branches. "Not the color, but the shape..."

"He what?" Pointe asks, and steps around the boy to peer at his face. "By the Writer," he says with awe. "And your lantern jaw."

Kintyre remains silent, but his face drains of all color, the red marks on his neck standing out in sharp, worrying contrast. He takes a step toward the lad, who straightens and thrusts his chin out, daring Kin to take a good look, to *comment*.

"*Why?*" Kin growls. Though of course, it's obvious *why* the child of the Pirate Queen Isobin would look like Kintyre Turn. Or at least, it *should* be obvious. I mean, Kintyre was there. We both were.

"Kin," I say softly. "Just... breathe for a second, please, and—"

"Why," Kintyre snarls now, stepping closer, nearly nose-to-nose with the lad. "Why didn't she tell me?"

"What for?" the lad sneers.

"What... what *for*?" Kintyre repeats, aghast. "You... you're my..."

"'M yer son," the boy says, and the truth of it smacks me between the eyes like a bag of rocks. "Go on, say it, hero."

"My son," Kintyre repeats, undeterred. "Why didn't Isobin tell me?"

"Would you have cared?" the lad challenges. "Would

you have *come?*"

"Yes!" Kintyre roars, and I can tell that this was not the answer the lad was expecting.

"Well, didn't want to share, aye?" he dithers, and then adds: "You know now. The capt'n'd only get fifteen years with me, anyway. You get the rest."

"The rest of what?" Pointe asks, looking back and forth between Kintyre and the lad, confusion writ large on his face.

"His life," I say. "Isobin doesn't let men serve on her ship. She barely tolerated transporting us. The moment the lad hit his maturity—"

"I was off!" the boy snarls.

"And what, she just dumped you on our doorstep?" I ask, aghast. "No note, nothing?"

"*His* doorstep," the lad says with a jerk of his head at my trothed. "And what need's a note when I can speaks for meself?"

"*Our* doorstep," I correct him.

"This is all yer fault," the lad says. "If you'd stayed out on the road, if you'd never shut yourself up like a stuffy prat, the capt'n'd never had nowhere to send me. But now, she wants me to grow up a *lordling.*"

"I highly doubt she would have bent her rule for you if we'd stayed adventuring," I scoff, and then I lift my hands away from my body, showing off the mud stains up my calves. "And do we look like we just shut ourselves up in the Hall?"

"Bevel, peace," Kintyre says softly, and I realize suddenly that I've been shouting. That I'm... angry. Angry? Yes, angry, I think.

Here is the child I've been hoping for, but no sweet babe to smother in kisses and raise with my values. Instead, he's a brawling, petulant, poorly spoken thug. How infuriating. How *unfair.*

"By the Writer's left nutsack," I say, after I've had a chance to calm down a bit. The crassness of the swear makes the lad snort, and then he covers his mouth with his hand, like he's annoyed he caught himself laughing. "You gotta be more careful with what you wish for, Kin—I think Pip's been Reading in. Seems our problems about a blood heir have been solved."

Kintyre chuckles at that, and I try not to be too hurt by how pleased he looks. He never really wanted a baby, anyway. I shouldn't be surprised.

"So, if you're Kin's kid, then why were you scarpering for the stables?" Pointe asks.

"Didn't ask to be dumped here, did I?" the lad mutters mulishly.

"So, what, you were just going to steal a horse and take off into the wilds? Live off the land and your sword?"

"Worked for Kintyre Turn, didn't it?" he says, jerking his chin at his father again. "Why not me, too?"

"First off, Kin wasn't alone," I say, pointing at my own nose. "Second, you're, what... fourteen?"

"Fifteen!" the lad protests. "Or else I'd still be aboard ship!"

"Kin was eighteen when he left," I say, deliberately not adding that, actually, I was just barely sixteen when I snuck away from the forge to follow the golden-haired lad who'd stopped to have his stallion shoed.

"Doesn't matter! I can take care of—"

"What's your name, son?" Kintyre interrupts, the question intent.

The lad gulps down the rest of whatever he was going to say and scowls. "Wyndam," he says after a mulish silence. "Wyndam Turn."

Pointe joins us for dinner, to give the report he had been coming to deliver in the first place, and to help us settle Wyndam into the house. Perhaps to frighten the lad into staying in the house, too, for after, he tells a tale about missing sheep in the back farthings and a wildly horrific story about a monster roaming the spit between the edge of Lysse and the Sunsong. It does its job, too, if the look on Wyndam's face is anything to go by. Like his... his *father*... Wyndam Turn is a shite liar.

It seems as if the new Lordling Turn has used up all his bravery—for one day, at least—which is a relief. We see the lad into the room that used to be mine, and the gossip in Turn Hall travels fast enough that by the time we've made our goodnights, Keriens, Velshi, and two footmen are waiting outside our room for us.

"In the morning," I tell them. "Details in the morning."

"Will he be here in the morning?" Keriens asks bluntly.

Kintyre and I exchange a glance, and then Velshi says: "Mr. Toflan has offered to, ah, keep an eye on the horses tonight. And Mr. Kartin"—the gardener, I know now—"has mentioned that he has quite a bit more pruning to do this evening than he thought. Might keep him up all night."

Recce the footman clears his throat and adds: "And I'm woefully behind on my boot blacking, I'm afraid, sir. Thought I might do it in the family hallway, if you don't mind, sir, where the lamps are brightest."

"Oh, by all means," Kintyre says with a smirk.

We bid our staff goodnight and head back to our room.

"So," Kintyre says slowly as we strip down for bed. "Thoughts?"

"I don't know, Kin," I say, settling down under the

covers. He curls against my side, head on my shoulder, and looks up at me through his lashes. "I feel sort of like we're holding him prisoner."

Kintyre scoffs. "I don't think Turn Hall could hold Wyndam any more than it could hold me. If he really wants to go, he will."

"You don't think he wants to?"

Kintyre runs one hand over my stomach—not sexy, just comforting, his calluses catching on my hair. "He could have broken Pointe's hold any time he wanted."

"Yeah, that's what I thought, too. So he wants to stay, but he doesn't want to admit it?"

"I think he's scared. I think he wants... comfort."

"Speaking from experience?" I ask.

"Leaving was the scariest thing I ever did," Kintyre admits. "Every night I wanted to turn around and go home. Wyndam's everything has been taken away from him. This is the next best thing. We can make it..."

"Home for him."

"Yeah. How are you feeling about all of this, Bev?" Kin asks, voice low, as if he's afraid to ask the question too loudly, afraid of Wyndam hearing the answer.

"I don't know," I say, equally low, for the same reasons. "All jumbled up, I guess? I'm happy for you, that the problem of an heir has been solved, that you have a son. And a son who seems to follow in your reckless, blowhard, soldierly footsteps. But I'm also mad at Isobin for keeping this secret, for keeping him from you. From us. I'm angry that we missed his childhood. But I'm relieved, too, because fifteen years ago, I don't think you would have... would have *stayed*. And I would have— you would have—"

Kintyre kisses that worry right out of my mouth.

"I might have stayed. You never know," he says, and I don't bother to tell him that the lie isn't as comforting as he thinks it is. "I'm here now, though. We're here now."

"We are."

"And I love you," Kin says simply, with a shrug, like it's the most obvious fact in the known world. And I guess, in a way, it is.

Kintyre Turn loves Bevel Dom. How silly of me to have forgotten.

"And you have a son."

Kintyre makes a noise into my armpit that I realize, after a moment, is a *giggle*. "I have a son," he says.

"A fine son, I think," I say. "Might be able to teach you a thing or two about hand-to-hand combat."

"Handsome son," Kintyre says. "He'll look excellent in Turn-russet. We should have something made up right away."

"Whoa up there, pacer. Perhaps let him get used to being here before you smother him in russet."

"Clever son," Kintyre challenges. "He knew to go for the horses."

"Mulish, stubborn, pigheaded, rude son," I counter.

"It's almost like we raised him," Kin teases.

"Yeah," I agree. Almost. But not quite.

Kintyre feels me go still, and sits up so he can look me in the eye. "Are you really satisfied with this?"

"Yeah," I say. "I am. I just..."

Kintyre cups my shoulder. "You wanted the baby."

"That seems like such a womanish thing to want," I admit. "The Lord Consort, the lady of the house, wants a baby."

"You're no woman," Kin says with a wicked glint in his eyes, his hand sliding lower. I bat it away before he can use that to distract me.

"That I'm not, Master Turn, but you're not derailing this conversation."

"One of those nights, is it?" Kin says with a put-upon sigh.

"I don't know," I admit, sitting up, too. The starlight through our window gilds my trothed in silver, and an ephemeral light that makes it look like he keeps sliding in and out of a fog. "I feel... wriggly. Unfinished?"

"*Not* superfluous. Not this again," Kin says. He picks up my hand to run his lips across my knuckles. "Because you know that you're—"

"No, I know," I say. "I know where I belong."

"Right here?" He kisses my knuckles again.

"Yeah, right here."

"But?"

"But," I agree. "But something. But... I don't know. I feel aimless. I was preparing to raise a baby, and now he's already half a man. So, now what?"

"Mother-hen the rest of Hain," Kintyre says. When I blink at him in confusion, he puts my hand down and sighs at me like I'm a particularly stupid villain's hench-man. "*The mask*, Bev. You still haven't put it on, have you?"

"No."

"Why?"

"I don't... I don't know. I'm scared?"

"Of?"

"I'm not sure. The mask burned Bootknife."

"Bootknife was a sadistic sonofabitch."

"Then maybe of becoming someone else? Of chang-ing? Of... not being this, *me*, anymore?"

"Forsyth didn't change," Kintyre points out.

"How would either of us know that? We barely knew him before."

Kintyre grimaces. I'm not wrong.

"I think you're scared because you're afraid you'll enjoy it," Kin says at length, in one of his rare fits of a philosophical mood. "You're afraid of having something that is separate from me, from us, from this." He makes a gesture between us.

"Hush," I say slowly. "That's... more insightful than I'm used to from you, trothed."

"Oh no," Kintyre scolds. "You know how much I like that word. Now I'm the one who won't let you derail this conversation. No 'trothed' nonsense until this is sorted, Bev."

I flop down on the bed, frustrated with my inability to articulate my frustration. *Again.*

"Look. I'll make it easy," Kin says, and climbs out of bed. He nips into my office and comes back with the mask. Yes. Of course, he would know where I had stashed it. I have no secrets from Kintyre Turn. I never have. "Put it on. Go have adventures without me. I'll be here when you get back."

"But I don't *want* to," I say, and the words, the honesty of it, catch in my throat. "Kin, I don't want to do anything without you. I don't want to live any part of my life without you. Not ever. Never again."

Kintyre pulls the mask out of the bag and holds it out between us, intimate and gentle. "You and I both know that you'll immediately come back and tell me everything. And Forssy said most of the job was done from home, anyway. We'll still do this together, only this time, you'll be the hero."

"Unnamed."

"Can't have all the glory," he teases. "Come on. I've been in the center of things long enough. It's your turn, Bevel Dom. I'll be here for you when you take the mask off at the end of each night. I always will be. This doesn't change anything."

"I..." I reach out and take the mask with the tips of my fingers. "Promise?"

"Always."

I nod once, firmly, not sure what, exactly, is calcifying in my throat, what emotion or truth is dying to crawl up my tongue and between my teeth. It's something good, though. Something honest. Perhaps something too honest. I can't say it.

I kiss Kintyre instead, relocate whatever it is in my mouth and put it into his, so he can taste it, so he can know. And he does. He is smiling when we pull apart, a smug, shit-eating grin that I have come to adore and loathe in equal measure.

"Is this it, then?" Kin asks, shuffling so that his legs are outside mine, bracketing me in like an ornery, over-protective living cage. "You put on the mask, you stop fussing like a woman, and we go back to the way we were?"

"Obtuse and self-important?" I ask with a snort.

Kintyre grins mischievously and pinches my stomach, making me jump and writhe. "No, *happy*. Arse."

"Happy?" I muse, turning the mask over so the face is pointed toward my lover. "Is that what we were?"

"Yes, of course," Kin replies, without the smallest hitch of hesitation. "Always."

"Even when we were annoyed with one another? Even when I was ready to wallop you?"

"Even then."

"Okay. Fine. *Happy*. Pah."

"Put it on," Kintyre urges. "Go on."

Under the careful watch of the one I care for most in the world, I raise the mask to my face. "You'll pull it off me if it starts to burn?"

"It won't. You're worthy."

"But if it does."

Kin huffs. "Fine, yeah. I will. If it does. But it won't. Stop stalling."

"I'm not stalling."

"You are *stalling*."

"No."

"Then say the Word."

I'm tempted to keep teasing him. To draw this out. But I also sort of... want it over with. The fear of it, the fear of what it might do to my flesh, what the duties of being the Shadow Hand might mean to my life, to my relationship with Kin, to my place in the kingdom... it's exhausting. I'm so tired of second-guessing myself, my worth, every hour of every day.

Time to give in.

"I love you," I tell him.

He smiles, but doesn't say it back. He doesn't need to. I already know.

In the quiet, ember-lit darkness of our bedroom, I Say the Word, and slip the cool, tinglingly magical Shadow's Mask over my face.

It feels like coming home.

HAPPINESS

This is the second of the stories I originally wrote to debut on Wattpad. Also in Forsyth's rambly POV, this one is set directly after the conclusion of *The Forgotten Tale*. Pip is downstairs, talking over what just happened with Elgar, while Forsyth has taken Alis upstairs to try to put her to bed.

(I love that I have the space to explore and celebrate not only the fantastical in this series, but also the small joys that make up the mundane domestic life of my characters, as well.)

When I was asked to write additional content, and after I had hit upon the shorts, and this format, it made sense to do a three-story set, placed, more or less, directly after the action of the centerpiece novels. The novellas are set in different parts of the chronology as a whole, but I decided that if I was going to write a story about a father speaking to his baby, then it made sense that I should also explore the immediate aftermath of the adventures said baby had just participated in.

Especially knowing, as I do, that Alis isn't likely to remember much—if any—of the events that are some of the most important moments in the lives of the people who love her most.

Well, now, my sweeting, how was that for an adventure?

"No!"

Hush, hush now. Don't sound so disappointed to be back, or you'll break your mother's heart.

"Mamamama!"

Yes, I know, all the interesting things are happening downstairs, and your terrible old da is making you come up here. Believe you me, my darling girl, all that we're going to do after you go to bed is have an extremely boring conversation.

Red wine and existential conversations with your... well, I shan't call him "uncle." Nor "grandfather." What shall we call him, my dear? This man who is something to you, but not what he wishes, and nothing that I am ready to admit. Not just yet.

"Bev?"

Wrong uncle, sweeting. But full marks for making the connection.

All the same, the point remains: downstairs will be important, but boring. Forget downstairs, sweeting.

Look at this—beautiful needlework, isn't it? Do you see? Right on the hem of your frock?

"Yah!"

I'll never break you of that, will I? You'll be saying "yeah" like a Bynnebakker blacksmith your whole life just to vex me, won't you?

"Yah! Yah!"

Of course. Look, see here, sweeting? Look at your frock. The little keys for House Turn, and the little sheep for House Sheil? Your grandmother—your namesake— embroidered this, you know. I wore it when I was your age. Your uncle Kintyre did, as well. I'm well pleased to have something of hers here, now.

And now... off it comes! That's right, arms up! Clever girl.

I shall preserve your frock, I think. Frame it, perhaps. I'd like to dry clean it first, but I haven't any idea if fairy-silk embroidery thread will hold up to the chemicals, and I would be sore disappointed if the needlework was ruined.

Now, my naked little wild thing, what do you say to a bath, hm?

"Wah wah wah!"

Wa-ter, sweeting. Do you think you can make it all the way to the end? Wa-ter. Oh! Such a scowl. Well now, you never learned that from me, I wager. Why don't you pick someone to go into the bath with you, hm? The duck? The submarine? The whale?

"'Derry!"

Ah, sweeting. I am sorry, but Capplederry is not here.

"'Derry! 'Derry!"

Oh now, please, Alis. Don't cry. I know, I know. I miss them, too.

"Bev n' Kin n' Wyn n' Bra n' Care n' 'Derry!"

That is an impressive list, sweeting. How about we—

"No, no! No no no!"

Oh. Oh, my poor wild thing, come here, come here. Cuddles, yes? Cuddles?

"Be-Behv. No no Bev."

Breaks my heart to see yours broken, my dear. It really does. I am so sorry. I am so very sorry. I miss them, too, you understand? I miss them very much, as well.

"Wah wah, Dah?"

Yes, that's right, my darling. Your da is crying. I don't think you've seen that before, have you? Your da is crying because he misses Bevel, and Kintyre, and Wyndam, and Bradri, and Caerdac, and Capplederry. And Lewko, and Pointe, and Dorthi, besides. But crying is all right, you see.

Because sadness is a necessary part of joy.

Yes, you are absolutely right to scowl at me like that. I

sound ridiculously soppy even to myself. Tissues for me, tissues for you... yes, I am utterly aware of the irony of drying your face only to put you into the bath. Okay. Hup, hup. The tub is all filled, and you have your... ah... dragon thing with the long neck. Well, don't look at me, my dear. I'm not the one who seems to think that you should be enamored with bizarre reptilian creatures with huge jaws and spiked tails and no ability to speak whatsoever. Such strange creatures, these dinos. I see no redeeming educational value in them, but who am I to deny your grandfather his delight in buying you these toys?

One arm—sudsy, sudsy—two arms... and these are your toes, my sweeting, and your feet, your ankles, the chubbiest calves and shins in the Overrealm, knees, thighs, bottom and tum, shoulders, neck, and dimples that could dim the sun, ears and nose, and here is your head! Now the baby's all clean, it's time for her bed! What do you think, sweeting? Should I write that one down in your Syth Rhymes book? Perhaps not. I just made that one up. I'm not certain your ma would say that counts.

Oh, you wiggly wee wild little thing. You giggly, gorgeous girl. Hold still, you squirmy, silly, slippery serpent. There now, all dry. Let's—Alis!

"Dah Dah Daaaah, 'ook, 'ook!"

Okay, yes, please let me catch up—when did you get this fast? I thought children weren't supposed to be quick on their feet for another few months, at least. What do you have there in your—by the Writer, *The Wizard of Oz*.

"'Ook! 'Ook!"

So imperious. Yes, I see it, sweeting. Okay, here, pajamas first, and then snuggles and bedtime reading. I'll take the book and set it by the—

"No!"

Alis? What's the matter?

"No! Noooo!"

Ah! Okay. Okay. I won't take it. You keep it, dearest.

"Dah! Daaaaah!"

Oh, honey. Oh, my poor girl. Come here, you. A blanket will do for now. Come on. Come have a cuddle with your da. Oh baby, shhh, shhhh. It's okay.

"Toto, Toto! Noooo."

Oh dear, more sniffles. I... see? Your da is crying again, too, my sweet. It's okay. Sorrow is a part of joy, remember? It's okay. You can be sad now. It's all right. We will never forget them, and that is the important part, isn't it, sweeting?

I miss them, too, but crying means that I love them still.

Shhh. Shhh. It's all well, my darling, my dearling, my sweet.

Sorrow just means that you were once happy, and that you will be so again.

Now then... now, now, then... hush-a-thee, hush-a-thee. Let's start at the beginning, shall we? I don't remember where we left off. Open the cover for me, Alis. There's a good girl. Read with me now?

The Wonderful Wizard of Oz, by Frank L. Baum:

Dorothy lived in the midst of the great Kansas prairies, with Uncle Henry, who was a farmer, and Aunt Em, who was the farmer's wife....

RHYMES

Being a Collection of Rhymes, Poems, and Prophecies from The Accidental Turn Series

One of the things you have to do when you create an entire world is remember that it can't actually read like it sprang, fully formed, from your head like a war goddess. There has to be history. Culture. Things like the little nursery rhymes and songs we sing to our children because they were sung to us, by parents and grandparents and extended family members who had the very same songs sung to them when they were children; things like the phrases and poems we read to mark the occasion of a wedding or funeral; favorite recipes and little sayings. The sort of shared sweetnesses and sorrows that show depth of culture and community in a few quick lines.

Tolkien knew well the power of song and poetry in world-building, and I made a point of using it, as well—not only because that's what Elgar Reed would have done, in imitating the Great Masters that came before him, but because I needed a world where it was clear that whole lives were being lived, that stories were happening off-page, in the places and parts of Hain and the Four Kingdoms that Elgar's Readers never saw.

Some of these poems were not presented in their entirety in the novels due to pacing, but I'm happy to say that you'll find the full versions here. In this instance, at least, not everything has to remain hidden in the margins.

FOR COUNTING TOES

One wee goblin, and one maid o' the lake.
One small dwarf, and one big krake.
One fairy, one centaur, one elf tall and wise,
and here is one dragon, king of the skies!
That leaves just two, love, this one and that,
one for your mother, and one for your da!

FOR SOOTHING SLEEPY BEASTS

Sleep now, my baby, and hear my sweet rhyme:
The Writer will come to us all in his time.
The books, they all close,
Our tales all conclude,
We're all for the Shelf, asleep and sublime.

So dream now, my child, of adventures to come.
Of laughter, of starlight; the moon and the sun.
Our children, our sequels
Spin out 'cross the years,
To continue our stories when our Chapter's done.

FOR MOONLIGHT AND SNUGGLES

Sleep now, sweet princess, my lady so fair.
There are charms braided up in your fall of sweet hair.
Sweet dreams, they wait, at the top of the stair,
Of ribbons and rainbows, and laughter to spare.

Sleep now, my darling, the sun's gone to bed.
So lay down, oh, lay down, your sweet little head.
Hush now, oh, hush now, believe in no dread.
For all of your troubles are turned out and fled.

Dream now, my child, of the stars and the moon.
Dream of adventures in ships and on dune.
Dream of a morning, for it comes all too soon.
And wake soon, my sweet, to the skylark's bright tune.

For Calling Children In From Play

Ah! The fields are dappled over, my love,
And the spring sings high and sweet!
Ah! The fairies flit and spin, my love,
And so it's time for us to meet!

The sun sinks ever lower, my love,
It marks an end to play.
So come straight to my side, my love,
Now at the close of day.

Come not through murky forest, my love
Where trolls and goblins bide.
Come not o'er standing pools, my love
Where kelpies wait and hide.

Come not through vasty deserts, my love
Where sun and djinn are cruel.
Come not through the icy wastelands, my love
Where reflections baffle fools.

Come not past cavern mouths, my loveCheck indents
When they issue smoke and steam.
For those are the homes of dragons, my love

Where they hoard things bright with gleam.

Heed not to the call of sirens, my love,
Nor any creature deep.
For they long to sing away children, my love,
To hold, to drown, and to keep.

Go not through the lofty halls, my love,
Made of fir, or ash, or pine.
For those are the realms of the elves, my love,
And to trespassers they are not kind.

Nor too, through the deep mountain kingdoms, my
love,
Though the dwarves are a good and fair race.
They like not surprise from strangers, my love,
When they find folk out of their place.

Oh, the road goes ever onward
No end to sea and sky.
And Quests may call you forward,
But many go awry.

Just promise, heed my word, love,
Wherever that you roam:
Ensure your eyes stay on the route,
For that will bring you home.

When you come to me, my dear sweet love,
Come safe, come sure, and come true.
For adventures are all well and good, my love,
But home is now calling for you.

Come only to the parlor, my love,
Come only down the stair,

Come to the fire with me, my love
And sit with your family there.

FOR SUMMONING A DEAL-MAKER SPIRIT

The Sigil that Never Fades
The Quill that Never Dulls
The Cup that Never Runs Dry
The Parchment that Never Fills
The Blade that Never Fails
The Desk that Never Rots
The Spirit that Never Lies

With these tools our world was born,
And with them can be broken.
Or born again.

FOR SUMMONING A DIFFERENT DEAL-MAKER SPIRIT

The Sigil that Never Dries
The Ash a Twelvemonth Still
The Heart of a Fallen Star
The Scale from the Siren's Lover
The Compass that Never Points Home
The Blood of He Who Calls
The Hearth that Warms a Shadow

With these tokens the sea awakes,
But be wary when you summon it,
For the Weather changes swift.

For Singing at a Wake

Far beyond the curtains of time and fate,
Beyond the misty vale of the Reader's tears,
The Writer sets down his quill, his intent filled,
The narrative played out, the ink bottle empty.

Here the story is finished, here joy abate
Here an end to pain, and an end to fears.
Here is the story told as He has willed.
Here the empty spot on the Shelf left for thee.

My heart fills with such a complex weight,
Grief, thick like syrup, in my breast appears,
My own tale, with you missing, I must rebuild.
Until my own The End also folds over me.

LULLABY

This rhyme has been featured once already in the book, but not like this!

You see, I have friends, and they are awesome friends, because every time a book comes out, they say, "How can we help?" One of these friends is Ashley Regimbal-Kung, whose name you'll see a lot in the acknowledgements in my books. We were talking one day about unconventional methods of book marketing, and I mentioned that I'd love to see my work inspire fan creators the same way I was inspired to create fanfiction and cosplay when I was younger.

I said that my fondest wish would be to hear some of the songs I'd written into this series scored and recorded by one of the myriad of extremely talented filkers out there. I didn't know it at the time, but Ashley started texting someone under the table.

And voilà, here we are, one year to the day of that conversation (almost), and my wish has come true. The wonderfully clever and talented Brigit O'Regan has created a version of Forsyth's lullaby to Alis that is so true to what I was originally thinking for this song that it's like she reached right inside my head and plucked it out. Almost like she used some magical Words on me.

But of course, there's no such thing as real magic. Right?

FOR CALLING CHILDREN IN FROM PLAY

J.M. Frey

As found in *The Forgotten Tale*

Ah! The fields are dappled over, my love,
And the spring sings high and sweet!
Ah! The fairies flit and spin, my love,
So it's time for us to meet!

The sun sinks ever lower, my love,
It marks an end to play,
So come straight to my side, my love,
Now at the close of day.

Come not through murky forest, my love
Where trolls and goblins bide,
Come not oe'er standing pools, my love
Where kelpies wait and hide.

Come not through vasty deserts, my love
Where sun and djinn are cruel,
Come not through icy lands, my love
Where reflections baffle fools.

Come not past cavern mouths, my love
When they issue smoke and steam,
For those are the homes of dragons, my love
Where they hoard things bright with gleam.

Heed not to the call of sirens, my love,
Nor any creature of deep,
They long to sing away children, my love,
To hold, to drown, and to keep.

THE ACCIDENTAL TALES

Go not through the lofty halls, my love,
Made of fir, or ash, or pine,
For those are realms of the elves, my love,
To trespassers they're not kind.

Nor too, deep mountain kingdoms, my love,
Though dwarves are a good and fair race,
They like not surprises from strangers, my love,
When they find folk out of their place.

Oh the road goes ever onward.
There's no limit to sea and sky.
Adventures may beckon you from your hearth,
But adventures can go awry

The world is wide and oh so deep!
Wish on stars from your window sill!
For the book of your life is still being written,
The author's hand rests upon the quill.

Just promise to heed my words, my love,
And wherever it is that you roam,
Ensure that you keep your eyes on the path,
For that is what will bring you home.

When you come to me, my dear sweet love,
Come safe, come sure, and come true.
For adventures are all well and good, my love,
But home is now calling for you.

Come only to the parlour, my love,
Come only down the stair,
Come to the fire with me, my love
And sit with family there.

For Calling Children in from Play

© J.M Frey

V.S.

not through vas ty__ deserts my love where the sun and djinn are__ cruel Come
not through i cy__ lands my love where re flec tions ba - ffle_ Fools Come
Not past ca - vern mouths my love When they is - sue smoke and steam For those
are the homes of dra-gons my love Where they hoard things bri ght with gleam Heed
Not the call of si - rens my love not a - ny crea ture deep They
long to sing away chil-dren my love to__ hold to drown__ to keep Go

not through lof — ty halls my love made of fir and ash or — pine For those
are the realms of the elves my love To— wan'-derers they are not kind Nor
too deep moun tain kingdoms my love though the dwarves are good and fair race They like
not sur prises from stran gers my love when they find folk out of their place The
Road goes ev er on - wards no end to sea and sky and
quests may call — you for - ward but ma - ny go — aw - ry Just

V.S.

4
73 C Bm Am D G
Pro - mise heed my words love Where- ev - er that you roam En -
77 C G Am B7 C D7
sure your eyes keep on route love for that will bring you home When you
81 Gm F Gm F Dm
come to me my dear and sweet love Come safe come sure come true For ad-
85 Gm F Gm D Gm
ven tures are all well and good my love But home is now ca-lling for you Come
89 Gm F Gm F Dm
on - ly to the par-lour my love come on - ly down the stair Come
93 Gm F Gm D Gm
to the fi - re with me my love and sit with fa - mi ly there

ORIGINS

his is another piece that was never actually meant to be shared. It was originally created as a reference document for the series, for my own personal use while writing *The Silenced Tale.*

See, if Elgar Reed was going to have to write a script, and then talk about what he wrote in said script in the novel, then it made perfect sense for me to just go ahead and write the script. That way I knew exactly what to reference where, and when, and from what page. Much like the rest of the world-building materials, it was all about internal consistency. And when it was done, I figured it would go into my filing cabinet of story notes, and that would be that.

It wasn't until I was reviewing material for this collection that I pulled this document, along with several others, out of that cabinet. When I read it again, I realized that it was, in fact, a complete story of its own, finished and capable of being read as a stand-alone. I even tested it by bringing it to a Con. Together with a bunch of friends, sitting around a hotel room, I read the script out loud. We howled with laughter the whole time, so I knew it had to be included in the collection you now hold.

Writing it as Elgar—who, as we all know, is a chronic overwriter (like yours truly) and far too flowery in his prose for the stark, to-the-point descriptions required for the standard screenplay—was both a challenge and a laugh, if not the most accurate reflection of what a true screenplay should be. Heed not, fledgling writers, this example should you wish to try your own hand at screen-writing.

That said, here you are: the script version of what happens directly before the first chapter of the first book of a series that I completely planned out but never created, as written by a fake writer who only exists in my imagination.

(My brain is convoluted, I know. Imagine living in it.)

Origins

by
Elgar Reed

Based on "The Tales of Kintyre Turn"
by Elgar Reed

Copyright © Elgar Reed, 2017

Kim McAvoy
Wellspring Literary
Los Angeles, CA

1 EXT.TURN HALL-FRONT COURTYARD.DAY.1

It is late afternoon in the Kingdom of Hain. In Lysse Chipping, in the northwest, nestled in a lush green valley sloping away from the chalky cliffs that border the Sunsong Sea, Turn Hall stands quaint and proud in the middle of a wildish parkland. No woman's touch has been felt on the house or its grounds in just under a decade——the fish pond is reedy, the covey forest dark, and the landscaping just a little too unkempt for a proper noble house.

The GARDENER is doing his best to remedy this. He is only one old man, however, and he's having a precarious time of it, balanced as he is on his step stool with shears.

He is trimming the hedgerow leading up to the grand front entrance of Turn Hall. Behind him, two FOOT-MEN——one on the roof and one on the ground——are hanging long silk banners along the front portico. A tug of gold tassel and they unfurl dramatically, fluttering in the breeze.

The banners are a rich russet, with gold borders. Around head-level, there is a massive embroidered emblem of House Turn: a lock, being lanced by an elaborate key.

Everything is calm and idyllic as the house prepares for a celebration tonight.

But then——the gardener slips! He's
going to fall!

CLOSE ON:

A hand shoots out and grabs the gardener's arm, keeping him upright.

                    GARDENER
          Oh! Oh, thank you--

The camera moves back, and we see the
gardener's rescuer: KINTYRE TURN.

Kintyre is built brawny. He is chiseled and incredibly handsome. His
hair is long, and flashes flaxen gold
in the sunlight; his teeth are white
and straight, unlike most of the people of Hain; his eyes are a clever,
adventurous blue.

He is dressed in black leather
breeches, a cream-silk shirt, and a
russet jerkin. He is freshly scrubbed
and shaved. The Turn Family Dagger is
at his belt, for today is his eighteenth birthday, and he is now a man.

                    KINTYRE
     There, now, Shofan. Watch your step.

                    GARDENER
     Yes, Master Kintyre! Thank you, sir!

                    KINTYRE
     No need to thank me, Shofan! It's
     my duty as the lordling to care for
               my people, eh?

                    GARDENER
               Of course, sir.

Kintyre flashes him another grin, then bends down and collects up a pair of very stuffed saddlebags.

GARDENER (CONT'D)
Oh, sir. Shall I fetch the groom to help you with that?

KINTYRE
No need, Shofan! I'm on my way back to the house now.

GARDENER
Very good, sir. And happy birthday, sir.

KINTYRE
Thank you, Shofan. That means... more to me than you'll ever know.

He claps the gardener's shoulder in a manly, friendly way, and squeezes once to show his gratitude. He lingers in the moment maybe a fraction of a second too long, overcome with the realization that he is going to miss these people.

GARDENER
Sir?

KINTYRE
Good day, Shofan.

GARDENER
Good day, my lordling.

Kintyre cuts through the hedgerow toward the house, ruining some of the gardener's careful work. The old man sighs, shakes his head, and climbs down the ladder to start push-

ing branches around to cover the new
hole.

2 EXT.TURN HALL-STABLE YARD.DAY.2

Kintyre was lying. He is not heading for the house. He approaches the
side door, but then pauses, looks
around to ensure that he's not being
watched, and breaks into a run toward
the stable.

A beat later, a skinny, weedy little
ginger creature darts out the door
after him. This is FORSYTH, Kintyre's
pest of a younger brother. Forsyth is
only eleven.

3 INT.TURN HALL-STABLES.DAY.3

Stormbearer, a brawny, dark stallion
with a fine arched neck and powerful
flanks, is stabled at the end of the
hall. He
is Kintyre's birthday present from
his father, and consents to be ridden
only by Kintyre.

The horse whickers and stamps as
Kintyre approaches, nose out to snuffle
and search for apples. Kintyre obligingly offers one out of his pocket.

As the stallion chomps, Kintyre
quickly saddles him up, throws his
saddlebags across the horse's rump,
and leads Stormbearer out the back
door.

A few seconds later, Forsyth steals
in, snags the lead of an unsaddled
donkey, and leads it out the back,

too, following his brother.

4 EXT.TURN HALL-THE COVEY FOREST.DAY.4

Kintyre leads Stormbearer through the forest, still on foot, pausing now and again to avoid being seen by his father's HUNTERS.

Forsyth follows.

Kintyre eventually makes it to the edge of the forest, where a low stone wall marks the boundary of the Turn estate. He mounts stealthily, and Stormbearer leaps the stone wall with ease.

Kintyre slips away into a wilder, darker woodland.

Forsyth, in his wake, hastily mounts his saddleless donkey, struggling. It refuses to leap the wall. Forsyth yanks his donkey around to follow the wall north.

5 EXT.CREEPY FOREST.DAY.5

In the twilight gloom of a significantly less cultivated bit of forest, Kintyre and Stormbearer pick their way toward a sheltered forest path.

6 EXT.CREEPY FOREST-ON THE ROAD.DAY.6

Stormbearer leaps one last bramble, and our heroes are back on the main path. They've emerged from the woods conveniently close to a crossroads. The sign indicates that Turnshire is to the east, Kingskeep to the West,

Erlenmeyer to the north, and the Urland border is to the south. Kintyre
wheels Stormbearer southward, and
they set off at a light trot.

From the north, a sweaty, fran-
tic-looking Forsyth, scratched from
nettles and muddy from an off-screen
fall, rides after Kintyre.

7 EXT.CREEPY FOREST-A CLEARING WITH A
SPRING.DAY.7

Some time has passed. Kintyre guides
Stormbearer to a calm, cathedral-like
natural clearing with an artistically
blue spring, lit with a golden light.
The space is, without a doubt, imbued
with magic. The air is syrupy thick
with the stuff.

FAIRIES glitter and glint in the
shafts of sunlight above the still
spring. A KOI FISH springs out of the
water and snaps one out of the air
like an unlucky dragonfly.

Kintyre chortles, amused, and dismounts. Stormbearer obligingly lowers
his nose to the water and drinks. The
same Koi fish eyes him up, but decides
the horse is not worth harassing.

Kintyre is feeling pretty smug right
now. He got away cleanly—or so he
thinks. He sits by the water, digs a
cup from his pack, dips it into the
spring, and drinks.

Kintyre takes a meat pie from a handkerchief in his saddlebag and takes
a big bite, relishing his ability to

eat with as poor manners as he likes.

The moment of magical peace is shattered when Forsyth and his donkey break into the clearing. Both are tattered and sweaty, scratched and bloody, and unbelievably displeased.

                    FORSYTH
          The least you can do is share!

Kintyre jumps to his feet, immediately angry.

                    KINTYRE
               Forsyth!

                    FORSYTH
        Brother! What do you think you're--

                    KINTYRE
          What are you doing here?

                    FORSYTH
               I saw you--

                    KINTYRE
          You wretched little sneak!

Forsyth, startled and wounded by Kintyre's sudden rage, slides down from the donkey. Kintyre jumps up and advances on his little brother.

                KINTYRE (CONT'D)
        How dare you?! You've ruined every-
                    thing!

                    FORSYTH
               I've... what?

KINTYRE
Why did you follow me, you pustule!

FORSYTH
I... thought you were... the party
this evening... Father told me to
keep an eye on--

KINTYRE
Of course he did! Loathsome bastard!

FORSYTH
Kintyre!

KINTYRE
Oh, don't pretend that you like the
bitter old troll any better than I!

FORSYTH
He's our father.

KINTYRE
Oh? Yes? And how's your wrist today?

Forsyth pulls his sleeve down over a
lividly bruised wrist, ashamed.

FORSYTH
He made me swear I would keep you
in my sights. Your valet has your
party clothes--

KINTYRE
Dash Velshi! And dash the party!

FORSYTH
You love parties.

Kintyre snorts and turns away. He
does love parties. But he's not interested in what Algar Turn has
planned for this one.

KINTYRE
They're no fun anymore. Father's
made them stifling.

FORSYTH
How can they be stifling when all
the girls want to dance with you--

KINTYRE
It's not the same now that they've
got their minds more on schemes
than on steps.

FORSYTH
But Father says you're particularly
to dance with the Lord of Fretta's
daughter, for she--

KINTYRE
That's exactly my point!

Forsyth, screwing up his courage and
standing straight as a little prince-
ling, stomps his foot.

FORSYTH
You must come back with me.

KINTYRE
Oh? Must I, Bossy Forssy?

Stormbearer paws and snorts ominous-
ly. The fairies have stopped to watch
the boys, tittering and still just
long enough for us to see that yes,
they are artistically nude women, but
they have multi-faceted, bulging eyes
like insects, and wings to match.

FORSYTH
If you don't, Father will--

                    KINTYRE
        Blast and dash that bloody old man!

                    FORSYTH
          Kintyre! Kintyre... please.

                    KINTYRE
        No. I'll not go back. Not ever.

                    FORSYTH
           Then I'm coming with you!

                    KINTYRE
              Absolutely not!

                    FORSYTH
        I know you're off to the Urlish
        border! I know you've got Uncle
        Alyk's jerkin in your bags. You're
        going to turn soldier and hide!

                    KINTYRE
                  (caught out)
        How do you know that? How? Have
             you been spying on me?

        Mulishly, Forsyth juts out his chin,
        crosses his arms, and stamps his
        foot——again.

                    FORSYTH
             You must come home.

                    KINTYRE
        Well, I shan't. I've renounced it.
        It's not my home any longer.

                    FORSYTH
                    Kin!

                    KINTYRE
                    No!

Overwhelmed with fear of his father
and his own childish anger, Forsyth
throws himself at Kintyre and tackles
him to the ground. The boys wrestle
and tussle, rolling back and forth.
Forsyth gets a good dunking in the
spring. They tumble against the side
of a rockfall and the fairies, as
one, spring into the air.

                    FAIRIES (overlapping)
          No! Stop! Look out! (etc.)

It happens so fast that Kintyre barely has time to see it.

A bit of ground underneath Forsyth's
feet crumbles and gives way. Screaming, clutching at his brother, but
ultimately failing to gain any handholds, Forsyth slips through the
earth and is gone.

Kintyre, stunned, drops to his knees,
fear in his face as he scrambles back
from the edge of the hole. He lays
along the edge carefully, testing
each patch of ground before putting
any weight on it.

                    KINTYRE
          Forsyth? Forssy?!

His voice echoes in the cavern below.
There is silence in its aftermath,
only the small plinks of stones falling from the rim of the hole.

8 INT.THE CAVERN.DAY.8

The only light is from the hole
above—a brilliant, harsh shaft. The

ground it illuminates glitters with
geodes cracked open by Forsyth's
fall.

Forsyth lays in the very center of
the patch of sunlight on the floor.
His head is bleeding sluggishly, artistically.

                    KINTYRE (O.S.)
              Forssy! Answer me!

          Forsyth stirs and groans.

                    FORSYTH
          Kintyre? (louder) Kin!

A shadow cuts into the sunlight, in
the shape of a head and shoulders.

                    KINTYRE (O.S.)
               Do not move!

                    FORSYTH
                     Kin!

                    KINTYRE (O.S.)
          Lie still. I shall fetch... someone!

                    FORSYTH
               ...Father...?

                    KINTYRE (O.S.)
              No. Of course not.

                    FORSYTH
                   (weakly)
                 Thank you.

                    KINTYRE (O.S.)
          Just... just stay still.

Forsyth lays his head back down.

> FORSYTH
> (dozy)
> Very well.

The shadow leaves the light. Forsyth startles back to awareness.

> FORSYTH (CONT'D)
> Kintyre!

> KINTYRE (O.S.)
> Yes, brother?

> FORSYTH
> Turn Hall's closest.

> KINTYRE (O.S.)
> I know.

> FORSYTH
> You'll have to... the healer woman...

> KINTYRE (O.S.)
> I know! Shut up, Bossy Forssy.

> FORSYTH
> Mmm. Very well.

He closes his eyes again.

9 EXT.CREEPY FOREST-A CLEARING WITH A SPRING.DAY.9

Kintyre, leaning over the edge of the hole, sits back and scrubs at his face, furious.

Then he stands, ties up the donkey, throws himself across Stormbearer's back, and rides hell-for-leather back to Turn Hall.

10 EXT.CREEPY FOREST-ON THE ROAD.
DAY.10

Kintyre and Stormbearer thunder down
the road. Before they reach the
crossroads, a small country laneway——
concealed when one is heading south,
but perfectly visible from the northward approach——opens before them.

Kintyre hauls Stormbearer to a stop,
contemplates it, and then wheels the
horse down the path.

11 EXT. CREEPY FOREST-AN ABANDONED
FARM.DAY.11

It is clear that nobody has lived
here for many years. The forest is
reclaiming the house, and the barn
leans precariously.

                    KINTYRE
     What! Ho! Halloo! Is anyone-- Ah,
       dash it. Hup, Stormbearer, hup!

He urges the horse to the barn.
Stormbearer hesitates at the threshold. Kintyre leaps down and recklessly throws himself into the tack room
by the gaping maw of the front door.

He gathers up as many coils of rot-
ting rope as he can carry, and swings
himself back up into the saddle.

As they ride away, the barn tips and
slumps into the vegetation, throwing
up splinters and dust in the late afternoon sun.

12 EXT.CREEPY FOREST-A CLEARING WITH
A SPRING.DAY.12

Kintyre returns to the clearing, ties
off one end of the longest coil of
rope to a tree, and then tosses the
other coil down into the hole.

13 INT.THE CAVERN.DAY.13

The coil lands on Forsyth's legs. The
lad stirs. He looks up in time to
watch Kintyre shimmy down the rope.
Kintyre jumps the last few feet down
and lands beside his brother.

> KINTYRE
> Forssy?

> FORSYTH
> Mmm... my head hurts.

> KINTYRE
> I'm sure it does. Hold on.

Kintyre looks around. He spots an
underground lake, still and shal-
low-seeming. He pulls a handkerchief
from his jerkin as he walks to the
lake's edge.

The lake is the size of a ballroom,
perhaps, and in the golden sunlight
streaming down from the hole in the
cavern's ceiling, the blue and purple
geodes that make up its bottom sparkle and dance.

Kintyre kneels to wet the cloth, and
then pauses. Something glints gold
in the center of the pool. Kintyre

straightens and moves as if to step
into the water, but then halts. He
looks back over his shoulder, guilt-
ily, to where Forsyth is now sitting
up, hunched over his knees and holding his head.

Kintyre returns to his brother's side
to doctor his head wound. Forsyth is
pale and shaking.

                    KINTYRE (CONT'D)
          Can you stand?

Forsyth shakes his head, then stops
abruptly, looking queasy.

                    KINTYRE (CONT'D)
          I'll have to lash you to my back,
                    then.

                    FORSYTH
          I'm too heavy.

                    KINTYRE
          You're a stripling. The axe I use
          for chopping wood for the kitchens
                    weighs more than you.

                    FORSYTH
          Mmm. Very well.

                    KINTYRE
          Just... get your bearings for a
               moment. I want to check...

He goes to the edge of the pool and
strips down until he is wearing
naught but his leather trousers. He
wades into the pool.

14 INT.UNDER THE WATER. DAY.   14

Kintyre dives and opens his eyes.
In front of him, the gold-and-white
thing shimmers and shifts. He reaches for it, but it is not within his
grasp——the clarity of the pool has
fooled him, and it makes the object
seem nearer than it is.

15 INT.THE CAVERN.DAY.15

Kintyre breaks the surface. He swims
a bit further out, checking below
him. He takes a deep breath and dives
again.

16 INT.UNDER THE WATER.DAY.16

Again the object eludes his grasp.

17 INT.THE CAVERN.DAY.17

Again Kintyre breaks the surface,
readjusts his position, takes a deep
breath, and dives.

18 INT.UNDER THE WATER.DAY.18

Third time's a charm. He's got it!

19 INT.THE CAVERN.DAY.19

The thing in his hand breaks the surface first. It's a sword!
But not just any sword——a gorgeous
sword. The pommel and grip are gold,
the hilt decorated with bloodstones
and rubies, the blade white-silver in
color, the edge wickedly keen. The
sunlight jumps and dances along every
reflective edge.

Blocky text etched in the center of

the blade, trailing down to the tip,
says FOESMITER. These words glow a
faint golden before settling down.

Kintyre breaches the surface next,
gasping for air, but grinning. He
wades to the edge of the pool, mar-
veling at the sword, turning it over
in his hand.

> KINTYRE
> (reading)
> I can't read this, but... it feels
> like... like it was made for me...
> just me...

Kintyre tests the balance and extension of the sword. They are perfect.

Forsyth makes a pathetic sound, and
the enchanted, magnetic draw of the
sword is broken. Kintyre gathers up
his clothes and moves to Forsyth's
side. The handkerchief is soaked with
blood, and, disgusted with himself
for getting distracted, Kintyre tosses it away. He rips the arms off his
shirt. He uses one to make a pad of
fabric for Forsyth's head, and rips
the other into strips to tie the pad
in place.

Kintyre quickly redresses. Then he
hoists Forsyth up onto his back,
lashes Forsyth to him with the second
coil of rope, jams the sword through
his belt, and ascends to the surface
once more.

20 INT.TURN HALL-KINTYRE'S APART-
MENTS.SUNSET.20

Kintyre, with Forsyth still strapped
to his back, hauls them both in
through his bedroom window. He leans
back over the bed and cuts the ropes,
plopping Forsyth down on the cover.

He stashes his saddlebags and——with
one last longing look——the sword under the bed.

Then he goes to the door and rings
the bell-pull viciously, while at the
same time, starting to wriggle out of
his damp clothes.

21 INT.TURN HALL-KINTYRE'S APART-
MENTS.NIGHT.21

Kintyre is in his dressing gown, his
hair brushed and mostly dry.
Algar Turn stands in Kintyre's apartments as Forsyth is being tended to
in Kintyre's bed by a WOMAN HEALER——
the lady who will one day be known as
MOTHER MOUTH.

Algar is clearly in the middle of a
red-faced, drunken tirade. Forsyth
cowers on the bed, but Kintyre takes
his father's anger on the chin.

                    ALGAR
     --running off, tonight of all
               nights!

                   KINTYRE
                (calm, dull)
     I was not running off, Father. I
       was anxious and thought a ride
     would soothe my nerves before the
                 festivities.

ALGAR
And you told no one of this, of
course!

KINTYRE
Forsyth knew.

Algar snorts.

ALGAR
Irresponsible wretch! I've half a
mind to not name you heir tonight
at all, to skip you entirely and
give everything to your brother.
At least the stripling brat has a
sense of propriety and familial
pride!

KINTYRE
I'd not mind it. The book-mouse is
more suited to studies and ledgers
than I will ever be.

Algar, in a towering fury, backhands
Kintyre. But Kintyre is a man now. He
is broad and brawny, and for the first
time, he realizes that his father is
small, and fat, and cruel. He touches his face, awed by this new truth,
then glowers at his father.

KINTYRE (CONT'D)
(growling)
You're right. I am a man now, Father.
And the next time you strike me like
that, I'll lay you flat. So help you
if you think I'm lying.

ALGAR
Don't backtalk to me, you useless
waste of an evening's tupping!

KINTYRE
How dare you speak of Mother--

Algar moves to strike him again, but
Kintyre grabs his wrist before the blow
can land.

KINTYRE (CONT'D)
I meant it. I'll match you blow for
blow, you cruel old bastard.

Algar, startled and, for the first time,
a little worried that Kintyre could do
it, pulls back and blusters.

ALGAR
You'll be downstairs in an hour,
boy. And suitably attired.

KINTYRE
(through his teeth)
Yes, Father.

ALGAR
(to Forsyth)
And as for you, you useless little
spare-- Better you stay out of sight.
You're no good to me like this.

MOTHER MOUTH
My lord, I hardly think Master
Forsyth is in any kind of health to
be--

ALGAR
Silence, you puffed-up hedge witch.
I didn't ask you!

Mother Mouth scowls, but obeys. Algar
sweeps out of the room. Kintyre, furious, goes to his wardrobe and flings
his somber but quality clothes onto the

chair by the fire, ignoring the glittering outfit already waiting on the nearby valet stand. Mother Mouth packs up her potions bag and goes, leaving Forsyth propped up on the pillows.

                    FORSYTH
          I'm sorry.

                    KINTYRE
          Shut up!

                    FORSYTH
          I didn't mean to ruin--

                    KINTYRE
          I said shut up!

                    FORSYTH
          Next time, we'll--

                    KINTYRE
          "We"?

Kintyre whirls on Forsyth, in the same sort of towering rage that Algar was in just moments ago and oblivious to the fact that this is just as terrifying to his hurt little brother.

               KINTYRE (CONT'D)
          There is no "we," little brother!

                    FORSYTH
          But... but we've always...
               together.

                    KINTYRE
          No more! This is all your fault!
          I could be away by now if it wasn't
               for you!

FORSYTH
(voice small)
But you're glad I'm well, aren't
you?

KINTYRE
(scoffing)
Truly? Right now I wish I'd been
an only son!

Forsyth is stricken.

FORSYTH
You don't mean that.

KINTYRE
I mean every word of it! Now, I am
bound to go downstairs to accept
the ring, and the seal, in front of
all the people of the Chipping, and
it will be official. I will never be
rid of it. And I'll never forgive you
for it, Forsyth. I'll never forgive
you. Never.

Kintyre gathers up his clothes and slams
into the dressing room next door. Forsyth curls up into a ball, holding his
bandaged head, and weeps.

22 INT.TURN HALL-THE BALLROOM.NIGHT 22

The ballroom is absolutely stuffed with
nobles. Every house is dressed in their
own signature color, making the room
look like a bowl of hard-boiled candy.
It is stifling, and the women's elaborate
hairstyles are wilting. The ice sculp-
tures on the sideboards are melting.
The musicians in the back corner are
napping. Only the eligible young ladies
are still rapt, their eyes turned up at

Kintyre.

Kintyre, dressed in russet-and-gold finery, stands on a dais beside his father. Algar is giving a long and rambling drunken speech. He holds Kintyre's hand out by the wrist, so that everyone assembled in the ballroom can see the shiny new signet ring—— stamped with the lock-and-key sigil—— on his pinky finger.

                    ALGAR
...and the pride I have in the fine, strong man my son has become. His mother, bless her memory, would have wept to see our boy so bonny and clever, ready to take up the mantle of Master of Lysse Chipping and Turnshire after me... (etc.)

Kintyre is bored, bored, bored, and hating every second of this.

23 INT.TURN HALL-HALL OUTSIDE OF KINTYRE'S APARTMENTS.NIGHT.23

The crush of the party audible behind him, Kintyre has snuck back up to his wing of the house. He is creeping toward his own door. Behind him, his valet VELSHI appears at the top of the stairs.

                    VELSHI
        My lordling Kintyre?

Kintyre whirls around, caught.

                    KINTYRE
        Ah! Velshi!

VELSHI
Is there something I can fetch for you, sir? There was no need for you to come upstairs yourself and miss the party.

KINTYRE
Ah, no, Velshi, I was... um, I just wanted to check on my brother, you see. I feel dreadful that he's missing all the hullabaloo below, eh?

VELSHI
Master Forsyth has been removed to his own apartments, sir.

KINTYRE
(with put-on surprise)
Oh, he has? Well, then. No reason for us to be up here at all then, is there, Velshi?

VELSHI
(suspicious)
No, sir.

KINTYRE
Right. So, um, you can... uh, go, Velshi.

VELSHI
Very well, sir.

Kintyre doesn't move.

VELSHI (CONT'D)
Are you sure there's nothing I can fetch down for you?

KINTYRE
Not at all! Goodnight, Velshi.

                    VELSHI
          Yes, sir. Goodnight, sir.

Velshi turns and goes back down the stairs. Kintyre sags with relief, and then enters his room.

24 INT.TURN HALL-KINTYRE'S APART-
MENTS.NIGHT.24

Kintyre retrieves the saddlebags and sword. He strips the bed linens, ties them into a rope, and is out of the window in a trice.

25 EXT.THE DOM FORGE.DAY.25

Kintyre, saddle-sore, cranky, caked in road dust and already regretting his first adventure, swings one powerful thigh over the saddle and hops down from Stormbearer.

He lands directly in front of a cooling trough in the alley between the tidy but rundown Dom family forge and a tanner's. This is BYNNEBAKKER, a village in the last Chipping before the Urlish border. It is small, and it is middling poor.

The roads are clean, but made of packed earth. The buildings are rundown, but well loved. The people's clothing is worn, but carefully patched.

Standing at the trough is BEVEL DOM, youngest son of the blacksmith, and apprentice to his father. The young man has navy eyes, sandy hair, and is corded with work-earned muscle. Bevel is sixteen.

Bevel is at the trough to soak a horse-shoe, and the hiss of the iron in the water catches Kintyre's attention. As soon as the horseshoe is out of the water, Kintyre comes over and dunks his head in the trough.

                    BEVEL
              What! Hey!

Kintyre pulls Stormbearer over, and the horse drinks. Kintyre pushes his long blond hair off his face, flicking it back in the sunlight, majestic.

Bevel, disgusted, turns to take the horseshoe back inside.

                    KINTYRE
              You there! Boy!

A beat.

                    BEVEL
              (annoyed and amused)
              You mean me?

                    KINTYRE
        Who else? My horse has thrown a shoe,
           and you must repair it at once.

                    BEVEL
              (sneering)
              I must, must I?

Kintyre's never been mocked before. He's not sure how to take this.

                    KINTYRE
              Well... yes.

                    BEVEL
                  Fat chance.

                   KINTYRE
              I beg your pardon?

                    BEVEL
                   (mocking)
        And you have it, my lordling prig.

                   KINTYRE
               Now, see here...!

                    BEVEL
        Oh, I see fine. No need to call
        attention to yourself. You were an
        elfcock the moment you dismounted.
                 I saw plenty.

                   KINTYRE
        How dare you! Do you know who I am?

                    BEVEL
        No. And I sort of suspect that's
                 the point.

        Kintyre sways on the spot, startled.

                   KINTYRE
              How... how did you know?

                    BEVEL
        Are you really that bloody new to
        the road? You look like a sodding
        pampered lordling to me, what's
        done crawled out of his bedroom
        window to go join the army, like all
        the rest of the idiot Prince Bloods
        what's been through here since the
        war got on. Hardly got the shine off
        your signet ring, yet. Didja just
             turn eighteen today?

Kintyre shifts uncomfortably and tries to hide his fidget in a stretch. Bevel watches this, eyes wide, mouth dropped—but it's not attraction. It's amusement. Even though Kintyre does paint a very pretty picture.

                    KINTYRE
          Four days ago, actually.

                    BEVEL
          Really.

                    KINTYRE
     Oh, shut up! Will you shoe my
          horse, or not?

Bevel, all annoyance burned away in the wake of the entertainment he's getting at the expense of Kintyre, turns and jerks his head toward a hitching post at the end of the alley.

                    BEVEL
  Tie him up there, my lordling prig,
       and I'll see to him in turn.

                    KINTYRE
       But I'm for the front now.

                    BEVEL
    Then I suppose you'll be walking.

                    KINTYRE
     You have a horseshoe in your hand
     right now. Why can't I just pay you
                    to--

He is interrupted with Bevel's laughter.

KINTYRE (CONT'D)
What now?

BEVEL
Oh, you really are pampered. Didja
really think a bit of clink would
letcha jump the line? My other
customers would be furious, and my
father would box me ears. Besides,
this shoe ain't gonna fit a
muscle-bound lug like your stallion
there. Just hitch 'im up, mi'lordling,
an' I'll get to 'im before the sun
sets, yeah?

KINTYRE
(whining)
And what am I to do until then?

BEVEL
There's a tavern up the street that
way. And a whoremongers' that way.

KINTYRE
And if I don't trust you with
Stormbearer?

BEVEL
Then you best come inside, mi'lordling,
and put on an apron. 'Cause if you're
keen to hang about here and make a
nuisance of yourself, then I'll make
good use of your 'ands.

Bevel takes a good long look at
Kintyre's hands.

BEVEL (CONT'D)
(dismissive)
Tsk. Soft, you is. Well now. We'll

get some calluses on those palms
soon enough. In you go.

He holds open the curtain that serves
as the alley-side door. Kintyre hesitates, then ties Stormbearer to the
hitching post and goes inside. Bevel
chuckles to himself and follows.

THE END

DELETED

Being a Collection of Deleted Scenes from The Accidental Turn Series

I always love getting to see what ended up on the cutting room floor, especially in films. Sometimes it angers me, because there's a line or a look in the removed footage that changes or clarifies character motivation or plot, and it frustrates me that the creators didn't think it was important to the story. Other times it delights me, because it shows that other types of creators can "overwrite," as well, and need to pull out things that are self-indulgent, run too long, or are just too precious.

So when I was asked to put together a compendium of companion materials for *The Accidental Turn* series, I knew that the inclusion of a behind-the-scenes, "Director's Cut" glimpse at the contents of my own cutting room floor would be a fun addition. Some of the scenes below were cut for being too long, or too rambly, but most of them are the starts or fragments of scenes-that-never-were. Chapters I started, and then abandoned, stories I tried to write and realized I couldn't, pieces that had to get dropped as the timeline of the narrative changed.

They're not all going to sync up with the books as they are now—don't try too hard to place them in the canon. Just enjoy them for what they were, and for what they might have been.

You'll notice as you read through this that there's nothing from *The Untold Tale* included. In some sort of cosmic miracle, the 2012 NaNoWriMo project titled "The Meta" somehow evolved into a novel where the first draft is—except for some judicious cuts to chapters eleven and twelve, and some added scenes to fill plot holes—nearly identical to the version you buy in the bookstore. The next two books had to be rewritten—or, in the case of *The Silenced Tale*, rewritten heavily—which is why most of the below content is from later in the series. But as I previously noted, the series itself was an "accident," so it's not surprising that I had to take a couple of attempts at some of the scenes or plot points before I figured out what worked best. That's what happens, I suppose, when you expand what was always meant to be a stand-alone novel into a four-book "trilogy."

This scene originally capped off *The Forgotten Tale*. It was the final moments of the novel. But it was cut because we agreed that the moment before this one was a better ending, and that this one hung the lampshade on the trilogy just a bit too obviously.

FORSYTH

Later, when Reed bids us goodbye—off in a cab to a hotel, for he does not wish to impose on us when we are so freshly returned home and has drunk too much wine to drive his own car—he makes me swear that I will call him again on the morrow. When he is gone, I curl up on my bed with my wife and my child, and together, we simply hold one another. If my fingers are a bit too tight in Pip's shorn hair, she says nothing, just as I say nothing about the way her nails dig into my arm.

When Alis begins to fuss, Pip pops downstairs for one of the bottles in the fridge, and I change Alis's nappy, toss her Hainish clothing into the laundry hamper in her room, and give her a quick bath and a story. She disdains the bottle when Pip brings it into the bathroom, but it is all we have. Tomorrow, we shall rally ourselves, brave the world outside our walls, and fetch some pabulum or porridge for her. She has become too used to eating what the grownups do.

As soon as Pip manages to squeeze a few drops of the warmed-up breast milk into her mouth, though, Alis's eyes widen with delight, and she latches on and sucks greedily.

"Enjoy that, kiddo," Pip says, wrapping Alis up in her towel. "That's the last of it. I dried up on the road."

"Oh," I say. "That's a shame."

Pip shrugs, and if it bothers her that she is no longer able to have that quiet intimacy of breastfeeding our baby, she says nothing about it. Instead, when Alis is dozy-eyed and burped, she kisses my cheek, hands off our child, and whispers into my ear: "I am *desperate* for a shower. Meet you downstairs when you're done putting her to bed."

Alis is very nearly asleep when I lay her down in her crib. It is large, so very modern, and as different from the Turn family crib as possible. I am glad Alis got the chance to sleep in the family cradle, though. It is where every scion and child of our house has slept—save for Wyndam—for generations beyond count.

As Alis squirms and gets comfortable, I sing:

Sleep now, sweet princess, my lady so fair
There are charms braided up in your fall of sweet hair.
Sweet dreams, they wait, at the top of the stair,
Of ribbons and rainbows, and laughter to spare.

Sleep now, my darling, the sun's gone to bed.
So lay down, oh, lay down, your sweet little head.

Hush now, oh, hush now, believe in no dread.
For all of your troubles are turned out and fled.

Dream now, my child, of the stars and the moon.
Dream of adventures in ships and on dune.
Dream of a morning, for it comes all too soon.
And wake soon, my sweet, to the skylark's bright tune.

Alis is fast asleep by the end of my warbling, and I back out of the room. My daughter is exhausted, and deserves a good long sleep in her own bed. In fact, I think everyone under this roof does, and I fully intend to suggest it to my wife.

I cannot *wait* to sleep in hideously late on our supportive mattress and between our ludicrously high thread count bamboo sheets.

When I come back downstairs, however, it seems as if my wonderful wife has other plans. Pip has locked all the doors and shuttered all the windows. The only light comes from the multitude of candles she has lit, which fill every surface of the living room. It is Solsticetide reborn. She is sitting on the sofa, her Hainish accoutrements stripped away, leaving her in only the Turn-russet sweater-dress I had gifted her with, a rich contrast against the black leather of our sofa.

And we are alone. Finally alone. Really and truly alone for the first time in a month.

Pip has also decanted a bottle of wine. Muscle-sore, bone-weary, but heart full, I sink down onto the cushions beside my wife. We wrap our arms around one another, legs tangling, ankles knocking, faces buried in each other's hair, and skin, and scent.

"Hello, *bao bei*," I say softly, kissing my favorite leaf. I run my tongue around its edges, making certain that it remains perfectly still.

"Hi back," Pip whispers, her lips dragging, warm and chapped, against the shell of my ear. "I missed you."

"I missed you, too."

But contrary to Pip's assertion that she is anxious for my company, she draws back to lean over my thighs and fetches two wine glasses, holding them out for me to fill. I do so happily, set the half-empty decanter back on the coffee table, and then take a long, lingering moment to taste my wife's lips before we taste the wine.

"To home," Pip toasts, and I chime my glass off of hers.

"To home," I agree. "The one left behind and the one regained, both."

We drink.

There is more sipping, more kisses, more running of hands through hair, and a general rediscovery of one another, a remapping of our bodies and love in a way that we have not had the ability to do in weeks, not while watching our backs and keeping one ear to the ground, listening for danger or approaching family, as we had been. Pip's hair is ragged now, a whole swatch missing from the back, no longer the sharp, precise bob she prefers. Mine has grown so long that there is an errant curl hanging down my forehead. There are bruises that make us each jerk and wince when we brush palms and mouths over them, small cuts that sting and burn pleasantly under tongues, and hushed, sweet moans that we keep low, intimate, trapped between each other's teeth.

When we are sated, and glowing, and the decanter is empty, I cradle Pip against my side, and we lay down on the sofa. Pip's head is tucked against my bicep, a small muscle that hasn't had as much sword practice as it ought. Recalling my thoughts on the matter in Pointe's own practice hall, I resolve to restart my regular sword training regime. Perhaps I shall even research fencing teams at Pip's university. Surely there must be some community center or private club that provides sparring space and partners.

I curl my arm around her ribs, and Pip drops a kiss against the knob of my wrist.

"Mmm," she says.

"Indeed," I agree. "And so, that is that. Is this The End, do you suppose, *bao bei?*" I ask, good cheer and the warmth of home, and love, and the honey-gold of post-orgasmic bliss, filling me with confidence.

"Maybe..." Pip murmurs. I wait for her to continue, but instead, she draws away, sits up slow as molasses. She pulls the throw off the back of the sofa and wraps it around herself, tucking it over her head, protective.

I sit up, the chill of the room slapping against the sweat still cooling on my bare skin.

"*Bao bei?*" I ask. "Pip?"

She walks over to the bookshelf, eyes wide, drinking in all the titles, gaze reverent, face open. Worshipful. She reaches out, slow, tentative, as if the books are birds she fears she might frighten into flight. Her fingers run over the spines of her books, fingertips bouncing and dancing across the love-worn and foxed edges.

"Maybe?" I repeat, her solemnity creeping into my mood.

Pip turns to face me, a forced, slim smile already withering on her lips.

"Maybe. The spell is still carved on my bones. It's not gone, even if there's no magic here, and... well... that's the thing with these sorts of adventures, Forsyth," she says, gesturing with gravitas at the fantasy novels level with her shoulder. "They always come in trilogies."

This deleted paragraph came from an earlier version of the epilogue to *The Silenced Tale.* I thought it would be hilarious to turn Bevel into the kind of whining man-baby who can't handle a cold. Unfortunately, that idea didn't pan out, as the epilogue was already as long as I wanted it to be, and I knew that I would have the opportunity to explore Bevel and Kin more in Magic. Unfortunately, this bit of plot never made it into that story, either. But I think this paragraph is too good not to share.

FORSYTH

Kintyre sleeps the sleep of the heavily medicated. Bevel, unfortunately, is not so restful. He is wrapped up in blankets on the neighboring chair like a miserable burrito, coughing in tiny pathetic mews that are all that is left of his voice. Unlike his husband, he was not pumped full of antibiotics to prevent sepsis as soon as he entered the hospital, and unlike me, his immune system was not given the benefit of a slow exposure and immersion into the Overrealm. Bevel walked straight into the Royal Jubilee Hospital, and into the nastiest bout of the summer flu the health network has seen in some years.

This scene was cut from *The Silenced Tale* simply because it repeated information that the reader already knew. But repetitive information was not the only thing sacrificed on the chopping block. Yes, at one time, the Piper family had a miniature schnauzer named Yin-se. I loved the idea that Forsyth would be striving for the domestic ideal of having a dog, but in the end, Yin-se just kept tripping up the plot's momentum in his leash.

FORSYTH

After a gray and miserable March, April warms to temperatures that I associate with an early spring in Lysse. My little Alis has developed a desire to be as helpful as possible around the house. Which, in Alis's case, often involves picking up whatever is left carelessly within her reach and hauling it to her reading chair. The books on the lowest shelves, a remote, Pip's keys, pots and pans—all have ended up stuffed under the chair, glittering additions to her hoard.

Alis and I are at the nearby dog park when my phone begins to play the fiddle-and-fife tune of Elgar's personalized ringtone.

Mei Fan and Martin's rowdy little miniature schnauzer pup, Yin-se, is running in circles around my daughter. They claimed the dog was for them, to keep wai po company on her daily walks, but the pup spends an equal amount of time at our house. Pip is unsure if she approves, but I, having grown up with only the hunting dogs that my father had reared into a snarling meanness, had always wished for a faithful hound of my own. I had imagined great adventures with this imaginary dog, and evenings of doggy cuddles that grew in the absence of any physical affection from my father and brother, once my mother had passed. I dreamt of a loyal, fierce protector to stand and growl between me and my father's fists when Kintyre had run away from Turn Hall, but alas, was never granted the reprieve.

Yin-se is delighted at the opportunity to be off his leash, and is trying to lead Alis in a merry chase, as far as I can tell. The pup is nearly the exact same age as my daughter, but as it is a dog, it is already far more coordinated than she. So Alis is spending almost as much time on her bottom, with her face being ruthlessly licked, as she is on her feet.

"Yin yin!" she cries in joy.

With both my daughter and the dog happily preoccupied, I pull the ringing phone from my pocket, cup my hand over the microphone to block out the ambient noise, and say, "Hello?"

My creator has called me near daily for the last week, as we have worked together to create his script. In the end, we had decided that he would write the moment when Kintyre first found Foesmiter. I had been present for that adventure—unfortunately—for it had happened on his eighteenth birthday, the day he ran away from home.

Terrified to have been left behind with our father and his temper, I had followed Kintyre, and subsequently gotten myself into a bit of trouble by falling down a sinkhole into a cavern. Pip tells me that my following and injury were meant to illustrate Kintyre's nobility and forthright morals as a Main Character, for he rescued me from the cavern and returned me to Turn Hall despite knowing that his plan to run would be foiled and he would be trapped. I remember him being petulant and abusive about the ordeal. And in the end, he had still run, leaving me alone and in my sick bed while our father raged and our mother was barely cool in her grave.

"Forsyth?" Elgar asks, and I can tell at once that something is wrong.

"I'm here," I say. I try to infuse the reassurance with as much firm support as I am able through the little device.

"Forsyth," Elgar says, his voice filled with thready fear. "Forsyth, I think... I can't be sure because I've never seen him before, but... no, no. I know him. I know I know him. My god, Forsyth, he's *here.*"

"Elgar, slow down. Who is here?"

"Jesus, Forsyth. The Viceroy. I'm sure of it. I just saw the *Viceroy.*"

The sun does not suddenly vanish from the sky, not in actuality, but all around me, the world tilts sharply, drained of color in an instant. Yin-se's yaps become tinny, and Alis's laughter muted. Goosebumps erupt all along my arms, needling into the back of my neck, and I am certain that all of my short hairs actually and honestly stand on end.

It's true. I know it with the same faith which I know the depth of my affection for my wife and child.

And it is a conversation that cannot be had in public, and certainly not one where I cannot focus the whole of my concentration on it.

"Are you safe?" I ask first, chasing down Yin-se and snapping the neon pink leash secured around my own hips onto his halter. The pup whines, but does not scurry away, seeming to understand with the empathy of all dear animals that now is not the time to fuss.

"Yeah," Elgar croaks. "Yeah, I am."

"Stay where you are, then," I say.

"No choice," he chuckles, but it is dry and strained sounding. "I'm in the hospital."

"You're *what?*" Panic splashes up my spine, as unexpected and shocking as being hit in the back of the head by a slushy snowball.

The desperate urge to *be safe, to not be outside and exposed, to have your back to the wall,* blooms inside my chest. I grab my daughter like a sack of flour and jog back toward the house, ignoring her indignant squeals and the way Yin-se yips and snaps at my heels as he is forced to trot to keep up.

Dreading the answer, I ask: "And where is... where is the Viceroy now?"

Saying his name out loud feels like an ominous summons, and I cannot help looking around at the perfectly normal Victoria street, as if I will be able to spot my brother's archnemesis peering at us through the branches of an ornamental bush. Ridiculous. If the Viceroy wanted to sneak up on me, I doubt I would see it coming. Shadow Hand I might have been, but field work had never been my specialty, and I am near on three years out of practice, besides.

"He left," Elgar says. There's the sound of shifting fabric, and I realize, starkly, that it is the sound of stiff, starched hospital sheets crinkling beneath him as he switches his phone from one ear to another. "That's what I don't understand." His voice goes quiet, the echo deadening; he must have cupped his hand around the bottom of his phone. Either he is being naughty, and he is not allowed to have his phone in the hospital, or there is someone else in the room with him, someone he doesn't want to either wake or to allow them to overhear what he is saying. "He was here... he could have... he was standing over me, Forsyth. We're in a hospital. It would have been so easy for him to find a... a scalpel, or... but he... left."

When we arrive at the house, I set Alis down. Immediately, she goes into full toddler meltdown mode, screaming and crying and tugging on my trousers to be pulled back up into my arms. Yin-se circles me, lashing my ankles together with pink nylon.

There's a telling pause on the other end of the phone, and I squeeze my handset between my ear and my shoulder as I struggle to unlock my front door with both my daughter and our borrowed dog fussing at my feet. Yin-se bolts inside, and I unsnap the leash from around my waist just in time to keep from being toppled. But Yin-se knocks over Alis, who lays on the ground and screams her displeasure to the world.

"What's going on over there?" Elgar asks.

"Chaos," I answer honestly. "Just a moment."

I scoop Alis up again, and shove my phone—our call still connected—into my back pocket. "Sorry, sweeting," I tell her, kicking the door shut and locking it behind me. Then I strip her out of her light jacket and muddy shoes, and haul my wriggling, writhing, red-faced child up to the playpen in my office.

When Alis realizes she's being abandoned to her fabric-walled prison while her da takes his telephone call to the master bedroom, she shrieks even louder. Downstairs, Yin-se is tearing around the kitchen, the metal clasp at the end of the leash scraping against the tile-work, nails clicking and scratching, adding to the din. I retreat into my bedroom and close the door.

I have a tablet resting on my bedside table, usually reserved for reading eBooks, and I snatch this up to open my note-taking app. Then I retrieve my phone from my pocket, put it on the bedside table, and turn on the speaker.

"Right," I say. "Start at the beginning."

"You know about the stalker," Elgar says, and it's not a question.

"Of course," I say, preparing my stylus.

A short pause, an intake of breath, and then: "How long have you known?"

"A month, or thereabouts. I have been monitoring the situation, but it seemed that your local police force had things well in hand. I am less certain now that you tell me you're in the hospital."

"Someone..." he begins, but then trails off, and I can hear how scared he is—his breath heaves, his throat clicks as he swallows hard, his voice becomes shaky. "Someone cut my brake lines."

"How?" I ask, boggled. "The police were monitoring your house. I read the reports daily."

Elgar groans. "It's my fault. Juan wanted to come to LA with me. So I thought, you know, it would be convenient if my car was at the airport for us. I thought... I'd hoped that... by the time we got back... that the stalker would have... I dunno. Left. Got bored?"

"If you really saw the Viceroy, if it is as you say, then

I am surprised that he did not—"

"I did," Elgar hisses. "I know I did."

"You've never seen—"

"*I made him up*, Forsyth. *Trust me.* I know him. Just like I knew you right away, too."

"Very well," I allow. Though he has never seen the villain in the flesh before last night, I accept that he would know him on sight.

Alis stops shouting soon after that, and I pause my conversation with Elgar—or rather, his horrified recounting of the events that prompted him to call—to check on her. She has exhausted herself with her anger, and lies sleeping on the floor of her playpen, flushed and miserable. Yin-se, also, is now quiet downstairs—a fact which fills me with dread. Normally, this means the dog has gotten into something. But when I peer over the banister of the stairs, I see that he is napping by the fireplace. Good, I seem to have worn out both my charges.

I return to my phone, and Elgar, and continue to make notes. "And your car?"

"Juan drove my car to the airport. We left it parked there while I was in LA."

"I'm missing something essential, Elgar." I rub the skin between my eyebrows with my thumb, trying to press back the headache I can already feel forming there. "What are you leaving out? Elaborate, please," I prompt, and, filled with surging adrenaline that he clearly has no other way to expel, he does. He tells me about the pantry, and the exploded desk, both of which I knew about. He tells me about a strange man in black watching him from every park bench he seemed to pass, about how the waitress in the diner's eyes seemed to flash green when he wasn't looking, how Juan had procured a new boyfriend who had lived in his house and utilized his devices, but whom Juan hadn't remembered inviting to stay.

"So, that is how he's doing it," I say, cold trepidation settling in my gut.

"It's more than that," Elgar whispers. "He... he did the most *awful*... poor Linux..."

"Your cat?" I ask.

"I just... I can't even... it was awful," Elgar says, his voice trailing off into a shaking sob.

"You do not have to recount it," I say, as gently as possible. "I will read the report myself."

"Thanks," Elgar says. "I just... I... what do I do, For-syth?"

"Heal," I tell him. "I will double your security at the hospital, and we will figure out what our next move will be."

"Thank you," Elgar says again. "Really, thank you."

"Elgar, believe me when I say that if this villain really is loose in the Overrealm, in possession of his magic or not, keeping you safe is the literal least I can do. Trust me."

"I do."

"Good." I can only hope my words sound more con-fident that I will be able to protect Elgar than I feel.

Originally, there were a few more moments to pause and take a breath during *The Silenced Tale* than we ultimately included. Most were removed to increase the pacing. This is one I particularly liked, though, as it high-lighted a moment of family-life amid the action. It may not have made it into the final novel, but it can at least live on here.

FORSYTH

Pip nods, and we change into our pajamas. Pip fin-ishes before me, and sits on our bed in her shorts and tank top, her arms wrapped around her legs and her chin on her knees. She picks up her cell phone from off the bedside table and fidgets with it, turning it over and over in her hands.

Ah, she wants to call and bid Alis a goodnight before we try for sleep.

"Put it on speaker-phone," I tell her.

"Do you think it's safe?"

I smirk at my wife, and bend down to bounce a light kiss off her forehead. "Your husband encrypted our signals before we left Victoria. To anyone trying to use our phones to track us, it looks like we are still in British Columbia. The phones are safer to use than the hotel line."

"What a lucky wife I am," Pip says, tilting her face up to demand a kiss. I am happy enough to oblige. When we part, she taps the screen and balances the phone on her knee.

"Ma!" Alis shouts from the other side of the country. One of her grandparents must have told her who was calling. "Hi, hi!"

"Hey, baby girl," Pip says down the line, a half-beat before my own: "Hello, sweeting."

"Dah dah!" Alis squeals in delight. Alis proceeds to tell us about her day, which seems to have involved a simply scintillating trip to the local hardware store with her grandfather. Mei Fan tries to fill in the extras from beside Alis, but Alis, annoyed with being spoken over, hisses an imperious "sshhhhh!" at her grandmother. Pip and I break into giggles so consuming, so relieving, that the phone tumbles off her knee and gets lost beneath our bodies as we roll and clutch at each other.

"Da?" Alis asks, clearly concerned that we are not hanging on her every word.

"I'm here, sweeting," I assure her, and she is off again on her ramble, to which I listen intently as Pip fishes for the phone. She finds it under her thigh and sets it on a pillow, and we curl around it like commas, listening and replying.

"'Isses night?" Alis asks us, and Pip makes the "muah" smacking sound with her mouth close to the microphone. "No!" Alis protests, and her voice is thick with frustration and sorrow, just on the verge of sobs. "Here!"

"Soon, sweeting," I promise her.

"Now! Alis 'isses now!" she shrieks, and I hear the sound of a tiny body hitting the ground, arms flailing.

"Sorry, Mom," Pip says hastily, sitting up.

"It's fine," Mei Fan sighs, picking up the phone. Alis is screaming full murder behind her. "You were the same."

"Then I'm *really* sorry."

"It's just the early onset of the terrible twos," Mei Fan says. "Too many big feelings for such a little body. It's normal."

"Buuu!" my daughter shrieks in the background.

"Is it?" I ask, sitting up as well, suddenly anxious. I have no experience with very small children, outside of Lewko Pointe, and he was always an exceptionally well-behaved young boy. He was Written as the perfect model of a child in the one scene Pip tells me he appeared in, in *The Tales of Kintyre Turn*.

"Yes, stop fussing," Mei Fan teases me. She finds my little quirks amusing and endearing. Thank the Writer for that.

"As my mother-in-law commands," I tease back.

"We'll let you go, Mom," Pip says. "Let you take care of the terrible terror."

"What's this? It sounds exactly like bedtime to me, jelly bean!" I hear Martin crow in the distance, and I can imagine him lifting my daughter up over his head and pressing blowing raspberry kisses against her cheeks until she is giggling instead of sobbing. I've seen him do it often enough before. Sure enough, Alis's screams become laughter and fade into the distance as Martin presumably carts my child off to bed.

"Bye, kids! Have fun!" Mei Fan says, and barely waits for our goodbyes before she disconnects.

For a moment, we both stare at the phone, aching for our daughter, missing her terribly. Eventually, Pip sets it aside on her bedside table.

"I'm glad she's not here," Pip says softly, and we resume our cuddle against the headboard.

"Me, too," I reassure her.

Pip then, eyes lowered to where she is picking at the lint clinging to her pajama pants, adds: "What do you think his plan is?"

I don't have to ask her which "he" she means. Like Pip, I am reluctant to speak his name aloud, strangely, tremulously fearful that it might summon him. That he might rise up into the sky beside our bedroom window, riding on a cloud of his mother's magic, hands glowing green, eyes alight with mad malice.

"Fear," I say simply, closing the last button of my top and sitting back against the headboard beside her. Pip curls under my arm, burrowing against my ribs. She pinches my stomach.

"Yow!" I yelp.

"That's not very specific. 'Fear.' What does that even mean?"

"From all that I know of the... of him," I say softly into the pseudo-darkness of our hotel room, "he thrives on the dramatic."

"You got that right," Pip says, thoughtfully. "He's definitely the sort for grand gestures. His vanity's about his ability to awe, to gain obedience through terrifying displays of power. That was always his undoing, too," she adds, a note of hope creeping into her voice as she wiggles an arm behind my back to squeeze me against her side.

"In a world where heroes always win and the narrative serves the main character," I say. "This is not that world. Do not get your hopes too high."

Pip gusts out a groan and buries her head in my pudgy little belly. Instead of saying anything, she stays there for a long few moments, face turned to my skin, accepting the comfort of my hand threading through her silky hair and down her back.

"Have we fallen right into his trap?" Pip asks me after a very, very long, and tensely thoughtful, silence. Her voice is muffled.

"You mean, have we allowed ourselves to be herded into the center of the maze like startled mice?"

"Yeah. That."

"Whether we have or not, we are here," I answer, pragmatic. With the hand that is not in Pip's hair, I stretch my arm out and touch Smoke to succor myself with the thought that it is well within reach.

"You're so comforting, tonight, *bao bei*," Pip says, biting at the same place on my stomach that she had pinched earlier.

"Yow!" I say again, but this time, it rides the air on a puff of laughter. "You're so cruel to me, beloved."

"They're love bites."

"I don't see what's so loving about abusing my tender bits."

Pip looks up at me with mischief glittering in her dark eyes. "There's lots of hot cosplayers at these things, and they'll be falling all over you 'cause you're the best Forsyth Turn they've ever seen. I'm just reminding you who you belong to."

"Only you," I murmur, tugging Pip up my body so I can get at her lips. "Only you."

In the original version of *The Silenced Tale*, Forsyth didn't travel to Seattle to catch the Viceroy at the hospital. Elgar traveled to ConClusion alone, with both Pip and Forsyth meeting him there. This exchange, then, is what happened in their hotel room when they first arrived.

FORSYTH

"You're really going gray, Forsyth," Elgar says, like it's something he had heard happened to older humans, but had never actually borne witness to it. As if his own hair wasn't entirely white by now.

"Just at the temples, like Mr. Fantastic," Pip says. "I think it's charming."

"Yes," Elgar says. "Very... literary, I guess. I just... I never thought..."

"That I would age? That I could? That I am forever that skinny, snot-nosed, bratty little-brother-to-your-hero in your mind?" I supply, gently.

Elgar colors a little, and though I know it's embarrassment that paints his cheeks pink, it's good to see them something other than the sallow parchment of exhaustion. "I guess."

"I am thirty now, well into middle age in Hain," I remind him. "And Kintyre is going silver, too. Not just white, of course," I add with an eye roll. "Because the Great Hero of Hain must be handsome even in his dotage."

Pip pinches my arm playfully. "Kin's not in his dotage," she scolds. "He's only thirty-seven."

"Silver?" Elgar asks, looking thoughtful.

"Yeah," Pip says. "All threaded in, too. It's handsome. Of course it's handsome. But it's... I don't know, dignified? Very Lord-of-the-Manor."

"And Bevel?" Elgar asks eagerly, sitting forward as much as his sore back allows.

"Still dishwater blond," I say, pleased that at least, if the little hedgehog has to age, he has not been granted the same grace as my brother and is not getting any more dignified looking. "And thinning on top."

"I wish I could have met them," he says at length, lowering his mug for a sip. By then, I've returned to sit beside Pip on the sofa by the window, and she puts a comforting hand on my thigh. He catches her movement in the reflection of the window, and turns to face us. "I don't mean it like that. I mean, I don't wish it had been them instead of you. I'm glad to know you, Forsyth. I just... wish I could have met them, too."

Pip and I exchange a glance, each of us thinking, surely, of the Viceroy. Of what we are facing, even in this lull. Of how useful Kintyre and Bevel would be, if only because they have faced him more times than we have, and probably understand him better, as well. Know his motivations, his patterns. Pip raises her eyebrow at me, askance, and I shake my head minutely.

We haven't discussed the possibility of finding a way to pull Kintyre and Bevel out of the books and into the convention, but surely we would need more magic to do it. Real magic. Deal-Maker magic. Or, failing that, the words of our Writer. It is a thought. Though it's one I would much rather discuss with Pip in private, before we suggest any plan of engagement in front of Elgar. Any action we undertake in that direction may be dangerously draining.

"Okay, you're weirding me out now, Elgar," Pip says, setting her coffee on the low table beside her and sitting forward on the sofa. "What's with all the broodful staring out the window and the intense inspection of Forsyth?

What's with all this talk about opportunities to meet Kin and Bevel—and in the past tense, may I point out—like you're already dead?"

"I'm not—" he begins, playacting at being affronted, but Pip and I can both see through him so thoroughly, and so obviously, that he just deflates. He takes a moment to sip his own coffee again, and then sets it down, as well. His shoulders hunch as he presses his hands, palm-to-palm, between his knees. "Honestly? I wasn't sure you'd come," Elgar says, staring down at his hands.

"You thought I would not come to aid you when you invoked the name of the Viceroy?" I ask, agog, and my mug joins the other two on the table. "Really, Elgar. Shame on you."

"But that's just it," he says, freeing one hand to gesture at me before tucking it back beside its mate. "You came for the Viceroy. Not me."

Pip and I exchange a glance, and matching confused frowns.

"I thought we'd settled this," Pip says.

"But you have the baby, the... the jobs. The... I don't know. All the stuff that has nothing to do with me. The house, and the hacking, and the life. And I thought, you know, when this was all happening, I thought, 'I can't tell them. I can't bring this to their doorstep. I can't lead this to them.' And I just... if the worst happens, well, then I don't want it to happen to you, too. And I thought you might think the same way."

"Elgar..." Pip begins, but she clearly isn't certain what to say next, so she pauses to lick her lips and think. "You're our friend."

"Am I?" Elgar asks, and perhaps I should be offended that he sounds so surprised. Mostly, I just feel a surge of pity. His eyes are wide and red-rimmed with lack of sleep and confusion. "I mean, watching Juan leave, I'm starting to... well, I'm starting to realize that... that maybe I'm not a good friend to have."

"All my life, I looked up at my father and wished, hoped that he would see me," I say slowly, quietly, holding Elgar's gaze with my own, gray on blue, so that he is sure to be paying attention. "That he would know me, and appreciate me for who I was. Not as his useless spare, or the bookmouse who could never hope to live in the shadow of his eldest son's legend, or even his own past military glories. But as me, wholly and completely Forsyth Turn. My whole life, I wanted him to delight and marvel in who I am, in what I do. I wanted him to revel in my accomplishments, to laugh at my joys, to weep for my sorrows."

"I'm sorry," Elgar says softly, taking my hands between both of his. "That's my fault, too."

"Yes, it is," I agree, but I keep my tone gentle, soft. "But I realized that, in resenting him so completely, I have also misplaced my anger and resentment onto you. You could not know that what you were writing was harming real people. You have accepted the consequences of the pain your carelessness wrought, and you have striven to make it up to me. And I have spat on the hand you've extended in friendship and peace, because it looks too much like my father's. But no more. *That* is why I am here."

Elgar squeezes my hands tightly. "Okay," he says, his voice caught in a hard swallow. "Okay."

Ahbni was originally created to be Pip's sidekick, but also as a means for me to point out the places where Pip herself still behaves problematically. (Pip is not a perfect feminist, and I wrote her that way on purpose. No one is perfect, and even Pip has more to learn.) In this version of the novel, Ahbni had a complicated story arc about the struggle of loving problematic material, and the way entitled fans can sometimes behave inappropriately toward creators. In the end, it bogged down the forward momentum of the plot, and was subsequently nixed.

The Viceroy was also originally meant to have acquired a sidekick, a hateful MRA/Sad Puppy type named Whisperblade. However, the problem of too many characters and not enough space on the page, plus the hope of creating an interesting twist, led me to conflate Ahbni and Whisperblade into one character.

This scene, which was meant to illustrate both Ahbni's fanaticism and the intractability that would lead her to stab Elgar to death, ended up being irrelevant to the plot itself. And I figured there were better ways than this to illustrate Ahbni's faults than a rehashing of Pip's tavern soapbox moment from book one (much as I do love my tavern soapbox moments).

You'll also notice that this scene is written in the third person present tense, instead of first person active. Way back when I was first writing *The Untold Tale*, I made the deliberate choice to make Forsyth's (and thus, later, Bevel's) tense as present and active as possible. As a fictional character who only had a "life" when he was on the page, I wanted everything that happened to him to be right then and right *there*.

So, when it came time to write Elgar in the Overrealm, a "normal" man in a "normal" world, I did it in third-person past, the most common tense used in modern-day novels. This was to differentiate not only between the characters speaking and narrating, but to make a clear division between how Forsyth sees himself, and how Elgar does.

My editor thought it was too different, though, to the point of being jarring, and so you'll see that Elgar's portions are now in the present tense (but still third person), as well. Just as they are in the final story.

For context, this scene is set in the con suite, right before our heroes go down to the viewing of the short film announcing *The Tales of Kintyre Turn* television series.

ELGAR

"Who?" Ahbni asks, looking up from where she's admiring the sword belt and sheath Forsyth has bought to go with Lucy's new sword. Elgar vaguely remembers there being a leather worker in the Dealer's Room, too, so he must have doubled back for it.

"Algar Turn," Elgar says. "His—that is, Kintyre's father."

Ahbni nods, and hands the sword back to Lucy. "Right, the drunk, abusive father thing."

"What thing?" Elgar asks, hackles rising.

"How all fathers are arseholes in worlds like yours. To get the protag out the door, right?"

"Algar Turn isn't—"

Forsyth coughs demonstratively.

"Oh fine," Elgar grumbles. "But it's not a thing. I only did it in one novel."

"You and every other writer. It's tired," Ahbni points out.

Lucy sighs and stands to strap on her new belt. "Okay, Ahbni?" she says, patting her shoulder as she readjusts the fall of her sword. "I get that you have a lot of opinions and stuff, but sometimes, it's all right not to throw them in everyone's faces. There's a time and a place."

"Ha!" Forsyth chortles. "That's rich, coming from the woman who called out a horde of barbarians to their faces."

Lucy sticks her tongue out at her husband, affectionate. "Where do you think I learned this lesson?" She leans down to give him a brief peck on the lips.

"But if we don't call it out," Ahbni protests, "then

how can anyone learn?"

"Call-out culture has its place, too," Lucy agrees. "But other times, it can be bullying, and can actually do more harm than good. You have to choose your language and your timing."

"I shouldn't have to police my tone," Ahbni huffs.

Lucy throws her hands in the air and huffs a sigh. Then, after a moment, she says: "Okay, but no." She turns to Elgar. "I actually have wondered about that."

"Thank you!" Ahbni blurts, throwing her hands upwards, as well.

"I mean, was your own father not... ?" Lucy starts, but then trails off, looking uncertain about where she wanted to go with this line of questioning.

"Not... ?" Elgar prompts.

"Well, kind," Lucy finishes.

"He was a good man," Elgar says, mantling at the insult. "He was great. What I remember of him, anyway. I was young when he died."

"Then why are all the men in your world so cruel?" Lucy presses.

"Not all the men!" Elgar says, and even in his own ears he knows he sounds childishly defensive. "There are hundreds of men who are good, and kind. Who are good fathers, good parents." He jerks his thumb at Forsyth.

Lucy frowns. "Just not the ones who made it onto the page."

"King Carvel!" Elgar counters, triumphant, jabbing a finger in Lucy's face.

"You still made him sell his only daughter to Gad-ot," Ahbni butts in. "She's been in Crownsnest since she was thirteen. That's young to expect a girl to get married. In fact, it's pretty gross. Just because she'd menstruated once? That doesn't make anyone a woman. That just makes her a girl with a period."

"But that's the way things were back then, and—"

Lucy puts up her hand to stop him. "Back then? Back *when*? This isn't a historical epic you invented, Elgar. This is a fantasy."

"*Bao bei*," Forsyth says softly, clearly attempting to diffuse Lucy's temper. It's not like Elgar hasn't heard it before from critics and reviewers and angry fans at Q&As, but somehow, having Lucy Piper say it to his face is different. This is, for all intents and purposes, his daughter-in-law.

"What if Kintyre had a daughter?" Lucy challenges, though it's immediately obvious that the girl-child she's really talking about is Alis. "Would you have sent her away to another Chipping? Would she have had to marry a lordling from Miliway or Ertse? Or, god forbid, a lord old enough to be her grandfather? Would you have done that to his child? Would you have done that to *mine*?"

"No!" Elgar protests, cold horror at the thought of sending Alis Mei Turn Piper away like that seeping across his face, into his voice. He couldn't imagine never seeing her again for the sake of a pact. "Of course not!"

"No, of course not," Forsyth parrots back, and Elgar is surprised to realize that Forsyth has had time to get furious in his own right. "Because he is Kintyre Turn, the Great Hero of Hain. He is the main character."

"Well, yes!" Elgar says. Confused, desperate to understand what has his friends, his family, so upset about a classic stereotype of fantasy novels, he hurries to explain further. "She would probably become a heroine, too."

"And would you rape her?" Lucy asks, voice low and crackling, eyes blazing. All of her attention is on Elgar now, and it feels a lot like being pinned under a laser. "Would you do that?"

There is no right answer to this question, Elgar realizes. So instead, he stays silent. Lucy waits. Finally, Elgar says: "Well, if I didn't know she was real, I might have—"

"And a woman needs to, what, know you, be part of your family, or belong to you, to deserve respect?" Lucy snarls.

"All those other women, all those other people—they're characters. They're not people!" Elgar protests. "I don't see why you're—"

"Not to me!" Forsyth roars.

"And not to me!" Pip adds.

"But that's only because you've *been* there," Elgar protests again. He jumps to his feet, feeling too twisted up, too hot under his lungs to stay seated, to stay in Lucy's line of sight. He never expected to be attacked like this over what had ultimately been an off-handed remark made in a single paragraph written two decades ago. "Only because you married—"

"No, not only," Lucy growls. "Because I am a Reader. I am a Reader, and I am a Fan, and do you know what you do when you do those things to the women in your books, Elgar Reed? You do it to me, too. Because everything in your work says to me, your female fan, that this is all you think women are good for. This is what you honestly believe that women are worth, what their place in the world is. You rape a female character to make her suffer; and you rape a female character to make a male character suffer. And in doing so, you tell me, the female reader, that this is all I'm good for. To suffer."

Elgar splutters, flabbergasted, and caught wrong-footed, and never in his life before in the position to have to defend his world-building choices like this. "I don't... I don't mean to..."

"I really do believe that it is subconscious," Forsyth says, and he stands, too. He places a calming hand on Lucy's arm. Lucy blows through her nose and grimaces at Elgar, refusing to be calmed. "I believe that my creator does not plan his world to be so heteronormative, so misogynistic, so completely lacking in racial diversity aside from the exotic Others introduced to be defeated or enslaved. I do truly believe that he has not meant to do it."

"But he does it all the same," Lucy snarls. "And you and I are the ones who suffer because of it. And now, he's going to end up dead for it."

"Uh..." says a small, confused voice from behind them, a slow drawl of confusion. The three people standing before the sofa turn to where Ahbni is watching them all with round eyes and a slack jaw. Elgar had forgotten she was even still in the room. "Why are you guys talking about this as if these people are real?"

Originally, the Viceroy really did attack our heroes at the end of the screening, but my editor rightly pointed out that this was too predictable, and it was changed. However, it seemed a waste not to use this high-action, alternate-universe/alternate-timeline moment, so here's how that originally went down.

ELGAR

But before the moderator can add anything, the ball of ice on the back of Elgar's neck blossoms. Something like a cold wind reaches forward and wraps him in a gust of misty haze. Elgar jerks to his feet as something impacts against the mist, whipping by his ear with a shrill whistle, just barely deflected. He yanks the knife out of its sheath at the small of his back and brandishes it in the direction he thought the blow had come from, but a second hit against his shield staggers him sideways, shatters the mist completely.

"Lies!" a voice booms, breaking over the heads of the startled crowd like thunder, amplified, but not by electronics. "Glorifying treachery!" The air crackles and snaps with static, and Elgar is reminded suddenly that the Viceroy's mother is a weather witch, a Deal-Maker with an affinity for water-magics.

"Pip, perhaps we should—" he half-hears Forsyth shout. A glance tells Elgar that Lucy is already in a defensive half-crouch. But before Forsyth can finish his sentence, the air thickens with the humid, cloying stench of ozone and danger. Something above everyone's heads sparks and crackles.

Elgar backs up so quickly that his chair overturns with a sickening bang. His arm burns where he holds the dagger out in front of him, ready to stab and thrust like Forsyth taught him.

Another crackle and boom rocks the room, and the fans surge to their feet, crying out as they stare upward. Someone screams. This sets off a chain reaction of pan-icked noise, so loud and sudden that it nearly drowns out the third and final crackling boom. Nearly.

The world flares bright. So bright that, for a mo-ment, it's impossible to see anything but white. Spots dance in Elgar's vision, and he jams the heels of his hands against his eyes, careful not to cut himself on the dagger. The aftermath of the light-show has left him dazzled, orbs and sparks shooting through his peripheral vision.

Elgar blinks his eyes open. Tears stream down his cheeks from the pain. He scrubs at his face, tries to orient himself again. The air has lost the ozone tang, the wet weight of potential magic. A dry crackling catches his ear amid the howling cries of thousands of people, among the bang and sharp metallic clacks of chairs being overturned and bashed together, amid the running and shuffling of thousands of feet on carpet.

A throaty *woosh* draws his blurry gaze to the back of the stage. Elgar collapses in a lump, cowering in horror, arm up in front of his face to try to block some of the heat.

The screen is on fire. The flames jump and crackle like lightning, unnatural and grasping. Worse still, the fire is green.

FORSYTH

Ignoring the stairs, I spring up onto the stage, suddenly glad that my wife bullied me into returning to those fencing lessons. I would not have been able to make the leap quite so limberly otherwise.

"Don't just sit there like a target!" I hiss, yanking Elgar up onto his feet with my free hand, and pushing him toward the wings.

"Wait!" Ahbni shouts, but she is on the opposite side of the stage, and Pip and I manage to hustle Elgar through the black curtains and down the wobbly metal grill stairs before she can catch up to us. I want to wait for her, but I want Elgar out of the line of literal fire more.

Pip plunges into the scattered crowd, shoving and shouting: "Get out of the way!"

"Where are we going?" Elgar shouts over the din.

"Back to the Green Room!" Pip answers. "I wanna get you somewhere that's not out in the open. Keep moving!"

Thankfully, my creator does as he's told. He puts his head down and bulls through the crowd in my wake. I wish I had a third hand, so I could have Smoke freed, and bared, and prepared, if need be, but it is better to have skin-on-skin contact with Pip and Elgar as I mutter Words of Invisibility, Words of Slipping, everything and anything I have learned as Shadow Hand that may help us pass unseen. I only hope that the Viceroy doesn't have the ability to sense where the magic is being siphoned off to, that he will not be able to pinpoint us *because* I am leeching power from Pip.

The crowd around us is surging in their panic, people shouting, calling for one another and for security, a dozen phones in the air as people try to capture footage of what is going on, as they try to *understand* it. Even if the hall itself is only a couple hundred feet deep, wading through five thousand confused, anxious, and fearful bodies makes for slow going. Doors at the end of the ballroom are flung open, and people surge toward and out of them like sand through the narrow neck of an hourglass. We three lone grains are buffeted along until Pip grabs Elgar by the sleeve and drags him to the side of the room. With our backs to the wall, we curl in small and wait for the stampede to ease.

I see Ahbni's head pop above the crowd, her brightly colored scarf a beacon. I presume she's climbed onto a chair to search for us among the chaos.

"Should we—?" Elgar starts, but I shake my head and grab his other arm to keep him from raising it, to keep him from waving to his temporary assistant to get her attention.

"I am unconvinced that she had nothing to do with this," I hiss into his ear, and Elgar goes still, and a little bit paler. "There's a service door, just up there, Pip."

My wife follows where I'm pointing, and we make our way down the wall to a small door. "Fucking locked!" she snarls, kicking the barrier.

"Here!" Ahbni shouts, rocketing past Elgar and me, pressing her whole body against the wall in an effort to stop fast enough. The keypad beside the door lights up and beeps, and Ahbni turns to glower at me. "Why'd you run away from me?"

"Hurry," Pip shouts, slamming open the door without checking to make sure no one was behind it. We stream into the confined space in a wave, fingers clenched together, Ahbni bringing up the rear. Pip directs us away from the stage, traveling along the other wall and back to the Green Room.

We hit a roadblock, however, in the form of a small mountain of piled cardboard boxes. They are clustered around a doorway, half-piled up a slight ramp that probably heads to a loading dock.

"Oh, for fuck's sake!" Pip screams, kicking one. "'Cause that's both fire safe and accessible!"

She flicks her middle finger at the pile, as if the magic of the crude gesture could suddenly make it vanish. Or make the people who thought it was a good idea to block the wheelchair exit more conscientious.

Stymied, we are forced to duck out of the cramped passageway and cross the floor. Luckily, we have emerged into the gaming area, and most of the people are focused on the cards in their hands, or the elaborate dioramas of battle on their tables. The pandemonium of the ballroom doesn't seem to have spread this far yet. But I can hear it coming, see it in the way that the people sitting at the gaming tables closest to the ballroom doors are starting to crane their heads to get a better view of what's happening.

Pip turns to Elgar and hisses: "Pull your hat down. We don't have time for you to get mobbed."

Elgar follows her command, hunching his shoulders in, as well, as if that could disguise his shape at all, and we make our move. Pip dodges around the folding chairs, hops lightly over satchels and glossy plastic bags of purchases littering the walkway. Elgar follows a few steps behind her, less agile, but motivated by urgency to move quickly. I follow, keeping my eyes on the people around us in the hopes that I can head off a mob if one begins. I can hear Ahbni behind me, keeping pace but out of my eye-line.

I would much rather that I could see her. The feel of

her gaze prickles on the back of my neck, and something is itching under my skin, something I don't understand just yet. Something I need to know, something I *want* to know, and damn Elgar Reed for Writing me to be so *paranoid.*

It's not paranoia if they're really out to get you, I think, recalling the clever poster I had once seen hanging in Pip's office back in Vancouver. At the time, I'd thought it a terrifying warning, before I understood that it was intended to be humorous. Now, I found it wryly appropriate.

As we pass the last gaming table, Pip pauses to scope out the best route to the doors, and then the Green Room from there. Elgar welcomes the chance to catch his breath. I, on the other hand, would prefer not to be so exposed, so obviously standing amid a sea of people sitting, literally sticking out from the crowd.

The food court lies before us, all open space filled with more tables and mingling people. It's the bored ones standing in line for the vendor carts clustered in a loose circle, the ones looking around, that are giving my wife pause, though.

Beside me, a young man cranes his head up and, in a deeply French accent, asks: "What is happening over at the ballroom?"

"Huh?" Elgar asks, and then starts. "Oh, hey, it's you. From the elevator."

And sure enough, there is the foursome we met yesterday on the elevator —the Frenchman with the cane; the shorter, rounder fellow wearing another pithy t-shirt; the young black woman with the funky glasses; and the older woman who had blinked so owlishly.

"Uh, hi, Mr. Reed," the older woman says, her attention stuck to my creator like day-old bubblegum.

✵

As I said above, I do love my soapbox moments (or, in the parlance of editing this particular series, "Pulling a Fucking Chapter Eleven"), and while Pip is a hardened adventurer and passionate academic, even I had trouble with the idea that she would stop in the middle of a climactic battle to have an academic debate. All the same, I hated watching this scene fall to the cutting room floor.

FORSYTH

"Okay, no, so like... how is this working?" Ahbni asks, wiping her mouth on her sleeve and standing. "How are you all... did you, what, come out of his head like Athena?"

"Who?" Kintyre asks.

"Not important," Pip says. "And no. You saw how it happened. Magic."

"But there's not... I didn't really think..." She touches the phone in her skirt pocket, and though I think she assumes it is a subtle gesture, I know that Bevel and I both catch it.

We flick a gaze up to one another that is as telling as an actual spoken conversation—*yes, I saw it, too. No, I don't trust her, either.* I cannot help but think of the Shadow's Mask, pressed against my chest under my jerkin.

"But how did you end up in the middle of all this?" Ahbni asks.

Pip turns to look at her and grins. "I was tortured by Bootknife, and the Shadow Hand of Hain rescued me."

"To be fair," I correct her, "the Shadow Hand of Hain sent the Shadow's Men into the Ivory Tower to steal back the books and tomes that the Viceroy had stolen first, and they found you quite by accident."

"Ooh!" Ahbni says, curling closer to ask, excitedly: "Did you meet the Shadow Hand?"

Pip smirks. "Yeah."

"Who was he?"

Pip jerks her thumb at me, smirk widening into a high-wattage grin.

Ahbni blinks, looking back and forth between us, and then sits back, mouth a perfect O.

"No," she gasps.

"Yes," I say.

"I put it in the books!" Elgar grumbles between us. "I don't know why everyone's so surprised. I put in the clues."

"But... Forsyth Turn." Ahbni frowns.

"Forsyth is so much more than his tropes," Elgar admits, a bit shamefaced. "He was supposed to be—you'll forgive me, my boy, for being brutally honest—the craven, envious sibling. The, ah, the one who might betray the hero out of greed and guilt. The Edmunds and Wormtongues. I even thought, for a time, that you might secretly be Bootknife," he says with a chuckle.

"Bootknife?" I echo with horror, and then touch the thin scar on my left cheek, covering it with my fingertips as if afraid that it would suddenly sprout limbs and give birth to the villain if I say his name too loudly.

"Turns out, you're Newt Scamander," Elgar chuckles. "The perfect Hufflepuff Hero. You talk people down instead of hurting them."

"Oh goody. Lucky us," Ahbni says, and sends a glare out toward the doors where it's clear she wishes I had been more a man of action. Then she returns to Pip. "So, what, he just talked at you?"

"Pip stayed at Turn Hall while she recovered, and I admit that I was attracted to her from the start. It is... more complicated than we make it out to seem, but in the end, we discovered a mutual affection, and worked together to form a partnership."

"The therapy helped," Pip teases.

Ahbni, however, seems to have lost her enthusiasm

for our love story. "Wait, you mean you creeped on her when she was in pain, and you think that's... romantic?" She turns her disgusted gaze on Elgar. "What the hell kind of people are you inventing?"

"Isn't it romantic?" Elgar hedges, uncertain as to why he's suddenly the target of her ire. "Love at first sight, and all of that?"

"No." Ahbni slumps back against the display, crossing her hands over her chest and scowling. "It's gross."

"Um, do I get a say in whether or not I found it romantic?" Pip asks, frowning at Ahbni's displeasure.

"Well, was it?"

Pip is about to shoot back an answer, but then she pauses and licks her lips. "Actually... not really."

"*Bao bei*," I gasp, hurt by this admission.

"I wasn't exactly in control of all of my own actions," Pip says. "Everything that encouraged your romantic attention wasn't, well... me."

"And so, you are saying that I was a horrible letch and a bo-boor for ta-taking your at-atach-m-ment at f-f-ace val-value? A-a-are yuh-yuh-yuh-you bla-ah-ming m-m-me?" I ask, my voice crackling on the last question, filled with an unexpected and sudden shame and pain that I had thought had been put to rest years ago.

Pip reaches up and cups my face in her hands. She kisses me, sweet, and apologetic. "You couldn't help it. It's how you're Written," she says quietly, and though the words are for me alone, I know both Elgar and Ahbni can hear them because Elgar makes an annoyed squeak and Ahbni scoffs. "Men in your world see a maiden and immediately evaluate them for a romantic or bed partner. And yeah, it's misogynistic and creepy, especially when I'm, you know, bleeding all over your mother's sheets."

"I'll say!" Ahbni says.

"But," Pip adds, turning to address Ahbni directly,

"once all of that was over, once I was in control of myself again, and once Forsyth had started back at ground zero, the relationship we built was real. It might have been too fast, it might have been under stress and pressure from the fact that the Viceroy was trying to kill us, we might have jumped into cohabitation too quick when I invited Forsyth to break out of what he was Written to be and come here with me, but we made it work. And we made a therapist very rich while we were doing it. Just because you don't see the hard work doesn't mean it wasn't there."

Ahbni colors and looks away. "Fine," she mumbles.

Pip reaches across Elgar to grab Ahbni's forearm. "Hey," Pip says. "I'm not scolding you. You're not wrong. It was kind of creepy and inappropriate. But it's not anymore. We did better."

"And what about them? How does that work?" Ahbni asks. "They're what, gay married now?"

"Just regular married," Pip says with a frown. "No need to add the 'gay' in front of it."

"But... they weren't. Not in the books. I know what you said about the subtext," Ahbni adds hastily, "and the cosplay and stuff. But that's not the same as... as Lord Consort Turn here."

Bevel fingers the string of the bow still slung across his torso. "Careful. I think I might be offended by that."

"No, no. I just mean..." Ahbni stands and sticks her hand in her pocket, fingers wrapped around her phone. "I didn't know things could change. That people could change." She peeks up through her lashes at Elgar, sucking on the corner of her mouth, thoughtful.

"They can't," Pip says. "Not really. Just... become more what they are."

"Are you sure?" Ahbni asks, and it's just anxious enough that Bevel and I share another look with each other. "Really sure? Or do like... do fanfics influence the world of the fantasy? Or... or other writing?"

What other writing is she referring to, I wonder. What else has she read that she thinks Pip would know, as well?

Pip, enlivened by this debate, is ready to keep the conversation rolling. Just as well, because I can see that Bevel is also carrying on a silent conversation with Kintyre. I don't know the extent of their wordless language, but I can feel the tension in the room growing more palpable. Ahbni and Pip, focused on one another, seem oblivious to it. But Elgar has perked up, and is watching Kintyre with a hawkish expression.

"I think it would take lots of fanfic to change it," Pip answers musingly. "But Forsyth says that the Reader's Eyes can interpret the lives of those below, so... I don't know... maybe?"

"*I'm* the author," Elgar protests, yanked back into the conversation by Pip's suggestion. "Only I can change the canon."

"Yeah, but fans have interpretations. And many fans can produce a belief in a fanon so strong that many believe it's actually true," Ahbni says. "Like how everyone named the stepmom in Labyrinth 'Karen' in their fanfics because they thought that was really her name. But in the credits, she's listed as 'stepmother.' One person called her that, and everyone took it for truth."

"But this isn't ancient Greece," Pip argues thoughtfully, warming to the debate. "This isn't belief becoming reality, or gods absorbing power from thoughts. This is a single reality authored by a single writer."

Kintyre and Bevel have moved back now, a subtle shuffling, pulling themselves from the conversation as Ahbni and Pip and Elgar close into a closer knot.

I am not so graceful as my brother, but I still remember the trick to moving without being heard that I learned as Shadow Hand, and I do my best to sneak toward their tête-à-tête without moving so quickly that it is noticed by Ahbni, whose back is to us all.

Pip looks up, possibly to confirm her protestation with me, and blinks to see that the three Hainish men have removed ourselves from them. I nod toward Ahbni, cut a glance to Pip's mouth, wag my eyebrows in a way that I hope conveys: *keep her distracted.*

"But it still went on without me," Elgar points out, oblivious to Kintyre and Bevel now in his effort to defend his work. "Lives went on. Time didn't stop. Things that had been set up in my books played out. Kintyre and Bevel—"

"But they wouldn't have gotten together if I hadn't meddled," Pip says, playing along. "So maybe? I don't know. I don't know if they were heading toward it naturally. I don't really think they would have gotten there if I hadn't forced them to tackle the issue head-on."

Pip shoots me a questioning look when Ahbni is distracted with thought, but I shake my head.

"But the point is that Bevel was pining after Kintyre the whole time. And when it was out in the open, Kintyre was open to it. Is that something you put in?" Ahbni asks Elgar.

"Definitely not!" Elgar yelps. "Not because, you know, there's anything wrong with that. Just... no, I didn't intentionally write my hero to be bi and his sidekick to be gay, and then have them sleep with and fall in love with women. I wouldn't do that."

"So then, maybe with fanfic, because the writers are not the Writer, it takes many stories to influence the world, but influence it, it still does," Ahbni muses.

"Like, it would take thousands of entries on an archive site about the Shadow Hand to make Forsyth feel confident enough to leave Turn Hall and do some legwork," Pip says, pointedly not looking over at me, the person who had only left to go on an adventure of his own after she had prompted me into that, too. But who had confessed to having had a slowly building desire to go out there and "be marvelous, myself" before she'd arrived. "It would have taken millions of entries to make Bevel brave enough to grab Kintyre by the hair and kiss the stupid fool."

"That's incredible," Ahbni breathes.

"It's horrific," Pip counters. She looks down at Elgar meaningfully. "It's terrifying enough to know that your entire personality and fate are in the hands of one flawed human being. But to know that the basic building blocks of your desires and sexuality and selfhood can be so... overthrown? By what is apparently a virtual committee? I don't know. That sounds like nightmare fuel to me."

And Pip has had nightmares enough about being puppeteered to know.

"We won't tell them," Elgar said, immediately and resolutely, looking up to where Kintyre and Bevel are now against the wall, holding a whispered conversation. Kintyre's hand is on the pommel of Foesmiter. "We can't."

"I think they're safe in this realm," Pip says. "I don't think the stories can touch them here. But I agree. We won't tell them. I don't want them worried about Wyndam, or Caerdac and Bradri, or the Pointes."

"Who are they?" Ahbni asks. She glances at Kintyre and Bevel, but doesn't seem perturbed that they're holding a conversation separate from her. I feel awkward, caught between the two groups.

"Nobody important," Pip says firmly. "And nobody worth telling stories about. For their sake. And for yours." Then she claps her hands together, rubs them swiftly, and looks around the room.

"Now, if you'll excuse me. I want to catch up with my brothers-in-law. Forsyth, I think Ahbni probably needs to check in with Ichiro, don't you? Can you help her find him?"

Ahbni clenches her jaw, mulish, watching Pip walk away.

"She doesn't need to dismiss me like that," Ahbni mutters. Then, not realizing the irony of her action, she turns away from Elgar. I cannot see what she's doing, but she strides to the door a moment after that, and is gone.

"Huh. Well at least one person is able to get some signal down here," Elgar pouts. "Lucky."

"*She what?*" *I ask, whipping around.*

"*Her* phone's working," Elgar says, as if I am the dimmest man on the planet.

And in that moment, I realize that I am. I must be. For how could I have missed that?

I race after the girl. But when I reach the ballroom, she is gone.

Deciding how many people to populate book three of the series with was an ongoing struggle. In one of the versions, I even thought I would bring Bradri, Wyndam, and Caerdac into the Overrealm to help fight the Viceroy. I thought this would give me a good opportunity for Wyndam and Kintyre to gain closure on their goodbye, and to repeat the act three pattern I'd established in the first two books of the dragonet and her rogue appearing just in time to conveniently impart much-needed information to our heroes. I also thought this would be ample opportunity to reveal that Caerdac had been a girl in disguise all along (because, you know, each epic fantasy plot has to have one!)

Unfortunately, as I plotted the climax of the novel, I realized that pausing the action to bring them out, and then use them, and then put them safely back inside the books again, was a poor idea. I really wanted to write them one last time, but it just wasn't meant to be. Is this, I wonder, what they really mean by killing your darlings?

You'll also note that Caerdac is speaking as if the two of them never worked alongside Forsyth et al. in act three of *The Forgotten Tale*. I was writing sections of books two and three at the same time, so this particular scene—though it was in book three—was written before I revised the third act of book two to make the rogue and dragonet a part of the team that rescues Alis. Originally, they met our party of adventurers on the road, gave them vital information to find the Viceroy as proof that narrative convenience really does befall Kintyre an awful lot, and then moved on, as they did in *The Untold Tale*. Before I could edit this section to reflect the fact that Caerdac and Bradri had joined the team, it was cut from book three.

FORSYTH

"Oh, it's you!" the rogue lad says, and his expression is torn between delight at recognizing us, and wariness. He puts himself between us and the dragonet who is now, a year later, over ten hands taller than it was at the shoulder the last time we encountered it. Its head used to be the size of a horse's, and now is easily the size of an elephant's.

"Is that—?" Kintyre asks, not bothering to complete the sentence before he snatches the sword out of the lad's grasp. He turns the blade over and, sure enough, right there in blocky Hainish runes, it says: Valorbringer. "But how—?"

"Oh," Caerdac says with a careless shrug. "The weather witch stole it. But when the Writer returned the stars, the totems returned, as well."

"Where did you find the sword, though?" Kintyre asks.

"That is, how did it come to find you?" Bevel cuts in, one hand on Kintyre's forearm, calming, as if he half expects Kintyre to whip Valorbringer behind his back like a covetous, mulish child and refuse to give it back.

"Pulled it from a rock, I did," Caerdac says, and rubs the end of his nose vigorously. "Was just sticking up from a crevasse. I feel like some poor blighter got it stuck there mid-battle and couldn't get it out in time to save his skin. There was lots of bones all around it."

"You... pulled it from a stone... ?" Pip echoes faintly, her freckles popping out again. She gropes backward for a chair and sits heavily.

"Why were you on an old battlefield?" I ask, more curious about the person from whom this sword might have come than how the lad found it.

"Easy pickings," Caerdac says with another shrug. "Jewelry, coin purses, gold buckles and jeweled pommels, and metal banner poles that any good smith would take as payment for fixing up our stewpot. The carrion birds get the flesh—Bradri and I take everything else."

Wyndam, still blinking around him, says: "Where are we, and how did we get here?"

"I thought we could do with a monster of our own," Elgar says with a smirk.

Bradri gasps in horror at the implication. "I am no monster!" she snarls, her scales peaking up in her ire so that she looks nothing so much as like a giant, scaly, affronted cat.

Did you know that Elgar Reed, the fictitious, best-selling mastermind behind *The Tales of Kintyre Turn*, has book reviews? I wrote these fake reviews to be read and referenced in either The Silenced Tale or one of the subsequent stories, but never found the right place for them in the prose. Deleted from the book, I give you: what the Overrealm thinks of Elgar's books.

"What Reed manages to do in this series is no less than provide the new generation of fantasy readers their own Lord of the Rings to covet, to examine, to love. It's precious!"
— Nathaniel Parker, *The New Fantasy Reader Magazine*

"With each successive book, Reed proves the power of imagination has not been killed by television. He's a first-rate storyteller, and I hope his readers continue to anticipate each of his books for years to come."
— Emily Dupuis, *The Dragon's Horde Book Blog*

"While you can't deny the mainstream appeal of Reed's *The Tales of Kintyre Turn* series, those of us fantasy readers looking for some substance to go along with our sword and sorcery will be disappointed. All Reed gives us is more Nice Guys™, more steel bikinis, more dopey sidekicks plodding along behind idiot heroes, and increasingly implausible situations. But the man is a bestseller, you can't deny that. And even if I don't like the messages behind the narratives, teenagers are reading; and it gives me a chance to share conversation with my kid. Well, forces me to, really. The stories are great, and the action literally leaves me and the kid breathless, but here's hoping that the next book in the series is smarter. I mean, c'mon, Mr. Reed. It ain't 1987 anymore. We've grown up reading your books—it's time for your books to grow up, too."
— Anonymous, *The Reading Dad*

"Derivative, but in a sort of entertaining way."
— *The Monday Evening Post*

"OMG, I love it! This is great! And Reed's clearly still got his slash-goggles on for Bev and Kin, which makes this book even moar fantastic! I've been waiting for it fivevaaaar. I am the happiest fangirl on the planet right now!"
—From *@EREEDFangirl333*

"Every time I pick up a new book in the Tales of Kintyre Turn series, I hope that this will be the book where Reed creates female characters that are characters, instead of plot devices. This book was not that book."
—Violet Wolfe, *Pub's Weak*

HEALTH

his is the third of the stories for Wattpad, the last of Forsyth's immediate-POV shorts. Much like the others, this one is set post-novel, a few days after the end of *The Silenced Tale*. (It also overlaps a little with *Magic*, which you'll get to in a moment.)

For this final entry, I wanted to fold Kintyre and Bevel into the close, domestic joy of the Piper house, and Alis demanding bedtime stories and snuggles seemed the perfect way to do it. But the end of the third novel presented a unique set of circumstances and challenges in terms of where best to set a moment like this in the timeline. Especially as these shorts had already established a pattern in their narrative approach, with each one being a story told to Alis. So how did I continue the rambly second-person POV with three other people breaking into the story?

Alis has a proven love of her uncle Bev's particular brand, so of course, I had to pull the Great Hero and his Paired into the tale. There simply was no other way to do it. And though this one definitely did my brain in, I think the result is a worthwhile blend of elements that captures both the quality of the previous shorts and the wider lens of additional characters. Although, dear Reader, I suppose you'll be the proper judge of that.

Ah, and there we are, my sweeting. Home at last. Home at last! Victoria has missed us, I am sure. I can assure you that I have quite heartily missed it, in return—at least, the parts of it that are home. My servers, my coffee maker, my own mattress... oh! What a great yawn that was, sweeting. Yes, I know. We're all tired. It's been quite a... a month, now, hasn't it? Quite a life, really, but of course, you wouldn't know that.

I don't suppose you'll remember much of these years, will you, Alis? Hain, or Uncle Gar, or... or any of it, really. Such a brief period of your life. It will all be gossamer, and fairy wings, and spiders' webs in your mind, and in mine... stone, and storms, and smoke. It boggles me that something so influential, so pivotal, so *weighty* will be nothing but dreams and mists to you.

Ah, yes, I know. Your da is being boring and introspective again. Don't tug so, sweeting. I'm coming. Where are we off to? Your ma has charged me with getting you settled for—ah.

"Unc Bev!"

"Hey there, polliwog."

"Bevel."

"Forsyth. What—oops, no, Alis, don't crawl on your uncle Kintyre. He's asleep, and I'd like to keep him that way."

"No!"

"Yes, I'm afraid, sweeting. Here, Bevel, pass her over to—"

"NO!"

"I can hold her."

Oh, sweeting, your uncle Bevel will spoil you terribly now that he is on this side of the books with us. Of this, I am certain.

"She is meant to be going to bed, Bevel. It's far past time."

"To be sure. How 'bout I tell her a story?"

Your uncle says it so nonchalantly, with a careless, throwaway shrug. But in his eyes, I see hope twinkle. His cheeks pink. He wants this. He wants to pamper and comfort you. He cannot pamper and comfort my brother while Kintyre sleeps, and he feels at loose ends. He feels useless in this Overrealm, this place where Kintyre Turn and Bevel Dom are naught but fiction, where swords are illegal and adventures happen only in books. Where, if he is no squire, no sidekick, no fellow knight, no trothed consort to a lord, then he has no idea who and what he is.

An uncle. He can be that. A brother-in-law. A husband.

There is no harm in encouraging that, sweeting. Though I fear it will make you the most doted-upon, spoiled child in all of Victoria, to have the full love and attention and focus of your uncles, your parents, your grand- and great-grandparents. A pity you will have no cousins to share the burden with. You certainly shan't be having any siblings. Sorry, sweeting, but it has already been decided. And no amount of begging you may do when you are old enough to understand that parents may be appealed to for such things will do you any good.

"Nothing violent," I allow.

Your uncle smirks and nods once, then moves to sit by his trothed's head. You squirm in his arms, as slippery and wriggly as the creature he has dubbed you. Kintyre stirs in his drug-enforced slumber, nuzzling into Bevel's hip. He moves onto his side, flings his tree-trunk arm around Bevel's waist, trapping you, my dear Alis, as well. He winces when you shift, and returns to resting on his back. Bevel settles you between them, slides Kintyre's nearest hand up and into his own. Yes, sweeting, that's very gentle of you, to cradle Uncle Kintyre's arm so. My, my, though! You can hardly get your own small arms around his bicep.

"Let me think," Bevel says, a finger to his lips, a mock expression of concentration on his face. "Do you know about Wisps, polliwog? I could tell you how the Wisps learned about lanterns, and why it's lucky to have a Wisp choose your home to light."

"Wis'!"

"Wisps, it is," Bevel says, a mirror to your enthusiasm.

"Ouch?"

"Ouch? No, polliwog, the lanterns don't hurt the Wisps."

"No. Kin's ouch."

Oh, my sweet, my darling girl. I see your mother in your worry, in your compassion, and it moves me so. I was turning away, would leave you to your uncles and this story in peace, but now I hesitate by the door. What will you do, I wonder. Perhaps I'll wait a moment more and see.

Your uncle looks to me for a cue on how I'd like him to answer. This story is his to tell you, however he likes to tell it. This, my dearest girl, is part of being a role model: the task of how to make awful things palatable.

Your uncle accepts the incline of my head as permission and reaches out to ever so slightly lift his trothed's sleeping shirt. I have seen the wounds, of course, sweeting. I was there when they were inflicted. I was covered in the blood they let escape. I have not seen them since they closed, however. And you have never before seen anything like this network of raised scars.

What will you do?

Ah! Ah! So sweet. My dear, I am more smitten with you each day. Your uncle is, too, it seems, for his eyes are warm and tender when you lean forward and gently, so gently, lay your face against Kintyre's tum. You are careful not to touch the scars, though how you know to do that, I cannot say. I have given you no such warning.

"Muah!" you say, whispering. "Muah, muah!"

Your uncle looks up at me, confused.

"In the Overrealm," I say gently, "they have a custom. When a child is hurt, one of their parents will kiss the place as a form of poultice. 'Kiss and make better,' they say."

"Kiss and make better," your uncle says musingly. Then he leans forward, presses his lips to the patch of unharmed skin over his trothed's heart, and echoes, "Muah."

And oh, your giggle is a delight, sweeting. Silly Uncle Bevel, to join you in your play. Silly Uncle Kintyre, lying so still as to let you kiss his tum.

"'Issess, 'issess!" you demand, and your uncle Bevel scoops you against his chest, flips you round as you squeal with happiness, and blows raspberries on your back. You kick and fidget, absolutely delighted, and I am delighted for you.

"Kiss and make better, polliwog!" your uncle says, and you lean over and smack another wet kiss on Kintyre's forehead.

Kintyre mutters in his healing sleep, but does not wake.

"Kiss and make better," Bevel says again. He heaves you over his shoulder like a sack of sugar.

"Come now!" I say. "You're meant to be calming her down, you great ninny."

"Da, da!" You laugh and squirm, arms out to reach me. I catch you up, and oh, you're getting so big, my sweeting! How much longer will I be able to lift you like this? How much longer will you let me?

"Yes, that's right. Come to Da, sweet girl. Bedtime for ladylings. I do not think you'll be getting sleepy in here."

You laugh, and squirm, and I take us back to the door.

"Goodnight, Bevel."

"Night-night, bye!"

"G'night," your uncle says, but he is distracted. His dark blue eyes are stuck like spellcraft on Kintyre's sleep-slack face. He leans down and kisses his trothed on the lips. "Kiss and make better," he murmurs.

AUTHORED

MAGIC

And here we are, at the last of the three novellas written to match the three novels. *The Untold Tale* and *Ghosts* are all about admitting things to yourself, finding out who you really are, and how the act of acknowledging that truth can change you. *The Forgotten Tale* and *Arrivals* are both about what happens when the Happily Ever After is over and real life steps back in. And Magic, companion to *The Silenced Tale*, is, much like its Paired novel, a story about the importance of imagination, the power of belief and community, the miracles born of hope, and the wonders found in the everyday.

My editor for this series—Kisa—warned me partway through editing this collection that she was getting sniffly, and I will admit, I was, too. With these stories—and with this novella in particular—I have been ever so slowly saying goodbye to these people, and this world.

You can't blame me if I want to hand them all heart-string plucking, comfortably sweet, Happy-Ever-After happy endings, can you? Especially since I put them all through so much.

PART ONE

While Kin is being sewn back together by strange
healers I don't know, Forsyth sits with me in a room filled
with uncomfortable chairs and despair. Other people
sit here too, crying or white-faced, waiting on news of
their loved ones. Some of them are the warriors from the
hall—Bob cradles both his wrist and his cane close, while
Kora hovers over him like a distraught chicken. Others
comfort and croon to each other. Many just stare around
at everyone else, like I'm doing. Nobody seems to want
to meet anyone else's eyes, everybody's faces slack and
bloodless with post-battle shock. The Soldier's Ailment,
Kin called it.

Pip went back to the inn to fetch clean clothing for
Forsyth and says she'll buy some for me. I'd never be able
to fit into Forssy's clothes—both of his legs together are
probably still skinnier than one of my thighs.

At least there's a water closet in this building, with
plumbing like they have in dwarven cities. I've already
scrubbed my hands and face clean. But there was blood—
Writer, so much blood—on my sleeves, on my chest, in
my hair. I'm desperate for clean clothing. It would give
me something to do, at least.

"Bevel, stop pacing," Forsyth says from his own
uncomfortable chair. He sounds weary, and looks worse.
"You do my brother no good by this."

"Better than just... just doing nothing!" I shoot back.

"I can't... Forssy, I can't just... sit still."

"Well, you're going to have to, brother mine," Forsyth huffs, looking around him. Nearly all eyes are on us, though some people pretend they aren't looking. It's like being back in the market in Turnshire. "You're attracting attention, and I really do not think you will appreciate the kind you will receive if someone realizes who you are," he adds in a hiss under his breath.

Someone dressed in volunteer-blue raises one of the small devices Forssy called a "smartphone" at me, and I turn away so they can't capture my face. Right, sure, I guess Forsyth has a point.

"Can't I see him?" I ask, and Forsyth shakes his head. "I don't want to interfere. I just want to *watch*."

"Trust me when I say that you do not," Forsyth says. "I've watched medical dramas on the television. It's not... as neat as if we were to do it, ah, *our* way. Come, Bevel, if you cannot sit still, then let us go for a walk."

"But the healers..."

"They will find us if they need to. We're hardly un-noticeable. Come." He gestures down the hallway. Huffing, so he knows just how annoying I find the act of following his suggestion, I slump after him. He directs us into a little shop filled with cut flowers, and brightly packaged foods that Forsyth calls sweets, and biscuits, and a delicacy of bread and filling called "sandwiches." There's fresh milk to drink, or hot tea, or something sweeter if I want it. There are stuffed toys for children. And along the wall, there's row upon row of *literature*. Pamphlets and bound leafs called "magazines"; puzzle books; adventure scrolls bound like spell-tomes that Forsyth calls "paperback novels."

Forssy is drawn to the novels, and I follow. Rifling through some stories to keep my mind off what's happening right now, and where I can't be, seems like the least aggravating thing I can do to distract myself.

It's not until I pick one up that I realize I can't read any of the thrice-damned things. They're written in the script of the Overrealm, and I can't interpret these runes. Forsyth, always the bookmouse, has obviously been studying them, because he reads some of the descriptions on the backs of the novels to me. Not because I want to choose a tale for him to tell me, but because the types of stories the Writers of this realm deem worthy of recording are—yeah, I'll admit it—fascinating. And I'm pole-axed to discover that most of them are *fiction*.

The magic and the worlds, and the people and deeds these books describe—almost *none* of it's true. None of it's *real*. But they're filled with fairies and enchanted swords and wizards. Magic does not exist in the Over-realm. And the fact that the denizens of this place seem to spend so much time making sure that everyone knows it doesn't exist is *fascinating*.

"They're stuffed with magic," I say as I pick out another for Forsyth to read to me. This one looks slightly terrifying—a giant goose in a kerchief is reading from a large spell-tome to a gaggle of docile-looking human children, probably luring them into complacency before devouring them. "Are these doorways to other realms, too?"

Forsyth leans on the shelf and takes the book from me.

"Perhaps," he says, and then makes that *face*.

It's the squinched, sour-looking one that I always thought was prissy and priggish. I understand now that it's a look of pain. Forsyth says he gets a tight ache behind his eyes and around his heart when he doesn't *understand* something.

He was Written to crave knowledge, but he doesn't just crave it. He requires it, like the rest of us need air, and water, and sleep. I was Written to be Kintyre Turn's perfect partner, and yet I'm out *here*, and he's in *there*, and I—I need to breathe. Panicking won't change anything.

"Or perhaps not," Forsyth amends, and his expression smoothes out. "There's no real way to know, I don't think. I have... searched on the Internet, but if there are other people in, ah, our *situation*"—he says it so delicately, like we're caught in the middle of an orgy and not just in a realm that's no longer our own—"then no one has come forward to confess to it. Or if they have, they are somewhere where the Internet is not accessible."

"Like a madhouse?" I snort. "That's where I'd suggest someone who said they escaped from a fairy-story should go, if I were still Shadow Hand."

Forsyth frowns. "You would? Really?"

I shrug, resettling my clothes on my shoulders, my skin itchy with his disapproval.

"Well, maybe not," I allow. "I would probably try to help the poor bugger first."

Forsyth nods, reassured. "Good. I would hate to hear that, had you been Shadow Hand instead of me when Pip was rescued, you would have locked her away instead of believing her."

Chastened, I gesture to the book in his hand. "I'm still surprised by how many of these are brimming with magic. The adventure tomes are overflowing with the stuff."

"And those are just the books in this shop," Forsyth says. "There is a much, much wider selection in the public libraries."

"Libraries? Plural?" I ask, and he nods. "And yet... nobody believes that magic is real. Nobody in the Overrealm even understands that the tales they read could be doors into other worlds."

"Perhaps," Forsyth cautions. "Or perhaps the magic of the Deal-Maker only works for us."

"Yeah, perhaps," I echo.

Forsyth reads summaries to me until we reach a shelf of books that he hesitates over. They're shelved so that I can't see what image is on their cover. But whatever it is the spines say, it's shocking to my brother-in-law. The blood drains from his face, and his eyes grow red, and wet, and tight around the sides. His mouth draws down into an absolutely agonized grimace, and he scrubs at his lips with the back of one bloodless, shaking hand. With the other, he props himself against the shelf, his knees buckling ever so slightly. Swallowing hard, he slips one of the books out of its snug place amid its brethren. He turns the back to himself, gasping a little at the photograph he finds there, which leaves the front unobstructed to my view.

I can't read the runes, but I recognize the man depicted in this painting. I know the line of his back intimately, the curve of his nape, the curl of his hair, the contour of thigh and calf. He stands heroically on a crag of rock overlooking the Sunsong Sea, his face turned away from me as he shades his eyes against the glare of the northern sun. Below him, *The Salty Queen* strides across glittering waves. And further out, I can see tell-tale specks that are the sirens.

"Writer's balls," I breathe, and pull another book off the shelf. This cover is a painting of Turn Hall from the rear approach, the Shadow Hand—*Lewko the Elder*, I remember, the memory having once been poured into my mind by the Shadow's Mask, and still there despite both the mask and I being stuck now in the Overrealm—waiting at the corner. Again, Kin is painted from the back, his face obscured by his hair and the angle.

His face.

I'm suddenly, overwhelmingly desperate to see my lover's *face.*

I yank the rest of the books off the shelf, piling them up in my arms as I flip each of them over, searching, searching, but no, no, Kintyre is looking away in every painting. His beautiful blue eyes are turned away from me, and I may never... I may *never see—*

I'm on the floor, suddenly, and I don't know how I got there. My arse cheeks sting, and my elbow throbs, and my chest burns, and I have to suck hard at the air to get anything into my lungs. Forsyth scrambles to prop me up, to rest my back against the shelf. Books scattered on the floor like dead pigeons. The proprietor of the shop looks annoyed, and in a blink, there's a healer stooped over me, her fingers pressed against my wrist. She's looking intently into my eyes, though what she hopes to find there, I have no idea.

"Breathe, Bevel," Forsyth says gently. "Go on, breathe, easy now. In and out."

"Kin—" I choke, trying to obey him, but the air feels like a burning lump in my lungs, and I can't dispel it. "His face... I can't..."

"It's okay," Forsyth says gently. "He-he'll be okay. You'll see hi-him ag-agai-gain-n."

"But I can't..." I don't know what I can't do, or see, or express. Only that it crushes my heart like a fully armored fist closing around it.

"All will be well, I sw-swear it," Forsyth says, and his determination helps set me at least a little bit at ease. Forsyth tries not to lie where he can.

The healer straightens and steps away. "He's fine," she says to Forsyth, as if I wasn't there. "He could use some sleep, and some fluids. Water, not caffeine."

"Yes, nu-nurse," Forsyth promises earnestly.

She quirks a smile at his seriousness, shakes her head,

and bids the proprietor goodbye on her way out the door. Forsyth collects me up off the floor, and we reshelve the books.

"I want to buy—" I say, but Forsyth interrupts me with a head shake.

"We have them all at home."

"But—"

"Bevel, I understand this impulse to have something of Kintyre to clutch close," he says gently. "But I promise you that you will soon be able to clutch *him*."

"Oh," I say, deflated, stunned by his insight and humbled by his compassion. I turn one of the paperbacks over and over in my hand, filled with nerves and wishing that I could... I could spar or wrestle or something to use up this jarring, clamoring impatience that zings under my skin. Forsyth looks away from my hands sharply. I look down to figure out why and... ah, his face looks back up at me.

He looks like Algar Turn. Same forehead, same nose, same beady, squinty eyes. Same beard. Same thick frame. But this image is not a portrait of my late father-in-law.

"Oh, Forsyth, I..." I begin, but I don't know how to finish. Forsyth turns his whole body away, covering his eyes. His shoulders seize upward, his mouth pinching, his other hand clasping hard at his stomach. In my panic about my trothed, I've forgotten that Forsyth has also lost someone dear to him today.

"I wuh-will c-co-cope," he says, his voice sounding like it's been wrung out of stone. "Just... let us-s-s re-tu-tuh-turn to the wai-ai-ting room, yes? But wuh-wa-water first, as the n-nurse comman-nds."

He grabs two clear cylinders from a glass-fronted cabinet, and then something off the bookshelf, and pays for them both with a small shiny rectangle. He explains, as we return to the waiting room, that he has bought a child's primer book, meant to teach younglings how to read and write the runes of this culture. He gifts it to me with a cheeky grin that doesn't quite dispel the lingering sorrow hanging over my head. But his thoughtfulness goes a long way toward melting the cold dread that's still frosting up my lungs.

My trothed will live. I have that, at least. And now, with this book, I have something to do. Some action to take. Some way to cure my own ignorance and to fill the horrible, stretching, silent hours.

But our Writer is dead.

Forsyth's voice and breathing even out, his sorrow sinking back behind his mask of concern. Though it ended worse for me, this trip to the shop was just as bad for him. When we get back to the room filled with chairs, we find Pip waiting for us.

"Hey, *bao bei*," is how she greets her husband. They kiss gently, quickly. It's casual and affectionate, and it makes my heart twist that my love is not here to bestow the same sort of kiss on me. *My* Turn is absent. My Turn is *hurting*.

She has two sacks of a slick white material, and she hands one to each of us with a watery smile.

"I had to guess your size," she tells me. "Go on. Go change. Just put your dirty clothes back in this bag, and we'll get them cleaned up later."

What I find when I go to the water closet for some privacy is a pair of long trousers made of blue canvas, more snug around the calves than I'm used to, and possessed of a strange closure that takes me a few moments of tugging at the metal tab to fathom. There's also a simple red shirt with short sleeves, made of a soft cottony material, with more of the indecipherable runes splashed across the chest. There's a sort of long-sleeved red house-robe with another of the strange, metal-toothed closures bisecting the front, and a deep hood that I choose to leave down. Nothing in this ensemble is Turn-russet or Dom-amethyst, and it breaks my heart to have to fold away my other clothes, to put them back into the strange slick bag.

How will the healers know that I'm Kintyre's family when they come out of their secret room now?

When I get back to the waiting room, Forsyth has already changed. He and Pip are curled against one another in the uncomfortable, hard chairs, his arm flung over her shoulders, and they're looking down at her smartphone together. Forsyth looks up at me, then grins and coughs out a chortle.

"*Bao bei,* you are a naughty, naughty woman," he scolds his wife. She smirks at him. I look down at my chest, wondering what it says. But I decide not to ask. Maybe it's better not to know.

Before I can start to get antsy and annoyed again, before I can even open the primer book Forssy gave me, a healer comes into the waiting room. He looks around, then heads straight for Forsyth.

"Mr. Piper?" he asks, and Forsyth stands and proffers his hand for the man to shake.

"Yes, that's me," Forsyth says.

"I'm here to update you on your brother. Are you... did you want to step away?" He eyes Pip and me carefully, clearly trying to decipher our relationship.

"No, we'd all like to hear what you have to say, if that's acceptable," Forsyth says. "This is my wife, Lucy. And this is my brother's husband, Bevel."

The healer shakes our hands, as well. "Mr. Turn, is it?" the healer asks me, and, not wanting to be sent away or excluded, I murmur my agreement. I don't mind the new surname if it makes it clear that I'm part of Kin's family. "If you three would follow me, I can show you where your husband has been put."

"Put?" I can't help but echo, and the words sound strangled even to my ears. *Putting* someone somewhere is the kind of verb I'd choose for a corpse.

"He's sleeping now," the healer assures us. Relief splashes across my skin. I woosh out a breath I didn't know I'd held in, suck in another, and for all that it tastes of the hospital's potions and sickness, it feels fantastic. "There was a lot of trauma in his abdomen, though, so we've decided to keep him asleep for the next few weeks. Give him time to heal up before he tries to use his digestive system or rips the stitches on his stomach, eh? But he came out of the surgery just fine. He's a fighter."

"You have no idea," I mutter, but I can't help the grin that's splitting my face.

"Yeah, I noticed his name. Kintyre Turn," the healer says with a chuckle as he leads us up a hall and to an open door. "Like the books?"

"*Exactly* like the books," Pip says with her own relieved grin, and then the rest of the world falls away, because there is my trothed—my *husband*, Forsyth called him, and perhaps men are allowed to *marry* in the Over-realm?—lying on a bed.

The healer stands by the door, talking seriously with Forsyth and Pip, gesturing confidently. I ignore them and cross the threshold. The room is small. Bereft of adornment. It contains only a small water closet, a large window, two chairs, and a raised bed ringed with strange devices and instruments whose uses I don't know. In the center of all of it, like the sacrifice in the middle of a summoning tableau, Kintyre lays silent and still.

The first thing I touch is his chest, just to be sure that it actually does rise and fall with breath. Under the thin sheet that covers him, his stomach is a bulk of what I presume are bandages and dressings. I lean down gently and, slowly, softly, kiss the mass of fabric. Then I take his large, square hand in mine—the back of which is pierced with some sort of metal needle leading to a clear tube of liquid—and kiss his knuckles. Someone has washed the blood off of his hands, off of his face. I find that I am grateful, though it accentuates the pallor of his skin. I kiss his cheek next, then each of his eyelids, then his mouth. His eyes flutter, but don't open. His mouth purses, an unconscious response, but doesn't curl into a smile.

He sleeps the sleep of the bespelled. A healing sleep, I hope.

"Sit, Bevel," Forsyth says next to my ear, and I don't know how he snuck up on me so quietly, or how he managed to get a chair behind me without my knowledge, but I'm grateful for both. I sit. "Drink."

I take the cylinder of water Forsyth presses into my hands, drain it dry, and hand it back. And then I begin a trothed's work of Speaking Words over the ill. The healers have completed their butchery. The vigil falls to me now.

"What's he doing?" the healer asks, his voice coming from the doorway.

"Praying," Pip lies to him.

"Ah," the healer says softly, understanding in his own way. "I'll leave you to it, then. I'll be back at the end of visiting hours to check up on the patient."

I pay the man no attention, because something... something is wrong. I'm clutching my trothed's hand and murmuring Words of Healing, Words of Strength, Words of Courage over and over again. I can feel the anxiety building, the panic clutching at my throat, because the Words aren't working.

Forsyth and Pip bid the healer goodbye. And then, as if he's afraid to startle me, Forsyth carefully lays his hand on my shoulder and says, sadly: "Bevel. Words can't be

Spoken here."

They could in the hall, in the battle, but not now, not with the Viceroy dead and gone. Magic doesn't exist in the Overrealm. Hells and blast it all. This is going to be a hard habit to break.

"How am I meant to hold vigil, then?" I snarl.

I hear Pip come up on my other side, but I can't seem to make myself look away from Kin's sleep-slack face. "Just be here," Pip says. "He knows it's you. I promise it will help."

"And the healing, what about that? And helping him shoulder his pain?"

"That's what the medicines are for. I promise, Bevel. He's safe now. It's fine. They're taking care of him. They're keeping him asleep so he can't tear his insides further. Look, see this line? They're even feeding him— you won't need to try to force him to swallow broth while he sleeps. He's well looked after."

"If you promise," I say gravely. Pip wouldn't lie to me, any more than Forsyth would. I have to trust her.

Still, I would prefer it if I could Speak Words. I would feel much better about this whole ordeal if I could help. But I can't. There's nothing for me to do. I won't even be needed to feed him, or clean him, if Pip's right. So I lay my forehead against my trothed's thigh, and close my eyes.

Kintyre Turn lives. Though I can't help him, Kintyre Turn will breathe yet. His heart beats. Mine beats, too. It says: *He is here. He is alive. He is alive. He is alive.*

Forsyth manages to get us a reprieve when the healers first try to push us out the door, using his charm and clever tongue to buy us a few more hours. But when the midnight hour is long passed, and the floor warden makes a round and finds me still in the chair watching Kin breathe, he makes it clear that I can't stay. And when he fetches a healer to confirm that I'm not allowed to sleep in the same bed as my trothed, and that I have to leave over the night, I'm horrified.

"No way!" I snap, when he tries to usher me out the door. I was asleep just before, so I'm still a bit cranky and fuzzy. And, all right, I probably take his declaration that "visiting hours" are far past over with more rancor than I should. All the same, I plant my heels as best as I can on the slippery floor tiles and hold my ground. "I'm not being separated from Kin!"

"He won't even know you're gone," the healer says, sounding both exasperated and like he's trying to be patient.

"I'll know!" I snarl. Pip took my sword back to the inn before we even came to the hospital. Right now, I'm dearly missing its familiar weight, and the way palming the pommel always made it very clear just how very serious I was being. I suddenly miss being Sir Bevel Dom, hero of Hain and Lord Consort of Lysse and Turnshire. My word would be law, then. Not this sniveling healer's.

"Mr. Turn," the healer says. "You need proper sleep in a proper bed, and a real meal. You need a shower. You can come back tomorrow when you've had those things. Visiting hours start at 8 a.m. I promise you, he's not going to get up and walk out without you."

"You never know," I say, but I can already feel myself deflating and giving in. My back hurts. I'm desperate for some decent sleep on a decent feather tick, and now that I'm awake, my stomach is growling like Capplederry. "This is Kintyre Turn we're talking about. Stranger things have happened."

The healer looks bemused. He holds his arm out toward the door invitingly.

I'm defeated before I can think of another protest. I napped, yeah, but I'm still utterly fagged. And I do want to be at my best for Kin when he awakes. And it's a "when," not an "if," thank the Writer.

Thank... well, thank *someone*.

I lift and kiss the back of Kin's hand one more time, and then lay it carefully over his heart. The front of his hair is still crusted with a little blood. I flick the last rust-colored flakes away, smooth back his hair, drop another kiss on his forehead. I murmur one last Word of Healing into his ear, just in case.

"It's odd," the healer says as he escorts me down the hall. Maybe he's just going in the same direction as me, but it does feel a lot like he's making sure I don't sneak around and double back. "Kintyre Turn. And your brother-in-law called you Bevel?"

"Yes," I say warily, waiting to see what he's digging at.

The healer chuckles. "He wouldn't happen to be named Forsyth, would he?"

"Er. Well, yes."

The healer stops in the doorway right before the waiting room, and turns to me, eyes wide. "What, really?"

"Really," I say.

"And did you grow up in the magical land of Hain?"

I nod gravely. It never does to lie to a healer. Not when they could one day hold your life in their hands. The man studies my face for a long moment, dark eyes narrowing, and then his somber expression cracks into a façade of mirth.

"Okay, okay, yank the other one," the man says, and he claps me on the back, like we're having one big joke together.

"Other what?" I ask, looking at his hands.

This sends the healer into an even bigger fit of laughter.

"Fine, okay," he says. "Big fans. I get it. You're too old for your parents to have named you after the characters—did you legally change your names? No, wait, never mind. It's none of my business." The healer waves his own question out of the air. "You have a good night, Mr. Turn. Master Knight Dom," he corrects himself with a theatrically gallant head nod. Then he shakes his head, shoves his hands into the large pockets of his odd white healer's robe, and returns to the warren of rooms. I'm firmly left on the other side of the swinging door, in the room of uncomfortable chairs.

Fantastic. How am I supposed to get in contact with Forssy to tell him I've been evicted?

"Bev!" a voice calls, and I look up to realize that Pip is waiting for me by the front entrance.

I raise a hand and trot over to her.

"Hey, bro," she says, and slings her arm around my shoulders. "Forsyth figured they'd be kicking you out right about now. C'mon."

"Where are we going?" I ask, not being able to resist turning back one last time to glance back down the hall to Kin's room.

"Our hotel's down the street. It won't be a long walk."

"I'm used to walking," I protest, in case she thinks I'm too tired or weak to make it there on my own.

"I know, Bev," she says, squeezing my shoulder. "It's fine. Besides, we have to pick up dinner on the way. I've already called in our order."

"What dinner?" I ask, my stomach grumbling again as we push through the front doors of the hospital and out onto the street. The humidity slaps me in the face, startling in the thickness of the air and the stench of hot stone, old urine, and cooking meats from a nearby market cart. I turn my nose toward the latter, wishing I had my string of coins with me so I could purchase one of the vendor's sausages right now.

"No, no. No street meat for you, Bevel Dom," Pip says, steering me in the opposite direction. "For your first real meal in the Overrealm, I'm introducing you to *pizza*."

Forsyth and Pip have a room with separate sleeping and lounging areas, and what I'm told is a very small kitchen, though there's no hearth and no pantry. We sit in the lounge and feast on flatbread with melted cheese, a plethora of spices I've never had before, and topped with chicken, mushrooms, and a strange tart-sweet fruit called pineapple that neither grows on a pine tree nor is the texture of an apple. Bloody vexing! The Overrealm's inability to call a thing what it is, is beginning to give me a headache.

After dinner, I'm introduced to another form of not-magic called a television. Forssy explains that it's like a play which is beamed—again, by not-magic—from where it's being performed to our room for our viewing pleasure. It's all very difficult to follow, and the narrative of the tale we're watching is unfathomable. Eventually, I just decide that I've been sociable enough and retire to the second bedroom to try to rest.

I lay down, and shut my eyes, and press my thumbs against my temples, and bite my bottom lip, and I *do not* weep. Eventually, I must fall asleep, because I wake with the dawn, though I don't feel rested at all. Hauling my aching body out of the bed is a task that feels as insurmountable as Mount Craeigspyre. The fantastical, overwhelmingly large and wealthy city outside the massive window in my bedroom is slowly coming awake. A pink dawn crawls up out of the harbor, and far below, I can see the dark specks of tiny people beginning to populate the walks.

Scrubbing my scruffy chin, I consider returning to what is probably the most comfortable bed I've ever had in my life, and...

Hells.

My shaving kit and valet are in Hain.

Fine. I've lived all but the last year of my life without a valet. I can bathe and shave myself alone. It takes me a few moments of fiddling, but I figure out how to use the dwarven-style plumbing, and the tiny square of hard soap that has been wrapped in more of the strange clear fabric that crinkles and tears easily. The rain-head takes a bit more fiddling to decipher, but when I do, I can't help groaning at how marvelous the miniature waterfall feels. Hot water and a thorough scrub go a long way toward making me feel human again, if not rested.

I'll have to ask Forsyth to pick up a new shaving kit for me. Mine is probably still sitting in my office where I...

And then it hits me, for the first time since this whole unbelievable mess began.

I will never see Hain again.

I mean, I knew that I could never go back, would never go back, when I... but the *meaning* of it really smashes into me for the first time. I stand in that bathing chamber and stare at my reflection and know, deep in my guts, that I will never again shave with the travel-razor Pa made for me. I will never again wear the gold-embroidered waistcoat that Kin commissioned for our trothing ceremony. I will never again revel in the pure bliss that is Dorthi Pointe's seedcakes. I will never see Wyndam wed, and I will never have the opportunity to ruthlessly spoil his children.

I've given up *everything*; every material thing I ever hoarded for the sake of sentimentality, every friendship I treasured, every relationship I had woven from the tapestry of blood and laughter. I have no wealth, no clothing, no *horse*. How am I to survive?

Can I be a writer here, knowing what it is a *Writer* is in this realm? Does the Overrealm need adventuring heroes? Can Kin and I thrive on the road, or will we be forced to impose on the hospitality of Forsyth and Pip indefinitely? And if we return to questing, can we stand it, with his injuries and our age?

Steam fogs the mirror, and I use one of the fluffy white towels to wipe it away. I look myself in the eye, honest and hard. By the seven hells, I look like an old man. I look exhausted. I am exhausted. I could sleep for another fortnight.

But no, I want to go back to the hospital, to sit by Kin's bed. I want to comfort him from this side of wakefulness. I want to be holding his hand when the healers deem it safe for him to open his eyes. I don't care how many days it takes, I will be there. And until he does wake, until it's safe to remove him from the immediate care of the healers to wherever it is that Forsyth and Pip live, I will push away worries of the future. Right now, Kin is my all, my everything, and he will be all I think about. He's all I have left of Hain.

And he lives.

That's a kind of magic in and of itself.

I spend the morning in the hospital being diligent with the children's primer book. It's either that or go mad staring at Kin's face, watching and counting each breath he takes. Pip sits with me in the hours leading up to lunch. She's a kind and patient teacher, with paper and a not-magical quill that never needs to be re-dipped in any ink pot. When my brain can't take any more study, Pip swaps out with Forsyth. He brings more wonderful delicacies from the take-away taverns of the Overrealm for our lunch, and we talk.

Before Pip, before the Shadow's Mask, before we spent a month traveling Lysse together with a cart pulled by a giant cat, Forsyth and I hadn't gotten along. We'd never even really spent a significant stretch of time together. We'd never had long chats, never sat in amiable silence in one of Turn Hall's many studies or salons, never made jokes about Kintyre at his expense, and in his hearing. I had six brothers already, then. I had no need to add Kin's whiny, cranky, fussy, bossy little brother to the mix.

Now, Bossy Forssy is the only brother I have left.

The realization makes my heart rush in my ears, and my lunch jolt in my belly. I swallow hard, blinking at the burn in my eyes. Forsyth just keeps talking, even when I knuckle them, giving me time to recover myself. He doesn't make a point of asking what's wrong. We both know. No need to make it worse.

As I take deep breaths, timed to match Kintyre's, Forsyth tells me how he's established himself here. We spoke about hacking and spying before, in Lysse, but now that I can *see* a smartphone, I understand better what he means. We dance around the topic of Elgar Reed, and the arrangements that, even now, Forsyth is undertaking. There's a lot of paperwork, apparently, in order to have our Writer's body prepared for travel back to his home kingdom for burial amid the bones of his blood relations.

When we've run out of things to safely discuss, things that won't make either of us avoid each other's gaze or make our words run dry, Forsyth shows me "the Internet." We're touched by the outpouring of grief from the Readers. Some of them have immortalized our Writer with images, and songs, and poems. A few of the images feature artistic interpretations of Kin or me, or both of us, prostrate with grief, lost in poetic mourning. It's all very odd, and at the same time, flattering. It helps to know that around the world, there are people who suffer Elgar Reed's loss as we do, who feel what we feel, who share in our sorrows. Still, it's a bit weird that people are puppeteering Kin and I to do it, though.

Forsyth sheds quiet tears during this, and it's my turn to fill the echoing silence of the hospital room. Chattering like a fishwife, I drown out the low pipping of the machines surrounding Kin's head with tales of the Hain he left behind. Lewko the Younger is seven now, and determined that, by the age of eight, he'll have learned everything necessary to take over the mantle of the Sword of Turnshire from his father. Caerdac, in the meantime, has turned out to be a disastrously eager apprentice to Sheriff Pointe. There was some grumbling along Lysse's northern border not too long ago about land rights and tax pickets moved secretly at night, but as soon as Pointe and

Caerdac had soared in on the back of Bradri to hear the complaints, the farmer had somehow suddenly recalled that he *had indeed* accidentally switched his neighbor's pickets for his own while taking them down to mow the verge.

Wyndam, meanwhile, had been taking Forsyth's advice to heart. He's been traveling the Chipping with Capplederry. The Great Cat seemed to have changed alliances back to House Turn once more, abandoning Law Manor for the stables at Turn Hall and the long, ranging walks that it went on with Wyndam each day. The Lordling Turn had explored every wood and glade of the Chipping, inspected every public market, wandered every communal building, and had supped, it seemed, at every hearth and table of every citizen of Lysse, from wealthy merchant to bookmouse scholar to lowly crofter.

"'I should know Lysse as well as I ever knew *The Salty Queen* if I'm to be her Captain,' was how Wyndam had explained this compulsion to me," I say.

"Smart lad," is Forsyth's pronouncement. "I hope the goodwill he's now engendered will stand him in good stead."

"I'm sure it will," I reply. "Though he wouldn't take the Shadow's Mask."

"He wouldn't?" Forsyth asks, scratching the scar on his cheek, surprised. "Odd."

"Hmm."

"Caerdac, then?"

"No, too enamored with the constabulary."

Forsyth looks at me, askance. "Then who were you grooming?"

"Gisella Gyre."

"Gisella Gyre," Forsyth repeats, astonished.

"Just because she's a woman—" I say, leaping to my secret protégée's defense, but Forsyth cuts me off with:

"Of course it is not because she's a woman! It's because she's a *Gyre*."

"Snob," I accuse him playfully.

He harrumphs and slumps back in his chair, folding his arms over his chest. "You must have been back and forth to Kingskeep quite often to tutor her."

"Oh no," I say with affected offhandedness. I love winding him up. "She lives in Turnshire now."

"She... I beg pardon?"

"She married Mamot Moslie."

"The *schoolmaster*?" Forsyth blurts, goggling at me. "Well... I'll be dashed. How ever did their paths cross?"

"They met at our trothing ceremony."

Forsyth runs his hand over his face and chuckles. We talk more of Gisella Moslie, of the Free School and the painter that Forsyth had sent off to Kingskeep when he was a lad, the pear orchard that Pointe's first apprentice eloped away to and now manages, and how King Carvel has begun to show signs of the palsy that afflicts all the older men of his line.

Eventually, though, we run out of topics. When our silences and our staring at Kintyre—still and pale in his bed—get gratingly long, Forsyth produces something called a "tablet" to entertain us. Though it's not made of stone.

"I thought you would like to investigate this world some more," Forsyth suggests. "Here, let me show you how to search for more short plays. You seemed intrigued that though there is no magic here, the people of this realm are enamored of it. Shall we start with some featuring that?"

What in the seven hells is he on about? "I thought you said there wasn't any, really."

"A different sort," Forsyth clarifies and shuffles closer so I can see the play more clearly. "Of a kind called 'stage magic.' Ah, here we are. You'll like this one, I think. The description states that the magician will cut this woman in half, and then reassemble her."

"Necromancy?" I ask, alarmed.

"The woman will remain alive and unharmed. She will only appear to be cut in half."

"They must go through a lot of stage blood."

"I don't think there will be any blood at all," Forsyth says. But he's staring at the tablet warily all the same. As if he's only just realizing that this might be a more gruesome act than he thought.

He taps the screen with a fingertip, and the play begins.

"How?" I ask again, amazed by what I'm seeing. "How is that done?"

"Stage trickery," Forsyth says. "Of a sort that involves misdirection, sleight of hand, smoke and mirrors. I'm not familiar with the specifics, exactly, but it's little different from what the King's Players can achieve, save that the mechanisms are more advanced."

"Amazing, yeah?" I say, riveted by the magician's tricks.

"Indeed. The tablet is set to autoplay—it will advance to the next video automatically. If there's a video you'd like to watch again, press this here... tap it lightly, yes, like that, and it will replay as many times as you like. If a red light begins to flash, it means that the tablet is about to... ah, lose power? It will become dormant and inoperable until it's charged again."

"Like a magical ward needs recharging occasionally?" I ask, making sure I understand.

"Exactly so," Forsyth says, pleased that I understand so easily, and so well. I may just be a blacksmith's boy, but I know how the world runs. Mostly.

There's lots in this strange new world that I can't

fathom, but bit by bit, it's beginning to make sense. It will have to—Kin and I are stuck here forever. But if Forssy can pick it up, then of course Kin and I will be able to get it, too. We have to.

Forsyth excuses himself from the room with a lingering, backwards glance at his sleeping brother. I crowd up next to Kin so he can hear the videos, even if his eyes aren't open. The healer told me that speaking aloud to one who's in a healing sleep is recommended, for it's proven that they can hear you. I describe the illusions as they play out on the video, and every few moments, I look to Kin, to see if he has woken, if he's following along. Then I force myself to tear my eyes off his slack face and turn them back to the videos. If I linger too long on him, I may get caught up in my own head again, and in my own despair.

Kin will wake. The healers all promised that they would let him wake when he's well enough to do so. He *will*.

After "visiting hours" have closed—and it's hateful that I'm being forced to leave my trothed behind in the hospital every night, alone—Pip takes me to a nearby bookshop that sells an array of marvels that far outstrip simple books. There, she gifts me with a children's magic kit. It's meant to teach younglings the basics of the stage trickery I've been using to distract myself. The simplicity of the language, when Forsyth reads to me the instructions for a basic playing-card trick later in the hotel, is insulting. But I remind myself that I'm not proficient in the runes of the Overrealm yet, and that eventually, I'll appreciate how easy the instructions are when I have to read them for myself.

For now, I'm feeling prickly, and after mastering the

first trick, I slump into the kitchen to have Pip show me how the cooker works. We dine on some sort of dish native to her mother's kingdom, and I barely taste it. In both a sulk and a pique, I go to bed, hoping to fall asleep to make the dawn, and the opening of visiting hours, come sooner.

So of course, I end up lying in bed, staring at the ceiling, feeling the emptiness beside me on the mattress with a piercing keenness. My guts feel hollow. My head is aching. I can't make my mind hush up.

I want one of Mother Mouth's headache draughts and rage a little when I remember that no such potions exist here. I can't sleep. I can't spar to exhaust myself; Forsyth has Smoke, and I have my sword, but there's no *space* for it here, and we're not allowed to take our swords into the hotel gymnasium. Being armed in public is, apparently, *illegal.* I don't even have Turn Hall's well-stocked wine cellar at my disposal; getting drunk would certainly help time pass faster. Bah!

For lack of anything else to do to exhaust me enough for sleep, I shove back the coverlet, drop to the floor, and do push ups until my arms tremble and sweat drips from the tip of my nose. But even that doesn't seem like enough to still my thoughts or exhaust my body.

I want Kin.

I want Kin beside me, and healthy.

I know how lucky I am. I know that if we were in Hain, he would already be dead. Dead and buried and decomposing. I *know* that I'm lucky. But right now, separated from him, stuck in a world I don't understand, with signage I can't read and kitchens that are infuriatingly complicated, and the mortifying ignominy of having to resort to books meant for children... I despise that I have to start all over again. I wish there was some magic to make this all easier.

Learning to read and write once was difficult enough.

In the morning, I chatter to my trothed about the world I see, the foods I eat, about the despair I feel, and the worry that his eyes will never open again, and, more than that, about the magic that is not. I tell him these things for no other reason than that it's innocuous and consuming enough to distract me from darker imaginings of worse things.

I ask the healer about a headache draught as soon as he comes by on his rounds. He gives me a packet of small white nubbins to swallow with water, and they turn somehow both chalky and mushy in my mouth, bitter and grainy. When I eventually get them washed down, they do the trick. But uhg. Vile.

"There's this famous duo, Kin, called Penn and Teller," I tell my trothed, swallowing against the aftertaste of the potion. Kintyre's eyes are still closed, his breathing still slow and even, his face still pale, his lips still bloodless. If I can't Speak Words of Healing, I can at least follow the healer's suggestions to talk to him as much as I can.

"They have a... a program where they challenge other magicians to perform a feat, and then they explain how the feat was done. And none of it's real magic, though it very much looks it. It's all parlor trickery, of course. Like something a child learning how to disappear objects does when he's first starting out as an apprentice. Floating things, and missing cards; stuff like that. Nothing so grand as setting wards, or changing the weather, or... or healing the sick."

I pull the hand that I never stop holding close to my face and buss my lips over Kin's scarred knuckles.

"Pip has bought me a children's magic kit," I chuckle.

I pause, by habit, for one of Kin's sarcastic observations to cut in, but my trothed says nothing. I swallow hard against the fear and the anger lumping up in my throat, burning the backs of my eyes. I add, with somewhat more desperation than I'm comfortable owning to: "Maybe when you wake, I'll be a master of sleight-of-hand tricks. Maybe all my practice in pickpocketing so we could purchase provisions has made me light-fingered enough already."

Again, Kin fails to make a crass comment. Again, I swallow hard.

The next few days pass in the same manner. I'm at the hospital every day for all twelve of the "visiting hours," and stay by my husband's side. (Forsyth's governmental trickery has given me a certificate declaring a marriage, and not just a trothing, which is moving and meaningful in a way I can't describe. To have my relationship with Kin be viewed as *equal* to that of a man and a woman fills my life with a security and peace I hadn't realized I was desperate for.)

Forsyth and Pip come in the afternoons to bring food, and books to study, and cables to recharge the tablet computer-thing that is not made of stone. In the evenings, they force me to go shopping with them for more suitable attire for the Overrealm, to pick things out for Kin to wear when he's awake, or to introduce me to new spectacles and cuisines that I wish I was experiencing for the first time alongside my husband. It seems so unfair that Kintyre, the one of us who adores architecture and art, isn't here to marvel at the soaring towers, and squat castles, and boggling art galleries of this city.

Pip seems to be elbows-deep in more paperwork than I ever had to do as Shadow Hand. It's all something to do with the tragedy, and the damage to the building, and something called "insurance." Forssy is just as busy, but his concentration is on making sure that Kin and I exist as citizens of the Overrealm, making sure that we have "bank accounts," and "social insurance numbers," and "medicare" to pay for Kin's bed and attention at the hospital.

Alis also arrives around this time. She's brought to this city by one of the "airplanes" that are also not-magic, and delivered to our rooms by her grandparents. My family is lost to me. But at least I have my niece here. And Forsyth introduces me to his father- and mother-in-law in the hotel. They are not my ma and pa, but they greet me just as warmly as if I were married to their daughter, and not simply married to the brother of her husband.

"Bev, Bev!" Alis bawls at me, arms out. She's on the ground as soon as she sees me, and manages to haul herself upright and wobble toward me by leaning on the coffee table.

"Hallo, dearling!" I say to my niece, and pick her up and settle her on my hip, like she demands.

"'Issis Bev!" she orders imperiously. "Now please!" I kiss each of her palms a dozen times.

"Look at you, all grown," I tell her. "And still demanding kisses like a frog, my little polliwog?"

Before I was summoned into the Overrealm, I didn't think I'd ever see Alis Mei Piper Turn again, I'll admit to that. The thought that I would miss out on the childhood of yet another small one dear to me had been painful. I had contented myself with the hope that Wyndam might have married early and would provide a brood of tumbling, rowdy little people to fill up Turn Hall while I was still young enough to roughhouse with them. But even that was a long shot. Wyndam's eye seemed to be turning toward Caerdac, and that was a—a girl, I correct myself before I can use the wrong pronoun—I could never imagine tying herself to hearth and home and cradle. But then, I had never imagined that of Isobin, either, and she had done a remarkable job in raising Wyndam.

"Hi," says the tall, travel-rumpled, sweaty man who had carried Alis into the hotel room. His hair is riotously ginger, his skin dotted with freckles, and his ears seem to be trying to escape in opposite directions. "I'm Martin, Lucy's dad."

"Bevel Turn," I say, enjoying the way the name flows across my tongue, and offer him my hand to shake, Over-realm-style. "Syth's brother-in-law."

"This is my wife, Mei Fan," Martin says, indicating the woman standing beside him. I drop a kiss on her prof-fered hand instead of shaking it. I know that's not the greeting here, but it makes Pip's mother grin and giggle, which is what I was aiming for. I'm not prepared to en-tirely lose my reputation as a charmer.

I see that Pip has inherited her strange features from her mother—the beautiful dark eyes, tilted upward in the corners, the planes of the cheekbones on a moon-round face, the gorgeous rich skin tone, the curtain of black hair. What a handsome people Pip's kingdom produces.

"Lovely to meet you."

"Yes, yes, lovely all around. Sorry, Bev, but I'm re-claiming my daughter now," Pip says as she plucks Alis out of my arms. Her eyes are red and sheened with tears, so I let my niece go. Pip and Forsyth retreat immediately to their bedroom to spend time alone with their child, and I can't blame them for it.

Mei Fan and Martin have been booked into a smaller room down the hall, so I make sure the not-magical card that acts as the key to our suite is in my pocket, and then help them move their luggage into their own space. They chat amiably with me about their journey here, about the surprise of the tragedy, how they hadn't realized that Forsyth had living relatives beyond Elgar, about how willing they are to help where necessary, and how much Alis missed her da and mum. About how happy they are to meet me, when they know nothing at all about me.

Rudding hells.

As I heft a bag onto a luggage stand, I'm struck again with the agonizing realization that I will never see my own parents again. No Pa and I bickering lightheartedly over the forge embers. No Ma scolding me for my shoddy darning job on my socks. No brothers teasing and wrestling, no sisters-in-law feeding me up, no nephews and nieces tumbling at my feet or dragging me off to the edge of town to show me flowers, and frog's nests, and their newfound ability with a toy bow-and-arrow. No more visiting Hey You in the stables and sneaking her apples. No more ales in the Bynnebakker pub where the friends of my youth brought their children to hear tales of my adventures from my own lips.

There is no blood of my blood, no flesh of my flesh, here. There's only Bevel Dom, and my line ends with me. Here. And so far from home that I can't even fathom it. Not really.

The truth of it punctures my soul. I can feel my spirit bleeding, sluggishly, invisible and unpatchable. I struggle to keep the smile on my face in front of these not-strangers who are also not-family.

"You must be exhausted," I say to the Pipers as my excuse to leave. It always worked for Velshi when he was helping us rid Turn Hall of unwanted linger-ers, and it works just as well, here and now.

"Yeah, thanks," Martin says, and I try to make it look like I'm not rushing for the exit.

Freed of my obligations, I return to the suite.

It's silent, save for the high sweet giggle of a child through the bedroom door, and the treble rumble of Forsyth singing to her.

I shut myself up in my own room and practice my reading until my brain is throbbing. Though it's not as tasty and effective as Mother Mouth's headache tea, I'm still pleased that the Overrealm has an equivalent medicine. I swallow two of the healer's chalky, horrible pills and go to bed.

For the next week, Martin and Mei Fan alternately visit with the friends and family they have in the city, showing off their granddaughter, and taking on the mundane chores of shopping and cooking so that Forsyth and Pip can spend time with Alis. I get my niece's undivided attention most evenings, as my daily absence makes me a novelty to her. I even have her all to myself once, when the Piper quartet goes out for a family dinner.

I was invited, of course. They never exclude me on purpose. But I wasn't feeling... sociable. And Pip, never one to waste an opportunity, suggested a "double date" with her parents and a little "Uncle Bev time" for Alis. I eat leftovers, Alis wears more of her own portion than gets it in her mouth, and we are both very diligent about her books until Alis nods off against my chest three pages into a hilariously terrifying picture book about sleepwalking in the snow titled, *Fifty Below Zero*.

Afraid to jostle her awake, and feeling lazy myself, I slide sideways on the sofa, settle my niece against my chest, wrap one protective arm around her to keep her from tumbling off me mid-dream, and let my eyes slip closed. She's a pliant, warm weight of the sort I've never allowed myself to fantasize about, not fully. Never allowed myself to admit that I covet.

The Pipers return from dinner to find us both asleep. I jolt awake when Forsyth lifts Alis from my arms. My hand goes immediately to my belt to—ah, but this is no stranger attempting to kidnap my niece, and I have no knife to hand, besides. Forssy nods, understanding what I had meant to do, approving of my hard-won protective instincts. I sit up as he whisks Alis into his room and to the cot the hotel had provided. I rub the grit out of my eyes.

"Here," Pip says, sitting on the coffee table in front of me. "We brought this back for you." There's a small paper box that smells of chocolate. I grin. Pip introduced me to the stuff, and we've bonded over the delicacy. "And this."

She next produces a small black device from her pocket. It's the length of her smartphone, but half the width, equipped with a touch screen and some sort of thin white rope emerging from the bottom like a lariat. Except the loop is broken in half by two bulbous little buds of hard white plastic.

"What's this?"

"It's a... a listening machine," Pip says. "These go in your ears, here, like that... is that comfortable?"

"Odd, but... yes?"

"Okay. And you press here... and *here*... so, there's music over here, and here... there are audio books."

"Audio books?" I repeat, and instead of explaining further, Pip taps the screen. A man's voice fills my head, as if he were speaking directly into it. He is clear, and crisp, and he's introducing a novel. He's reciting it, as a bard might recite a poem in a tavern.

Pip pauses the voice, and tugs one of the buds out of my ear. "I've preloaded it with a bunch of books I thought you'd like. Music, too. There are some classic books... but here, look, I made you a folder of books about magic. There are some biographies, and some histories, and some fiction. I really enjoyed *The Prestige*. I think you'll like that."

"I... I don't know what to say," I tell Pip, because it's true. I'm overwhelmed, again, by the thoughtfulness, the cleverness, the generosity of my sister-in-law. I'm no great reader, I'll admit to that. But I need something to help me pass the time until the healers think Kin is well enough to wake. And this will help.

"Just don't break it, okay?" Pip says with a laugh. She claps my shoulder affectionately, and then takes herself off to bed.

That night, I lay awake until dawn, listening to an absent man tell me a whole story, straight into my head, as if by magic.

The next new person I'm introduced to is a handsome, charming, but devastated man named Juan. He's accompanied by his "boyfriend"—the Overrealm term for one's Romantic Paired—a quiet, distinguished-looking older man named Gil. Juan is miserable, cloaked in the sort of walking-corpse grief that I've seen too often shrouding those who have lost shield-brothers on the battlefield. Gil is faring better, and from the way his gaze lingers on Juan, I know he wishes his Paired were free of whatever obligation brings the young man to Kintyre's bedside.

They wanted to speak elsewhere, but I refuse to be absent during visiting hours, not when I already have to abandon my husband every night. Pip had pressed for us to go to a nearby park to have this talk. I'm wondering now if I'll regret it. This Gil, when his eyes are not on his lover, has his gaze greedily latched onto *mine*.

And though he tries harder than his Paired, Juan can't seem to keep his eyes off of Kin, either. Like the healer in charge of Kin's recovery, it's not lust or admiration that colors Juan and Gil's gazes, but confusion and wonder.

Here, before them, are Kintyre Turn and Bevel Dom, and they can't allow themselves to believe it. For magic does not exist in this world, and there's no other plausible explanation for our existence and appearance—and *names*—that these people can accept.

In a fit of pique and overwhelming culture shock last week, in one of my low points, I had accused Forsyth of being ashamed of his heritage. I had seen his taking of his wife's family name, his adopting a new diminutive, as *shameful*, and cowardly, and a rejection of all that we are when all that we are is all that we have *left*. I'm starting to see now that he was perhaps the wiser one for it.

Bev and Kin, though, we'll stay. I couldn't bear to call Kin anything other than his name. And I don't think the oaf would remember his new name, anyway. Maybe we'll adopt a new patronym. Taking up "Reed" might be a suitable way to honor our fallen Writer. If Forsyth allows. And if Kin agrees—I won't do something as drastic as change my husband's name without asking him first.

"Juan?" Pip prompts gently, bringing his attention back around to those of us who are awake in this room.

"I... uh... there was a will," Juan says. "Syth Piper and family are the main beneficiaries." He hands a piece of paper I can't read to Pip. But I don't need to be able to read the paper, I can read her expression. Her mouth drops open, her skin blanches, her freckles stand out against a creeping flush.

"Holy tallulah," Pip says, eyes wide. "This is an *absurd* amount of money."

Gil snorts. "And there'll be more once the TV series is out. Royalties from that, plus a cut of the merchandising, plus the surge in book sales from people who want to read it before they watch it."

"*Bao bei?*" Pip asks Forsyth, and I'm not sure exactly how to interpret her glance and the question implied in her use of Forsyth's pet name, but his answer is something I understand well enough:

"I have already set them up with bank accounts. It will be very easy to ensure the royalty payments are funneled into my brother's reserves instead of our own." He smiles at his wife, a thin attempt at good humor in the face of the grim reality of just where this inherited wealth is originating. "And of course, I shall set aside enough of it to ensure Alis's education is paid for, and her life a comfortable one."

"And there's the matter of the... the house," Juan adds damply. "The estate is yours, Mr. Piper, but if you don't mind, I'd like to... there are a few mementos I'd... if that's okay, I mean. And you'll need to hire someone to clean it—the police have been through it for... for evidence. I can give you Elg—Mr. Reed's... uh... the weekly cleaning service's number," he finishes shakily, his voice damp. "Though I don't think I could... help you sell it. I couldn't stand it."

"We shan't be selling it, I don't think," Forsyth says, with a meaningful look in my direction. "I find myself in need of two houses, suddenly."

"Is your manor not large enough to accommodate just two more?" I ask. I was under the impression that their household was well-shod and stable.

Pip snorts. "'Manor' my arse, Bev. No one has manors. It's too expensive to keep staff. Our whole place could fit inside your Great Hall, with room to spare."

"Ah," I say, understanding. It would be a shame to ruin my suddenly amiable relationship with my only remaining family by cramming us into too tight of quarters. I know that danger well. I liked my own brothers much better when they married, moved out, and lived a village or two away.

I've been accused of being crude and thoughtless, but

I do have enough sense to wait for Juan and Gil to leave before broaching the next question. It's burning on the tip of my tongue as they linger over their farewells. Forsyth must see it there. He thanks Juan and Gil for coming all this way to hand-deliver this news, and promises to meet with them to finalize the hand-overs with a lawyer.

Juan tears his eyes away from Kin on the bed, shakes our hands, and goes. But Gil lingers beside me.

"Forgive me," he says. "But I can't... I just... listen, you are uncanny. Elgar never said that he based his characters on real people, and you and... this guy"—he waves at Kintyre—"you're just perfect. Your accent. Your bearing. You even have that damned little scar under your eye." He leans close to point to it, finger almost near enough to touch me, and I jerk my head back, blinking challengingly at him. "Right, sorry. I just... look, here's my card. Come to set, okay? I'd love to have both of you on set when he's on his feet again. Just... come consult, or something?"

"Consult?"

"You're familiar with the *Kintyre Turn* books?"

I can't help it. I snort. "Intimately."

"Then come to set. Please. See how TV magic is made."

"There's no such thing as magic," I remind him.

He grins at me. "Oh, this is going to be fun. I like you... *Bevel.*" He forces a little rectangle of thick paper into my hand. I want to read what's written on it, but it would take me an embarrassingly long time to do so, and I don't want to mortify myself in front of strangers.

"I make no promises," I warn him.

"No, I get it," he says. "I do. I don't... let me be clear, I don't want you to replace Elgar, okay? Nobody can do that. You're not runner-up to him. But you... you *both*... please. When he's up and around. What a resource you could be." He looks up, catching Pip's eye. There's something extra in his gaze there, something going on behind the scenes that I don't know about. "Just think about it?"

"I will," I say, and then, with hurried handshakes all around, Gil is gone.

"Well," Pip says, slumping into the chair beside Kin's head. She reaches out and brushes a lock of hair off my husband's forehead. "That was a circus. You sure missed something just there, Kintyre Turn."

The casual, affectionate touch and the breezy way she addresses Kin puts a lump in my throat. I hand Forsyth the rectangle of paper, and he explains that it's contact information.

"Should I?" I ask him. "He wants me to help. "

"Only if you want to," Pip says. "Once Kin's up and at it, you two will want to do something to keep you busy. I know you don't miss being Shadow Hand, not the way Forsyth does, but you're going to have to find some way to occupy yourself. This might be a good opportunity."

I can't help another snort. "You know as well as I that Kintyre Turn will never be content with simply telling people how things must look or happen. He will pick up the prop sword and wade into the choreography himself. " I rub my forehead, trying to massage away the building headache. "And I will have my hands full with the ruddy great brute while he does, won't I?"

"Will that be so bad?" Pip asks softly. I look up to find her patting Kin's arm. "Just like old times, right? Just like that time with the King's Players."

"Yeah," I say, and then excuse myself. I have a desperate need for a smoke, and the hospital doesn't allow pipes inside its walls. After a while, and after my bowl is packed and lit, Forsyth joins me in the hospital courtyard.

"There was another question," he ventures, after I've made a good half-dozen smoke rings. "I saw it in your face. Ask it now."

"It's a bit crude, but... how much wealth is a lot of wealth?" I ask. His forehead wrinkles as he thinks about how to answer, and I interrupt with: "I mean to say... I've... there's a magician," I start, not quite sure where to begin this conversation. Blast it. I hate being on the back foot. "I'm listening to the audiobook of his life, and he... he has a husband."

"Yes?" Forsyth asks, patient, while I chew on what to say next. On how to say it.

"You say there's no magic here, and I believe you, so this must be a science beyond my understanding. But in this book, this magician, he and his husband are able to produce... they have... there are *children*."

Forsyth leans back against the wall of the hospital, understanding at once what I'm aiming at. I've never been as grateful for Forssy's ability to infer things from scant facts and truths as right now. It's nice to not have to say it out loud, when I've got no rudding idea how I would even begin to articulate it.

"Yes, Bevel," he says, reaching out and squeezing my shoulder, reassuring. "Yes, there is more than enough money for that... that sort of magic."

"Explain it to me," I say, and I'm not ashamed of how eager I sound.

PART THREE

At the end of the month, the healers wean Kin off of the medicine keeping him asleep. He wakes in fits and starts, eyes open for only a few short minutes at a time. He smacks his mouth because it's so dry, snuffles, and then closes them again before I can force any water into him. The first time it happens, it startles me. I hadn't expected him to wriggle and twitch the way he had. The easy way he slips back into sleep each time fills me with a stab of fear that he's slipping away for good. I hide it. I mean, I hope I do. And if I don't, then at least no one is rude enough to point it out.

It takes a day or so, but eventually, Kintyre wakes enough to actually focus on the room around him. That damnable wrinkle appears between his eyebrows as he stares up in confusion at the ceiling, around at the devices crowding his head, and down at his stuck hand. It only smooths away when his eyes find my face. A dopey smile spreads over his lips, and this time, I know he's really awake. "Bev," he croaks.

"Shhhh," I say, my own voice as hoarse and quivering as his, though for different reasons. I hold the water glass so he can sip. "Now try."

When he's wet his tongue, he says, "Bev," again, and then, "Hello."

"Hello, my sleeping prince," I say softly.

"Oh? A prince am I?" he chortles.

"Only to me. You're a pain in the arse to everyone else."

Kin snorts at this, and then winces and tries to curl around his wound, which just makes him jerk and grunt in surprised pain. "Writer's nutsack," he growls. "Hells, that hurts." He tries to stretch, and groans again. "That hurts, too."

"It ought to hurt," I say, feeling tart. "You've been in a healing sleep for nigh a month. What were you thinking, Kintyre Turn? Getting yourself disemboweled like that?"

"Disemboweled?" he repeats, startled. "A *month*?"

"Yes," I snip at him, and sit back. I cross my arms over my chest. The knot of *something* that's been sitting behind my rib cage, keeping me from restful sleep, and being able to talk, and... and... any kind of *enjoyment* crumbles like old ash inside my chest. A sob bubbles up my throat, and I swallow it down hard, refusing to let it out. So what if my chin wobbles and my eyes burn? "You *left* me. Alone."

"I didn't—" he starts, but then interrupts himself with another wince.

"You *died*."

He freezes, and takes his time looking up at me. When he meets my eyes, it's with the deep guilt of a little boy who knows he's been caught out.

"I couldn't let the Viceroy—"

"I know," I blubber, and Writer's balls, what in the seven hells is wrong with me? "But you still died, Kin. Right there, on the floor. Blood everywhere. You made me watch that. You made me *live* that. It was awful of you." I want to say more, to say everything, to vomit out every measure of anger, and terror, and hurt, and loneliness, and disconnect I've felt without him for the last month. But the enormity of it all congeals into a ball against the root of my tongue and blocks anything else.

"I'm sorry," says my trothed—my *husband*, though he doesn't know it yet. He defies the pain to reach out, snag my hand, and bring it to his lips. "Forgive me."

"Only if you promise to never die again," I grump at him.

"I promise," he says.

"Wretched liar," I say, but drop a matching kiss against his knuckles. Then I free my hand so I can help him drink a little more water. "You can never promise me that."

"Then I promise never to be disemboweled again," he says solemnly between sips.

"See that you do," I tell him. Then I stand, press a gentle, meaningful kiss on his mouth.

"Mother Mouth around?" Kin asks when we part.

"Ah, about that," I say with a wince.

Kin frowns at me.

"Don't be mad, Kin," I say softly. "But I had to... I had to make a choice, and you were... it was either go home to Hain where the magic is strong, but help might not have arrived quickly enough, or stay where the healers were already..." I swallow hard, annoyed with my own cowardly prevaricating. I sound like Forssy. "I... well, I chose the Overrealm."

Kin coughs, and harrumphs, clearing his throat. I wait in agony for him to start yelling.

Then he says: "Good."

"Good?"

"Good choice," he says, and he reaches out and wraps his fingers around mine. "I won't mind the Overrealm, I don't think."

"You say that now," I scoff. "We'll see how you feel when you have to navigate the subway." I bury my head in his shoulder, breathe in the smell of his neck and unwashed hair, the staleness of him from so long without a proper bath, and shudder out a sigh of relief. "I'm going to go fetch your healer. Just relax."

"I'm exhausted," Kin says. "I've been sleeping for a month, you say, and I'm *exhausted*. Ruddy unfair is what that is. I want to stay awake with you."

"You've been getting well. That takes a lot of effort." I circle the bed, but before I can reach the door, Kin grabs my nearest wrist.

"Hey," he says softly. "I'm sorry I nearly died. I'm sorry I left you alone for a month."

"I had Bossy Forssy," I say, forcing a shrug and a tone of casualness that I don't actually feel.

"Ha!" Kintyre says, and then lays his free hand over the mass of bandages on his stomach, trying hard to hide his wince. "I bet that was tedious."

"Some nights," I allow. "But Forsyth's family has been good to me. We're in their debt, Kin. They're very generous, and they've been very kind."

He lifts my hand and kisses the tips of my fingers. "I'm desperate for some poppy milk," he says low, his voice gruff.

"I can fetch the healer if you just let go," I reply, and reluctantly slip my hand out of his.

"Never," he says, and we both know he isn't talking about our linked fingers.

The healer talks about *physiotherapy* and s*kin treatments* and *dietary restrictions* and all manner of things that Kin will have to do to regain full use of his body—but, the healer adds, regain it, he will. And that's the important thing. He's pleased with Kintyre's progress, pleased by how alert he is, pleased that Kintyre is hungry, though he can only promise Kin a thin broth and perhaps some form of parritch for his dinner—if, that is, Kin can remain awake long enough for it to arrive.

I summon Forsyth via the tablet. Shortly after the healer has imparted all this news to Kin and me, he's in the hallway repeating it to Forsyth. Who, I'm sure, is taking careful notes of all the healer's dictums. The fussiness of it would have annoyed me in the past, but now, I can appreciate the meticulousness of Forssy's habits—it means I can consult him later if I need. I don't have to keep anything in my head but Kin, and all the things I've been dying to say to him.

Kin does fall asleep before his food arrives, and I wake him again when it's in danger of growing too cold to be palatable. He whines and whinges that it's nowhere near as savory as something I could have prepared for him, even if I would have been forced to make the food simple for his sick bed. I wish, suddenly, that I had my sword belt and its little cylinders of spices. I could at least make the food taste a bit more like home.

That's something I've missed. For all that the many cuisines of the Overrealm are interesting, intriguing, and tasty, they don't season the food the same way here. I can't wait until we're back in the town called "Victoria," where Pip and Forsyth live, so I can assemble some comfort food. So I can use my own spices, my own mixes, my own travel-proven receipts.

After he's eaten, and I've helped Kin wash his face and neck, we talk about Wyndam. We talk about Caerdac as Sheriff, and Gisella as Shadow Hand, about how I had no time to tell anyone the Word that unlocks the mask, that it doesn't matter because it remained with Forsyth, cut off forever from the magic that used to power it, and now just a useless bauble. We talk about how someone is going to have to forge a new one, and how they'll have to begin to amass all the knowledge of the known world anew. We talk about the Sword of Turnshire, and how fine a lad Lewko the Younger is growing to be. We talk of how well Gisella Gyre has fit into Turnshire and her role as Schoolmaster's Wife, and how, as a scion of the House of Gyre, she will be there to guide Wyndam in the duties of a lord, if he needs it.

We talk about all we have left behind, and all of the things we will never see, or hold, or taste, or do, or cherish again. We talk about how my decision did not let him say his farewells. We talk about how I didn't really get the chance to make my own farewells, either. We talk about what will become of Turnshire, if we think Hain still exists with our Writer dead (it must; the Readers recall it; it must still be there; our friends and families are safe; we have to believe it), and what we will do with our lives once Kintyre is well.

A few days later, when Kintyre is well enough to stand and walk a little with my help, several things happen in quick succession. The healer gives me Transfer of Care papers for my husband, which will let him "come home" to Victoria, British Columbia, where he'll enter the care of a different specialist healer whose focus is to make sure Kin heals up the way he should. Forsyth presents us both with airplane tickets and identification papers. He's also made us some digital boxes where our Internet mail can be delivered. When I open mine, the first email to my new address (Bevel.Turn@gmail.com) is a confirmation for the tickets. The second is from Juan the assistant, verifying the details of Elgar's estate. The third is from Gil, of the television program, repeating his offer to have us visit the production set when Kintyre is able to.

Lastly, and in great secret, I arrange a consultation via email—all on my own!—with a company in the harbor city of Vancouver. I've been researching how two men may father a single child between my studies in Over-realm runes and stage magic. (I can only say a heartfelt thank-you to whomever it was that invented the assistant program that reads text on a webpage aloud via the computer. It's been an invaluable feature for me as I bash my way through learning to read a second time). I don't tell anyone else about my research or appointment yet. I want to discuss it with the expert first, before I decide whether or not this is something I want to suggest to my husband. There's no point in pushing him on this, and then deciding, later, that it's not to my taste.

We travel from the hospital in Toronto to the airport in a caravan—Kintyre and I by one of the white hospital trucks, and Forsyth, Pip, Alis, Martin and Mei Fan in a taxi van. I'm glad for the porters who accompany us through the airport, transferring Kin from the hospital's wheelchair, to the port's wheelchair, to the airline's. If they weren't there to help us with our tickets, and to guide us through the maze of checkpoints and scans, I might have lost my temper. It's all just so... circuitous. And *impersonal.* I find myself absurdly longing for the gruff tolerance of Pirate Queen Isobin. She never put her hands all over you when you tried to board her vessel. Or at least, not without enthusiastic and willing consent.

Forsyth, it turns out, hates flying. He hates the indignity of the security process, and the queuing, and the cramped seats—though they're an improvement to even King Carvel's finest carriage—and the sensation of taking off, and the view of the world far below us. I can't say I like the feel of the not-magic of this method of flight, either, but it helps that I have Alis to distract myself with. Kin, bizarre man that he is, spends the whole flight twisted awkwardly, and in exactly the way the healer told him not to, so he can press his nose against the glass that's not glass and watch the world speed by below.

"It's faster than Bradri," Kintyre tells me, more than once. "Do you see the way the landscape rolls over the horizon? It's gorgeous, Bevel. Where are my charcoals? Does someone have paper?"

Pip and I eventually trade seats so I can be closer to Alis's bag of necessities, and so Pip can chatter with Kintyre. I only half-hear it when she tells him the science behind our flight, and the names of the towns and rivers below us. Eventually, the servants produce a crude, cheap pencil and a small notebook for Kin. Pip sketches out the shape of this world for him, and shows him where we are in it.

Disembarking is another long process of shuffling, cattle-like, through corridors and security doors, and it's utterly draining in a way I've never experienced before. All I did was sit for seven hours! Why in the bloody hells am I so tired?

On the other side of yet another long, circuitous trek, we're met by representatives of the Royal Jubilee Hospital. Kin and I are whisked away to a private room in the airport so the specialist healer may assess Kin after our long, long journey. Martin and Mei Fan—who insist that we call them Mom and Dad, as if we were related by more than just a license—bid us adieu. The rest of Forsyth's—*our*—family waits for us, and Pip laughs at the pout on Kin's face when he needs to be levered up into the taxi van. I told him not to twist his torso to look out the window, but he didn't listen, and now the healer is mad at him.

We find that while Kin was getting scolded, Forsyth has asked his in-laws to go ahead of us and prepare the guest room for my husband and me (where I'm finally allowed to sleep next to him, thank the Writer). In short order, we are all in the house, Alis has been put to bed, and the ever-present magic of Telephoning for Take-Away meals has occurred. Kintyre stays awake long enough to shovel some of the food into his mouth, and then retires for his pain-blocking medicine—more not-magic in pill rather than potion form. I follow soon after him, exhausted by worry and travel, and am finally able to fall into a deep, restful sleep.

Kin sleeps late, and I let him. Today, we plan on nothing more strenuous than attempting a bath, now that the wounds on his stomach have closed up. In the evening, if he's up for it, Pip suggested we might take the carriage—the car—to a nearby park that Alis is fond of. It'll give us the chance for some fresh air, and let Kintyre walk around a little if he wants to.

My niece wakes soon after I slip downstairs. She howls down the house demanding her da, her ma, her breakfast, her "'ooks," and, once she's seen me, her "Bev!"

I don't mind being her climbing frame while Pip attends to her morning toilette. I mind even less when Pip trusts me enough to leave us alone together while she pops out to the local marketplace. We're going to need a lot more provisions now that we're settled for the foreseeable future. At the very basic, we'll need food for the kitchens, and some of the devices the healers recommended Kin acquire to aid in rebuilding his muscle and reacquiring his balance after so many days on his back, and so many injuries to his core.

For the first time, I realize that we haven't got any material wealth to offer Pip in recompense for all that she's buying. My few remaining gold coins were lost in the battle, I've got no jewelry to sell, and no way to access the wealth of Turn Hall to pay for its lord's upkeep.

Never before, never since I ran away to follow

Kintyre Turn to the Urlish Wars, have I ever wanted for anything. Kintyre's status as Lordling always ensured that we could credit a stay at an inn, or a purchase with a merchant, with a simple press of his signet ring to warm wax. And after the war, our renown as heroes was usually enough for folks to buy us meals and drinks at taverns, offer us beds in their houses or haylofts, or gift us with new clothes and weaponry as thanks for rousting a villain or saving a crop. And even if we couldn't barter or borrow, a trip to Kingskeep and to my printer was enough to ensure we had coin enough to furnish ourselves with whatever it was we wished to purchase. If we were really desperate, we just went to Turn Hall. Bossy Forrsy never turned us away, and we always left feeling well-rested, well-washed, and well-provisioned. Something I don't think I ever really appreciated when we were in Hain together.

And here Forsyth is, giving us a roof, a bed, food aplenty, and protection—again. Only, in this realm, the vast wealth of House Turn is also lost to him. He doesn't have an inheritance to keep his coffers padded.

Sheepish, and feeling like a burden in a way that I haven't experienced, haven't thought about since I left my ma's hearth, I hitch Alis up onto my hip and mount the stairs to Forsyth's study. He bids us enter, takes his daughter from me, and motions me to a chair. Alis babbles and garbles and giggles, clearly in the seat she loves best in the whole world: her da's lap.

"Forsyth," I say, with perhaps more gravity than he's ever heard from me, because he blinks at me in surprise. "I... I want to, ah..." I swallow, the oddness of both apologizing and begging boon from Bossy Forssy strange and unnatural to me. "I, uh, I know that, ah... Kintyre and I are... well, we're a burden on your household, and I wanted to..." I trail off, hoping that Forsyth will take pity on me and interrupt, say that he understands, say that it's no hardship at all.

But the brat has a smirk on. He's *enjoying* watching me wriggle like a worm on a hook. Prat.

"I... well, I, uh... I wanted to express my thanks," I say, fumbling on the words, everything coming out more formal than I really wanted it to in my awkwardness. "I know the wealth of our Writer will one day be ours, but until the estate has been settled, I have... I have nothing with which to repay you for what you spend on our upkeep. So, I thank you for that."

Forsyth nods once, seriously, acknowledging what this gratitude has cost me. I'm mortified to be in his debt. But at least he's good enough not to press the advantage and tease or humiliate me. My brother Vulej would have made a production about it.

"All that I have is yours, brother," he says gently. "And trust when I say that I have acquired enough wealth through my clever spywork that you needn't worry overmuch."

"I'll pay you back," I grind out between clenched teeth. "That I vow."

"That I know," he echoes. "In the meantime, I am laying the groundwork for your new lives here. I have been setting up citizenship for you. Kintyre will have to be Canadian, if he is to be my brother, but you shall be American, so that you may be made the inheritor of E-Elgar's es-estate with-with-out com-pli-complica-*blast*," he snarls, and presses his hand over his eyes.

I reach out and squeeze his shoulder gently. I don't know what to say, what platitude to trot out. They would all be patronizing, anyway, so instead, I just stay silent.

Forsyth buries his face in Alis's neck for a moment, hugging her tight to his chest and composing himself. I give him privacy—I stand and walk over to the wall where

Smoke has been mounted on a wooden plaque. The blade is pocked with chips and gouges from our battle, but still shines silver and ever-sharp with elf-magic.

That's something, at least.

When Forsyth looks up again, his eyes are red, but his cheeks are dry.

"Here," he says. "Come, Bevel. Sit by me, and together, we will construct a false life for you. The best lies are based on truth—tell me the names of your parents."

We spend the morning in this illegal activity, and by noon, Kintyre has woken with a fierce hunger. We feast on parritch and other easily digestible foods that Pip has left out for us, and then take our time carefully running a bath, cleaning his long hair, and scrubbing away the last of the battle and hospital from my husband's skin. When he's clean, I drain the dirty, cool water from the tub, and refill it with fresh and hot. I climb in behind Kin, so he can lay back against my chest, rest his head on my collarbones, his arms on the tent of my legs on either side of him.

And if, perhaps, our mouths find each other's a little too often, our hands wander a little too much, and we spill a little of the water on the floor, then what of it? It's been over a month. Kintyre and I haven't yet had the opportunity to engage in our traditional post-battle celebration. It's long overdue, and I am *famished*.

The next while isn't all smooth sailing and clear skies. While Kin had slept in the hospital, while I had distracted myself with tricks and illusions and this new alphabet, Elgar Reed's body had been attended to. As his closest living relative—at least, according to the falsified records that Forsyth had produced—my brother-in-law gave permission to Juan to organize and control the settling and arranging of Elgar's funeral. Were we back in Hain, Elgar would have had to be buried in Toronto, and quickly, to prevent putrefaction.

But here, the not-magic of medical science extends to even, apparently, the preservation and transportation of corpses. Between Forsyth from Toronto and Juan in Seattle, it was arranged that Elgar Reed's viewing and visitation would happen in his hometown. I had assumed that even then, Elgar Reed would be underground before Kintyre woke from his medical sleep. But apparently, the embalming the corpse has gone through will preserve it for the six weeks necessary for Kin to be well enough to participate in the wake.

Elgar's body has been available for viewing at a funeral home in Seattle for the past two of those weeks. The site has become a pilgrimage center for fans from around the world. But they have been holding the final goodbye until Elgar's "family" were well enough to attend.

Thus it is that, at the beginning of the sweltering Overrealm month of August, we make our way southward to say our farewells to the man who Wrote us.

Pip rents a van and drives four adults and one toddler across the border and to Seattle rather than put us all through the rigors of flying again. Besides that, it gives us a chance to see some of the landscape we'll have to get used to, as citizens of the Overrealm. It's much more populated than Hain—or any of the Four Kingdoms, really. The roads, as I've noticed in Toronto and Victoria, are a marvel of straight pavement, and every stop is filled with restaurants, way stations, and inns.

We take a ferry from the island to the mainland of Canada, which Alis does not enjoy at all. She flops in my arms, boneless, backwards, and wailing. I have to stand in the center of the boat to keep her from tantruming herself right overboard. Once we're back on dry land, she's pure as unicorn piss again. Definitely related to Kintyre, the little faker.

From there, we drive to the border. I'm amazed by how quickly we move. What would have taken our Capplederry-cart days to traverse will, Pip assures us, only be about five hours, if we have a meal break.

Kin and Pip are in the front of the van, with Pip driving. The middle bench is devoted to Alis and I, where I'm entertaining her by practicing the not-magic trick of making a coin appear in her ear. Behind us, Forsyth and his computers have the final bench to themselves. What he does back there, I don't know, but it keeps him quiet, which is a blessing, honestly. I'm learning to appreciate Forssy in ways I never did before, but that doesn't mean I have any more patience for his *droning*.

Kin and I are quite familiar with keeping ourselves occupied as we travel, so any fears Pip might have had of boredom and inaction turning us cranky and fractious have, at least so far, been unfounded. Besides, we five had been on the road together before. We know what to expect from each other. Though, last time, Kin and I had the opportunity to ride ahead if we were saddle-bored. Now, we're all trapped together in a single contained carriage.

Still, we arrive at the crossing between kingdoms before anyone can become too frustrated.

"Passports?" the bored soldier in the custom-house requests when we pull up. Forsyth hands five small books to the front of the vehicle—four black, and one blue. Pip hands them to the soldier, who pages through them. "What's the purpose of your trip?"

Pip has cautioned us to let her do most of the talking, unless we are directly addressed. In that case, she's given us a few phrases to memorize. She says: "Family funeral."

"Whose family?"

Pip turns to Kintyre. "My cousin," he says, just like she's coached him to do. "You've heard of him? Elgar Reed?"

The soldier jerks his head up, startled. "The writer? Aww, man. Yeah, I heard about that. You're related to him?"

"Yes, through his father's family."

"I'm so sorry to hear it, bro," the soldier says. He turns his back to us then, which, I can tell from the look of surprise on Pip's face, is unusual. He reaches into his little custom-house and turns back to us with a book in his hand. "He signed this for me a few years ago. He was an awesome writer."

"He... he—" Kin says, his voice catching in his throat. He coughs. "Yes. He was that."

The soldier frowns sympathetically. "Hey, bro, sorry to hear it. Be safe on your drive, okay? And, you know, give the man my respects, will ya?"

"Absolutely," Kintyre croaks. "Thank you."

The soldier hands back the little booklets, and then takes a step back so Pip may drive on. Before she can, he leans forward again and says, "Hey, bro, anyone ever tell you that you look exactly like Kintyre Turn?"

Kin smirks. "All the time," he says.

The soldier nods, as if they've shared a secret between them, and then waves us on.

Kin twists in his seat as we drive away, to address his brother. "Do people tell you that you look like Forsyth Turn?"

"Sometimes," Forsyth replies. "Though less since I've stopped wearing russet in public, and have changed my hairstyle." His hair is cropped much shorter in the Overrealm, that's true.

Kin's wearing a Sheil-purple t-shirt with a series of hand-language symbols that spell out *HAWKEYE*, and his hair, though still long, is now piled on top of his head in what Pip calls a "man-bun." He's also stopped shaving as diligently, and, with the aid of an electric beard trimmer, has begun to cultivate a fetching layer of "scruff." I enjoy his scruff immensely; the delicious beard burn on the inside of my thighs is proof.

Me, on the other hand, I've relished the ability to stay clean-shaven and smooth-faced without the fuss of needing Keriens and going through the hour-long process every morning. My own hair is shorter than I've ever worn it in the back, but with an artful swoop at my forehead that Pip asked if she could try out on me.

That people think that Kin still looks like, well, Kintyre, even with these changes is worrisome. We're about to wade into an entire crowd of *Kintyre Turn* fans. Will we be mobbed? Will we be photographed and harassed to aggravation, like Forsyth was?

"Don't worry," Pip says, catching our silent exchange. "I have a feeling people are going to be pretty subdued and respectful at this shindig. And if they're not, we can always just leave."

"It's not proper to leave," Kin says, but drops the discussion after that. Besides, it's not like we haven't had to deal with adoring women and enthusiastic hangers-on before. Not in the numbers that are expected at tomorrow night's wake, perhaps, but it can't be that much different. I hope.

After a few long moments of silence, where Kin keeps his eyes out the window and Alis begins to fuss and whine for a "'ook! 'Ook, *Bev!*", Kin asks: "Is the rest of the country all but barren? To have so many people living along the roadways."

"Sorta?" Pip replies. "There're big prairies and ranches in the middle of the continent—most people live on the edges, though. Or, in Canada, along the southern border. But there are much bigger cities than Victoria and Toronto, too. Not much bigger than Toronto, but bigger. The population on this continent can be measured in the billions."

"The billions," I repeat, aghast. "How does your king ever manage to ensure that everyone is well cared for?"

"Ah," Pip says, waffling. "*Bao bei*, you wanna take that one?"

We spend the rest of the journey learning about revolutions, representative governments, voting, and the political parties of our respective new kingdoms—nations. It's boggling, and a bit baffling, and, I realize, a big responsibility as, as a voting-aged citizen, we will need to be well informed. There's even *more* reading I'll have to do. Blast.

The not-magic of the map machine chirps more and more often as we get closer to our destination. We pull into the driveway of a home not unlike Pip and Forsyth's just around the dinner hour. Juan is standing on the front portico, waiting for us. He looks drawn and solemn.

"Hey," he says as we all climb out. "I've ordered in some pizza for you guys. Nice to meet you awake, man," he adds, extending his hand to Kintyre for a shake. It's even more awkward because Kin is still walking with a cane, and he has to switch hands.

"Ah, yes," Kin says, trying not to be fuddled about it.

"C'mon in," Juan says, pulling Pip's luggage out of her hands for her. Normally, Pip would complain that she was perfectly able to carry her bags herself. She's always been very vocal about how no special accommodations need to be taken simply because she's "a chick." But she's tired enough from driving to let him.

The house is, of course, not Turn Hall. Some small part of me almost expected it to be, or at least for the décor to be all Sheil-purple and Turn-Russet. Instead, it's the sort of white-stone-and-gray-marble generic that I've seen on the television. The foyer is not even remotely grand. A pokey little door leads to a pokey little bit of tiled floor and a pokey built-in wardrobe. To the left is a "living room," which is a kind of small salon with blue-gray carpeting and a lumpy old blue sofa. A patchwork quilt is thrown over the back of it.

Beyond that is a small kitchen clad in pale wood, cool with disuse where Forsyth's kitchen is rich and warm and lived-in. There's a hallway beside the pantry door that leads, Juan tells us, to an office and a small washroom, and a staircase. Upstairs, Juan leads us to the master bed-room with en suite bath, and a spare bedroom.

Forsyth hesitates on the threshold to Elgar's cham-bers. "I... I don't know if I can sle-sleep on h-his..." Forsyth says.

"I had the sheets changed," Juan says softly. "But I can show you how to set up the pull-out sofa downstairs if you—"

"This will be fine," Pip says, and bullies her husband into the room. "It will be better for us to have the en suite, with Alis." Her tone is brash, brave, but her touch on the base of Forssy's spine is gentle and compassionate.

Forsyth sighs deeply, nods once, and forces himself to walk through.

Kin and I stow our bags in the guest room, and then follow the delicious smell of melted cheese, tomatoes, garlic, and herbs down to the kitchen. Juan shows us where the dishes are, the beer he put in the fridge, and the wine. He puts a set of keys down on the kitchen counter.

It's not until he's halfway to the door that I realize he intends to go.

"Stay," I say, catching up to him and touching his elbow. "Dine with us."

"I shouldn't," Juan says, and his eyes are red-rimmed

and bright with emotion. "This isn't... this is your house now. I'll just be in the way."

"Nonsense!" Kin calls from the kitchen. "You were a friend of the Writer. Stay. Break bread with us and tell tales!"

"I was his employee, not his—"

"Nonsense!" Kin repeats, louder.

Juan snorts out a laugh. "Jesus. Okay, I see why Elgar wrote Kintyre Turn the way he did." But he comes back to the kitchen with me, and lets me pour him a glass of red wine.

I have the same, and Kintyre takes one of the tiny bottles of ale from the fridge.

"Should we wait for the others?" Juan asks.

"Syth needs some time, I think," I say. "They won't mind."

We toast Elgar Reed—the first, I know, of many toasts that are to come over the next few days—and dig in.

"This wine is..." I say, peering at the glass and trying not to make a face. "It's... tart. Not fruity."

"Dry," Juan says. "That's what Elgar liked."

My taste in wine doesn't match my creator's? That's a bit... huh. Ridiculous? What an odd thought. Why would he ever write me as liking something different from him? Not for the first time these past five weeks, I wish I'd had the chance to really talk to Elgar Reed.

"Bev likes something that tastes like jam," Kin says around a mouthful of pizza.

I shouldn't be touched when my husband remembers stuff like that. After all, most spouses do know that kind of thing. But I'm used to the old Kin, the Kin who only cared about himself, his own pleasures. This new Kin is marvelous and lovely, and just a little bit eerie, I'll be honest. One year of a new habit doesn't erase seventeen years of another.

"Here, I've got a Gamay," Juan says, as if that should mean something to me. He pours my remaining wine into his own glass. Smart man. He then fetches a clean one, the other bottle, and gets me furnished with a new drink.

"Much better," I tell him, after a tentative sip.

We eat for a little while longer in silence, and then Pip, Forsyth, and Alis come down to join us. There are tear-tracks on their cheeks, and their eyes are a little raw, but on the whole, they look calmer than they were when we went up.

Alis is at the stage where she wants not only what is on the plates of the adults, but *exactly* what is on our plates. When she sees Pip putting a kind of red sauce on her pizza, Alis points and shouts, "Me, too! Same-same!"

"It's hot, sweeting," Forsyth cautions.

"Same-same!" Alis insists. Her newest issue seems to be a dogged determination that everything should be identical, and everyone treated equally.

Forsyth sighs, theatrically put-upon, and puts a little of Pip's sauce on one of the chopped up pieces of piz-za. Alis jams it in her mouth and chews lustily, in defi-ance of her father's warning.

Then she screeches and spits the piece back out.

"No!" she yowls. "Ouch! Bu!"

"Papa warned you," Pip says, trying to smother a laugh, and gives Alis a bit of milk.

Kintyre decides he'd like to try the sauce, and snatch-es up the bottle of red sauce.

"Show-off," Pip accuses. "It's not actually macho to eat things that are too spicy for you, you know."

Kin only grins. But his scowl, and the speed at which he spits out his mouthful a few seconds later, matches that of his niece. Forsyth snorts at his brother's pain. It's the first time Forssy's cracked a smile since we got up this morning.

As is only right, we show up to the funeral home late the next morning monstrously hungover. We stayed up late with Juan, trading stories and learning all about the life our Writer had lived before he picked up the proverbial quill. Juan ends the evening by asking if he can keep the quilt off the sofa—it was made by Elgar's aunt, apparently, and Juan holds fond memories of it—and the remainder of the cat accoutrements. Forsyth and Kintyre agree. They don't have an emotional connection to those things, and Juan clearly does.

Now, the lot of us are tumbling out of the rental van and into harsh daylight.

"Uhg, why couldn't this have been one of Seattle's famous rainy days?" Pip whines, squinting against the sun.

The parking lot of the funeral home is bisected with a winding rope labyrinth. We bypass that and head straight for the glass doors. "What's that for?" I ask.

"To control the lines," Pip says. "Keeps people organized. The news said there were over four thousand people through here yesterday alone."

"Writer's nutsack," Kin cusses. "That's a damned lot of people."

Pip gives him a funny look. "Okay, maybe don't... say that kind of thing today?"

"Swears?" Kintyre asks.

"Things about 'the Writer,'" Pip clarifies. "We're going to be surrounded by Elgar's fans all afternoon. It'll be... odd."

A man in the Overrealm version of a somber formal suit greets us in the carpeted foyer of the house, and introduces himself. I have no head for his name, though, because through the doors behind him, I can see a coffin.

It's heavier, bigger, more ornate than any coffin I've ever seen before, except for maybe that of King Carvel's brother. Prince Partel had fallen on the battlefield during the Urlish wars, and had received a state funeral a few days after Kin had been knighted.

From everything I've heard about it, our Writer has been given a state funeral of his own. It seems appropriate.

And now he's... in there.

I've never been afraid of corpses. Unless, of course, they were liches. Or zombies. Growing up as I did in a poorish village far from the kingdom's capital, I'm no stranger to death, or bodies, or burials.

But this is... this is my *Writer's* body. This is my *Creator*. Not my God, not in the way the people of the Overrealm worship insubstantial beings that seem, at least to me, to be more rumor than fact. That seem to be embodied excuses to behave poorly toward fellow humans. No, though I never really believed it, my Writer was real.

When I met him before, alive and grinning, flushed with glee and triumph, he didn't scare me. He was a man—flawed, and genuine, and fallible, but so, so honest. Now... he's less than a man, and more than a spirit. He's *beloved*, and he's *gone*. And there's that curling dread in my guts that where I came from might be gone with him.

But no. I've seen the books. I've watched the footage from the television series. Hain's sun rises and sets, the stars wheel. Wyndam, and Gisella, and Pointe, and Dorthi, and Lewko, and my parents, and my siblings and their wives, and their children... they all live. They live in the eyes and the minds and the hearts of the Readers.

And yet.

And yet, I'm terrified to go through that door, to cross that threshold and... and be witness to the death of... not my father, but perhaps the closest thing to a father I could have had in this world. The sharp pang of missing my family, and the sharper agony of knowing I will never see them again—that they will never know what became of me, that I lived a peaceful and happy life in the Overrealm—threatens to escape from my belly in a groan. I put my knuckles to my mouth to stifle it.

Cross the threshold, I must. Enter the room, I must.

With Kintyre's arm tight around mine, our elbows pressed together, fingers twined, wrists connected at the pulse points, we brave it. Forsyth, Pip, and Alis form a tight knot behind us. Forsyth is shaking in Pip's arms, his face dry, his eyes screwed shut. He's trying to say something, but his stutter is so bad right now that all he's saying over, and over, is: "Buh-buh-buh-*bao*—"

"I'm here," Pip croons, smoothing her hand through his hair, cupping the back of his skull, scooping him against her heart. "It's okay. Just breathe. There's no rush. We'll do it when you're ready."

Kin and I leave him behind to work through his humiliation and grief with his wife, in private. The man in the suit follows us in, walking like a cat-footed creature, silently padding. He steps to the side of the door, waiting with his hands folded respectfully in front of him, eyes turned down and away to give us our own privacy.

A security guard I hadn't noticed moves from a chair in the corner of the plushly decorated room. He stands, takes a few steps toward the head of the coffin, and then stops. He, too, turns his eyes away. But his presence is an unmistakable message: no matter how famous and loved—or reviled—this man was in life, his corpse will suffer no indignity.

Kintyre ducks under the red velvet rope that is just a little more than an arm's length away from the coffin. The guard tenses; the man in the suit shakes his head minutely, and the guard relaxes. I join my husband at our maker's side.

In his coffin, Elgar Reed does not look like he's sleeping. People who describe the dead as looking merely asleep are at best fanciful, and at worst, horrible liars.

He looks like he's dead. His jowls sag backwards, his cheekbones are more pronounced. His flesh has just started to take on the tinge of gray that even the not-magic of Overrealm embalming could not halt. His eyelids have molded to his decaying eyeballs, shrunken inward a little, already. His hair and beard are neatly combed, and rigidly, unnaturally styled, with not a wisp or a whisker out of place. His chest does not rise and fall.

He is dead.

Finally, horrifically, shockingly *dead*.

But... it's also a *relief*. I haven't seen Elgar since I was pulled away from Kin by the paramedic healers, and then, my only thought had been to follow them, to keep my trothed in sight, to not allow us to be separated. If Kintyre was to die, then I was going to be by his side when it happened. I would be holding his hand. I would be holding his Writer-be-damned *guts* in, if I had to. And I would probably find a way to follow him onto his Shelf not too soon after he was filed there himself.

And in all of that, Reed had been many hours a corpse by the time help had gotten to him. You can grieve a person gone from your life forever. You can prod at the vacancy until it throbs like tender gums where a tooth has been yanked out. But being able to be witness to their gone-ness with your own eyes, to be able to touch their parchment flesh, the same temperature as the air around them and stiff, makes that separation almost bearable.

Almost.

For the horror of death is not the death itself, not really. The pain, the grief, the agony of it is that you will never see them again after this one last parting. No more hugs. No more smiles. Nothing. Never. Empty. That's what grief is.

Not the death.

The loss.

The gap where that person used to be and will never be again.

Kintyre leans over the side of the coffin, and murmurs something quiet and secret into Elgar's ear. I know they're Words; I can feel the surge of their power as they're Spoken, feel the magic of them strangle, still-born on Kintyre's lips in this not-magic world. But beyond that, I have no idea what he's said. Then he straightens, places one palm on Reed's forehead, and closes his own eyes. Kintyre sways a bit on the spot as he breathes, but otherwise is completely still.

Then he steps back.

I take his place beside Elgar's head. His lips are the wrong color. The cosmetic paint they've used to keep him from looking too ghastly isn't quite the right shade. In life, his lips were ruddy and plump with self-assurance and ready smiles. Now, they're nearly orange.

I chuckle. I should be indignant on his behalf, but I think Elgar would have been rueful about this last bizarre indignity, instead of mad. He would have, I think, laughed at himself. I hope he would have.

"Thank you," I say to him, simply. I'm filled with the urge to say more, to clarify, to add to it, but everything else I want to say rushes up out of my belly so fast, and all at once, that I can't. It jams together in a crushing tangle in the hollow of my throat, and I have to swallow the lump back, hard. The backs of my eyes burn, I can feel my ears flushing, and I blink to banish away the tears that threaten.

Instead of speaking, I pick up his hand, kiss the back

of it gently, reverently, gratefully.

"Thank you," I say again, setting down Elgar's hand and taking my husband's instead. Kintyre squeezes back until I feel my bones grind together, as if he can anchor me in my grief, and I in his, with the sharpness of the ache. "Thank you."

I don't say, I can't say... *for giving me life, or, for giving me this love, or, for so many wonderful adventures, or...* or any of it. I can't. But I think he knows it.

Forsyth and Pip come into the room. Alis is between them, holding one hand of each of her parents, toddling on unsteady legs. Kintyre and I move aside for them. Pip hoists Alis onto her hip, so the child can look down into the coffin.

"Gar gar?" she asks, sucking on one finger and looking back and forth between the coffin and her mother's face, uncertain.

"Say bye-bye," Pip says, and her voice is tight and damp. "Bye-bye Uncle Gar."

"Bye-bye, Uncle Gar," Alis parrots. Pip's sorrow breaks through, finally, and large fat tears start to roll down her cheeks as she sniffles and snorts and tries to pretend she's not crying. Alis, moved by her parents' grief, though she doesn't quite understand why, starts squirming and wailing: "No! Noooo! No!"

Pip shoots me a grateful look when I let go of Kintyre and scoop up my niece.

"Come on, polliwog," I say to her, tucking her face against my neck and beating a hasty retreat out of the room, glad for the excuse. "Let's give your ma and da a few minutes alone."

In Hain, we would have had the viewing of the body and the wake in one. Usually, the body is laid out in one room, in its coffin and directly after being washed and dressed by the deceased's family, and in an adjacent room, friends, family, and neighbors gather to grieve, sing, dance, drink, and celebrate the life that is now gone. When the sun rises on the first day without the deceased, the mourners leave the wake and follow the undertaker to his ossuary for supplies and where—still drunk, exhausted, and miserable—they take turns, one by one, to shovel dirt into the grave, until it's closed up.

In the Overrealm, the body is viewed separately, and this viewing is then followed with a great fat load of speeches, and *then* a procession to intern the body, but everyone leaves before it's actually buried, leaving strangers to tuck the deceased into their last bed, which is just *wrong*. And *then* comes a gathering of people, and the drinking, and the songs.

Juan speaks before a crowd of thousands, who have piled into the funeral home's largest hall. A parade of hundreds of cars follows the undertaker's vehicle and our own van to the graveyard, and there, Forsyth speaks eloquently, and with hardly any stutter—he's cloaked in his Shadow Hand persona—of family and of what Elgar meant to him.

And in the great hall that Forsyth rented to accommodate the masses of mourners, where the alcohol flows freely and fans sob in the corner, Kintyre and I stand on a table—Kin leaning heavily on me due to his pain and his level of drunkenness—and *sing* as one ought:

Far beyond the curtains of time and fate,
Beyond the misty vale of the Reader's tears,
The Writer sets down his quill, his intent filled,
The narrative played out, the ink bottle empty.

Here the story is finished, here joy abate

Here an end to pain, and an end to fears.
Here is the story told as He has willed.
Here the empty spot on the Shelf left for thee.

My heart fills with such a complex weight,
Grief, thick like syrup, in my breast appears,
My own tale, with you missing, I must rebuild.
Until my own The End also folds over me.

Our efforts are met with raucous applause. Soon, another group takes up the song. They sing songs near and dear to my heart, set to tunes I've never heard before. Songs from Hain, recorded in my own scrolls, printed in the novels here, and set to music by Readers who could only guess how they may have sounded, how the melody might have gone.

It's eerie, and fantastic, and Kintyre and I stay late into the morning, greeting the sun properly: with our bellies on fire from whiskey, our throats hoarse from song, and the damp blanket of grief thrown off our shoulders. Today is the first dawn in a world without Elgar Reed's magic. And we are ready to face it.

PART FOUR

I won't bore you with regaling the three months following the funeral. In that time, Kintyre regains his muscle mass and flexibility quickly—more quickly than his specialist healer had ever seen before. Forssy says that he suspects it has something to do with Kin's being a Main Character. Though there's no magic in this realm, we each still retain something of the traits which our Writer imbued us with. Forsyth will always be scarily clever, and able to absorb and deduce from disparate pieces of information with deceptive ease. I will always be a storyteller, brash and crass, good at crafting a dazzling meal from nearly nothing and getting people to trust me implicitly. Kintyre will always be strong, in good health, fast, a moral paragon, and utterly charming to the opposite sex. It is as we were Written, and in the absence of our Writer, I find it a measure of comfort that some small bit of him remains.

We go for longer and longer walks each day, exploring first Forssy's neighborhood, then the city of Victoria itself. Kin and I practice reading signs, and taking the bus, and buying strange new foods with small plastic squares, from horrifyingly large and brightly lit indoor marketplaces until the strangeness, the newness, of it all starts to ease, at least a little.

When the leaves turn, Pip returns to her place as a teacher, in a school of higher education. I'm impressed with her prestige and the amount of work she's done to achieve her status, now that I finally understand it. Forsyth continues to methodically and slowly build identities for Kin and me, and it seems that each day we are presented with a new form of proof that we have always existed in the Overrealm: bank accounts, credit cards, passports, a marriage license, and paperwork that indicates where and when we were born, and to whom. In creating his own identity, Forsyth had, at Elgar Reed's request, made himself distantly related to our Writer—the son of a cousin of Reed's deceased father. Kintyre shares this relation, on paper, and as his husband, so do I.

It takes longer than I thought, but eventually, the deed for Reed's home and small patch of land transfers to Kintyre. His wealth is deposited into first Forsyth's, and then Kintyre's bank account. And Kintyre and I prepare to give our farewells to Forsyth and Victoria, to move into a home of our own and, for the first time, to fend for ourselves.

What happened at ConClusion very quickly passed into legend. And thank the Writer for that. Especially since it grew more fanciful and more elaborate in the telling. The constabulary of Toronto called it a terrorist act using hallucinogenic gas as a weapon, and a madman determined to perpetuate a slaughter. And they are not entirely incorrect, at that. Since the Viceroy had cut the hotel and convention center off from what Forssy calls "the digital communications grid" when he locked down the building, there was no security camera footage to either confirm or deny this story.

Oh, there's shaky video and blurred photos from the attendees, but most are shaking so badly they're out of focus. And no one victim's account meshes with that of another's. Fantasy and science fiction fans, it seems, have vivid imaginations, especially when they're "drugged." And if any reports of the official sort veer a little too close to the truth, well... social media sites have viruses and glitches all the time.

Forsyth Turn is not a master hacker for nothing.

Our secret was safe, our privacy ensured, and the safety of those who'd suffered the most, who'd been the most affected, was paramount. So, it comes as a bit of a surprise when it's not a fan who outs Kin and me, but an eagle-eyed assistant in a lawyer's office. Nobody really believes that we're the real Kintyre Turn and Bevel Dom. Our identification names us Kevin and Barry Turn, but it's the combination of our surname, my email address, and Elgar Reed's estate that pricks the assistant's interest. She declares on her web-journal that Elgar Reed based his books on us—his cousins—and suddenly, every website in the geek kingdom is carrying the ConClusion story again, this time with photos of Kin and I leading the battle at their head.

"Blast," Forsyth grumbles, and he spends a long night corrupting pixels, dashing out viruses, deleting whole articles, and not sleeping. "What vicious magic social media is!" he snarls when I bring him a coffee, late into the night. Or early into the morning, depending on how you want to count the day.

But the stories propagate faster than Forsyth can quash them. Eventually, around dawn, Bossy Forssy concedes defeat. With the aid of Juan, who has also been awake all night, working alongside Gil and Flageolet Entertainment to minimize the damage to their television series, they draft something called a "press release."

In it, Forsyth speaks on Kintyre's behalf and confesses that, yes, the Turns—Kevin and Syth—are cousins to Reed, and that their cousin based his main characters on the two young boys he'd watch grow up, and that, yes, we were all in attendance at ConClusion in order to celebrate the release of the short film and the television announcement with Elgar. He doesn't name or even speak about me, which I think is smart. He says that witnessing the death of their cousin at the hand of a crazed fan was traumatizing in the extreme, and begs compassion and privacy from fans and the press. It rankles Forsyth to have his private grief so callously aired, but it seems like there's no help for it.

The "mainstream" media picks up the story. A to-do is made about how the cousins of Elgar Reed, the living embodiment of his characters, were by his side when he died. That they rallied a rag-tag army of cosplayers to repel the mad terrorist in what the fans have begun to call "The Battle of Hall H."

And with this fame comes something that Kin and I never had to deal with when we were recognized and swarmed in Hain: paparazzi.

Kin and I stay inside the Piper house to avoid them, and Pip is forced to take a holiday from work because the school doesn't want the madness to follow her to campus.

"No offense," our sister-in-law says to us while we help her to draw the blinds, "but I can't wait until you losers move out."

Kintyre wordlessly opens a bottle of wine and pours her a glass.

"It's not even noon," Pip protests. But she takes the glass, anyway.

After a few days of taking the same unsellable photos of a closed-up house, and a remarkable spate of parking tickets and disturbing-the-peace violations being issued ("Where are these coming from?" I hear one of the reporters by the door ask a photographer, bewildered. "My wife says they keep showing up in the mail, but I don't see any cops around here tagging the cars. It's like goddamn magic. I owe, like, two thousand bucks!") we are left in peace. Forsyth has all the satisfaction of a sailor who got his dick wet in a siren and survived when he finally emerges from his office.

"Bravo, *bao bei*," is the last thing Pip says before she hands Alis off to me and drags her husband back upstairs.

By now, Kin and I have figured out the not-magic of the television and the Netflix. We put on the next in Kin's favorite series of tales, and drown out Pip and Forssy's celebration with the sounds of lightsabers, murderous bear creatures, lasers, and the defeat of the dastardly Empire.

The "media circus" dies down a little after that, but not completely. Which means that our first visit to the set of the *Kintyre Turn* television series isn't as... *stealthy* as Kin and I had hoped it would be.

"I guess all press is good press," Gil sighs when he picks us up at the airport in Los Angeles, on a temperate day a few weeks before Solsticetide. Kin still walks with a cane; not because he needs it, really, but because he's being—at my nagging insistence—*cautious*. He's regained his health, for the most part, but sitting for long periods, like on a plane, makes him sore and liable to wobble on his feet. Gil helps him into a long, fancy black car, handing the cane in after him, and I follow quick to avoid the swarm of photographers who have finally spotted us and are rushing along the curb to try to grab a photo.

"Hotel first, dinner tonight, and then to the set tomorrow?" Gil says.

"Sure," I reply.

Juan is in the car, too, already peppering Kin with the sorts of polite small-talk about his travels and how he's enjoying Victoria that Kin despised when he was a lord, yet still excelled at. Kin's face is tight with pain and exhaustion, but if the Overrealm has taught my husband anything, it's *patience*.

Pip warned us that the production company would try to woo us spectacularly, so I'm not surprised that the room we're given is huge, ornate, and has an awe-inspiring view of the city. There's a large gift basket including the Overrealm form of whiskey, which is tasty, but not the same as Drebbinshire's Best. There's also a soaker-tub large enough for both of us facing a floor-to-ceiling window.

I chivvy my cranky husband into a hot bath, pour us both a tot or three, and climb in behind him. We watch the sun set in the bubbles, talking about dwarves, and our last visit to Chasmshine. We both skirt around how angry I was, how envious of the queen and her spouses. I can't help running my fingers over Kin's flat belly, feeling the ridges of scars, both old and new, as I palm his belly button. I wonder what it would be like if my husband were pregnant—how cranky and bitchy he'd be about the whole affair, how he'd hold it over my head for the rest of our lives, I'm sure. I wonder what it would be like to be pregnant myself, to feel life fluttering against my organs, kicking at my ribs. To hold and to shelter my own child in the fortress of my flesh.

The urge to tell Kin what I've been up to is strong, all of a sudden. The surprise I've been keeping from him sits like a hot coal on the root of my tongue, begging to be spit out.

No, no, now's not the time, I remind myself. Instead, I kiss the back of Kin's neck, the top of his head, the shells of his ears. It's as much to distract myself as it is to pull him out of his sulk.

Dinner is quieter than it would have been had Kin not been lingering sore and slightly fuzzy-headed from his medication. Gil and Juan take us to a place that is, I'm sure, meant to impress. And it does, but not because of the name on the outside of the restaurant.

The décor is sumptuous, more rich than anything I ever saw in any king's Great Hall or ballroom. Everything is crystal, and mirror, and gilt. The fabrics are elaborately embossed. The food is art on a white-plate canvas. Kintyre leans over when the first course is delivered to our tables—thank the Writer Gil asked if he could presume to order for everyone, for it saved Kin and I from the mortification of trying to read our menus—and says he wishes he'd thought to bring his sketchbook.

Even the other members of the "creative team" are impressive. They have done incredible things, it seems, in translating the world in which Kin and I were born into something like what I've seen on television. Andy, the director, shows us the short film meant to depict Kintyre finding Foesmiter on his tablet. After the death of Elgar Reed, the creative team was left at a loss as to what to do with the short film. It was meant to be released on the Internet, and to preface films in theaters right after the Con. But with our Writer only a few months dead and buried, Gil had worried that it would be disrespectful to release the teaser as if nothing was wrong. Especially since it was the last thing Elgar ever wrote. That Flageolet wants to be considerate, and not "cash in" on his death endears me to the team.

But what impresses me most is the open and affectionate way Gil and Juan behave. In our months in the Overrealm, Kin and I have learned that, while same-sex Romantic Pairings are common, legal as marriages and not a second-tier trothing the way they are in Hain, not all the world nor all its peoples and cultures feel that it's entirely natural. (How love of any sort is meant to be unnatural baffles me, but it seems that the Writer's realm hasn't been created by as methodical a world-builder as my own.) Same-sex Romantic Pairings are rare in Hain, to be sure, but not entirely unheard of. So it should follow that in the Overrealm, where they're more common, and more celebrated, they should be, by extension, more accepted.

But I've seen news reports of absolute horrors being perpetrated on people who dare to love where others think they shouldn't. It's enough to make me wish that carrying a sword in public was allowable—and that so was hunting down and running through the dastardly cowards who inflict such pain. I don't like being idle while innocent people suffer needlessly.

We are scheduled to be in Los Angeles for a week. And for that whole time, Kin and I are pursued by hounds with cameras. We are followed all over the city: to the studio where they are designing and building the props and costumes (What we see there is not perfectly accurate, but I sort of like the messy, scrappy "dishabille-aesthetic" the designer tells us about. While I don't mind taking creative license on the page, it seems odd to see another's interpretation of my own everyday clothing, and to know that it is, well... wrong), to the restaurants where we have a parade of impressive meals, to the studio where the stuntmen practice their swordplay in advance of heading to Newfoundland for the on-location filming. It is there that they, vultures that they are, manage to catch Kintrye on film with a sword in hand. Just as Pip and I predicted, the bloody great lump couldn't help but take up one of the foam practice swords and show off to the stunt team. I, of course, am no better—the incredible plastic bows are like nothing I'd ever seen before, and I had to get my hands on one. It only took running through one quiver-full for me to get the hang of the new grip and pull, and then I was back to my usual spate of bullseyes, and making a cheeky leg to the impressed team applauding them.

(Kin and I decide to find ranges and training space when we move. As soon as we return to our hotel, Kin painstakingly taps the tablet Forsyth gave us to search for practice spaces in Seattle, and finds hundreds of martial arts dojos. "Wouldn't it be fun to learn a whole new form of grappling?" he asks me, showing me videos of what is labeled Brazilian Jiu Jitsu. It looks like the whisking, circular tumbling that Wyndam used in combat.)

The photographers even follow Kin and I to the beach, on the one day Juan has scheduled us for fun rather than meetings. Kin and I purchase very scant "bathing suits," which cover significantly less than the drawers we wore under our leather riding trousers, and which I am sure Forssy would consider immodest. Kin looks incredibly sexy in his, and I am a very, very happy husband. It's glorious to see so much of my lover in bare daylight. His skin is tinged with honey in the guilding effect of the sun, his blue eyes glowing with mirth and light, bluer even than the sky, and his hair glitters gold with just a bit of dashing silver at the temples.

His older scars are white and softly pink, a crisscross against his left shoulder, around and down his back. The rake of a siren's claws along his ribs, an arrow-puncture in his upper thigh, the score of a cat-o-nine-tails on his back, the stab wounds from Cassiopith's subtle little dagger against his collarbone, the burning brand of a witch's coal-hot hand on his ankle—each of them the mark of a time when I would not let someone else take him from me. And now, there's a still-red, pitted and puffy scar in a wide, thick slash along his belly. It begins just below his bathing suit line, dances on the crest of one hip, tumbles upward along the chiseled muscles of his abdomen, skirts under his belly button—bisecting, sadly, that trail of golden hair leading down to his privates that I like so much—and curling upward to end just below his left nipple.

I spend maybe more time than I should kissing my way up that scar in the searing heat of the sun. With each kiss, I thank the healers and medicines of this world that he lived, that the wound didn't fester, thankful that, in our final battle with the villain who had plagued us our whole lives together, I didn't lose him. Of course, the photographers end up publishing ribald photos of us in the surf, my hands very clearly in a place on my lover that is not appropriate in public.

Pip sends us a copy of the photo with the accompanying blog article before we even finish showering the sand out of our hair back in our hotel room. The headline on the article says "#BINKYLIVES," and though it takes us a good half hour of teamwork to read through the entire thing, it fills us with delight to learn that the Readers of the Overrealm had secretly always suspected that a romance between my husband and me was inevitable.

When we get back, it's decided that we'll stay in Victoria until after Solsticetide. We'll move into Reed's home in Washington in the new year when, hopefully, the furor around our identities will have died down, and ConClusion has stopped being newsworthy. Directly after we move out, Pip and Forsyth intend to shutter their house in Victoria and rent a flat in a city on the other side of the continent, so Pip can be closer to her new position as Story Consultant for the television series. So this holiday is the last time the whole family is going to be together for a few months, at least.

I've never been more than a week's journey from my family before, and while traveling with Kin, we were back to Turnshire or Bynnebakker at least once every few months or so. It's going to be weird, being able to see my family now through screens, and talk to them via text, but not be able to touch them unless we want to travel a distance larger than the whole of the Kingdom of Hain. At least with the Overrealm's cars and planes, the journey itself won't take more than a day.

During our last few weeks in Victoria, Kin and I have been put to work as manual laborers for our brother's estate. We spent four solid days in the backyard, putting up a new fence, pulling out a scrubbly old hedge, and building a flag-stone lined fire-basin. Now, as the sun sets on the Night of Light, and Forsyth and Pip are inside, finishing the food and decorating, Kin and I are sweating in our winter outerwear as we clear snow from the stone bowl and build a bonfire.

"Not too big!" Pip reminds us, sticking her head out the patio door. "This is a suburban neighborhood! No flames taller than the fence, okay?"

"Spoilsport!" Kint shouts back, but it's with a grin. He waits until Pip goes back inside to say, "Here, Alis, hand me more."

"'Kay," she says, and balls up more old newspaper for Kintyre to stuff in the base of the split-wood base I'm making.

"Kin," I say warningly, but he just leers at me and shows Alis how to place the twigs we've torn from the remains of the hedges. The logs from the hedge we tore up are still too green to burn this year, but they've been split and are seasoning against the fence, under a tarpaulin.

As soon as I've finished stacking the kindling, I shove my numb hands back into my gloves. "Fwah.

Forssy warned me that it got cold in this realm, but I didn't expect this," I say.

"Not as bad as Erlenmeyer," Kin points out. He's got Alis by her ankles now. She's screaming in delight as he lifts and lowers her like a construction crane so she can drop twigs down the holes between the stacked kindling.

"No," I agree, "but still colder than Bynnebakker ever got. Or Lysse, for that matter."

"We had mild winters while you were there," Kintyre says.

"I'm glad we're moving further south," I say. "Not certain I could tolerate Los Angeles in the summer, but Washington should be just perfect."

"Hmmn," Kin agrees. "All done. Down you go. Off inside, now."

Alis, clever thing that she is, points at the net bag of firewood we purchased, waiting beside the basin. "More!"

"That's too heavy for you, polliwog," I tell her.

"No!" This is one of her favorite words.

"You're welcome to try, then," Kin says. Alis scrambles up from where he'd plopped her in a snowbank, and toddles over to the bag. Her mittens are made of a slick, waterproof material which makes it hard for her to get a grip.

Kin picks up one log with his strong fingers, and holds it out over her arms.

"Put your arms like this, Alis," I say, tucking my elbows into my ribs.

Alis copies me, and Kintyre lowers the log just enough that she can feel the weight of it, but not so much that it tumbles out of her grip and onto her foot.

"There!" Alis commands, and shuffles toward the basin. Kintyre keeps his grip on the log, letting her direct where they take it.

"Throw it, now. Ready? One, two, three!" Kintyre

says, and makes the log fly end over end to land exactly where it needs to, on the top of the kindling.

"Again!" Alis demands.

Kintyre obeys. Though I'm shivering as the sweat under my outer clothes dries, I stand against the house, leaning back on the brickwork, and watch. It takes three times as long as it would if Kin just did it himself, but he lets Alis transfer every piece of wood over to the fire-basin, patient and kind. It doesn't matter that the pile is now over-stacked and will never burn well—we'll remove most of the logs before we light it at midnight. Alis will probably be in bed by then, and won't be there to pitch a fuss about her uncles dismantling her hard work.

Babies, he doesn't understand, but Writer, my husband is marvelous with children. He doesn't think so, but he is. He's never been less than generous and kind to them. He listens to them seriously, doesn't dismiss them, speaks to them as if they were reasoning adults in their own right. He treats them, in short, the way his father never treated him. To this day, he holds a soft spot for Thoma of the *Pern*, and though he complained theatrically of Lewko, he would never let any harm come to the boy, nor any real scorn.

And though he's never said it out loud, I think Kin feels robbed of Wyndam's childhood, just as I do.

It makes what I'm about to give him for our Solsticetide gifting all the sweeter.

When my two troublesome Turns have finished their tasks, I usher them both inside for baths, changes of clothes, a warm bottle for one, and mulled wine for the other. Alis, when sleepy, prefers her father's embrace to anyone else's. She crawls up Forsyth's leg and perches on his hip like it's her Writer-given right to be there. Dressed in our Solsticetide finery—all in shades of russet, gold, and amethyst—the five of us toast to the New Year. We toast to our wishes for what's to come. We toast to the health of those who can't be with us, and to the peace of those whose books have been Shelved forever. It's an emotional moment, and though I don't like to own to it, Forsyth's quiet, staid tears are not the only ones shed as we each sip the spiced wine.

"Elgar gave us this spice sachet," Pip says after we have all drunk, her voice wobbling. "Seemed appropriate to make it tonight."

We raise another silent toast, and drink again.

"Come upstairs, Kin," I say. "I have something for you."

Kintyre leers at me, eyebrows waggling, and Forsyth makes a disgusted sound.

"No offense, brother mine," Forsyth says, "but I truly cannot wait until this house is solely ours again."

"Miss the sofa-sex, *bao bei?*" Pip teases him, just so she can watch his face go red and splotchy.

"Pip!" he says, aghast.

"'Cause I do." She tugs the wine out of his hand and puts both their glasses down on the coffee table. "Come have a cuddle with me before our guests arrive."

"Absolutely not!" Forsyth protests, but he lets his wife lead him to the sofa, anyway. They drop Alis into her playpen on their way, where she's surrounded by a bounty of board books and Library the stuffed lion to complain to.

"Oh, I can't wait either," Kin says, squeezing one of my arse cheeks hard enough to make me yelp. I nearly spill my wine.

We set both our glasses on the mantle, and I have to dodge Kin's hands all the way upstairs, laughing as we go. I let him catch me at the threshold of our borrowed room. We tussle a bit, eager and full of the urge to reaffirm that we're alive after so grave a reminder of the existence of death. I let it get as far as mussed sheets, rumpled hair, and reddened, puffy lips before I put a stop to things.

"Aw, Bev, c'mon," Kin whinges, grabbing a double handful of my arse this time and grinding our hips together. He's so hard it feels like he's going to bruise my stomach, and I laugh and swat at him again.

"No, no, this isn't my Solsticetide gift," I say.

"S'not mine, either," he smears against my neck, sucking a bruise under my ear where he knows everyone will be able to see it. Bastard.

"You first, then," I say, wriggling away so I can straddle his waist.

"Yours is that good then, yeah?"

"Yeah."

"You'll have to let me up," Kin scolds.

"I could tie you to the bedframe and never let you up again," I tease back. "Go looking for my gift on my own."

"You could," Kin says with a splotchy blush of his own. "I'd let you, too. But how would you ever be able to do that thing to me you like so much?"

"Oh, I can work out a way to get you on your knees with your rump in the air well enough with your hands still bound, Kintyre Turn, don't you doubt me on that." I sneak a hand under him and pinch the delicious rump in question. He heaves and snorts. "So, where's my gift?"

"Under the bed," he says.

Reluctant to get off him, enjoying the press of his sword against my thigh, I stretch and twist until I can get my hands on something long and thin, and wrapped in fabric. I tug it out by one corner of the wrapping, and as I do, the fabric slides away.

"Oh," I breathe, dazzled by the loveliness of my gift. "Kin. A bow? Is it made of wood?"

"Mahogany. I commissioned it as soon as we got

back from LA, from one of the show's bowyers. I told him I wanted a functioning replica of Bevel Dom's prop bow from the show. He enjoyed the challenge."

"By the Writer, Kin," I breathe, stunned by the beauty of the oiled-leather grip. It's not strung, but a beautiful plastic packet is tied to the grip, a black string waiting for me to bend the bow for the first time. "Arrows, too?"

"Greedy," my Paired, my trothed, my husband laughs. He pinches my side, and I squirm and giggle, and hold the bow over my head like a trophy. "Arrows are in the top of the closet. Now me."

"Stay put," I say, and swing off Kin to lean my new bow in the corner, where it can't fall over. Then I dig into the bottom of the laundry pile for a thin, flat package.

"You hid my gift with the dirty clothes?" he asks, propping himself up on his elbows, head tilted to the side like a charming, curious puppy.

"Exactly where you'd never find it," I say, coming back to the bed to hand him the envelope. "You never do the laundry."

"Women's work," he huffs while he takes the package.

"*Never* let Pip hear you say that," I admonish, sitting on the side of the bed by his knee. Noticing how nervous I suddenly am, Kin sits up. He pulls a cardstock folder out of the buff-colored envelope. It is, by a marvelous coincidence, purple.

"What's this?" he asks.

"Read it."

Kintyre frowns at me. Kin's ability to read is coming along shakily, but he's able to understand the words on the cover when he carefully sounds them out: "Gr-Great-Greater Van-Vancouver Surr-o-ga-cy Cli-nic." He scowls. "I understood half of that. What's surrogacy mean?"

"It's... open the folder, Kin," I say, where I know there's a picture that will help my explanation. "It's a service. They... look, you know how I've been going to other meetings when we go into Vancouver for your special medical tests?"

"Yeah," Kintyre says, looking askance.

"I found... I mean... so, there's a not-magic here, in the Overrealm. I heard about it in one of my magician audio books. This not-magic lets the... the doctors, the scientists... well, they take the seed from a man, or from two men, like... like you and me, Kin. And they take the part that's needed from a woman, and they put them in a dish, and they mix them together, and they... well, they make a baby."

Kin's brow draws downward, from confusion to concern to disbelief. "Two men making a baby?"

"Well, yes! And then they put all that goop back into a different woman, one who's agreed to, you know, carry and birth the baby. But she's not the mother, she's got no claim to it, so it's just like the two men made the baby all by themselves. They both get to be the father, and there's no mother. No... no complications."

Kin lets the folder fall against his lap, his expression going dark. "And you've been having meetings about this?"

"Yes! See, if you... if you just flip to this page here, see? I've, ah, I've paid for the, um, the first round of assessments and treatments already, and... um... I've selected some potential egg donors. I thought, of course, you should help pick the final one, but look, here's a whole page of women who... see, doesn't she look just like your mother?"

My husband doesn't lower his eyes to the page where I'm pointing. He doesn't say anything, either. He just... stares at me.

I swallow, suddenly, and for the first time, doubting. In all my joyful planning and fantasy-spinning, I hadn't considered that Kin wouldn't be *pleased.* "Well. So, um, Happy Solsticetide, Kintyre."

"You did all this?" he asks, and his voice sounds small and broken. Not at all the boisterous joy I expected.

"Yes?"

"Without asking me?" he adds, and now he's starting to sound a little dangerous.

"Well, that's the point of a surprise, isn't it?" I ask, desperate for the levity we had just a few moments ago. "Surprise!"

Kintyre throws the folder at the wall and leaps to his feet, looming over me. He knows I hate it when he does that, when he tries to bully me with his superior height and muscle mass, so I kneel up on the bed until we're eye-to-eye.

"You can't... you can't just..." he says, stumbling over what it is he's trying to articulate.

"Just what?" I ask, resentment beginning to flare up in my guts. He wasn't supposed to react like this. This was supposed to be... be good. "Just work for months? Just worry about you discovering the paperwork and completely ruining the surprise every single day? Just do all that I can to replace what we've lost in Hain? When I'm the one who made the decision, without giving you the chance to decide for yourself, that we would stay? Just that?"

"Replace!" Kintyre roars, aghast. "You can't... you're trying to... you can't just *replace* Wyndam!"

"I'm not looking to replace Wyndam," I roar back. "I'm just trying to—! Writer's nutsack, Kin, we're old men! Don't you understand that? We're old men living on the wealth of another old man, and when we die, we will leave nothing and no one after us! There is no flesh of our flesh, no child to hear our stories, no human being to remember us as we were in life! We will just... *cease.*"

"There are fans!" Kintyre says, throwing up his arms. "There are hundreds of thousands of fans!"

"Who don't know us," I shout. "They don't *know* us, Kin. They're not family! They only know what I wrote in those scrolls! What Elgar Reed wrote in his books! That's not the real us. You know that!"

"I don't see why—"

I reach out, clutch at his sleeves, wishing to press my forehead to his, to get it through his thick skull. "Two men in this realm can be fathers together, Kin! What a gift that is! What a magic! You can't honestly tell me that you don't want—"

"It's you who's always wanted kids!" Kintyre bawls, taking a step backwards. The fabric of his Solsticetide shirt slides out of my surprise-limp fingers. The physical space between us is like a tear, a rift. I can feel the ragged edges of it in my flesh, in my lungs. "I've never—"

"Of course I do—" I climb to my own feet, take a step toward him, try to heal the... the gash between us. But he takes another step back.

"Writer, I've never met a man so baby hungry," Kintyre spits, and if he meant it as an insult, he's missed the mark.

"I'll own to that!" I reply. "Of course! Do you think I'm ashamed of it? I came from a large family, Kin. I love my nieces and nephews. I love Wyndam. I adore kids. I think they're the Writer's most glorious and brilliant creation. Why in the whole of the great green world do you think I would be ashamed to admit that? Because I'm a man?"

"It's womanish!"

"To want to procreate? To want to watch your own flesh and blood grow and laugh and be filled with joy? To have someone to teach, and cherish, and to pass down the traditions of your House? To have an heir? A legacy?"

"A *burden*—" Kin spits.

"I am not your father, Kintyre Turn," I remind him, wagging a finger in his face. "And neither are you. There is no Chipping to hand down, no rules to follow, not here. Just our own happiness."

"And what in all seven of the hells makes you think that forcing me to accept another responsibility when I am finally, for the first time in my life, free of them, is going to make me *happy*!" Kin snarls.

And then he is out the door, and pounding down the stairs. Pip squawks from the living room, and Alis shouts after him, but he doesn't stop. The back door slams hard enough to shake the entire house.

The only reason I don't punch the wall is because it's my brother-in-law's house, and not mine.

PART FIVE

Downstairs, Forsyth welcomes the first of his neighbors, and though his voice rings up from the foyer, expansive and cheerful, I can hear the strain in it. Of course they overheard us shouting. I'd be surprised if the whole block hadn't heard it.

I should have gone down to be with Forssy. The head of the house greets the guests, but the rest of the family is meant to be his support, to whisper names of neighbors and tenants in his ears, to smooth ruffled feathers and bypass political dramas. To pass him water and wine, as needed. To support.

But I could do none of these things for Forssy. I don't know his neighbors, and they don't know me beyond being Forssy's hurt brother's husband. The slightly useless one who just watched the baby while Pip and Forsyth worked, and Kintyre was working toward recovery. Which, okay, yeah, that's uncharitable to myself, but I'm feeling a bit...

I don't know how I feel. Lovers fight. It's inevitable. Forsyth and Pip battle, my parents tussled and shouted, even Kin and I have sniped and snarled at one another a time or two.

But this... this feels different.

This feels... final.

Sitting on our bed, with the heel of my hand pressed against my chest, trying to shove down the aching dread building behind my heart, I can't seem to tear my gaze away from our presents. My bow, shining seductively in the corner, and his papers, scattered all over the carpet.

Kintyre gave me something I didn't even need to ask for. He knew I wanted my bow, missed my bow, and he went out and made it happen. And I... I gave Kintyre something that I wanted, something I assumed he did as well, but did I really know? Did I really ask?

Writer, of all the dumb, selfish, self-serving, *blinkered* things to...

After a few long minutes of—yeah, I'll admit to it—*sulking*, I scoop up the papers and shuffle everything back into the Sheil-purple folder in the right order. I linger over the photos of the women who look at least a little bit like his mother, and the one I'd slipped in that looks a bit like my ma.

How had I gotten this so wrong?

How could I have been so... was *selfish* the right word?

The anger surges again, petty and vicious, the way it had when we'd first been Paired and Kin hadn't been able to see how much his casual dismissal of our bond had hurt me. I want to be a father, a husband, I want a family, and I... I...

But it isn't all about me, now is it?

I was the one who took the choice away from him, the decision to go back to Hain (yes, and probably die there), and I'm the one who's been trying so hard to give back everything I took from him. But Kin isn't laid up anymore, isn't flat on his back and white as the pillows around him. Maybe I need to stop doing things for my husband, and start doing things with him.

Writer, my ma would be annoyed with me. How much more obvious and oblivious could I be?

The doorbell rings again, and I set the folder down

carefully on our tousled pillows. Then, considering the possibility of nosy neighbors, I slip it underneath the pillows. In the Overrealm, children put their lost teeth under pillows and hope that a fairy that doesn't exist will exchange them for money. I wonder what will happen if I leave the folder there, like a childish wish.

What would it grow? What would this non-existent fairy exchange it for?

What have I sold away in exchange for that dream?

I am gasping, making an ugly choking sound, before I even realize I am having trouble breathing. The bubbling ache behind my heart is growing, vomiting up out of my mouth, spilling out of my eyes, and I shove my face down into the comforter to muffle the noise.

By the Writer's Quill—what have I done?

Kin and I have had ample practice acting in tandem despite a tiff, of watching each other's backs while spatting. We'd have both been long dead on the battlefield if we hadn't had the ability to leave the domestic complaints at the camp. I just didn't expect to have to call on that practice on the Night of Lights.

I can't hide upstairs forever, so I dry my face and fix my hair, and endeavor to ignore the throbbing headache. When I hear Kin's voice rising above the crowd, I gird my loins, fix a genial smile on my face, and head down. Without missing a beat, Kin slips his arm around my waist, presses my wine cup into my hand, and continues his conversation with the wide-eyed spotty kid from down the street who loved Elgar Reed's books.

It's agony.

There's so much I want to say, to ask, to *apologize* for, and I can't do any of it. Pip circles around the crowd, Alis on her hip, wide-eyed and enchanted with everything around her. There are a few other children, as well, tumbling between their parent's legs, laughing and chasing each other under the table groaning with culinary offerings from all of Forsyth's family and friends.

The scent of sweet and spice catches my attention, and Kin lets me steer us to the table. As he takes my cup so I can fill a little plate, I take a fortifying breath, intending to—

"No," he whispers.

"But—"

"No," he says, a little more forcefully. "We are not doing this right now, right here. Not to Forssy."

The consideration for his brother's feelings leaves me blinking, cutting an end to the spat before it really begins.

"I still want to—" I finally try when I've got my voice and wits back.

"Later."

"But—"

"Later, Bev." He starts to lean down toward me, instinctual, instinctive, then hesitates for a very brief second—long enough for me to notice. Then he makes up his mind and presses a soft, lingering, sweet kiss against my temple.

It's not an apology. It's not forgiveness, either.

"I love you," I whisper.

"I know," he mutters into my hair.

I can't help but snort. I elbow him gently in the ribs, well clear of his new scar, and say, "Pip should never have showed you those films."

"I like the Ewoks," Kin says, and straightens up. "Try some of these dumplings. Pip's mother's mother made them."

Kintyre knows that *wai po*'s cooking is my new weakness. Maybe it's a peace offering; maybe he's only pointing them out because he wants me to stuff my face until I can't speak. Either way, there are dumplings to eat, and people to meet, and wishes to make, and wine to drink, and a fire to enjoy, and a folder and a bow upstairs that will still be there in the morning.

When the last guest is on their stumbling way home, and the fire has died down to crackling embers, and Pip is upstairs convincing Alis that she really is tired enough to sleep, Kin and I start packing up the leftover edibles in the plastic containers that are a small magic of their own in this realm. The real challenge is figuring out how to fit them all in the fridge.

"Just put it in the snow," Kintyre grumbles, when I ask if there's space for yet another partially drunk bottle of wine. "That was good enough during the feasts at Turn Hall; it's good enough for here. The local wildlife is a lot less pesky than a bunch of fairies taking off with an amphora, too."

Figuring that if one of the local raccoons can figure out how to get into a screw-cap wine bottle, it deserves to get drunk, I plunk a line of bottles into the snowbank by the kitchen door.

"Not that one," Kin says, plucking the last bottle out of my hand. He hunkers down in the doorway, on the step, letting all the cold air into the house, and unscrews the cap. He takes a swig from the bottle, and then, without looking, hands it up to me.

Right, I think. *Now it is, then.*

I take the bottle and sit beside him. Kin wraps his arm around my shoulders, and for a few minutes, we pass the wine back and forth and watch the fire die down. From over the fence, the sunrise starts to turn the horizon a dusty pink.

"Pip and Forssy are on the front step making their

wishes," Kintyre says at length, making it clear that we're alone. "What do you wish for?"

"That I'd chosen a different Solsticetide present for you," I say, though it burns like bile to get the words off my tongue. Resentment and self-recrimination have been jammed up in the hollow of my throat all evening, and it hurts to force it out into the open air. "What do you wish?"

"That I'd reacted better," Kin admits.

I jerk my head up to scrutinize his expression, but he is working hard to hide it from me, eyes gimlet and face pointed toward the sunrise.

"You think that children are a burden," I say softly. "That's how you feel. That I'm imposing them on you against your will."

"Well, no," Kintyre protests, just as softly. "But you— Bev..." He hesitates, reaches up to run his fingers through my sweaty hair, and pushes gently until I am snugged up against his armpit, my ear on his chest. "Bevel, you didn't ask."

"I know. I'm sorry. I'm an elfcock—"

"Let me finish."

"I don't need to hear you itemize everything I did wrong. I get it. It was a bad idea, and—"

"I never said it was a bad idea!"

"You didn't have to! You threw the folder at the wall and stormed out!" I struggle to sit up, and he yanks me back down. "I think that message was pretty clear!"

"Well, when you put it like that—"

"Damn straight, when I put it like that!" I snarl. "You over-defensive, rotten, self-denying—"

"Okay, now," Kintyre says, holding me at arm's length so he can study my face. He puffs up, ready to retaliate, but then the color drains away as he deflates, realization dawning in his eyes when he sees how hurt I really feel.

"Okay, I'll admit, I haven't taken this surprise very well."

"I worked on it for months!"

"I know. I think I was just... startled. I came at it the wrong way. I've never really thought about—"

"Oooh, you narcissistic liar!" I hiss at him, and let my fist fly. It strikes Kin solidly in the sternum, though I pull my punch. I don't want to crack his ribs. "Don't tell me that you weren't thinking of taking Gisella Gyre up on her offer, Kintyre Turn. Don't you dare lie to me about that."

"For the sake of the bloodline!" Kin protests, letting go of one of my shoulders and tipping me to the side on my thigh as he rubs the rapidly forming bruise. I can't see it, but I know it'll be there when I strip him down for make-up sex, when the rest of the household is abed.

"And only for the sake of the bloodline?" I ask, eyes narrowed and jaw clenched so hard my teeth squeak.

"No..." he admits at length. "No, not just for the sake of the bloodline. But with Wyndam, it seemed like... I don't know, like it wouldn't be fair to him to, you know... have another child. It might seem like... we were... that he wasn't enough. And I—I never wanted my son to feel like he wasn't enough. Not like... not like my—*blast.*"

Kin covers his eyes with his hand and heaves a deep breath. The emotion of his confession and my surprise suddenly shaking him. I lean him back against the door-frame, tucking myself up against his side. The shaking turns rapidly to tears.

"I miss my son! I miss him!" Kin sobs.

"Shh, shh, I know, Kin. Me, too," I say, cradling his head against my shoulder. There's something cathartic about sorrow, and I will admit that, despite my own sob-bing earlier, I do cry along with him this time, too.

Wyndam is a good lad, and he will do good things with Lysse, but he was also troublesome, clever, mischievous, and compassionate. Not being able to see him every day, not being able to mark his progress, the inch he's grown, or the lesson he's learned, or the kindness he's doled out, or the secret he's discovered, or the joy he's found in some far-flung corner of Lysse—it is a scream-ing ache, a gaping wound in my chest, all day, everyday. It is there, bleeding, bleeding, and yet somehow, I don't die. I wake each morning, and I feel the wound, and some-how, I still draw breath.

We grieve, and the sun rises, and still, we draw breath. Together.

"What's your real wish, then?" Kin asks damply, when his sorrow has wound down to moist sighs.

"I don't know," I say. "No point in wishing for what I can't have—and I have all that I could want here."

"Not all," Kintyre says.

"All," I repeat, stubborn, chin thrust forward in that way that makes Forssy call me a bulldog.

"Twat," Kintyre chuckles.

"Go on. What's yours, then?"

"I wish that I had a baby," Kintyre says softly. "Some-one to teach, and to love, and to leave a legacy to—not just money, or land, or a title, but stories. Someone who will remember us, the real us, when we are Shelved. Someone I can cherish as much as I cherish my husband."

"You don't have to wish it just because I want it—" I start, but Kintyre leans down and stops my protest with his wine-sweet mouth.

"I want you to be happy," he says. "And I think it will probably make me happy, too. I'm sorry I was a total arse about it."

"I'm sorry I sprang it on you," I counter.

"Then we're both sorry," he says. He kisses me some more, making promises with his lips. Then we readjust our clothing, smooth out the wrinkles, tidy up our hair, and watch the sunrise.

"Well," Kintyre says at last, when the bottle is empty and the new year has arrived. "I suppose, if we're going to make a baby, we should get on that."

I laugh, feeling lighter, freer than I have all night, the bile and burn in my chest turned to bubbles and butter-flies, my head light as fairy wings. "That's not quite how it works, Kin. We can't actually make the baby ourselves."

"Won't know until we try," he says, and waggles his eyebrows at me, and the Writer knows, I can't say no to that.

The move to Seattle is plagued by paparazzi camped on our front lawn, but luckily, Bossy Forssy's not-magic hacking powers extend to the United States of America, too. Soon enough, the photographers find themselves under injunctions and restraining orders and up to their eyeballs in parking tickets and tax evasion inquests. And we are left in peace.

We arrive in mid-January to wet, gray weather that is still better than snow. Juan has paid a charwoman and a gardener to keep up the house, and save for the few sentimental tokens he has taken, the furniture, clothing, and possessions of Elgar Reed have all remained.

It's several emotional days' work to clear out his wardrobes. We donate a majority of the clothing to a local shelter for vagrants, send a few small items—ties, a hat, and all of the buttons and pins which name Elgar the nominee or recipient of this or that award or honor—to Forsyth. His trophies we take from his office and display prominently on the mantle in the salon.

Very slowly, we shift the layout, the placement of things, the arrangement of the shelves and rooms. We watch online videos and television programs about home redecoration and tutorials for "DIY." We paint the bedroom, alter the window coverings, and swap the linens. We build a fire-basin in our backyard, and plant a vegetable patch, which, of course, Kintyre leaves to me to weed, the lazy arse.

We find and join a local archery range and a dojo, and at night, we practice with our own swords in the backyard, where the high fences keep peeping neighbors from reporting us to the police. Foesmiter is not as nimble in this world, not quite as intuitive, but inborn magic doesn't entirely fade in the Overrealm. The Viceroy was proof of that.

Together, we review the surrogacy paperwork. We choose an egg donor. The service has branches in Seattle, and we go to the clinic to provide our half of the goop. The technician is red-faced and flustered when we emerge from the same private room with our sample cups, but children are meant to be created through an act of love. What did she expect? That we would wank separately? Never.

Begin as you mean to go on, Forsyth's always said.

We are cautioned that the potion doesn't always take the first time, but—with the sort of Turnish luck and Narrative Convenience to which those I love dearest are privileged—we are blessed.

Our surrogate is pregnant right away. Her name is Maddie, and she's a waitress.

Amid our frequent trips to the Isle of Newfoundland to visit the set of the television series, or to Victoria to visit with Forsyth's brood, we now add bi-weekly trips to Maddie's house on the other side of town to ply her with groceries, help her fill her prescriptions, or to accompany her to her medical appointments.

When I ask her why she chose to be a surrogate, she says: "Lots of bad has happened in the world through me. It's not my fault, but it happened. I'd like some good to come of it. You know, balance it out."

And then, of course, through the miracle of the not-magic of the Overrealm, it's time to see our baby for the first time. I'm told that there's going to be a black-and-white image on a screen of the child—a gel and a not-magic wand combine so we can look through Maddie's flesh and into her womb.

The creature on the screen, cradled in the dark gray sides of Maddie's innards, is hardly baby-shaped at all. It's small, and all head, just like the books on baby-rearing have warned us. But there is a wee nose, and even smaller bones of the vertebrae, and a fluttering pulse that the technician tells us is our child's heart.

"It's kind of like magic, isn't it?" the ultrasound technician muses as she moves the wand around to find a better angle.

"Kind of like," I agree, whispering in awe. "A child."

"A child?" the technician says, pointing at a second small blob on the screen. "Better make that plural. Congrats, boys. You're having twins."

The grin Kintyre flashes at me is blinding in its joy. "Let's name them Luke and Leia," he suggests, and guffaws when I pinch his arm hard enough to leave a bruise.

We hadn't meant for the Meeting of the Interested Parties to happen at our house in Seattle. But yet, somehow, I found my soon-to-be-publisher, Lynne, her assistant Adam, my agent Kim, as well as Gil and Juan, all descending on us for a long weekend in November. Kin and I can't fly to New York, or down to Los Angeles, not with Maddie so very pregnant, so it made sense to promise a few good meals and enough space around our massive dining room table to negotiate some contracts, show off our renovations to Elgar's house, and indulge in a bit of cookery for those whose job it was to ensure we kept making money.

Kin has become annoyingly adept at the barbeque, now that it's a delight, and not a chore for the side of a road before we can bundle into sleep. I still won't let him at my carefully hoarded canisters of Hainish spices, though. This is where I assume he is—ridiculous apron with a buxom woman's torso printed on the front, hand clutching the tongs as if they were Foesmiter, discussing with Gil and Juan his "inspirations" for (what we otherwise properly call "memories" of) the great Urlish battle that caps the television miniseries, my first scroll, and Elgar's first book—when he gets the call.

The news that Maddie is in labor comes in the form of Kintyre barreling into my office, where I'm supposed to be having a closed-door meeting with Kim and Lynne. Adam, the harried assistant, comes tumbling in the door on my husband's heels, his own eyes wide, his cheeks flushed with excitement.

"Now?" I ask, leaping up from the desk, not caring one whit where the contracts fall in my wake.

"Your boy has called the car service," Kintyre says, jerking his thumb at the assistant. I still can't quite convince him to stop speaking about the hired help as if they were full-time live-in servants. Neither of us has learned to drive yet, either, Elgar's car neglected and rusting in our garage. But we have money and eccentricity enough in our corner to pay someone else to do it, just as we used to with the servants.

I turn back to my publisher. "Will you and Adam—?"

"Juan will show us out," Lynne says, collecting the papers we'd been reviewing from the floor. "We'll pick this up later."

"But you flew all this way," I say. Kintyre is dancing in

the doorway, the overnight bag we had carefully packed slung over his shoulders. The two baby car seats are also already assembled and waiting by the front door.

She laughs. "I'm not going anywhere until these are signed, don't you worry about that. I have more than enough manuscripts piled in my hotel room to do me for a few days. But babies wait on no man. Or woman. Contracts can."

"Bev!" Kin chides. The doorbell rings, and Adam ducks back into the hallway to, I assume, help Juan load the car seats. Gil is around somewhere, too, likely having removed himself to the kitchen to stay out of everyone's way.

Someone throws my coat over my shoulders like a scarf, I manage to half-jam my feet into my shoes, and then I am being hustled out the door. It's not until I'm seated between the two car seats in the back that I realize I am still wearing my crappy jeans and a wrinkly t-shirt with a stain from lunch on it. And Kin is still in that stupid apron.

"Oh," I say, wrinkling my nose at the state of my clothes. "This isn't what I wanted to wear."

Kin cranes his head around from the front, and the driver says nothing and keeps staring ahead. "The babies won't remember."

"But I will," I said. "Only one chance to make a first impression, as they say here."

Kin rolls his eyes at me, reaches into the bag in the footwell beside him, and pulls out a carefully rolled dress shirt. I've never seen it before, but when he tosses it over his shoulder to me, I can see that it's made of a fine, closely woven cotton. And it's Dom-amethyst. He pulls out a second shirt, and this one is Turn-russet.

"Kin," I breathe, feeling my chin wobble with his thoughtfulness, and the impending realization that this is what I'll be wearing when I meet my children. Which is followed swiftly with the gut-punch realization that, *by the Writer, I'm about to meet my children!*

The driver is unperturbed as Kin and I both strip from the waist up and don our shirts, wriggling in the confines of the car like worms on the end of a hook.

And then, somehow, we are in the hospital, and Forsyth is on the phone with Kin telling him that the Pipers are already on a flight from Vancouver, and Kin is cursing his brother roundly for being such a nosy busybody that he knew that our babies were being born before we did, and then I am standing in a room, smothered in flimsy garments to protect both my clothes and my arriving children—what was I worried about the damned shirt for again?—and then Maddie is screaming, and Kin is letting me squeeze his hand until it's got to be near to breaking, too frightened of everything that is about to happen, about to start, to really remember to breathe while my husband gleefully sticks his head between Maddie's legs to get a really good look at the fascinating process of it all. And then Forsyth is there, bringing us all water and forcing me to let go of Kin's hand so he can wrap it because I probably sprained Kin's finger, and then, and *then, and then—*

Something small, and pink, and squirming and shrieking, and still kind of gross and bloody, and covered in white stuff, is plopped into my arms and, *holy fucking shit*—as Pip might say—it's my *daughter.* And because the universe loves a Main Character, and because narratives love symmetry, and because any child of Kintyre Turn is genetically predisposed to be impatient, a few moments later, a matching squirming red and pink and white thing is given to Kintyre, and it is our *son.*

I assume other things happen around us at that point, but all I am aware of is Kintyre and I staring at each other in matching shocked wonder as the babies wail. At the same time, as if we were twins ourselves, our gap-mouthed shock transforms into poleaxed wonder, and then gleeful, blinding joy. Someone in plastic gloves plucks my daughter out of my arms, and before I can make a protesting sound, Pip is there to soothe and promise me that it's only to clean my daughter up and give her a weigh, as Pip starts to chivvy me to a loveseat under a window—we had spared no expense in this and were not sharing this room—where she orders me to take off my shirt.

"But it's Dom-amethyst," I protest weakly, still too exhausted (though I didn't do any of the work) and emotionally wrought to do more than bat feebly at her hands as she plucks at my buttons.

"Skin-to-skin contact is clinically proven to reinforce bonding."

She barely has the sentence out before Kin is shucking his soiled hospital greens and his own shirt. It occurs to me then that I don't know where our son is, although, obviously, he's been taken aside for a clean up, as well. In the bed, Maddie is speaking low, sleepily content Spanish with her father, a man I've only met a handful of times. The team is helping her, as well, getting her cleaned up and prepared for rest, so they can wheel her bed out of the room and leave us with the babies she's protected and nurtured for us for nine months. We'd already agreed that this would be the plan, and that, if Maddie wants, she can swing by and see them every now and again. She's earned the right to be a part of their lives, if she wants to be, we figure.

In my forty-some-odd years, I have carried many things. Horseshoes and ingots in my pa's forge, a sword and a bow at Kin's side, scrolls and quills along the road, and eventually, the heart of the man who is more dear to me than anything—*anyone*—else in the world. But when the room goes quiet, and everyone retreats save for two nurses, each with a babe in their arms, my arms feel heavy, and hollow in a way I never could have expected.

And when they come back, when my daughter is placed in the crook of my elbow, it feels like a homecoming, like an obvious conclusion, like the whole of my life, anything else I had ever carried or lifted and cradled had all been training for this, this, *this*.

Leaning against one another, skin bare and hearts thumping in what must be tandem beside the little, perfect—Writer, they are *perfect*—ears of our children, Kin and I cuddle them close and weep like the big stupid heroes we are. The nurses help us with bottles and burping in hushed tones, and our children soon stop making noises like wounded dragonets, as they drop off into a milk-drunk stupor, tiny chests rising and falling so fast it looks like they're panting as they take their first in-the-world naps.

After a while, I realize the four of us are utterly alone.

Kin is still looking down at them both, expression greedy and humbled, so I decide that I'm the one who is coherent enough to go fill out their birth certificates. We'd chosen their names long ago, though we hadn't shared them with anyone, wanting to keep the power of it to ourselves until just now.

"You take them," I say to Kin, my throat crackling. How long have we been sitting here? "Take 'em both. I wanna go see if Maddie's okay, and let the Pipers in on the news, and get us some water."

"I can't—" Kintyre says, starting to stand, curled protectively around the tiny, trustingly limp bundle of red wrinkles that is our son.

"Stay put," I say, making a point of nudging him back down into his chair. "You're doing fine. Haven't dropped him yet."

"I've only been holding him for a few minutes!" Kin protests, breath racing in panic.

"Exactly," I say. "Imagine how good at it you're going to be in a few hours. A few days."

"A few years," he murmurs, looking down and frowning in concentration as I reposition our son and slide our daughter carefully into his other arm.

"A few lifetimes," I agree, and press a kiss to his forehead.

"Writer," he gasps as our daughter wriggles and yawns in her little knitted cap.

"What are you feeling, Kin?" I ask, watching him take in both of our children in his arms, one small head in each palm, their tiny toes tucked into his elbows. "What's it like?"

The act of tearing his eyes away from them seems nearly painful, and he does it so slowly that I can damn near hear the air tearing. Those big blue eyes find mine, and his smile crinkles up—more creases in the corners than there used to be, more scruff on his chin, more silver in his hair—those same eyes that once met mine across a horse trough of water and hooked hard into my heart.

I feel that hook sink deeper, a warm and wonderful ache, accompanied by two smaller barbs, attaching themselves into the muscle in my chest as easily as breathing. And it feels good. It feels so *good*.

"It's magic," is all he says.

PRIDE

his short story was a little bit written as a thank you to a reviewer who has been one of my most vocal supporters during this series (and who I may have also slipped into the story you're about to read, here). His enthusiasm and approval means a lot to me, especially since I am neither a bi nor gay man, and I tried very hard to write my bi and gay male characters authentically. His insights were extremely valuable.

Also, I wanted a peek into the future for our heroes, a place where everyone is healthy, happy, and doing what they love. What better way to put a bit of a rainbow-colored bow on the whole series? So, of course, Bevel is a best-selling novelist, as well.

What, you're surprised?

"I don't know how I feel about being an international queer icon," Kin says as I carefully paint a blue-purple-pink trio of stripes on his cheek.

I peck a kiss off the tip of my husband's nose. "Tough shit. There's no putting that djinn back in its lamp."

Kintyre threads his fingers into the loops of my jeans and tugs me between his spread thighs. "I love that you still use the phrases from home," he murmurs quietly, moving the kiss to our mouths. He doesn't need to explain what he means by *home*. We both know he's referring to Hain.

"Gotta keep 'em in my mind," I say, pushing back to finish the last stripe on his cheek. "My publisher would be annoyed if I started to forget 'em."

"Not to mention the fans," another voice cuts in.

My years of being a warrior are far enough behind me that I'm ashamed to admit I'm startled enough to jump, spilling the paints all over my hands. Kin, the smug bastard, just squeezes my arse cheeks and grins over my shoulder at Adam, our liaison from my publishing house.

"Ready, love birds?" he asks, jerking his thumb at the float waiting in the parking lot behind the pile of sound equipment boxes Kin and I had taken advantage of to sit for a moment. On the top of the float, our twins are sitting on a giant rainbow made of flowers.

Ettie has a stuffed unicorn clutched tightly between her knees, and seems determined to keep her ice cream from dripping onto its head. She's so concerned with haphazardly chasing the drops that she's not paying attention to how quickly the rest of it is melting. Terse is licking his ice cream mathematically, keeping what remains corralled in a perfect sphere even as it diminishes. The Writer help me, there is so much of his uncle Forsyth in that boy.

Strange that Forsyth got a miniature version of Kin in Alis, and we got a replica of him in our son. At least we both know better how to handle our children thanks to the many mistakes—and apologies—we've had to make on all sides as adults.

Another liaison from the publisher watches over the twins, holding out futile napkins that neither child can be bothered with.

As Kin stands, and I try to wipe the paint off my hands, he asks: "Does that thing have seat belts?"

Of all the people in the Overrealm to become an

insufferable worrywart upon having his newborn children deposited in his arms, I never expected it to be Kintyre Turn, Lord of Lysse, Great Hero of Hain, and royal pain in my arse. But Kin has become a fusspot. He never fussed over Wyndam as much. But then, Wyn was already sixteen when he came to us, trained in the deadly arts of piracy and accustomed to his independence.

"There's a rail," Adam says. "And there will be lots of people from the office there to keep anyone from going overboard."

Kin frowns, but jerks his head in a nod, and we all cross the lot to clamber aboard. The float itself is shaped like a stack of books—one in each color of the rainbow—with an open book as the platform where we're all to stand. Some of the more athletic-looking young folks have staked out perches on the ladder of books, but my family will be staying on the lowest level, where it's safe.

Ruddy hells. Maybe Kin's not the only worrywart fusspot, after all.

"Daddy!" Ettie says, overjoyed and raising her arms to be lifted by Kin as soon as we're aboard. Instead, Kin plucks the cone from her hand and licks all around the bottom to clean it up. Ettie gasps in horror. "Daddy, that's my ice cream!"

"Daddy's tax," Kin says, and hands it back to her.

"No such thing," Terse replies, but he's already handing Kin his cone.

"Papa's tax," Kin says, and offers it to me.

I copy my husband—*mmm, mint chocolate chip*— and hand the cone back to Terse.

We have to wait in the marshaling area for another twenty minutes, during which our kids finish their ice cream. I am grateful that one of the folks with us has wet wipes handy to clean up their faces, and I sign about ten copies of *The Riveting Return of Kintyre Turn*, book one of the new series, for the people on the float. Kintyre has near about three heart attacks trying to keep Ettie and Terse from clambering down the giant wheels under us, or eating the candy necklaces we're supposed to be throwing to the crowds along the route, or deciding to play hide-and-seek without telling us and suddenly vanishing.

Adam, who's been keeping an eye on our little hellions, waggles his eyebrows at the back of the oversized stack of books. I can see Ettie's stuffed unicorn peering around the corner, as if my kid would be able to spy on her brother through its plastic eyes. Yup, that's Kin's daughter right there. But she reminds me a lot of Vulej, too, my next eldest brother, in her carefree joy and determination to never miss out on any of the simple pleasures that life has on offer.

Terse, I can't spot, however. I'm not certain how they think they can play hide-and-seek when there's only two of them, but they're seven, and they seem to have a secret and special way of doing things between themselves which only makes sense to them. Pip calls it a "twin thing," and Alis calls it "stinking unfair" when it means their older cousin gets excluded.

A cheer rises from the waiting crowd around us, and a whistle shrieks over the blare of dance music that gets cranked up. Kintyre reaches around the stack of books and lifts Ettie up by the back of her shirt, hefting her onto his massive shoulder. Ettie squeals with glee, the unicorn flying. Adam catches it before it can sail over the edge of the float.

Predictably loath to be left out of anything, Terse squirms out from his hiding place behind the barrel of candy necklaces and scrambles up the side of the books to take his rightful place on his da's other shoulder.

"Oh my god!" one of the other people on the float squeals, and those ever present bloody cameras and phones all start snapping and clicking. Kin flashes his movie-star smile at them, and the twins strike poses with their arms in the air. Kin flexes his biceps, the glorious show-off, bracketing Ettie and Terse so they can't slide off when the massive truck pulling the float lets out a deep honk and begins to slowly roll down the street.

"Pa!" Terse commands indignantly when I stay where I am, admiring the picture my family makes on the colorful float, instead of joining them. "Come on! You're missing it!"

"All right, Lordling Terse, all right," I chuckle. We call him that not because he is the heir to anything we can claim anymore—besides, his half-brother Wyndam is still above him in precedence—but because he likes things Just So. He keeps tabs on everyone, has a head for names, and faces, and is the most proficient small-talker I've ever seen in a seven-year-old. If we were all still in Hain, I might have started to worry that Gisella Gyre might snatch the boy up for her apprentice courtier and secret Shadow-Hand-in-Training.

Ettie—sweet, boisterous Ettie—would probably be kissing frogs, and tumbling through the wheat fields, and brandishing toy swords alongside Lewko Pointe. I would probably have to talk her down off Capplederry every night so she could sit with us for dinner. And Cook would always be in despair over the state of the young Ladyling's frocks.

And Miss Alis, well, someone would need a chain and a hook to pull her out of the Turn Hall library and force her to go to bed. There is not one event, or family picnic, or day at the beach, where Alis hasn't wandered off for a bit of alone time with a novel. Pip calls her an introvert who just needs time away from people to "recharge her batteries," and says she's very much the same. I'm not sure how that behavior would have been taken in another

Great House, but I hope that at Turn Hall, we would have made it clear that we had no problem with Alis's bookishness. Of course, it's well-balanced by her reckless sense of danger-hunting, as well. For all that she reads like a bookmouse, she is also the first one of her friend-group to jump off the highest diving board, to try wall-climbing, to beg her Uncle Bev to teach her how to string a bow and shoot an arrow.

Were we all in Hain, I think Gisella would have been scheming marriage matches already. Alis is only eleven; it would have been too soon to entertain any such thing seriously. But Alis has grown up pretty—very pretty—if a bit rumpled like her father, and wind-blown like her Uncle Kin, and it would have been about time to start thinking about where to send her for her Finishing. Which school she attended would have had a big impact on which daughters of which Great Houses she was flung together with, which would have put her in the path of their brothers eventually, which—*uhg*.

I'm suddenly glad that this is not something we have to worry about at all. In the Overrealm, the only scheming we need do for our children's future is the kind where we make sure they are happy, well-cared-for, and have the funds and ability to be and do anything they want in life.

"Pa!" Terse commands again, pointing at his other father's side, and I start, realizing I've been woolgathering. Bollocks.

Obligingly, I grab one of the barrels of candy and haul it closer to my family. I pass up a handful of necklaces to each kid. Ettie flings the whole lot into the crowd at once, and Terse tries to make sure he tosses one to each child he sees.

"Be more generous, Terse," I say. "There's lots." Then, to his sister: "And you be less generous, fairy-cakes."

"Where's Uncle Syth?" Terse asks, eyes scanning the crowd.

"He's in there somewhere," Kin says, grinning at the crush of people along the parade route, knowing that his brother despises the crowds.

"More like up there somewhere," I say, gesturing at the balconies of the hotel rooms that look out over the city streets. "You know he'll have gotten one with a good view."

"But I want to see them!" Ettie whines from her perch. She's trying to slip a candy necklace into her pocket. It's the third one she's jammed in there, and she's out of room now. I frown at her, and she slumps and rolls her eyes before she tosses it to the crowd.

"We're meeting your brother and his family at the restaurant for dinner," Adam reminds us. He's looking forward to chatting with "Forsyth Turn," and his fannish enthusiasm is a bit flattering, in a roundabout sort of way. Adam only knows him as Elgar's inspiration for the Forsyth of his novels, and the character who sees the fictional Kintyre and Bevel off on the *Adventure of the Seven Stations* that happens in my second novel. Forssy had asked not to be in my series, and except for that one appearance—done mostly so I could fix the misconceptions about the kind of man my brother-in-law really is—I've honored his wish.

Still, some people's favorite characters are the ones with the least amount of screen time, I've learned, and Adam has said more than once that he identifies with Forssy. Probably, though I don't want to cast aspirations, because of the way both men felt so out of place in their youth.

Which brings my thoughts circling back to the parade. The twins are squirming down, now, tired of being on top of their da, and scrambling up the book staircase with the help of—and under the watchful eye of—Adam. From there, they can see everything, and throw candy to the crowd with joyous abandon.

Kin pulls me to the front of the float, where he and I can stand on the open book platform.

"Kin, I can see just fine from where we were st—" In full view of the crowd, my lover, my trothed, my husband and partner, dips me low and plants the kind of kiss that wouldn't be out of place on a Hollywood silver screen. The people on the street holler and whistle, and behind us, the float erupts in applause.

"What was all that about not wanting to be a queer icon, you ruddy great lump?" I ask dazedly when he lets me back up.

"Ah, to all seven of the hells with it," he says, and when I turn the tables and flip him around to give him the same dipping treatment, he comes up grinning, and to the thunderous approval of the crowd around us.

"Gross, Da," is Ettie's pronouncement, as she squirms between our legs and wriggles past us. From the front of the float, she waves to the crowd, and within moments, Terse is there beside her, leaning over the rail and smiling tightly, still methodically dispersing candy.

"I don't think it's gross," I say. "I like kissing your da."

"Gross," Terse agrees.

"Not," I say, dropping a kiss on the top of first Terse's head, then Ettie's, "gross."

"Super gross," Ettie groans. But there is a smile curling at the side of her mouth, happy. She pulls Kin's free hand onto her shoulder.

"I guess we're just gross, then?" I ask Kin, and he loops his free arm around my waist, fingers hooking into my belt loops. I return the favor, and bracket Terse into the family the same way, my hand on his shoulder, too.

Between us, Etaphemia and Tersavan lean back

against our thighs and crane their heads to smile up at us, adoring, and trusting, and just the most Writer-be-blessed perfect little human beings.

"Super gross," Kintyre Turn agrees, and kisses me again.

ACKNOWLEDGEMENTS

For the last time, I get the privilege of being able to highlight the wonderful humans who have helped make The Accidental Turn series what it is today.

Firstly, thank you to Ashley Ruggirello and Kisa Whipkey at REUTS Publications for stepping up and saying, "We want the book that nobody else did, and more than that, we want three of 'em!" Without your enthusiasm for not only *The Untold Tale*, but the world and additional stories that you could see in it before I ever did, this collection wouldn't exist. You opened my eyes to the possibility that there were many other places I could explore, many other lives I could live through, and many other struggles to illuminate. Thank you for trusting this book, trusting my worlds, and trusting me.

Thank you to my mother and father, for being wonderful beta-readers and copy editors, when they never thought they were signing up to do so. I'll keep your little notes with corrections in your handwriting forever. It means so much to me that you're involved and invested in something that means so much to me, simply because it means so much to me. I love you, I love you, I love you.

My aunts, uncles, grandmother, brothers, and cousins who have come to my launches, bought the books, recommended them to friends and neighbors, and have just generally been very supportive of me following this very difficult, very rocky, very uphill path of my passions. They have been there to hand me walking sticks, push me up inclines, and kick rocks out of my way. I love you all. Thank you.

My friends: Adrienne, Stephanie, Karen, Ashley, and Brienne for getting me through the rough patches, and drinking wine on my balcony when I needed the support, to spitball ideas, and to celebrate.

If you've noticed the beautiful maps of the Four Kingdoms and the ConClusion convention space in these books, they are the work of the very talented Christopher Winkelaar. Most authors who write fantasy are smart enough to draw a map while they're creating said fantasy realm, and I did, too—on a whiteboard wall in my office. And because the series was only supposed to be one book, when I'd finished my final go-over with it and sent it off to my agent, I... erased the map. Like a complete nincompoop. I didn't even photograph it first! When the book became a series and I realized we'd need a flyleaf illustration, Christopher provided a beautiful one that went far beyond my whiteboard scribble. He was very patient when I had to keep going back to the text to verify distances and locations, which inevitably meant he had to change something. Luckily, I had the map all ready for book two, and I learned my lesson and kept my map scribble for book three for him to use as a basis. I'm very grateful to have Chris as both my illustrator, and my friend.

The work in this collection is not solely mine this time, and to that end, I want to make a point of thanking the artists I collaborated with—Kelly Fesmire (another-wellkeptsecret.tumblr.com) and Brigit O'Regan (brigitoregan.com)—for their interest, their enthusiasm, and their professionalism. Working with each of them was an utter delight, and a complete breeze.

And once again, my dear Readers, the very last thank you goes to you. Without you, without your enthusiasm and support, without you falling for the characters, writing about them on your blogs, creating university classwork around them and teaching them to your students, without you asking conventions to have me come speak, without you requesting these books at libraries and festivals and bookstores, I couldn't—I wouldn't—be here, writing the final words of series.

Thank you.

ALSO BY J.M. FREY

(Back)
Triptych
City By Night
The Dark Lord and the Seamstress, a coloring storybook
Hero Is A Four Letter Word,
short story collection
"Whose Doctor?" in *Doctor Who In Time And Space:
Essays on Themes, Characters, History and Fandom,
1963–2012*
"How Fanfiction Made Me Gay," in *The Secret Loves of
Geek Girls*
"Time to Move," in *The Secret Loves of Geek Girls
Redux*
"Bloodsuckers" and "Toronto the Rude" in *The Toronto
Comic Anthology vol 2*
"The Promise" in *Valor 2*
"TTC Gothic" in *Amazing Stories vols 1-4*
Lips Like Ice, as Peggy Barnett
Time and Tide

The Accidental Turn Series
The Untold Tale
The Forgotten Tale
The Silenced Tale
The Accidental Tales,
more stories from the Accidental Turn series

The Skylark's Saga
The Skylark's Song
The Skylark's Sacrifice

ABOUT THE AUTHOR

Photo by Marion Voysey

J.M. Frey is an author, actor, and professional smar-typants. She's appeared in podcasts, documentaries, radio programs, and on television to discuss all things geeky through the lens of academia. J.M. lives near Toronto, surrounded by houseplants because she is allergic to fur. She's a tea and wine nerd, and her life's ambition is to one day set foot on every continent (3 left!)

Her debut novel *Triptych* was nominated for two Lambda Literary Awards, nominated for the CBC Book-ie Award, was named one of *Publishers Weekly*'s Best Books of 2011, was on *The Advocate*'s Best Overlooked Books of 2011 list, received an honorable mention at the London Book Festival in Science Fiction, and won the San Francisco Book Festival for Science Fiction.

www.jmfrey.net

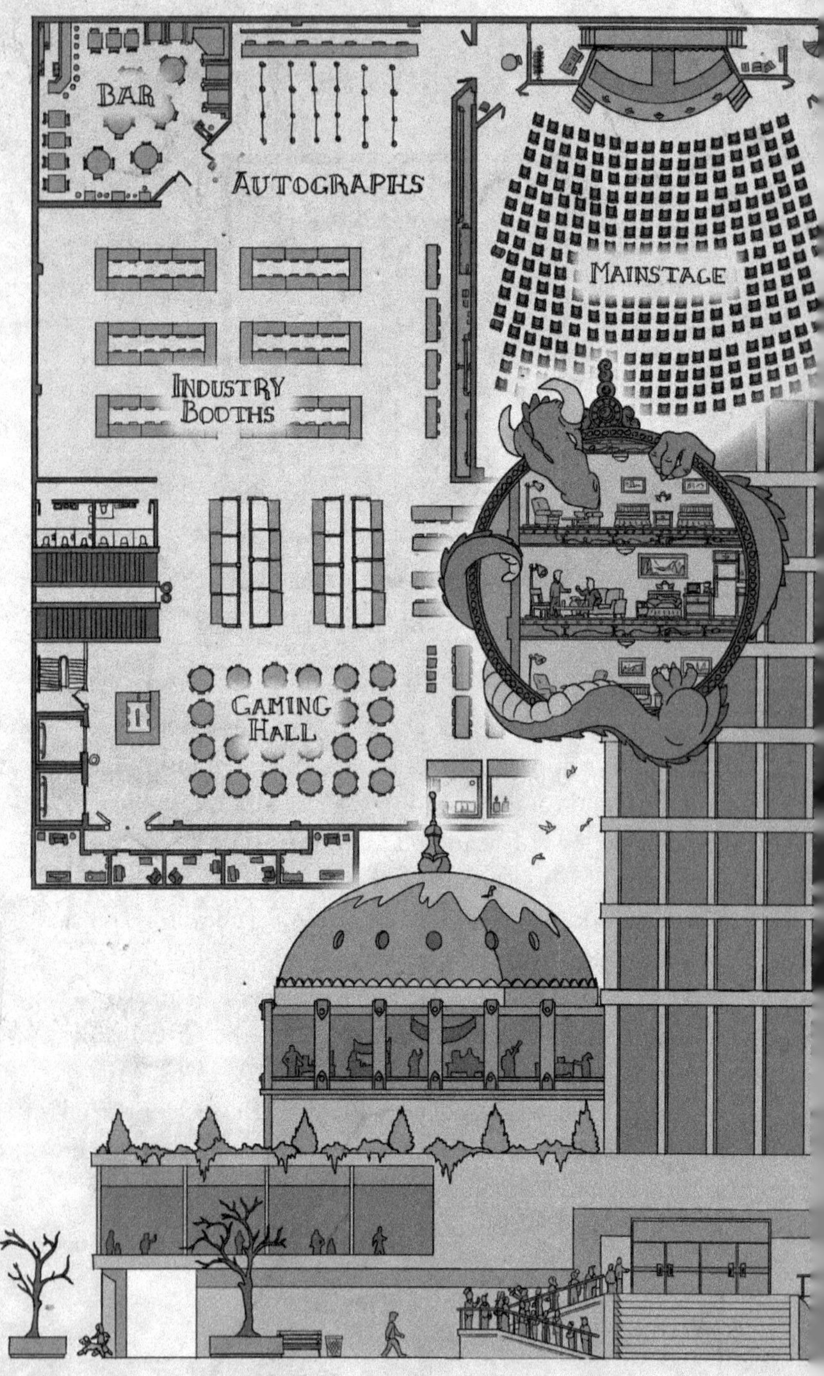

BAR
AUTOGRAPHS
MAINSTAGE
INDUSTRY BOOTHS
GAMING HALL